"Thi ries . . . Any it] is an entertaining, exciting realm." —*Midwest Book Review*

"Highly sa n- joyable inst t, soul, adver a character-d e last book, I e

"Chock-full of adventure . . . it's tautly written with a surprise around every corner." —*All About Romance*

"Aguirre's writing is tight, and the characters have plenty of depth . . . This isn't just a run-of-the-mill military science fiction story with some obligatory romance thrown in . . . Ann Aguirre is quickly becoming one of my favorite writers, and *Aftermath* is a big reason why. I am looking forward to reading all the books in the Sirantha Jax series." —ScienceFiction.com

"Why do I love this series so much? Ann Aguirre is an amazing storyteller. She started with this crazy sci-fi world, but what she really has given us are unforgettable characters."
—*Smexy Books*

"Aguirre has created a fleshed-out futuristic world and, yes, a strong heroine to lead us through it. There's always something new to learn about, and the characters—the supporting cast—are also well worth the trip." —*Giraffe Days*

KILLBOX

"Fraught with action, farewells, and sorrow . . . Fans of this series won't be able to put *Killbox* down . . . Ms. Aguirre has left the reader hanging with a finish that guarantees the reader will be on pins and needles waiting for the next installment." —*Fresh Fiction*

continued . . .

"A fabulous book . . . Fans of the big SF flicks out there, from *Serenity* to *Star Wars*, will find everything they love about those stories in this one. Princesses, spaceship battles, monsters, lasers, and aliens, *Killbox* has it all and is poised to thrust this series into a strong, tight spin to its (I hope) victorious end."

—*BookLove*

"Rife with huge, tender emotions, rough anguish that makes me cry, and moments, snatches of joy, that make all of that anguish worthwhile . . . This is the kind of story that makes the emotional roller coaster of reading so appealing."

—*Lurv a la Mode*

"Oh wow! I literally inhaled this book, and I could not put it down . . . an epic space opera . . . five out of five stars!"

—*The Book Pushers*

DOUBLEBLIND

"The world-building was not only tight but excellent. Ms. Aguirre weaves some amazing cultural, environmental, and physical details into the Ithtorian world that I found fascinating, and it is what made this book stand out for me."

—*Impressions of a Reader*

"One of my favorite aspects of this series is Jax. I love her as a heroine, and this book really allows Jax to shine . . . If you are a fan of this series, you know the ending will have you flipping through the calendar to see when it is time for the next in the series. This book puts things into motion, [and] I cannot wait to see where they go from here. Rating: five stars."

—*Smexy Books*

"What marks this series as excellent is the complexity of character . . . Plus, there's the fact that Ann Aguirre tells a good story, plain and simple . . . *Doubleblind* was a fantastic installment in the series, and, while being immensely satisfying, it still left me wanting more in the best possible way."

—*Tempting Persephone*

WANDERLUST

"Fast-paced and thrilling, *Wanderlust* is pure adrenaline. Sirantha Jax is an unforgettable character, and I can't wait to find out what happens to her next. The world Ann Aguirre has created is a roller-coaster ride to remember."

—Christine Feehan, #1 *New York Times* bestselling author

"The details of communication, travel, politics, and power in a greedy, lively universe have been devised to the last degree, but are presented effortlessly. Aguirre has the mastery and vision which come from critical expertise: She is unmistakably a true science fiction fan, writing in the genre she loves."

—*The Independent* (London)

"A thoroughly enjoyable blend of science fiction, romance, and action, with a little something for everyone, and a great deal of fun. It's down and dirty, unafraid to show some attitude."

—*SF Site*

GRIMSPACE

"A terrific first novel full of page-turning action, delightful characters, and a wry twist of humor. Romance may be in the air. Bullets, ugly beasties, and really nasty bad guys definitely are."

—Mike Shepherd, national bestselling author

"An irresistible blend of action and attitude. Sirantha Jax doesn't just leap off the page—she storms out, kicking, cursing, and mouthing off. No wonder her pilot falls in love with her; readers will, too."

—Sharon Shinn, national bestselling author

"A tightly written, edge-of-your-seat read."

—Linnea Sinclair, RITA Award–winning author

Also by Ann Aguirre

Sirantha Jax Series

GRIMSPACE
WANDERLUST
DOUBLEBLIND
KILLBOX
AFTERMATH
ENDGAME

Corine Solomon Series

BLUE DIABLO
HELL FIRE
SHADY LADY
DEVIL'S PUNCH

ENDGAME

ANN AGUIRRE

THE BERKLEY PUBLISHING GROUP
Published by the Penguin Group
Penguin Group (USA) Inc.
375 Hudson Street, New York, New York 10014, USA
Penguin Group (Canada), 90 Eglinton Avenue East, Suite 700, Toronto, Ontario M4P 2Y3, Canada (a division of Pearson Penguin Canada Inc.) • Penguin Books Ltd., 80 Strand, London WC2R 0RL, England • Penguin Group Ireland, 25 St. Stephen's Green, Dublin 2, Ireland (a division of Penguin Books Ltd.) • Penguin Group (Australia), 250 Camberwell Road, Camberwell, Victoria 3124, Australia (a division of Pearson Australia Group Pty. Ltd.) • Penguin Books India Pvt. Ltd., 11 Community Centre, Panchsheel Park, New Delhi—110 017, India • Penguin Group (NZ), 67 Apollo Drive, Rosedale, Auckland 0632, New Zealand (a division of Pearson New Zealand Ltd.) • Penguin Books (South Africa) (Pty.) Ltd., 24 Sturdee Avenue, Rosebank, Johannesburg 2196, South Africa

Penguin Books Ltd., Registered Offices: 80 Strand, London WC2R 0RL, England

ENDGAME

An Ace Book / published by arrangement with the author

PUBLISHING HISTORY
Ace mass-market edition / September 2012

Cover art by Scott M. Fischer.
Cover design by Lesley Worrell.

For information, address: The Berkley Publishing Group,
a division of Penguin Group (USA) Inc.,
375 Hudson Street, New York, New York 10014.

ISBN: 978-1-937007-74-4

ACE
Ace Books are published by The Berkley Publishing Group,
a division of Penguin Group (USA) Inc.,
375 Hudson Street, New York, New York 10014.
ACE and the "A" design are trademarks of Penguin Group (USA) Inc.

PRINTED IN THE UNITED STATES OF AMERICA

10 9 8 7 6 5 4 3 2 1

For Suzanne McLeod,
who heard my cry for help and said, "Of course."

ACKNOWLEDGMENTS

Thanks to Laura Bradford. She accomplishes the impossible and makes it look easy. She is not only my agent but a dear friend, and I am lucky to have her as a partner in my career.

Next, I thank Anne Sowards, who built Jax into the heroine you see today. Her keen insight takes each book and makes it exponentially better. I adore working with someone with such great knowledge, experience, and instincts.

I appreciate my copy editors, the Schwagers. I cherish their diligence in making me look good. They polish my prose without changing my voice; that is an incomparable skill.

Thanks to my amazing personal proofreader, Majda Čolak.

Thanks to my friends in the Loop That Shall Not Be Named. Without y'all in my corner, my head would've exploded this year. I heart you all.

If you enjoy the way this series plays out, thank Sharon Shinn. She gave me the idea how to tie everything up, and I think it works beautifully.

Mega-thanks to Myke Cole for helping with some critical plot issues. He also recommended *The Sling and the Stone* by Colonel Thomas X. Hammes, USMC, to enhance my understanding of this theme; it was an invaluable resource, and I highly recommend it. Additionally, to write this novel, I learned more about guerrilla warfare from Robert Taber's *War of the Flea*, and Che Guevara, who led that rebellion in Cuba and wrote *Guerrilla Warfare*, a combination manifesto and practical handbook. Farah's character is based loosely on the man, at least in the sense that she, too, started in medicine, became sickened by the excess of the Nicuan nobles, and became a combatant to fight for her people.

Thanks to my family. I tend to be a workaholic; I devote long hours to my books, but you're always in my heart. Take this as proof I love y'all. See, it's in writing, so I mean it.

Readers, it's hard to believe Jax is finis. Thanks for sticking with us. *Endgame* marks the end of her journey, but don't worry; I'll revisit this universe with a new SF project. In the meantime, your e-mails thrill me—please keep writing. That's ann.aguirre@gmail.com.

CHAPTER 1

This is not a love story.

It *is* my life, and as such, there is love, loss, war, death, and sacrifice. It's about things that needed to be done and choices made. I regret nothing.

It's easy to say that. Harder to mean it. Sometimes I look back on the branching paths I took to wind up here, and I wonder if there was another road, an easier road, that ends somewhere else. Yet it all boils down to a promise.

That's why I'm on La'heng, after all.

The La'hengrin have been enslaved too long. It's time to change the status quo.

But after six months of futile appointments and following procedure, I'm ready to tear my hair out. Instead, I sit obediently outside the legate's office, as if this meeting will turn out any different. The Pretty Robotics assistant monitors me with discreet glances, as if the VI has been programmed to see how long people will wait before storming off in a fit of rage. So far, I've been here for four hours. I hear a door open and close down the hall, and I recognize the legate as he tries to slide by me.

It *is* around lunchtime, so I push to my feet. "How lovely of you to make it a social occasion," I purr, falling into step with Legate Flavius.

He's caught the assignment to deal with all of our appeals, which makes me think he pissed somebody off. His favorite tactic is avoidance, but since I've caught him, he can't dismiss me without calling for a centurion to eject me from the premises, and I have a legal right to be here. In fact, I have some grounds for a discrimination suit since he made an appointment, then refused to honor it, as he wouldn't do to a Nicuan citizen.

"Come along, Ms. Jax," he says with weary resignation.

"Where are we going?"

"There's a place nearby that does an excellent salad, and they have truly superior wine. None of the local shite."

Fantastic, so he's a snob, and he thinks nothing on La'heng could be as good as what they import from elsewhere. I make a note of that and walk beside him, mentally lining up my arguments. He makes polite, strained small talk on the way to the restaurant, which is atop one of the towering structures nearby. The floor rotates slowly, granting a luxurious view first of the harbor, then the governor's palace in the distance. In Jineba, the buildings are like Terran trees, where the rings reveal their age; you can judge a structure's age by the architectural style and which conquerors designed it. The Nicuan occupation results in a series of colonial buildings, where pillars and columns mask the modern heart.

The penthouse dining room shares that quality, and there are La'hengrin workers instead of bots. They take our orders with quiet humility, and I loathe their subservience because someone has ordered them to labor here. It wasn't a choice, and they don't receive wages. Whatever the nobles call it, this is slavery. Since human interference on La'heng, this has been the situation on their homeworld; their "protectors" have not treated them well. Over the turns, La'heng has changed hands multiple times—sold off like a corporate asset—and currently, Nicuan nobles hold the power. They treat the planet like a vacation colony, complete with native serfs.

Legate Flavius orders for us without asking what I want. To a man like him, I suppose it doesn't matter. Once the niceties are attended, he steeples his hands and regards me across the white-linen-covered table. "Make your case, then."

"Under the Homeland Health Care Act, ratified by the human board of directors in 4867, the natives of La'heng have the right to the best possible treatments, including and not limited to experimental medications. Carvati's Cure ameliorates damage created by widespread exposure to RC-17." When humanity seeded the atmosphere with a chemical that was meant to keep the La'hengrin compliant, we didn't factor for their adaptive physiology. It's been centuries now, and the effects linger still. "Therefore, the Nicuan council actively prohibits a treatment that will improve quality of life for the La'hengrin, which is unlawful according to article thirty-seven, codicil—"

The legate sighs faintly. "Yes, you've inundated my office with claims about your miracle drug. Unfortunately, you haven't passed licensing through the drug administration. As I recall, there have been *no* trials. What kind of monsters would we be if we permitted you to use the La'heng to test your product?"

The kind who makes the La'hengrin your slaves, like the ones you have at home.

I grind my teeth, holding the retort. "We applied for permits to begin trials three months ago. They were denied due to lack of residency requirements."

On Nicu Tertius, the slave trade is legal. There's also a complicated caste system and petty aristocracy constantly warring for the emperor's purple robes. Many nobles posted on La'heng exude a smug superiority that grates on my nerves. This legate is no exception, and it taxes my patience to deal with him.

Flavius smiles. "Ah, yes. Unfortunately, you must achieve residency on La'heng before you can expect to receive rights that come with citizenship."

I want to come across the table and punch him in the face. Instead, I bite my inner lip until I taste copper. The pain focuses my anger into a laser.

"I applied for citizenship," I say carefully. "And my request was denied."

The unctuous smile widens. "I did see that. Your regrettable past makes you rather . . . undesirable, Ms. Jax."

"Excuse me?" I bite out.

"First, Farwan Corporation charged you with terrorism—"

"Those accusations were entirely baseless," I snap.

"As if the business with Farwan wasn't questionable enough, your military career ended in a rather colorful fashion, did it not? To whit, charges of mass murder, dereliction of duty, and high treason."

"I was acquitted. It's illegal to deny me services due to crimes the court judged I did not commit."

"Hm," he says, feigning concern. "Well, feel free to appeal within the Conglomerate courts. Since we are, at least in the tertiary sense, subject to their laws and jurisdictions, if they deem our denial to violate your rights as a Conglomerate citizen in good standing, then we will certainly reconsider the decision."

He knows that will take turns, damn him. Turns to appeal the rejection. Turns to get another application approved. Then I'll have to start over with the permissions to initiate drug trials. They're trying to kill the resistance with blocks and delays.

Assholes.

Holding my temper with sheer willpower, I say, "So you allege that you're denying progress with the cure for the good of the La'heng."

There's that awful, hateful smile again. "Certainly. We take our duty as their protectors very seriously."

"Sure you do." I shove back from the table and stalk away. There's no way I'm spending another minute with this jackass, now that I know it's another dead end. In the past six months, I've met countless trifling bureaucrats who get off on jerking people around. The Nicuan Empire is full of stunted dictators who have secret dreams of being the emperor, and so they rule their tiny department with an iron fist. The fact that they've been sent to La'heng often only increases their despot tendencies. They fall into two categories: those who want to be here because the rules are more lax and those who have been exiled for some transgression. The latter tend to be the most difficult.

Inwardly seething, I depart the restaurant and make my way down to the street. Public transport carries me to the house Vel bought, which serves as our headquarters. Once I hop off the tram, I walk some distance as well. We're off the beaten track for obvious reasons. As I trudge the last kilometer, I reflect that Vel can try to reason with assholes like Flavius. Vel may prove harder to block as he lacks my tarnished reputation. He was a bounty hunter known for his compliance with all regulations, then he commanded the Ithtorian fleet to great personal acclaim. But it's so fragging disheartening to think of starting over; it would mean refilling all the paperwork, permissions, and applications in his name.

And maybe there's no point.

My old friend, Loras, with whom I have a complicated relationship, woven of mingled affection and guilt, thinks going through channels is a monumental waste of time, but he let me do it while he puts other plans in place. Sometimes I can't believe it's been so long since we first met; he was part of the crew that broke me out of the Farwan prison cell on Perlas Station, and for a short while, I owned him, which was pretty horrifying. Then I left him to die, which was worse. I feel like I owe him, in addition to caring about his cause.

But rebellions aren't born overnight. They foment over time with careful nurturing, and while I waste my time with Nicuan officials, Loras is working other angles. By the time I give up the whole thing as untenable, he'll be ready to move. In a way, I'm his stalking horse. While they're screwing with me, the nobles won't expect problems from any other quarter.

"How did it go?" Vel asks, when I walk in. He gets back from flight school before I finish up my work in the city, and it's nice to have him waiting. Before coming to La'heng, we agreed that we'll explore the galaxy together, once our business here is complete. To make that happen, I need a pilot; he needs a navigator. Symbiotic.

An Ithtorian exile, he's over two meters tall, covered in chitin, with hinged legs, and my mark on his thorax, a character that means grimspace in Ithtorian. His side-set eyes and expressive mandible no longer seem strange to me though people on La'heng sometimes stare if he's out of faux-skin.

"For shit," I mutter. "Who I am is actually working against us. Or at least, they're using my past to block my petitions."

"I am sorry, Sirantha."

When we first met on Gehenna, Vel had taken a job to retrieve me for Farwan Corporation. He slid into a friend's skin and figured out a way to get me to go to New Terra with him willingly. That could've ended badly for me. Fortunately, Vel was as honorable a bounty hunter as he is in every other regard, and once he realized the Corp was using me as a scapegoat, he became my biggest ally. Now, he's my dearest friend . . . with nuances of something else, maybe, someday. But he doesn't look for promises any more than I'm looking to make our relationship more complicated. His mere presence defuses some of the tension and frustration that comes with the territory. He's always supported me, believing the best of me even when I screw up, even when I don't deserve it.

I shrug. "Loras warned us it would be like this, but . . . I'm not used to such abject, consistent failure. I keep thinking I'll stumble on the magic handshake and get somewhere with these assholes."

He crosses to me and runs his claws down my back, more comforting than it sounds. "It is unlikely."

"I know." My mouth sets into a firm line. "They'll regret it. Someday."

"You gave them a chance to do the right thing. They are more interested in maintaining their own luxurious lifestyles. I shall not care when we raze them to the ground."

His quiet assessment of their prospects makes me laugh, partly his calm tone, and partly because that day seems so far off. But I'm capable of playing the long game, as the Nicuan will discover.

CHAPTER 2

I've consulted with Suni Tarn, the former chancellor of New Terra, previously, and it's time to bring Loras into the loop; however, it's best we aren't associated in public, hence the secrecy. The former politician arrives by private aircar. He has the credits and connections to permit such an extravagance whereas the Nicuan wouldn't grant me a license to buy a pet. A spring afternoon, though not as warm as it would be on other worlds, the sunlight is faint, and it has a sharpness like crystal as it falls across his face. To make things more interesting, he's brought his partner, Edun Leviter. The two men step from the vehicle and cross the yard toward the house. At my behest, the door swishes open, permitting them entrance.

To my astonishment, Tarn was already here when I arrived with Vel. He joined Leviter, who amuses himself by playing with the noble houses, causing some to rise and others to topple; for him, it's a hobby, a sideline to his true trade. As I understand it, he'd gone into partial retirement since he paired up with Tarn, taking less dangerous work for his partner's peace of mind. When we offered him a chance to do some real kingmaking, he couldn't sign on fast enough.

Through the windows, the sky overhead is a gauzy blue. Even in the city, air traffic is light since only the elite have access to the sky lanes. Out here, it's even quieter, as the La'hengrin can't own their own vehicles; they can only operate them for their masters. This injustice has me plotting with a former politician and . . . whatever Leviter was. From Tarn's veiled hints, it was something awesome . . . and dreadful. I never thought I'd see Tarn again, but our paths crossed my first week on world, and to my surprise, he didn't shy away as if I had the plague. He holds no grudges, despite my decision to alter grimspace beacons, creating endless complications for him.

Today, we'll discuss the petitions.

In the foyer, I murmur something polite and shake Tarn's hand. His partner is tall and slender; he greets me with a firm handshake. Leviter looks clever and sly. He has a narrow face with dark eyes, capped with well-groomed silver hair. A neat goatee frames a thin mouth, and his mien gives away none of his thoughts. From their body language, the two are more than friends though Tarn's never discussed their relationship. They're both private men—and tremendously useful. More to the point, they look happy, comfortable even, which means they've been together a while.

"Your reputation precedes you," Leviter says.

I figure he's giving me fair warning what to expect from him. "Only half of it's true."

Leviter flashes a sardonic smile. "That's more than enough."

"Is Loras here?" Tarn interjects. "I look forward to meeting him."

"Yes, the others are in the ready room. This way." I gesture for them to follow me.

Outside the city, the house is perfectly situated for skullduggery such as this, and it's large enough to house everyone—Loras, Zeeka, Constance, Vel, and me—without any trouble. Since the property lacks a pool and formal garden, however, most nobles found it too provincial, and Vel got a good bargain; it had been on the market for a while.

"Any luck?" Though it's not a specific question, I know what Tarn's asking.

I shake my head. "I didn't imagine it would be easy, but it's worse than I expected."

"Have you cited the legal precedents, as I suggested?" Tarn asks.

"For all the good it does. The Nicuan are entrenched."

As we walk, Leviter says, "I trust Suni told you I have some ideas of how to start?"

"You're committed to the cause then?"

Leviter smiles. "I specialize in this sort of thing."

I decide not to ask; sometimes it's better not to question your allies. The resistance is a grassroots movement with a few volunteers filling out forms and holding poorly attended rallies. At this point, the Imperials don't even take us seriously enough to shut them down.

Tarn nods. "It's true. If anyone can help you get the job done, Edun can."

"Excellent news. We can use all hands." This is true enough, as my own efforts have been spectacularly fruitless.

"Ultimately, you know that the civilized requests will go nowhere." Leviter speaks the words with grave caution, as if he wonders whether I'm the sort of person who believes you can change the world through peaceable means.

I would like that to be true, but it's not. That's an idealist's dream, and I'm too far past my starry-eyed youth to put my faith in fairy tales. Yet we must start somewhere, and I want it on record that we tried lawful measures before we escalated.

"I'd be surprised if anything came of them since the nobles run all the courts on Nicu Quintus." That's what the nobles call La'heng.

I step into the ready room, where Loras is waiting. At the moment, Vel's at flight school, and Zeeka is tinkering upstairs with something that will explode if he's not careful. It has been delightful exploring the galaxy with the grown-up version of Baby-Z. Before getting to know the Mareq, I never could've imagined such a bright and cheerful soul.

Loras stands and offers his hand to the two men. He's average height, thin, with blond hair and azure eyes. When I first met Loras, he had an unearthly beauty, which made his face disturbing because it made me think he couldn't care enough about events to be affected by them. In fact, that untouchable aspect came as a result of the *shinai*-bond, which makes his people reliant on others for their protection. When you're prevented from having experiences, you look young; it's natural cause and effect. In the turns I've known him, he's lost that deceptive innocence, and since he took Carvati's Cure, Loras has changed. The *shinai*-bond kept his integral savagery at bay, but over the last turn, he's become fierce and driven, hardening into the steel he'll need to lead this rebellion.

I remember the promise I made to him, before the Morgut War. At the time, I was trying to apologize for leaving him to die and to explain how much I valued him as a person. In response, he asked the impossible of me: "The only way you can prove that is to set me free." From there, it went to impossible research and a remedy for the damage done to his people. Though it took turns, we have that cure now. It's not enough that Loras is a free man; his people deserve the same liberty. This injustice cannot stand.

Shaking off the reverie, I perform the introductions. Afterward, I take a seat; and the others follow suit. Leviter's dark eyes hold a hardness except when they touch on Suni Tarn. If the man has an Achilles' heel, it's sitting beside him, hand on his knee.

After the courtesies, Loras asks skeptically, "Will Jax's petitions do any good?"

Leviter addresses the question. "So long as you have realistic expectations, it will not prove a useless exercise."

"Oh?" I arch a brow. This is why Tarn brought his partner in; he's the idea man, while Tarn has always been the mouthpiece.

"I'll keep tabs on the situation. See how various nobles react to the emancipation proposal and requests to open centers where the La'hengrin can openly receive the cure."

Tarn nods. "Then we'll know whom to approach. Whom to bribe later. There may well be sympathizers who think what's happening is wrong. They just don't dare act."

"Maybe," I say.

I fetch us all some *kaf* from the kitchen-mate. The tray comes with all the fixings, but Tarn drinks it straight. Playing hostess, I serve and observe while Loras asks a number of pointed questions regarding their interest and commitment.

After the brief interrogation, Leviter scrutinizes Loras. "You aren't what I expected."

To me, it's clear what he means. Loras has a hard quality you don't usually see in the sheltered La'heng, who are treated like children and not encouraged to think for themselves. Unlike children—due to the RC-17 disaster—they can't rebel. Loras has been off world, traveled extensively, and under the care of his last master, he fended for himself quite a bit. His time with Hon left him angry and bitter, but it made him stronger, too, determined to do whatever it takes to free his people. I envy his passion because I've only ever felt that way about grimspace, and that seems less worthy.

Loras meets Leviter's sharkish gaze squarely, then he shrugs. "Does it matter?"

"Not really. I came to La'heng for a new playground. This cause will suffice."

"What do you mean, 'playground'?" Loras demands.

Tarn says, "Did you hear about the sex scandal in the governor's palace? It ended in two suicides and a change of fortune for the noble they appointed to the office."

Loras nods. "Of course. It was all over the planetary bounce."

"That was my work," Leviter says softly, proudly.

Holy shit.

"And you did that for fun?" I ask, trying to understand.

"The old governor was a perverse pig of a man," Tarn mutters.

I raise a brow. "Do I even want to know?"

Leviter eyes me with cold calm. "That depends. How do you feel about men who prey on girls less than twelve turns, who can't defend themselves?"

"I hope he's dead," Loras snarls.

Tarn smiles. "He was the first suicide."

Something in that look makes me wonder if Leviter had something to do with it, if it was a murder so convincing that the best Nicuan examiners missed the clues. The man's flat smile gives nothing away, and I decide not to press. It only matters that the bastard's dead.

"Who was the other?" Loras asks.

"His procurer."

That's an especially satisfying answer.

"Let me guess," Loras mutters. "He bore the title of protector."

Tarn rubs his fingers against his brow, as if the system pains him; Leviter sets a hand on Suni's shoulder to comfort him. Then the former chancellor asks, "How did you know?"

"Because it's disgusting. And too common." Loras clenches his jaw, staring at the screen across the room, more for the distraction than from true interest.

The news is on, showing some dignitary proceeding in entourage fashion toward his next entertainment. A La'hengrin girl walks six paces behind the Nicuan noble. She can't be more than eleven, and she's loaded down with packages, treated like a beast of burden.

And that's the least of what you see in the capital on a daily basis. The La'hengrin have no rights on a planet that belongs to them—that we stole from them. The "protection" of the *shinai*-bond masks so many offenses, so many abuses, that it took a forty-eight-page memorandum to document everything I've seen. Not that I expect the court to care.

"You sent in the citizenship appeal today?" Suni asks.

"I did. The Conglomerate rep said they'll review it and respond within sixty days."

"It will be more like a turn," Loras mutters.

Leviter shakes his head. "Six months. I can pull a few strings."

"He has a way of collecting favors," Tarn explains.

"That will be helpful down the line." I drain my *kaf.*

Leviter didn't touch his drink; I wonder if he's the paranoid type who never eats anything he didn't prepare himself; he gives off that vibe. Seems like it would be hard to love a man like that, but he's probably different, alone with Tarn. He'd have to be.

"I'll be in touch," Leviter says.

CHAPTER 3

Life is damned frustrating at the moment.

It's been nine days since my aborted lunch with Legate Flavius, four days since we consulted with Tarn and Leviter. I feel like getting stone drunk, but that won't help. Instead, I have a meeting with the people Loras has been working with; they form the core of our rebellion. He's picked up support quietly in the city, offering the cure to those who want it and are willing to fight for the cause. Zeeka works in the lab with Loras, producing the cure in small quantities. It's illegal, but at this point, I don't care.

The justice system is totally fragged.

Zeeka, a fine specimen of adult Mareq male, follows me on bare, webbed feet. He eschews clothing when we're at home though he conforms anytime we go out. Which means he's got on a shirt and trousers today. His hide is mottled green with brown spots, and he has a pale belly. Huge, muddy eyes dominate a round face, and the curved slit of his mouth makes him look like he's perpetually smiling. He can also puff out his throat if he's pissed off or feeling playful. It amazes me that I've known this kid since he came out of an egg. He's got an eagerness and a zest for life that never fails to move me.

I face forward, keeping an eye on Vel and Loras in front of me. To be honest, I don't even know where we are. Loras leads us through a complex system of tunnels below the city streets. Along the way, Vel disables a few bots and wipes their memory cores, so they won't show a record of our passage. Loras taps a code on a security panel, and the door slides open. There are forty people in the room, an open storage chamber with scuff marks on the floor and trails in the dust to show that things have been moved recently.

Vel leans in. "They keep furniture here for formal state occasions. They have set up for a ball up top, and this room will be vacant for several hours."

It's just storage, but spyware won't penetrate walls this thick, and you can tell at a glance there's nothing present. No panels to slide aside, no holes hiding video equipment. That reassures skittish volunteers that they won't be arrested as soon as they walk out the door. The fear on their faces reinforces the risk we're taking. Yet none of them leave, even as others join us.

At last, all fifty of the La'hengrin arrive. At this point, Loras outlines his plan. While I was trying to work within the system, he cured people; he recruited and convinced them he has the wherewithal to change the world. He is . . . amazing.

A lovely, red-haired woman puts up her hand. "Is the base completed?"

Loras has been quietly requisitioning supplies and equipment, constructing our secret ops center in a mountain range to the north. I haven't been there yet, but it's nearly ready to go. From there, our intelligence division will coordinate strikes and relay messages.

"It will be sufficient for us to commence operations in a couple of weeks."

"Do we have enough personnel?" I ask.

If we hit hard and fast on multiple fronts—with the right spin, the Conglomerate will declare La'heng a red port, which means local conditions are unstable to the point of being unsafe for interstellar travel. They'll lock La'heng down, giving us the freedom to fight without worrying about reinforcements from Nicuan. And Imperial forces can't take on the whole Conglomerate, even to help their beleaguered colonists. That will give us time to deploy the cure to the La'hengrin and train them to fight back on their own behalf.

"Enough to run the first mission and get the planet coded red. I'll need Leviter's help with that. You're still in touch with him?"

I nod.

"Contact them. I'll go over your agenda with you privately."

Which I take to mean, *Shut up and let me talk.* I comply; Loras is awesome when he shifts into command mode. Zeeka puffs his throat at me in an affectionate taunt, and I grin back. Mary, it feels good to be starting phase two. I'm not naturally patient or tolerant.

It takes another hour for him to run down assignments, then the crew breaks up. I won't see everyone again until we move to the base. I hate to leave the house Vel bought; it's been as much a home to me as anywhere I've lived in the last ten turns. Which isn't saying much, I suppose. I've been on ships since I was thirteen, apart from a hellish six months at boarding school and my stint at the nav-training academy on New Terra.

The red-haired woman lingers until I make eye contact. Then she offers her hand. "I'm Farah."

The La'heng are an attractive people, but Farah's skin glows with a luminous quality; her eyes are the green of a verdant hillside. And her hair gleams like pure, untarnished copper. When you combine that with a heart-shaped face, full lips, and a pointed chin, it's hard to look away from her.

"Nice to meet you." I figure there's some reason she's introduced herself.

"He told me"—she jerks her head at Loras—"that you once held his *shinai*-bond."

Oh, Mary. I can't imagine this conversation leading anywhere good.

"I did. Not on purpose, though. It kind of just happened."

I *did* help him. On Lachion, when he was dying from damage inflicted by the savage Teras, I saved his life when the others paid him no attention at all. In most ways, my lover, March, is a good person, better than me, and if I were capable of hating him, it wouldn't be for wrongs he's done me—there've been some over the turns—but for how March treated Loras when he held the *shinai*-bond. At the moment, he's on Nicu Tertius, raising his nephew to be a productive member of society, despite powerful Psi ability that might otherwise cripple the kid. The long-distance aspect of our relationship has been tough. But in regard to Loras, he had a blind spot—and he treated our mutual friend with the casual discrimination that's excused because everyone does it.

But it's still not all right.

Farah watches my face while these thoughts tumble through my head. What she sees makes her smile. "I wanted to thank you for that."

"Really?" I ask, surprised.

"Yes. If not for you, I wouldn't be free. Your guilt drove you to help your friend, and the result makes up for what came before."

From her insight, it's clear that Loras confides in her. She's somebody I need to get to know better, when time permits. But he's already at the door, beckoning me, every bit the impatient general. I murmur my excuses and stride away.

"Come," Loras orders. "I'll brief you on the way."

After I hear him out regarding the interdiction on La'heng's ports, I nod. "I'll contact Leviter and Tarn tonight."

"Excellent." He turns to Zeeka. "How are you coming with the demolitions training? I need a specialist."

The Mareq gives his wide, openmouthed smile. "As best I can. It's hard to locate helpful texts. The ones I do find are old or outdated."

Yeah, for obvious reasons, the Nicuan nobles don't want the La'hengrin having access to that kind of information. Though they can't fight, I'm not clear on how far the boundaries stretch. Could they trap an expanse of land? The result would certainly be aggressive, but since they wouldn't be doing it directly . . . well, I'll have to ask Loras. It might be a loophole we can use out in the provinces.

Zeeka goes on, "But Vel is helping me."

On some planets, you could totally get an annex class in *How to Blow Things Up*, but La'heng isn't one of them. The nobility controls credits, policy, and education, all the better to keep the natives ignorant and subservient. There's an underclass among the Nicuan, too, but they had the opportunity to learn before they arrived on world, along with the rest of the house retinue.

Loras nods. "Keep at it. I need you ready to go in three weeks. Will you be set then?"

"I will be." This kid—he's an adult, but it's hard for me to think of him as such since I've known him since he was a tadpole—gives 110 percent.

The Mareq have relatively short life spans. They're grown by five, middle-aged by twenty, and die between forty and forty-five turns. Fortunately, they breed and gestate fast—and in large numbers. They also possess the J-gene, which is rare and lets them navigate faster-than-light ships. Few humans have the capability, and NBS—Navigator Burnout Syndrome—has led to a dearth of jumpers who can take ships safely through grimspace. It's possible that in a hundred turns, the Mareq will solve the navigator shortage; the star roads will be full of Mareq. When I realize I'll likely live to find out—via the experimental nanites that prevent normal aging—the epiphany startles me.

Damn. Loras is talking, and I've missed half of it. I glance at Vel, who inclines his head. He'll catch me up if I pretend to be current for the rest of the conversation. I tune in with renewed focus.

". . . so it all hinges on Leviter and Tarn. This attack, in and of itself, won't be enough to get the planet locked down."

"There will be damage on multiple fronts," I say, "but not the kind that closes ports."

"Exactly. We need spin."

I nod. "Leviter's specialty."

"March is coming, isn't he?" Loras asks. "Four or five days from now?"

Oh, March. At last. Mentally, I do a happy dance, but I don't show any of my euphoria or trepidation. Outwardly, I'm cool.

"His visit won't affect the timetable. He's staying for two weeks, and you have us scheduled to move in three."

"I wasn't questioning your right to have visitors, Jax." Loras aims a smirk at me.

"I sounded defensive as hell, didn't I?"

Zeeka says, "Pretty much."

This can only lead to ribbing, so I zip my lips for the remainder of our walk. When we get back to the house, Vel updates me with the rest of Loras's strategy, and it's solid. Though I'm not a tactician myself, I appreciate a cunning plan.

In the morning, I set up a meeting with Tarn and Leviter. It doesn't take long to explain what we need, and Leviter agrees to do his part. On the bounce, he can make the attacks look worse than they are, and he can pull the strings on high-ranking officials to push for getting La'heng classified as a red port, no ships in or out.

Without a single shot fired, the war has begun.

CHAPTER 4

March strides toward me like a conquering hero.

Instinctively, the people between him and me clear out of his path, recognizing the determined demeanor of a military man even if he doesn't sport a Conglomerate uniform anymore. I quicken my pace toward him, a walk becoming a run, until I close the distance between us. He catches me up in his arms and swings me around.

I've dreamed of this moment for a turn.

Vid-mail tided me over until the next time I could see him, touch him. He waited so long for me, five times this long, in fact, but I'm impatient as hell, and it feels like an eternity since I walked out of his apartment on Nicu Tertius. He promised we'd comm—that he'd visit—but this is the first time I've seen him since that day. Work kept me busy, but deep within their compartmentalized slots, my yearning for him—and grimspace—never faltered—twin insatiable addictions.

He cups my face in his hands and kisses me like my lips will save his life. An ache springs up, and I wrap my arms around him, heedless of the jostling passersby in the spaceport. He tastes of mint and a darker tang, expensive liquor. I lose myself in March, as I've always done, then I hear his voice in my head: *Mary, I missed you.*

Me, too, I think.

March leans his brow against mine until the kid, his nephew, intrudes. "Are we going to stand here all day? People are staring."

Stepping back, I glance around March to greet Sasha. He's less timid than he was when I came by for dinner. Taller, too. I don't know enough about kids to be sure if he's big—or small—for his age, but I glimpse the gangly promise of the young man he'll become—he's twelve now—and definitely not as childish as he seemed before.

"Sorry," I say. "I really missed your uncle."

"I get that," he mutters, but it's not fear or even hostility I see in his face this time. It's just simple distaste for being part of a public spectacle.

"It's good to see you," I say because it is, as it means March is here.

At last.

First order of business is to get out of the spaceport and take him home. We have *two* glorious weeks together before Sasha's school term resumes; he's doing well enough for Psi Corp to sanction a trip. Unlike when March dragged him to Gehenna, this journey's been vetted and approved. This holiday falls during the calm before the storm. Since Flavius forewarned me with his taunts, I know it's going to come down to my lack of citizenship. When they block my latest petition—and I foresee no other outcome—then we have no legal recourse. Which leaves illegal ones.

Loras has always been prepared for that eventuality. He understands that you can't negotiate with those determined to strip a planet of its resources and who prefer to keep the native populace in chains. Historically, no homeworld has been occupied so often.

Putting those dark thoughts aside, I lace my fingers through March's, noting he's got their bags slung over one shoulder. He's taller than I remember, but just as ugly-handsome, with a strong, harsh face, golden hawk eyes, and the bumpy, oft-broken nose. It doesn't look like he's cut his hair in months; I wonder if he did that for me. I've always preferred it long.

Of course, he tells me.

A warm shiver quakes through me. Two weeks aren't enough. It's going to half kill me when he leaves, but until then, I have fourteen days with him. Resentment flares that he can't stay—just a spark—quickly quelled. Intellectually, I understand why he must go. He has to look after Sasha. So I'll store up memories to last. I tell myself I'll be busy forging ahead in the liberation of La'heng, then put the prospect of another farewell, another separation, from my mind.

I smile up at him. *The things I'm gonna do to you in thanks . . .*

"You're talking silently," Sasha guesses, as we walk. "That's rude, you know."

March grins down at the kid, and my heart actually stutters a little. I've never seen him so . . . free. Words like contentment and peace didn't use to apply to March, but they do now. My resentment fades; it's impossible for me to doubt his choices when parenthood so obviously agrees with him.

"We're not talking about you," I assure him.

"Then it's sex stuff." Sasha sighs.

I'm not sure if I should show amusement, but March gives me permission with a nudge in my head, and pretty soon, all three of us are laughing like mad, loud enough to draw a few looks from other travelers, but this time, Sasha's in on it, too, and he doesn't mind the attention. From what I remember of being a kid, mood swings like that are normal. You're surly, then not-surly, all within half an hour, thanks to the crazy hormone cocktail running amok in your bloodstream.

"So where are we going?" March asks, for Sasha's benefit. He's gleaned everything he needs to know, and more besides, hanging around my head.

"I've got a place."

Guilt surges. I refused to stay on Nicu Tertius with him, but here, I have my first dirtside residence since Gehenna, when I worked at Hidden Rue and lived in a garret above Adele's place. I miss her so much; and I know that Vel is still hurting. It's ironic that the same woman meant so much—in different ways—to both of us; doubtless she would argue that's evidence of the divine. For him, the pain bleeds on and on until such a time when he doesn't feel like it's killing him, measured in tens of turns. He's good at covering, but he's heartbroken, and I make an imperfect consolation prize.

I wonder what March will make of the fact that Vel and I are roommates. It made sense to take one place, divide up the space, and share costs. Loras, Constance, and Zeeka are there, too, so it's not like it's a romantic arrangement.

It's all right, he tells me silently. *I understand* why *you're here.*

Right. There's a mission involved, and he knows that. It's not like I decided to ground myself because the weather's nice, and the scenery's pretty. La'heng is a cold world; the flora and fauna are pretty uniform. The trees go brown if it's dry, but they don't shed leaves. Instead, needles drop during the drought. There are four seasons: Warm (Ferran), Cool (Ayfell), Dry (Taivan), and Wet (Shoofu). The weather definitely isn't the same as New Terra's because the patterns are more consistent, something to do with the moon and tides.

In fact, I'm already going nuts here. March senses it. If I hadn't augmented all the filing of motions with training Zeeka to jump, I might have lost my mind entirely; Dina was kind enough to provide us a nav-training chair and simulator before she took off. All told, it's been a long, fruitless turn, and I can't *wait* to get March home alone. That thought cheers me as I step out of the spaceport and fasten my jacket.

"Is this yours?" Sasha asks, when a silver aircar zooms up to the platform.

"Yep."

"I've always wanted to ride in one of these!"

It's a sleek model, sexy and aerodynamic, not boxy like some of the hover cabs. You feel like a million creds when you're driving this thing, not that Vel let me more than once, after I scraped the paint. He's rather possessive of this ride—and I don't blame him. March cuts me an amused look. The door lifts up with a hydraulic hiss, so we can get in.

"Good to see you again, Commander," Vel says.

"It's just March now. And you, too, Vel." He chucks the luggage behind the rear seat.

"Sit up front," I tell Sasha, who's bouncing.

I hope he's learned better TK mastery in the last turn.

"Really?" He doesn't wait for confirmation, just scrambles

into the seat next to Vel. He's definitely braver than the kid I met, because the Bug doesn't spook him a bit. Instead, the kid studies the buttons and lights on the control panel, then he turns to Vel with a bunch of questions.

Hope this won't be awkward. I don't want it to be.

For a second, I forget that March is in my head. His surprise feels like a cool chill, then he asks, *What?*

Vel and I came to a new understanding. It's not the same relationship I have with March, but there are *feelings*, and we've been together for the last turn. I'm not sure how March is going to react to that, if he'll think he's got competition, which seems silly, considering Vel and I aren't even the same species. It's just not the same. Hopefully, March is enlightened enough to get that.

He skims these messy thoughts, and then there's silence. Not an exodus, but he locks down like he doesn't want me to feel what he does. And that worries me.

March?

I'm jealous he gets to be with you, he says finally. *But I'm not upset that you care about him. You care for Loras and Zeeka and Constance, too. I don't want to keep you in a glass box, Jax. You'd never survive it.*

There's a pause.

Unless you want to sleep with him. In which case, yes, I mind. I mind to hell and back. I'm not that *enlightened. Your sainted Kai probably would've given his blessing.* Touch of ire, there.

How funny, he's still envious of a dead man.

It's not *funny.*

He wasn't a saint, I point out. *Kai would've said my desire for someone else meant our time together was finished. He wouldn't have fought for me.* You *would. You have.*

March turns to me, smiles, and laces our fingers together. For a few moments, I just listen to the ask and answer going on up front. Maybe I should have expected it, but Vel is good with Sasha, patient without being patronizing.

We'll make it, March promises me. *I know there are challenges, but we've come too far together to give up now.*

He's right. We've faced worse than this. And the next two weeks will be glorious.

CHAPTER 5

At his first glimpse of the house, March turns to me with a questioning look. "It's bigger than I expected."

"Vel bought it. Good price, too." The place is located in the mountains north of Jineba; from here, the view is spectacular.

"It's beautiful."

Vel depresses a button, opening the door to the storage bay adjacent to the main house. Within, there are a number of vehicles in various states of disrepair. Though he doesn't have Dina's fine touch with machinery, he's nonetheless excellent at fixing broken things, courtesy of his turns on Gehenna. Like Loras, Dina was part of the team that first rescued me on Perlas Station. She's not with us anymore; she put together her own crew, and she runs her own ship. I miss her.

While March helps me from the aircar, Vel looks after Sasha. I haven't asked him to entertain the kid, but this is the way it's worked out. The boy wants to see the shuttle Vel's modifying. I don't look forward to the day when we use it for the first time; I've had enough of war, and yet here I am again, ready to fight. I don't want to. In war, people die. But I didn't cut the cards this time, and I *will* play the hand I'm dealt.

March follows me into the house, where Zeeka and Loras

are watching a news program. Constance, my PA, is sitting with them, but she's data scanning something, based on the rapid movements of her eyes. She started her existence as a small sphere; she's evolved to running ships and inhabiting a Pretty Robotics body since then. And I couldn't get by without her. I've seen her in two different casings, and this third one looks to be permanent. At least, I hope she won't encounter any difficulty. I bought her a Paula from Pretty Robotics; this time, she's a grandmotherly sort of woman with a round build, a friendly face, and a crop of short silver hair. Constance likes this form because it removes the issue of sexual attraction from most sentient species, and people are predisposed to treat her with respect. They also don't suspect her of having diabolical plans behind her kind brown eyes.

To March, Loras offers a lazy wave in greeting, his demeanor laced with subtle attitude. He remembers being *shinai*-bound to March, no doubt. And he's not thrilled about it though it would be worse if March had been one of those bastards who came to La'heng to pick out a pretty slave. March's great-uncle held Loras's bond before; I've never asked what sort of man the great-uncle was, or what he did with Loras. I fear the answers.

"Come to join the rebellion?" Loras asks lazily.

"Just for a visit." But March's tone reflects regret. It goes against his nature not to fight. He's a bit quixotic in that regard, always taking other people's causes as his own.

"You may not remember me, Commander March, but I'm glad I got to see you again, so I can thank you."

That always astonishes me—that Zeeka claims to recollect what happened to him when we took him—he was so tiny. I wonder if he recalls the pain of his death as well, but I've never summoned the courage to ask. It's enough that he appreciates his second chance, and that he doesn't blame me for what I did to him.

For once, March is pretty close to speechless. At last he manages, "For what?"

"Caring for me."

"Anyone would have done the same. I'm glad to see you're well," he answers.

I grin, deciding I've let Zeeka discomfit him long enough. "Come on, I'll show you the upstairs."

"But Sasha . . ."

"You'll notice if he gets upset, right? He's safe with Vel."

"True. His distress isn't subtle."

He follows without protest, the luggage over his shoulder, and I take him directly to my room. When the door swishes shut behind us, he drops the bags and pulls me into his arms. This isn't a hello kiss, like the one at the spaceport. It's far more visceral, and I need his touch so desperately that I can't think. I'm not made for long periods of celibacy.

Neither am I . . . and it's been a long dry spell, Jax.

Yeah, those five turns where he didn't know where I was— in my defense, neither did I—then we reconciled and had to wait another turn. Nobody ever said our path would be easy, I suppose, but it seems to me it's been harder than most. His kisses drive me until I'm wrapped around him, arms and legs, about to lose my mind.

"Well," I say aloud. "I could show you the rest of the house . . . or—"

He cuts in, "I like 'or.' I am *in love* with 'or.'"

While Sasha is occupied now, he'll probably come looking for us at the worst possible moment. "We have to be quick."

March yanks my shirt over my head. "I guarantee that won't be a problem."

His trembling makes me believe he hasn't touched anyone else, just like he said he wouldn't. I gave him permission, but he didn't take it. Like me, he's been focused on other things. No sex, until now.

Yes, there.

He bites down on the curve of my throat. I scramble out of the rest of my clothes, too impatient to let him undress me. March is clumsy in his haste. I can see he's been working out; his stomach has new definition, and his arms are even bigger than before. I imagine him using fitness machines to sweat out the desire that haunts my own sleep, and he nods, still a quiet warmth in my head.

I can't go slow. Tell me you're ready.

My assent is all he needs to bear me back on the bed, touching and stroking with hurried, desperate hands. I dig my fingers into his hard shoulders; and then he's inside me. He holds there, kissing me ravenously, then his movements begin with unpolished need. His longing fills my head, a blistering, white-hot crackle of desire, until I'm breathless and groaning beneath him. My legs curl around his hips as I urge him faster, deeper, harder, then, for the first time, he leaves me behind.

March arches and shudders, his eyes squeezing shut. I don't know that he's ever lost control like this with me before. I'm frustrated, obviously, but also a little moved. He wants me *this* much. I hold him and stroke his hair, his back, while he gets his breathing under control. A few moments later, he makes it up to me with fingers and lips, and I come undone with a quiet scream.

Afterward, he holds me, peppering gentle kisses against my brow. "I'm sorry. I'll do better next time."

"I have no complaints."

"You have to say that, or you'll destroy my fragile male psyche."

I lever up on an elbow to bite him. "Have I ever given the impression that tact is one of my greater gifts?"

He laughs. "Point."

With a sigh, I say, "We should shower and get dressed. Sasha is being remarkably understanding, but I don't want to tax him."

He sobers, his amber gaze going bleak with remembered pain. "He noticed how sad I was after you left."

"It was hard for me, too," I whisper.

"I tried to put up a good front, but I didn't eat much for the first month, and I barely slept."

The March I remember wasn't quite this open. He found it easier to show his feelings with forays into my head, but he didn't *talk* about them. Being a parent has taught him emotional candor, I suppose. You can't raise a kid to confide in you if you don't muster up the courage to do the same.

I can offer no less than the same bravery. "I focused on work . . . but I lost four kilos after I arrived on La'heng."

"You didn't need to." He runs exploratory hands down my rib cage, noting the slight difference in my build. "You feel almost fragile now."

"I'm not."

He nods. "Let's get that shower."

Cleaning up leads to bathroom sex, which leaves us both shaky, then a real shower. We do so individually because showering with him might mean death by dehydration. By the time Vel's call comes, we're dressed again. Mostly.

"Jax, Sasha has finished examining all the vehicles and is wondering where the two of you are," he says.

"We'll be down shortly," I promise.

To give credence to the lie I intend to tell Sasha, I take him on a quick tour of the house. He only pays cursory attention, then we join the others in the ready room, where there's a comm center, comfortable furnishings, and a big screen to monitor the Imperial response to our petitions.

"Did you see anything you like?" March asks.

Sasha nods with enthusiasm. "Tomorrow, Vel is going to show me how to modify a short-range shuttle for in-atmosphere use."

"There are some ruins nearby. If we finish overhauling the navigation system, we can go for a test drive . . . with your uncle's permission."

"Can I? Please?"

March tilts his head at me like I *asked* Vel to do this. "Of course, as long as the weather's clear."

More alone time, he says silently, and I beam in response.

CHAPTER 6

March has been here four days.

The time passes in a beautiful blur of eating, laughing, talking, and sex. Though it can't last, I'm desperate to drink him in. Store up good memories to tide me over during the dark times to come. Deliberately, he and I don't speak of the parting that will occur in ten days. It's like we're in a bubble, where nothing bad can touch us.

Or at least, we pretend.

"What's a normal day for you like?" I ask.

It's late, and we're in bed. His arms are wrapped around me, and I'm snuggled against his side. Such moments without threat of attack or interruption seem like they've been scarce.

He regards me thoughtfully. "Why?"

"I'm curious."

"I get up, make breakfast—"

"You mean you program the kitchen-mate."

"And?" March eyes me with a half smile.

"Go on."

"Then I see Sasha off to school. After that, I work out. Do some household chores. When he gets home, I help with his homework. We eat dinner together. Watch some vids."

"Do you have friends there?"

He considers. "Friendly acquaintances, people I talk to at school functions."

"But you're not close to anyone." It's not a question.

March strokes my back lazily. "Are you worried I've met someone?"

"No." *Okay, maybe a little.*

"I'm not seeing anyone, Jax. That would be pointless when I'm so in love with you."

The night passes swiftly after that, but we don't sleep much.

The next afternoon, we're all in the ready room, watching the result of the hearings. March senses my nerves and laces our fingers together. Sasha is sprawled on the floor, playing a game with Zeeka. Vel isn't around; he's in the storage bay, working on the shuttle. I wonder if he's doing that on purpose—giving March and me so much space. I need to talk to him, I think.

Loras looks resigned as we await the verdict. The pretty, dark-haired presenter on the vid stands outside an enormous, opulent structure that serves as the governmental hub, near the governor's palace. Like the surrounding structures, it's not of La'hengrin design, as it was built when the first wave of invaders occupied the planet. Loras growls beneath his breath.

"Today, the Imperial board of governors are expected to rule on the final appeal for the widespread availability of Carvati's Cure. This miracle drug is purported to restore La'hengrin autonomy and would obviate the need for any Imperial presence." Maybe I'm imagining it, but she seems sympathetic to the cause. From her appearance, she's an ONN—Omni News Net—talking head, not bribed by Nicuan authorities. That means we have a shot at some fair coverage on the bounce.

Then, as we watch, a squadron of centurions march up behind her. Their uniforms shine in the sunlight; it's not metal, but a synthetic polymer burnished to appear so. I glance at March, wondering if he ever wore that armor; I know he fought on Nicuan for many turns. Wrapping an arm around my shoulder, he shakes his head.

I never worked for the same noble that long. Mercs become

eligible to be promoted as centurions after ten turns in the service to the same house.

I glance at him in sudden interest. Other than the story about how he left Nicuan, I don't know that much about his time there. *You never stuck with any house?*

They paid well, but I hated them. So I had a tendency to get them killed.

My brows shoot up. *On purpose?*

He shrugs, and I turn back to the screen, where the presenter is struggling with two centurions. "You need to come with us, ma'am."

"Why?" she demands. "This is violation of the Free Press Act, my diplomatic status as a journalist, and—"

They stop playing nice, then. A centurion claps a hand over her mouth as the presenter thrashes, and the drone-cam changes angles, likely following its simple programming to stay out of reach and keep filming. The soldiers solve this dilemma by shooting it. Red light sparks, then the feed dies. They permit twenty seconds of static before a new presenter takes over in the same locale. I can tell by his haircut, however, that he's Imperial personnel, not ONN.

"The fringe group that has been harassing Imperial authorities for the last turn was formally denied this morning. The Imperial governors have chosen a course that is best for La'heng, offering the most stability in the region. In other news—"

I sigh. "Well, Flavius warned me. I'd like to stick a knife in that rat bastard."

Loras cuts the power. "Looks like things are about to get interesting."

"What're you talking about?" Sasha asks.

He looks between Loras and me, his face a picture of innocence. This once, I don't glance at March for guidance. Kids deserve to have answers to their questions if they're brave enough to ask them. I fold myself down onto the floor next to him, so we're on the same level. Zeeka already knows the story, but he seems just as attentive.

"A long time ago, when the humans first came to La'heng, they covered the world in a chemical that changed the natives. It made it impossible for them to fight. So for their 'protection,' humans took over. Otherwise, the La'hengrin would have been easy prey."

Loras takes up the narrative. "Since then, my people have been 'protected' by a number of species. They strip our natural resources and treat us as slaves. Jax funded research that led to a cure, permitting us to become self-sufficient again. But the current rulers don't want us to be free."

"That's not right," Sasha says indignantly.

It's really not.

I go on, "So we've been trying to get legal permission to open centers where the La'hengrin can come in for treatments."

"But they don't want to let you," the kid guesses. "Because once people get free, they'll kick the helmet guys off the planet."

Succinctly put, he encapsulates our problem. There was no way we could ever drum up enough support to deploy the cure legally. It doesn't matter; it was worth trying. I live for the day that people surprise me by doing the right thing.

"Well said," Loras says.

"What's your plan?" March slides to the floor from the couch, drawing me back against him.

I contemplate prevaricating, but there's no point. He can dig it out of me; he doesn't have to ask. So I lay it out for him, step by step. And when I finish, he's shaking his head.

"Guerrilla wars are seldom won, Jax."

Loras cuts in, "That depends on how you define it. I can name several where the invaders were driven out because holding that colony became too expensive."

I nod. We've looked at the historical precedents. Well, Vel and Loras did. In this one instance, I'm content to be led.

Sasha aims a chiding look at his uncle. "Don't tell them they can't win. When I competed for the blue ribbon, you said I just had to believe I could do it. Were you lying?"

I seam my lips together as March squirms. "Of course not. But this is—"

"The same thing," the kid says implacably.

One of these days, he'll be a force to be reckoned with. But then, any kid with such strong TK, raised by March, couldn't turn out any other way. I like him more this time; he's at the age where you can reason with him. He's a small person instead of a bundle of agitated impulses.

"Fine," March mutters.

I know better than to expect he'll shut up without having his say. He just does it where Sasha can't hear. *I don't like this, Jax. It's dangerous. You don't have the equipment, experience, or personnel to mount this kind of ground war.*

Teach us what you can in ten days. Loras has been studying guerrilla warfare for the last turn, but you can help him figure out what strategies are practicable.

March doesn't want me fighting a war without him, but he can't stay; the conflict threatens to tear him in two. Under no circumstances could he choose to stay here with Sasha, under these conditions. But he *wants* to. And his pain is staggering.

All right.

This isn't how I planned to spend his visit. I thought we'd roll around in bed the whole time and come up only for a few bites of food. But it'll give the rebellion a better chance if March assesses installations, analyzes the battlefield, and tells us where we can create the most chaos. He mutters, "I'll help while I'm here."

"I knew you would," Sasha says proudly. "In fact . . . we should stay, shouldn't we? They need you, and I can help, too. You're always saying I have an obligation to use my powers for good. What could be better than—"

"Enough, Sasha. I'm retired, and you have to get back to school." Wisely, March doesn't say it's too risky for them to linger on La'heng. Nothing rouses a kid's interest faster than a whiff of danger.

Even so, from Sasha's expression, I suspect we haven't heard the last of this.

CHAPTER 7

Later, after a long planning session and we've retired to my room, March pulls me into his arms.

He's sleeping with me, of course. For the short time we're together, I won't have anything between us, not even a wall. After he's gone, I'll deal with the heartbreak, just as I did before. The separation hasn't been easy, but I didn't expect it to be. Anything worth having is worth fighting for.

"Do you think we have any chance of pulling this off?" I ask softly.

He thinks for a few moments. "With any other team, I'd say no. But I know what you and Vel can accomplish together. So . . . maybe?"

"I'd prefer more confidence." I poke him. "It's not just us, you know. Loras has quietly been building underground resistance. There are more supporters of an independent La'heng. They're just not under this roof."

"You need a face for your rebellion," he says, pensive.

"We have one," I say at once. "Loras. He was the first to receive the cure. He's free of the *shinai*-bond, the first La'hengrin to have free will in so many turns. His people will think he's a hero even before the fighting begins."

March nods. “Perception is everything.”

“Not everything. But it matters a great deal.”

“He’ll work,” he says. “He has charisma and resolve.”

“Did I share the most interesting thing?” I project a gossipy tone, prompting a quirk of amusement from March.

“No. Do tell.”

“The former chancellor, Tarn, is on world.”

He arches a brow. “Really? Why?”

“I’ve no idea, but he’s been helping with the petitions and appeals. I was surprised as hell to see him.”

“That’s . . . interesting. Does he have another job here as well?”

I shake my head. “That’s why it’s so odd. But without him, we wouldn’t have gotten the motion as far as we did.”

“Only to be blocked in the High Court,” March mutters. “Imperial bastards.”

His bitterness is a tangible force between us, like a serrated blade. I remember the story he told me about losing so many men on Nicu Tertius, the pain of the endless war and betrayal. When March worked as a merc for these Imperial bastards, it meant a fat paycheck waited at the end of each contract, but at such cost. And irony is, those turns cost him his sister, who tired of waiting for him to save enough credits to buy a ship and save her, a sin for which March will spend the rest of his life trying to atone.

But I’ve got my ghosts, too. Doc haunts me still. He comes to me in the night, gone but not gone, so long as his memory lingers in the neurons and electrons that comprise my brain. You’d think the dreams would be nightmares, but he only talks to me in the way he used to—with dry humor and quiet wisdom.

Then I imagine living on Venice Minor, where he died, and I have to ask, “How do you stand living on Nicuan?”

I’d think the memories of failing Svetlana would be even stronger there, as that’s where March was when she died.

“It’s best for Sasha,” he replies simply.

That makes sense. He can expiate that grief by doing better for her son. With effort, I tamp down my emotional turmoil and go on with the conversation. “But I *did* think it odd that Tarn is here. I wondered if he intends to make up for the fact that Conglomerate tried to hang me out to dry.”

"I'm sure he feels a little guilty over that," March admits. "Mary knows I do. But then I remind myself they were your choices. If you'd gone about it a different way, I could've shielded you." There's tension in his tone, even after all this time.

"Hey," I say, sitting up. "I am *never* going to ask you to give an order that could result in my death. You couldn't live with it."

He's been inside my head so many times that I know exactly where his stress fractures lie. And failing to protect those he loves—starting with his sister, Svetlana? That's a wound he wouldn't recover from. Yes, he might be strong enough to send me to die, but then, *he* would, too. And I'll never let that happen.

"You know me too well," he says softly.

"Not as well as I used to. Fatherhood has changed you."

"For the better?"

I consider this. "You're calmer. Less hard-edged. So, yes, I think so. When you're inside me"—I touch the side of my skull—"I see that he's finished the healing I started on Ithiss-Tor. Those dark, disconnected places are whole again."

"It's remarkable what perfect trust can do. He thinks I'll never fail him."

"Because you never have. And you never will."

He exhales a soft breath. "Your faith in me is terrifying."

"Welcome to my world." I curl into his side, unwilling to sleep even though I'm tired, but I resent the need. Each time I close my eyes, I lose six or seven hours with him, and they are too few. The ache threatens to overwhelm me.

March wraps his arms around me and rubs his cheek against my hair, which is not silky or smooth. The curls are coarse and wild, as they ever have been, and he tangles his fingers in them possessively. I kiss the column of his throat.

"Can we really do this?" he asks, sotto voce.

"What?" It's cowardly, but I pretend I don't know where his mind has gone because I don't want to talk about it.

"How many turns will we be apart, Jax? One was . . . endless."

That parting came on the heels of a longer separation, where he didn't know if I was alive or dead. I feel guilty doing this to him, but it's not better on my end. I could lie. I could say any number of things, but that's not my style. So I choose brutal honesty instead. If he wants to end this, I won't try to talk him out of it, no matter how much it hurts, no matter that it's his voice I hear in silent moments.

"It will get worse," I reply. "Once we force the Conglomerate to limit space travel, and La'heng becomes a red port, you won't be able to visit."

By his flinch, he hasn't let himself think of that. "They'll probably lock down the comm, too."

I nod. "No messages in or out until it's over, once we begin."

His arms tighten on me. "Mary, I hate feeling like this."

"Like what?" As if I don't know.

March can't bring himself to say the words aloud, but he doesn't have to. *That despite how much we've been through, this is it.* This *is what we can't surmount. You can't leave Loras . . . he needs you here. And I can't stay with Sasha. It's too dangerous.*

I share his foreboding. *I wish I had a solution or a magic pill. But I don't. So just know this—I love you. And I always will.*

"No more of this," he says hoarsely.

"We have time yet. Let's make the most of it."

And we do.

The next day, I work with March to coordinate assaults that will do the most damage. I hand him the datapad with the intel the resistance has collected and he skims it, brow furrowed as he analyzes the probability of victory. "No. No. Too much ground resistance. But here, they've reduced sentries because of budgetary considerations, and the damage to the infrastructure would be considerable if you pulled off a successful strike."

I make a note of where, and we move on. The morning passes in that fashion, and, in the afternoon, we meet with the rest of the team to talk strategy and resources. March works with Zeeka on explosives while Vel puts in a word or two to clarify. The Mareq soaks it in all in, learning fast, while Constance logs everything. She will be our hub, making sure the left hand knows what the right is doing.

March and I spend our nights loving as if there's no tomorrow, yet the time goes too damn fast. I resent each sunrise because it draws me nearer to the day when he returns to the spaceport to take ship away from here. The Imperial bastards have grown complacent since the ruling. By the increased centurion presence, I think they expected some form of peaceful protests, mobs in need of dispersing. But lulling them is only the beginning of the plan. Once they stop expecting an attack—and after March and Sasha are safely away—then we strike.

On the eleventh day, Sasha talks March into taking him for a ride in the shuttle Vel has finished modding. Vel has taken him out before, but the kid wants some time with his uncle. He's not whiny; it was a casual request, or rather, more of a challenge to "show his stuff." I wonder if March has ever piloted for Sasha. All his adventures must seem far removed from their normal life.

Vel finds me surrounded by maps with targets marked. I've prioritized with color codes, so I won't forget which facilities need to go first.

But he doesn't want to talk about the coming war. "Are you well, Sirantha?"

No doubt he's referring to the imminent departure. "I'll be fine."

"Will you?"

I'd tolerate that kind of prying from nobody else. "In time. You forget . . . this is what I do. I lock it down and move on. I was made to be broken."

"I do not forget." A layered statement.

"Does it bother you to have him here?" That's a silly, human question, and I know his answer before he voices it.

His mandible flares in honest denial. "Of course not. March makes you happy. That is all I require. If that ever changed, if he *hurt* you, then I would kill him."

That's not an empty promise, and it makes me smile, though maybe it shouldn't. But it would take a better woman than I not to be pleased he cares enough to kill for me. Vel's devotion is precious and rare; I'm lucky to have him. Lucky to have them both.

Unfortunately, I'm not the sort of person whose luck runs hot long.

La'heng Liberation Army signal-jack ad: Profile One

UNA

[A girl with fair skin and wide blue eyes stares at the camera, blinking nervously.]

Male interviewer, off-screen: Don't be scared, Una. Tell us who you are. The world needs to hear your story.

[She clears her throat and then nods.]

Una: It's bad here. I can't remember anything else. I hear it used to be better, a long time ago. Now, there's never enough food. I didn't see an aircar until I was fifteen.

Male interviewer: What changed?

Una: A nobleman came to the provinces looking for a pet and took me from my family. It's a status symbol, if you have a pretty La'heng to serve you.

Male voice: Did he pay your family?

Una: Yes. He didn't have to since he had a dispensation from my protector. My mother cried. She said it was wrong to take credits for me, but the young ones were starving. The man said it was a privilege to be chosen—that it meant I could get better work, travel, and learn lots of languages. It didn't *feel* like an honor.

Male voice: What was your new life like?

Una: At first, it was all right. I went to school. I learned many languages, just like he promised. I liked it . . . and it was easy.

Male voice: But . . . ?

[She lowers her head, hair veiling her face.]

Male voice: Continue whenever you're ready, Una.

Una: When I turned sixteen, everything changed. He . . . hurt me. When I pleaded with him not to touch me anymore, he said I owed him for sending me to school, like a lifetime of indentured service wasn't enough. I couldn't fight. I wanted to. I hated him. But I *couldn't*.

Voice-over: And *that's* who you're fighting for, LLA. Contact the comm code at the bottom of your screen to find workers with the cure.

CHAPTER 8

I've been called a terrorist before, usually by a government trying to pin something on me that I didn't do. This time, I'm earning the title.

In the morning, March and Sasha left; I dropped them off at the spaceport myself. The pain nearly killed me. My love's anguish exacerbated my own, and Sasha was mad as hell, muttering beneath his breath about taking the coward's way out. I don't envy March the journey back to Nicu Tertius.

Yet their departure frees us to act. The plans are in place.

Loras touches me lightly on the shoulder, grounding me. "If we hit this pylon, it will take out terrestrial communications in this sector."

True. This is one of the targets March designated before he left. He lingers even as we move forward, his experience driving our initial assault.

Vel adds, "They can bounce messages to a near-orbit satellite, but transmission will take considerably longer, and Leviter will be working simultaneously."

I nod. "So that buys us time. But the charges will take out the building next to it . . . you're sure there are no La'heng inside?"

"Positive." Loras checks his handheld just in case. "I sent a message on the subchannel, advising all service personnel to avoid the premises until further notice."

"Based on comm chatter," Vel puts in, "I would say your message has been disseminated. The Nicuan masters are agitated that their slaves are unavailable."

"After tonight, they'll see that as a warning sign," I mutter.

By distant lamplight, Loras looks more human than I've ever seen him. His fine features are touched by fear, weariness, and regret, but he doesn't hesitate. "We'll find a way around it. This has to be done."

But he doesn't sound any happier about it than I am.

"With Leviter's help, tonight should get the planet locked down," I say. "With La'heng decreed a red port, there will be no ships in or out until we finish our work here."

"It could take turns," he warns.

I shrug. "So be it. We can't fight those on world, plus the collective might of Imperial forces fresh from Nicuan. They built an impressive fleet during the Morgut War."

Loras scowls. "And lost few. Wretched cowards."

It's true that while Nicuan promised ships and a legion to crew them, they didn't send their centurions to the front in time. Others bore the brunt of battle and sacrificed for the greater good. The current Nicuan emperor, Tacitus XVI, could muster almost enough ships to threaten Conglomerate control. They ought to be watching them carefully, but I don't trust the new chancellor. While Katrin Jocasta might be a skilled diplomat, she lacks Tarn's steel.

But that's not my problem.

For my last public appearance, I will be playing the Hero of La'heng, and then it's time for a final bow, and the curtain will come down. I'm *so* ready to lead my own life. It's what keeps me going in the middle of the night when I am desperate, aching, and already lonely for the man I love. It's only been a few hours. The next turn will feel endless, but even in that, I am luckier than March; Vel, Loras, Constance, and Zeeka remain with me. I'm not alone. He only has Sasha, who loves him but can't support him. March can't lean on the kid. He can only be strong for him.

The fact is, I don't care what history makes of me. After

the bombardment on Venice Minor, I'd have sworn I was done with bloodshed, done with war. The cost is just too high. But sometimes, it's the only choice that remains; and some things are worth fighting for.

My friend's freedom is one of them.

So I give the order. "Red team Alpha, go."

And the explosives detonate, lighting the night sky in a vermilion corona. Metal quakes and topples in shards. Raid sirens sound as emergency lights come on. People scream as chunks of building slam down, leaving pocks in the pavement. We're far enough away that I can't make out the details, but I know what it looks like. Some images I can never get out of my head.

The same thing is going on in cities all over La'heng. Multiple strike teams, multiple detonation sites. The chaos will be splendid.

"Success," Vel tells his handheld. "Imperial comms have gone silent."

It is the first step to outright rebellion. Since we're vastly outnumbered and have fewer resources, we'll depend on good intel, calculated sabotage, and the occasional ambush to throw their infrastructure into disarray. There's a battle plan back at headquarters, mostly due to March, Vel, and Constance. Though I sat in on all the planning, I'm not much for strategy sessions; I'd rather be fighting.

But we can't take them in a head-on battle. They have too many soldiers, and we face the challenge of distributing the cure to the La'heng. Once we do that, we can count on a world full of savage warriors, furious over generations of enslavement. But I can't inject everyone on the planet at once, and I won't do what my predecessors did—and gas everyone without their consent.

Change on this scale takes time.

Until we devise a solution, we'll utilize guerilla strikes. Make this an uncomfortable place for Nicuan nobles to holiday. It's not an ideal solution, but in a perfect universe, this never would've come to pass. Humans wouldn't think they knew best—that their ways are superior—and it gives them the right to destroy somebody else's culture.

Odd. As I sprint from the scene, I realize I've used that

pronoun for humans, as if I'm *not* one. I won't think about that disconnect now. I have to focus on eluding the centurions pounding the pavement behind us. They're fanning out to search the area, confident they'll have the culprits in custody soon.

I slow enough for one of them to get a look at my back. A shout goes up from the centurion, and he fires. I slide around the corner of a building as chaos escalates. Breaking cover, Loras and Vel shoot back, but clumsily, permitting the two centurions to close. They think this fight will be over quickly.

And it will—for them.

As the centurions round the corner, I launch myself at one on the left and take out his kneecap with a ferocious kick. The patella pops, and his leg won't hold him. I'm on him in a second. But then, if I meant to kill him, he'd already be dead.

I jab the hypo into his neck. *Bastard. I hope it hurts.*

Within seconds, it's lights out. Vel subdues the other one, then doses him. He hefts one; Loras shoulders the other, and I cut a path through the alley to where our shuttle awaits. Once Vel chucks his hostage in back, he slides into the pilot chair. He passed the pilot-training course. As of now, he has the credentials to fly any class of ship from shuttle all the way to M, which I secretly think stands for massive. The centurions are key to the next step in our plan: infiltration.

I tap the comm. "Mission accomplished. Red team Alpha, meet us at base."

Before the attack commenced, we packed up and moved on. They'll find no sign of where we've gone should they find the house. From here on out, we work from the hidden ops center or in the field.

"Acknowledged." Zeeka's voice is unmistakable, mostly because I picked out the tone of his vocalizer.

"You got away clean?" I ask.

I can't help mothering him a little. I didn't want to send him with the crew to plant the charges, but he feels like he has something to prove. Everyone else has been with me longer; they've done more. We have *history*, he says, like that's a bad thing. But I guess you can expect that attitude from a young male of any species.

Zeeka replies, "No witnesses. RTA out."

I glance back, checking on Loras and the prisoners. "They're still unconscious?"

He inclines his head. "Should be for a while yet."

As Vel powers up the shuttle, he says, "Strap in, Sirantha. Drones have locked on with instructions to prevent any air traffic by any means necessary."

I comply, then flick a switch to take control of the guns. This is a sweet ride; without Dina, it took longer to whip it into shape, but Vel did a good job, and Zeeka was eager to learn. Vel finished it up last week, with Sasha and Z assisting.

"On 'em."

Behind me, a captive whimpers, trapped in narcotic dreams. I don't feel sorry for him. He made his choices. We all do.

From conversation with March, I recall that most Nicuan centurions start as mercs. After ten turns in service to the same noble, they receive a permanent assignment, a rank, and a retirement fund. That's rarer than it sounds because so many soldiers die on Nicuan; they don't survive long enough to become centurions, let alone get a cushy post on one of the colonies. In all official documents, they call this colony by its Imperial name, Nicu Quintus.

Which enrages the La'heng. But they can't show it. Instead, they follow orders and hoard their hatred. When we work out the kinks in the cure's delivery system, the planet will rise up behind us.

Until then, it's up to us.

But then, isn't it always?

CHAPTER 9

After takeoff, I focus on the drones.

Four of them bear down on us, nearly in weapons range. Shuttles don't usually have offensive capability, but Vel retro-fitted this little beauty with some guns from a junked skiff. We have other vehicles for air travel as well, but none quite so nice.

It feels odd to fire from the console instead of a proper gun pit, but there's no room in a ship this size. I tap furiously, lining up my shots. The shuttle's size means I can feel each swivel of the lasers. When I have one square in my sights, I loose the first shot. I have to be fast. If these drones have a chance to bounce any visual footage to the satellite, Imperial forces will know what they're looking for, and we'll have to scrap the shuttle. Our resources are finite, not due to lack of credits, but because we're limited as to what we can buy on world without attracting attention.

Red zings through the sky, outside my line of sight, but I catch the echoed light in my periphery as I line up the next shot. *Boom. One down.* My hands are steady even as Vel angles the throttle, delivering more altitude to evade the onslaught coming from the remaining three drones. I clip the second, and it careens into its cousin. They explode in a shower of sparks.

One left.

"Looking good," Loras says. "Finish it before we get adds."

"Yes, sir."

I'm too busy to make a rude gesture or sketch a mocking salute. His laughter tells me we're really friends, and he's forgiven me at last. I feel a little lighter as I take the last shot, and more metal rains down on the centurions below.

Vel takes us up, zooming away from the scene into a cloud bank. We use that to confound anyone tracking us from the ground. He stays at that altitude until we reach the base, located in the mountains four hundred klicks outside the city.

At this altitude, the flora is evergreen, like that found at the frost line on more temperate worlds. Which means it's thick, green, and prickly. And it offers great cover as Vel descends with a skill that belies how short a time he's been flying. Light snow dusts down on us, melting beneath the thrusters, as he maneuvers us into a shallow cave. Any significant surface installation would be reported to the Nicuan overseers—and that's why we built into the mountain itself. Using quiet laser drillers and the natural tunnels already in place, we've constructed an impressive base of operations in the last six months, projecting that our final appeal would fail. Sometimes it pays to be a pessimist. The doors seal behind us, hiding energy emissions that would let them track us.

As I step into the shuttle bay, I marvel that it doesn't look at all cavelike. Instead, the walls have been finished, and it looks like any other building, provided you can forget you're buried beneath several tons of rock. It gives me a little trouble, but as long as I concentrate on other things, I get past it. I tell myself that it'll pass, anyway, once I get used to the place.

Right now, I've got to unload the prisoners. There are one hundred of us at the base, which I feel is a decent start, given how long we've been under way. Loras has compelling skill in convincing the La'heng to join our ranks, but he can only reach them in limited numbers. That's why it was so vital to take down Imperial comms.

That changes tonight.

"I want our message on the air in ten minutes," I say, as Vel and Loras haul the two centurions from the back of the shuttle.

They're stirring, so I dose them again, just to be safe. Best not to delay our plans with complications that could've been avoided. The Nicuan government can't censor our message this time. That surgical strike removed their ability to deny or approve what comes in on satellite. If we time it right, in the next nine minutes, all the La'heng who have access to public comms will know what we're fighting for—what's at stake.

Two liberated La'heng stride toward us. With fine features, the La'heng are more attractive than the average human, a hint of extra elegance and refinement. Yet that beauty masks a savage nature. A few have died taking Carvati's Cure; they succumb to the bloodlust and have to be put down. So far, our casualty rate is holding steady at 5 percent.

Loras accounts it tolerable, considering what's at stake. I wish I could do better, but over the turns, I've accepted that perfection is a dream. In the end, there's mud and blood, and you can only hope you can live with the stains when all's said and done. I wouldn't be able to stand myself if I didn't try, here.

The first rebel is taller than his companion. I remember Zhan because he has a red streak in his hair. He added it after he survived the cure. First thing, he picked a fight. It breaks your heart to watch them roughhouse just because they can, throwing punches like flowers, joyous laughter ringing out.

Right now, I can't remember the other one's name; it doesn't matter. There's no time for chat. With hands raised in greeting, they carry the two centurions out of the bay to be dealt with later. Vel nods, staying with the shuttle to check it over—as Dina would have—and Loras jogs toward the communications suite.

I follow because this was my idea, and I'm playing cameraman. Well, at least, I'm programming the cam for him. I unlock the door with my code to be sure nothing's been touched, and Loras stands in front of the flag, a blue background with a red circle and the old La'heng coat of arms, which had been printed on everything from art to flags to money, before we *changed* them.

This is a new flag for an independent La'heng. We spent

hours designing it, just as we did the Conglomerate uniforms, and I'm positive we got it right. It also provides the perfect backdrop for our opening salvo.

Quickly, he changes from his black-ops gear into less sinister, more neutral attire. "How do I look?"

"Like the perfect spokesman for the rebellion."

He frowns at me. "I'm serious."

"So am I."

"What if I screw this up?"

"You won't. You've practiced the speech a hundred times, a thousand even. Now you're going to say it with more conviction than you ever have, knowing that in a few hours, people all over La'heng will be hearing you . . . and seeing what you can do."

"That's not helping."

Oh, shit, stage fright?

"Take a breath, then, and pretend you're talking only to me."

Loras relaxes visibly. "Better."

"Camera's recording in three . . . two . . ." I hold up one finger so my voice doesn't wind up on the sound track, and the red light comes on.

"This is the first communiqué from the La'heng Liberation Army," Loras says, gazing directly at his audience—or at least, that's how they're going to feel, five hours from now. I wonder if they'll have shivers, too, like I do.

"Humanity has stolen everything from us: our self-sufficiency, our pride, our cultural heritage. They have enslaved us. Oh, they call it by benevolent names, but in truth, they have turned us into helpless children. But there is a solution, called Carvati's Cure. I've taken the treatment, and I say to you, my brothers and sisters, be slaves no longer. I will show you the way. I will show you proof."

That's my cue. I splice in the clip of his fight with Hon, courtesy of Dr. Carvati on Gehenna, and then training clips later on. It's indisputably Loras, fighting, impossible for a La'heng. Yet, he's kicking the dread pirate's ass.

I imagine the impact this footage will have on the rest of La'heng.

And then it gets better.

Zhan steps into the room, his face in shadow. This is scripted, but the audience won't know that. They throw a few punches, live and streaming; there's a distinctive watermark on a live broadcast so the audience knows there's no special effects involved.

Perfect.

Because when they conclude the match, Zhan faces the camera and bows, making it clear that, he, too, is a free La'heng; and then he steps out of frame. Loras goes on, "You want what we have. There's so much hopeless anger trapped inside you. I can help you. But you have to be brave. You have to reach for it. Watch the comms for more instructions on how to join the La'heng Liberation Army."

Grinning at him, I turn off the cam, cutting the bounce-feed. "That was amazing. You just started a revolution."

CHAPTER 10

After the broadcast, I run into Tarn in the hallway. "Did it work?" I ask.

"I timed the message perfectly," Suni says. "My old Conglomerate contacts will hear straightaway about the tremendous civil unrest."

I fall into step beside him. "Will that, coupled with the damage from the attacks, be enough for lockdown?"

"It should be once Leviter finishes spinning it."

"He could get the planet coded red with a vid message," I mutter.

"Probably," Suni replies seriously.

"How did you meet him?"

"You wouldn't believe me if I told you." There's an intriguing softness in his smile.

Tarn leads me to a conference room, where Leviter is waiting. It's a small risk, permitting them to know the location of the base, but one worth taking for their help. Leviter needed a secure site to work his magic, somewhere his efforts can't be traced. Besides, if it comes down to interrogation, Leviter can probably kill people with a sharp look, and I've no doubt he'd end anyone who so much as stared sideways at Tarn.

"It went smoothly," he says without looking up from his handheld. "Well done."

I acknowledge the praise with a nod. "You did your part?"

"I lit up the bounce-feed, as promised. They're already talking about the rebellion in the forums and the news-net channels. It helped that you hit several different installations, giving the impression of large, organized resistance."

"You can really make so many people off world believe the situation is dangerous, unstable, and dire?"

But Tarn wouldn't lie. He's not that kind of politician.

Leviter tilts his head back to study me, his expression quietly amused. He has the eyes of a shark, flat and hard, with darkness at their depths. "One doesn't need to control reality, only the *perception* of it. And I'm not doing it alone. I have agitators with various Conglomerate officials, reporting 'first-hand' information from the attacks."

Mary, I'm glad Leviter's on our side. "What's the next step?" I ask.

"I've requisitioned buoys, warning all vessels away from La'heng space. They should arrive within the next twenty-four hours."

Tarn nods. "In anticipation of the Conglomerate ruling."

"Will that work?" I imagine a beacon that shouts, *Go away*, into the silence of space, while ships ignore it.

"The buoys are also SDIs," Leviter explains, as if I'm slow. "Any ship that attempts to violate the Conglomerate edict will be blown to bits."

Aha. That makes all the difference, I decide. "So the space above the planet becomes a minefield. Nice."

Leviter continues, "Once the Conglomerate codes La'heng red, if the Nicuan Empire attempts to breach the no-fly zone, it will be tantamount to an act of war against all Conglomerate worlds. They have a fine fleet, but they can't take on all the tier worlds."

"Excellent. The centurions must be cut off, left to the mercy of the legates on La'heng."

"Who are all morons," Tarn mutters.

Yeah, mostly. This is the assignment older centurions on Nicu Tertius beg for because there's no actual fighting—or there *hasn't* been in many, many turns. So it's a cushy gig, where they get to attend parties as show dogs in dress armor while their employers eat and drink like swine, all while plundering La'heng and stealing from its rightful rulers, while the La'heng serve and follow orders.

I'm getting mad all over again, just thinking about it.

"Easy, Jax," Tarn says. "Save that fury for the enemy."

I muster a half smile. I'm tired, cranky, and missing March. But there's more work to be done.

"Are you two heading back to Jineba?" I ask.

"Soon," Tarn replies.

Nodding, I push to my feet. "Be careful. They'll be looking at all air-traffic logs. And thanks again for your help."

Leviter smiles once more, and it's fairly alarming. "No thanks needed, Ms. Jax. We're just getting warmed up."

Once I leave the conference room, I go looking for Vel. As I expected, I find him with the prisoners, who are awake . . . and in a fury over their incarceration. "When my prince hears what you've done, he'll make you beg for death."

On another planet, serving a prince would be impressive, but in relation to Nicuan, such claims to royalty mean less than nothing. There have been so many emperors over the turns that pretty much all the noble houses can claim royal blood. His boss is no more important than any other.

I address Vel instead of the captives. "The tall one, right?"

To replicate somebody's face, Vel needs to study it. A glance from across the plaza in the dark won't suffice. Once he's perfected the man's appearance, he can slide into his life. Hence, Slider, the somewhat derogatory nickname for Ithtorians . . . but when I first met him, that's exactly what he'd done with my now-deceased friend, Dr. Solaith. Doc.

Mary bless and keep you, Doc. Wherever you are.

"That's the plan," he answers.

Of course. That will be easier for him and less painful.

But the centurion he indicates looks terrified, not as full of bravado as his squad-mate. He glances between us, trying to figure out our plan. It won't help.

"Have you checked his personnel file?"

Vel reminds me, "Communications are down."

Right. I touch the intercom. "Constance, we're ready for you."

My PA has been at the base since March left, facilitating completion and organizing resources. She's also the head of R&D, along with a number of other responsibilities. Only a VI—or maybe AI is more accurate—would be capable of multitasking with such efficiency.

"On my way."

"Who are you people?" the smaller soldier demands. "Torture won't work. We will *never* reveal any of our prince's secrets."

Oh, the poor bastard. He still thinks this is some petty, house-related coup. If he had any inkling just how big the plan is, he'd piss his pants. I smile at him, which seems to make his fear worse. They're bound to their chairs, with wrists lashed together behind their backs. If I hadn't wasted a turn of my life trying to reason with men just like them, I might feel a flicker of pity.

Before I can reply, Constance arrives with an armload of machinery: cords and discs and a console to monitor the whole process. The guards go from anxious to terrified, but it's not what they think. In some ways, it's worse. This is an insidious device, certainly, but not for the reasons they believe.

"Which one first?" she asks.

"The tall one." I turn to the La'heng waiting just outside. "Take the other one back to his cell. We'll deal with him presently."

Separation will ratchet up his fear as he tries to envision what horrors his friend is suffering. If we let him watch, that mental preparation might give him an edge later. Not that I've ever seen anyone resist this machine. Still, there's no point in bettering the man's odds.

Once the La'heng guard hauls him off, struggling and kicking the whole way, Constance gets to work. She attaches wires to the centurion's skull in proximity to the various pleasure centers of the brain. Then she discovers the perfect current through trial and error. There's no pain, only incredible pleasure of varying levels.

Oh, there are various truth-serum drugs, but most of them have side effects, and they leave the person hostile once the effects wear off. With this device, by the time we're finished, this centurion will think we're his best friends. He'll believe anything we tell him—anything at all—to keep the pleasure coming. And that's why I called it insidious. When Constance concludes this session, she will have added a loyal foot soldier to the La'heng Liberation Army. In theory. This is experimental tech, so we'll see how well it works.

The first jolt startles a sensuous moan out of the prisoner. His eyes go glassy, his mouth slack—too intimate an expression to see on a stranger's face. She'll continue the treatment until he's utterly seduced and ready to tell us anything at all. I leave Constance to it because she doesn't need my supervision. She's willing to do whatever it takes, so long as Nicuan forces occupy La'heng. I will not pity them.

Vel accompanies me back to my quarters. The space I've been allotted is small and sparsely decorated in shades of gray; it's all one room, with a bunk, a comm terminal, and a sitting area comprised of a small sofa and one chair. It's been a long night, the first of many. He settles on the couch and invites me to join him with a flourish of his talon.

Many would find this scene oddly domestic, especially the easy way I curl up beside him to better view his handheld. We're close enough to touch, but I don't. Sometimes even I'm not sure where the boundaries between us lie.

He's captured several images of the man he will replace. Later, he can spend more time in the centurion's company, memorizing the angles and lines, to reproduce them perfectly. For now, the pictures will get the process started. The guard is nearly two meters tall, with dark hair, gray eyes, and a weathered complexion. He has squint and frown lines, more than those that come from laughter.

"Will you have any trouble?"

Vel glances at me. "No."

"I've never understood how it works."

Skin is one thing, but hair has a different texture. I've seen him become someone else, but watching it doesn't help me understand. Once, I'd have felt unable to pry, worrying that he'd take it the wrong way. Now I understand there's nothing I can't ask of him.

"The human body creates different types of matter," he says. "Usually with the intent of cleaning or eliminating waste."

I nod. I'm with him so far.

"What I do functions on a similar principle . . . I simply have better control over what form it takes."

"So you command it, like on a cellular level." That's pretty damn cool.

"Essentially, yes."

"Wow. No wonder Ithtorians think humans are savages."

"We have had longer to evolve," Vel says modestly.

"What do you think of the target?"

He considers. "He is a serious soul."

Or he used to be, before Constance got ahold of him.

Everything she does, she does at my behest. She's still my PA, no matter how sophisticated she's become. When I first reactivated her, after the time she spent locked in Dina's data chip, I asked if she was sure she wanted to return to human form. She'd seemed content as a ghost in the machine—first on the ship, then on Emry Station. I'd worried I was being selfish by wanting her back in my life in a more tangible way; maybe she was happy manipulating those vast data streams, and it would be wrong of me to make her go back to a limited life.

She replied, "Now that I've known both, I prefer being a person, where I can interact in a more meaningful manner."

And here we are.

"On a scale of one to ten, how much hope do we have of pulling this off?"

"Negative two," Vel replies. But his mandible quirks, telling me he's joking.

"I'm not kidding."

"What do you mean by 'this'? The infiltration or the war effort in entirety?"

"Both."

He gives the question solemn consideration. "As to the former, I have done it many times. People never want to believe there could be something wrong, so they write off any behavioral changes, ascribe it to stress."

"So you're telling me not to worry."

"Precisely."

"I can't help it." I feel odd and raw. "I don't know what I'd do if I lost you."

"You won't. This is my forte, Sirantha."

Knowing that intellectually doesn't dim my worry any. Because after he goes inside, Vel will be out of touch, beyond my help. As a copy, he'll live this centurion's life while the original babbles Imperial secrets as fast as we can record them. And if this guard doesn't know what we need, then we'll take someone else. This is only the first sortie in the war.

"I know. But imagine if it were me."

"I could not bear it," he says quietly.

"But I'm expected to? Not fair, Vel."

He furls his claws in subtle response. "That is a childish complaint, Sirantha."

"Sorry." But I'm not, really.

Constance interrupts before this can become an issue. Vel feels like the last person in the universe who belongs to me. There's March, of course, but he's gone, and not all mine. There's a large portion of him bound up in raising his nephew, and I have no role in that.

"There's a small problem." She never wastes time on a greeting.

I invite her to make use of the other chair. "What's up?"

"Infiltration of Titus's life may prove problematic."

"Why?" Vel asks.

"He is recently married."

CHAPTER II

This is indisputably a snafu.

A new bride pays attention to things a wife of many long turns ceases to notice. She'll expect regular sex from Vel, as they don't call it the honeymoon period for nothing. There will be little in-jokes that he's expected to remember and understand.

"Damage control," I mutter. "How do we fix this?"

"He'll be useless as a centurion," Constance replies.

True. The machine she used on him is wildly addictive. If we cut him loose at this point, he'll go mad wanting that pleasure again. He's ours to keep, now.

"The solution is simple," Vel says, after a few moments' thoughtful silence.

"It is?"

A flicker of amusement twitches his mandible as he reads my doubt. "I can take the second one's place," he offers.

Since the man is short and compact, as Doc was, it will be physically painful for him to compress his body, but he's done it before. Vel is willing to suffer for the cause. I just wish he didn't have to. But our first choice is off the table, so we'll work with what's left.

"Constance, see to the second prisoner," I order. "Find out if he has any dangerous demographics. Then report back."

"At once, Sirantha Jax."

After she departs to deploy her infernal device, I sigh. "All told, it's not too bad."

"There are worse disasters that could befall us," Vel points out.

"Will the op require surveillance?"

He lifts a shoulder. "It might."

Someone should watch his back if he's in the field alone. Unfortunately, Vel has the most experience stalking targets, but he can hardly guard himself. Which means I'll do it for him. I can be quiet and patient, if I have to be; I just can't get too close or arouse suspicion while I'm there. Whatever the mission requires, Vel will do it properly. I can count on him. Vel's here because of me, and I didn't even have to ask. That's a type of friendship of which I've known little in my life.

Constance returns an hour later. "The second centurion is single. He has no close family on La'heng. He was recently punished for something he did not do, and he has a mild addiction to chem."

Nothing in those facts will make Vel's mission more difficult. It's within acceptable parameters, so we'll greenlight the mission. I turn to him, but he's already come to the same conclusion.

He says to the PA, "I need detailed images of the subject, and take some molds, if possible. I will also need to study him at length once I process the initial data. So keep him in good condition for a day or two."

Stay of execution for the centurion. He won't be beaten or killed while Vel needs to learn the lines of his face. Still, that's a pretty grim reason to be alive, and if the soldier's not connected to Constance's device, it will be hellish. His addiction proves his brain chemistry tends toward dependency already; that inclination will worsen his final days. I can hear him screaming now that she's stopped as his body deals with the sudden loss of dopamine.

"Acknowledged," Constance says. "I will prohibit the free La'heng from making sport of him until after you complete your assessment."

After all the La'hengrin have suffered at Nicuan hands, I don't blame them, but I still shiver at what lies ahead for that centurion. I turn to Vel. "Are you good with plan B?"

"I will make it work, Sirantha." That doesn't tell me anything about how he feels about going undercover alone, however, or how much pain he'll experience compacting his form for long periods. I've noticed he's never chosen such a build, apart from that one time with Doc, when it was unavoidable.

Shortly thereafter, Vel excuses himself. There are nights when I wish he didn't leave, but if he stayed, it would cross a boundary in my head. Right now, the only reason I don't hate myself for loving two such different males is that the relationships operate under disparate parameters. Vel cuts me a look as he goes, like he suspects some of these inner workings, but he doesn't call me on it.

I don't know what I'd do if he did, if he said, *Let me stay, Sirantha.*

It wouldn't be for sex, but maybe in some regards, my pleasure in his presence might be worse. Because it means it's real and lasting because I feel better just knowing he's beside me, and March must've seen as much before he left. We didn't talk about it. At some point, we must, rather than tiptoeing around our issues like we live on a thawing iceberg.

Vel once told me that the heart isn't like a cup of water. You can't drain it dry. It's more like an endless well, and the more you love, the more it pumps out. I'm remembering imprecisely at the moment, but it's late, and I'm tired. That's the gist.

Once he's gone, I wish he hadn't, but I'll never say otherwise. I can't be the woman who loves the one she's with. I don't want to be fickle and inconstant; I don't want it to be true of me that the longer the object of my affections is out of proximity, the less I think about him.

But maybe it is.

Maybe, no matter how I try, I'm not destined for a great love. I'm just constantly compartmentalizing and adapting, and it prevents me from giving my heart completely. In one way, that's good, I suppose. It means I can survive anything.

I put those melancholy thoughts aside and get some sleep.

In the morning, I rise and eat breakfast with the La'hengrin and our few human supporters. Since we brought the cure and started the formalities to begin large-scale testing, others have flocked to our banner. They treat me with an awe that makes me uncomfortable. Here, I've made no friends like Dina, Argus, and Hit. I have only the ones I brought with me: Loras, Zeeka, Vel, and Constance.

The Mareq jumper joins me before I finish eating. Because I know it bothers him, I refrain from praising the successful mission or his safe return. He wants me to treat him like any other soldier, but it's so hard when he's been a child with me twice; the last time, he actually ate from my chest. Is this how *normal* mothers feel?

It's the closest I'll ever come, I suspect.

"Good morning," Zeeka says.

He's assimilated human customs as best he can though his appearance marks him as other. Fortunately, most people don't realize how rare he is, the only Mareq ever to venture off world. Z says it was his destiny, and that if we hadn't come, someone else would have. Maybe somebody who wouldn't have felt guilty enough to give him a second chance. Cloning is a tricky business. It's not like he's the same person that the original Baby-Z would have been, but he has identical DNA, and he had the same environmental markers. To *his* mind, he is the same person, reborn, and I don't feel qualified to argue.

Doc would have, I suspect.

I miss him. Along with Rose and Evie. If Mother Mary has a sense of humor, they're all together in the afterlife, and Doc has some explaining to do. What I wouldn't give to hear it, too. But it's not my time, and if the nanites have anything to say about it, I'll have many turns before my body wears out. Vel's remarkably cheerful about that. I suppose I would be, too, if I'd lost as many friends as he has.

"Morning," I reply.

"I heard you're going back to the city with Vel. Complications?"

"You could say that." I fill him in as he eats, explaining how the first choice was a no-go, and we've had to make do with the second centurion.

"Have you scouted a location where you can watch over him?" Z asks.

Unlike Vel, he has a modern vocalizer, which translates with less formality. It makes him more approachable, I think. Less intimidating. Plus, it's hard to be frightened of anyone with such liquid eyes. Zeeka radiates innocence; by looking at him, you'd never guess that he laid the charges that took down an Imperial installation last night.

"No, all our intel and preparation was for the first target. But I'll figure it out when I see where the guy lives."

It was an unfortunate turn of luck that resulted in the first centurion's having gotten married since we observed him last. Nothing in his behavior led us to believe a happy event was imminent. The man got up, went to work, and socialized little. From a distance, he seemed like the perfect choice, down to the correct build.

Because I can't help myself, I add, "You don't have to be here, you know. You're qualified to jump on your own, now."

Z laughs. "Grimspace isn't going anywhere, Jax."

I accept that as truth. How amazing; he has the skill set without any hint of addiction. Since I've never raised a Mareq, I don't know if I should insist on pushing him out of the nest, so to speak. He's so eager to learn—and to help—that I'm unwilling to crush that spark. I can't tell him, *Get lost, kid. We don't need you.*

We do. Or the La'heng Liberation Army does. At this point, we're so few against so many that all are welcome, whatever their species or motivations.

CHAPTER 12

Things just get more complicated.

Constance pokes me awake in the middle of the night—not that you can tell what time it is outside the mountain except that we've programmed the environment to match planetary cycles. The lights inside the LLA base have a special fuse that compensates for lack of sunlight. Those with skills unsuited to combat will be here a long time, running support on missions, and we had to factor that into the design.

I sit up, shoving the hair from my eyes, and frown up at her. "What's wrong?"

"Urgent message, Sirantha Jax."

What the hell . . . nobody has the codes here. This can't be good. I sit up.

"Do I need to—"

"No, I recorded and downloaded to my internal systems."

Even with that warning, it's still a fragging terrible shock for March's voice to come out of Constance's mouth. I stare, unable to believe what I'm hearing.

He's too smart to identify himself, but it's definitely him. "We . . . missed our flight. It's complicated. I'll explain when I see you. Now the spaceport's locked down. I went back to the house, but you've already vacated. I need to get Sasha someplace safe. Come when you get this. We're not going anywhere."

"How did this come in?" I demand.

"It was bounced to the shuttle's comm code."

Right. I remember now. Vel took Sasha to see some ruins in the mountains; the kid rang the house to tell March how awesome it was, but we scrubbed all records from the comm suite before we left. Which means one of them remembered the codes on screen from that single call. It's the kind of thing I expect from March, actually, attention to detail that makes any operation he plans go smooth as silk.

Constance goes on, "A maintenance worker forwarded it to me. He guessed it was important though he didn't know the particulars."

Mary bless you, sir.

I can't risk sending a return message, but there's no question I'll go get them. Shit, March must be so pissed. I thought they were long gone.

The days we spent together during his visit let the Imperial forces drop their guard after the final ruling. The centurions spent a week and a half on high alert, and just before I dropped March at the spaceport, the Imperials reduced patrols and went back to business as usual, assuming our group had been defeated. People who file motions generally don't have a backup plan that involves destabilizing the government.

"Wake Vel," I tell Constance, who looks worried. "I'll throw some clothes on and meet you in comms."

The Paula unit is capable of fifteen basic human facial responses, and she's programmed herself to reflect the one she deduces is most suitable for any situation. She's come a long way from the little round gizmo I first encountered on Lachion. Most people can't tell she's a bot, in fact, unless they're familiar with the model.

She doesn't argue, just leaves my quarters without wasted words.

It takes me only a few seconds to throw on black trousers and a light-armored flex-shirt. It's formfitting but provides great ease of movement. Quickly, I strap on my weapons and tie my hair up. I need to be ready to move once I get Vel.

There are few people in the dimly lit halls. Most went to sleep hours before; there are just a few wildly dedicated La'heng who have barely slept at all since they took the cure. I understand their feverish devotion to the cause; if I were them, I'd feel the same way.

"Is he on the way?" I ask Constance as I stride in.

"There was no answer. I have tried several possible locations—to no avail."

If he's not in his room, he's awake. He's not in the docking bay, tinkering, or he'd have heard the incoming message himself, and he'd have woken me. It's not the sort of news he'd trust to an intermediary. The base sprawls over a kilometer of ground, with different areas of concentration.

After a moment's thought, I say, "Buzz R&D."

"This is Devries," a male voice replies.

"Is Vel there?" I ask, leaning over Constance toward the mic.

"He is. I'll put him on."

Thank Mary.

"Something wrong, Sirantha?" I'd be asleep at the moment if shit hadn't gone sideways, so it's a fair question.

I summarize, then add, "Meet me at the shuttle in five minutes."

"Less, if I can." He cuts the comm connection.

"Hold the fort," I tell Constance. Then I sprint for the hangar.

If Loras and Zeeka wake before I return, she'll fill them in. This is a mission that doesn't require numbers. Vel might be able to handle it alone since he's both a pilot and a badass former bounty hunter, but there's no way I'm delegating this task. I won't rest until we're back at base, human cargo in tow.

I'm out of breath when I arrive. The shuttle door's ajar, waiting for me to board; Vel's already in the pilot chair. I clamber in and hit the button to seal the cabin. That much I can do, though I'm useless otherwise . . . unless he needs a gunner. Mary, I hope we don't. This needs to be a silent run.

"Do you think they've connected me to the bombing yet?"

"Unlikely. With systems crippled, it will take them a couple of days to narrow down possible culprits manually," he answers, checking the instrument panel.

"Even with a VA's help?" Though true AIs are prohibited, due to humanity's fear of machines running amok and enslaving them, virtual assistants are popular, having more limited programming and protocols. They're often used for tasks too monotonous for people to tolerate, like sorting endless registries of names and looking for matches. "I'm a natural suspect after the way I harassed Legate Flavius—"

"But *my* name was not used in any of your motions," he reminds me. "And I purchased the house."

"But you're a known associate of mine."

"True enough. But as long as we slide in and out, there should be no complications."

"Should be," I mutter, strapping in.

He completes his check, and I take a deep, worried breath. The danger comes when we open the outer door that seals any sign of our facility from the outside world. There's always risk, and we've tried to minimize it by coming and going during the night. Fortunately, it's still dark, and the Imperial forces should still be working on rescue and recovery, not hunting down those responsible yet. Not scanning for unusual energy emission on the surface in a region where there's nothing at all.

"Try not to fret, Sirantha. We will get them out safely."

"The timing could've been worse for a rescue," I mumble.

Vel nods as he maneuvers the shuttle out through the tunnel. At first we hit the wind and drop; despite my anxiety, my pulse leaps. I *love* to fly, even within the atmosphere. The thrusters burn as he throttles up, yielding enough altitude to clear the mountains ahead. I hope the Imperials won't be watching the sky or monitoring air traffic too closely right now.

For safety's sake, he should be running lights so we don't collide with another craft. Instead, Vel relies on the external sensors, and we'll quietly avoid anything we see up here. The base is remote, so there's nothing in the sky tonight anyway. I mutter my thanks for that as he closes the distance to the house.

"How mad do you think March is?" I ask quietly.

He angles me a look of amusement, punctuated by the movement of his mandible. Great, Vel thinks this is funny.

"Let me sum up: He is stranded with his young nephew, whom he would do anything to protect, on a world in which a war is brewing, and they have no means of escape, no way of returning to the safe, comfortable life they have built."

"That's what I figured."

"But no matter how furious he is, he would never lay a hand on you, as long as he is in his right mind."

It goes without saying that Vel won't let that happen again, not after Ithiss-Tor. He blames himself, I think, for the marks that required his tattoo around my throat, color to hide the bruises from when March tried to kill me. That will never happen again, and I shiver a little at the thought of the two males I love coming to blows. I won't let them hurt each other in my name.

"He'll be mad when we find them, but not crazy." I try a smile, but Vel is somber, a little troubled, I think.

I settle back and wait because there's nothing else I can do just now.

Imperial Public Service Announcement

[A ticker runs on the screen, listing the names of the missing and the dead. The Nicuan presenter looks suitably grave, dressed in a dark suit, his hair just disheveled enough to suggest restrained, noble grief.]

It is official. By the time order had been restored in Jineba, the edict came down from the Conglomerate. They have locked down interstellar travel until local affairs stabilize. The Nicuan Empire assures you that our centurions are the best trained soldiers in the civilized world. They will not rest until the culprits responsible for these egregious terrorist acts have been apprehended. The investigation is ongoing, and we expect to have the criminals in custody soon.

In the meantime, you will notice some changes to security procedures in urban areas. This is for your safety and protection. Loyal citizens have nothing to fear from these measures. We will be increasing drone security in outlying areas, and there will be a curfew implemented in all urban zones. We urge caution to anyone traveling outside these safe zones as we cannot guarantee your security in the provinces. At this time, patrols have been assigned to those areas most densely settled by Nicuan citizens.

In conclusion, respect the curfew. Be vigilant and report any violation of new security laws to the legate in charge of your borough. Remember, safety is everyone's business.

[End PSA]

CHAPTER 13

The shuttle has good vertical maneuvering capability, so Vel puts us down within a stone's throw of the house. For obvious reasons, we can't be here long. Every second increases the chances that someone will notice readings out of place even though this property is isolated. I vault out, check my weapons, and follow Vel.

I'm nervous.

Logically, I know Vel's right; the Imperials shouldn't have tracked me to this property purchase yet. Which means this isn't a trap. March and Sasha truly need our help.

On approach, the windows are dark. They could be asleep; it's been a while since they bounced the message. That doesn't seem like March, though. I bet he's standing guard while Sasha rests. If I know him, he's looking for me, watching the sky.

Vel checks the perimeter. "It looks clean."

"Then let's go in after them."

"In and out," he agrees.

The codes haven't changed; that's a good thing. With my thumbprint, a retinal scan, and the pass code, I get us into the house. Vel could crack it if March reprogrammed the system for greater safety, but it might cost time we need to make our escape. Hopefully not. Vel and I split up, and I creep through the dark house toward the bedrooms.

Movement catches my eye, but I can't nail down where the shadow came from. Then March touches my mind tentatively. *Jax?* His thoughts echo with exhaustion, anger, and fear, though not for himself. I skim his mind, seeing just how long he's been awake.

But at least they're here. Safe. Relief surges through me in a tidal flood. Until this moment, I didn't realize how worried I was that Imperial forces had snatched them up to be used as leverage against us, crippling the resistance before we get off the ground. While they might not connect Vel immediately, I'm high-profile. ONN has kept an eye on my involvement in case things got interesting . . . as they tend to when I'm around. And everyone knows about March and me. So while he's here, he's a target.

Get Sasha and meet me at the back doors, I tell him.

On my way. He mutes his emotions, holding explanations for a more appropriate time. I glimpse a number of things in his head, but it's not clear. I lack March's aptitude for skimming information quickly and efficiently.

I tap the comm to advise Vel, "I found them. They're on the way down." Then I spin, retracing my steps.

"Copy that. I will be waiting in the shuttle."

"Don't start it up until we arrive."

The house seems spooky, with all the electronics shut down; it's so quiet I hear each whisper of movement. At first just noise, then they become shadows, then shapes. Sasha stumbles, and I reach out for his shoulder. To my surprise, he doesn't shrug away. Maybe he's just tired and disoriented.

"Glad you're safe," I whisper to them both.

"We'll talk later," March says.

Sasha mumbles and follows me to the shuttle. I signal Vel as we approach, and the rumble of the thrusters sets the greenery on fire in the field behind. That'll leave a huge clue, assuming the Imperials ever find this place. I wonder if we should burn it all.

Sadly, I'm not kidding.

I help Sasha into the back of the shuttle, and March follows. Then I swing into the seat beside Vel.

"Do you think we need to torch the place?" I ask.

Vel checks readings, whether other craft show on the sensors. "That would draw more attention, I think. Most of their attention is well occupied to the south."

"Is there anything left in the house that could help them find you?" March asks.

"We scrubbed it thoroughly, wiped all the data."

"If it was my op, I'd blow the place. With luck, they associate it with the other strikes and consider Vel a victim, not a culprit."

I glance at Vel. "What do you think?"

"A bold plan, not without risks. Do you feel up to a firefight, Sirantha?"

I nod, glancing back at March in inquiry. "Are you sure you want us doing that with Sasha on board?"

"I don't want to be here at all," he mutters.

"It's not Jax's fault. Don't take it out on her for what I did."

I blink, certain I can't have heard the kid right. "What'd you do?"

"Uhm." In the dim glow from the instrument panel, Sasha looks chagrined. "Well, maybe I crushed some engine parts so our ship couldn't take off."

"Mother Mary. Why?"

"Because he wants to join the resistance," March snaps. "It looks glamorous when you're twelve."

"You wanted to stay, too, Dad. So I made it work out for both of us."

Yeah, I'm not getting in the middle of this for a billion credits. I listen to them argue while Vel takes us up.

Eventually, March swallows his anger and answers the question I've almost forgotten I asked. "Weapons hot, Jax. I trust you."

With his nephew's life—that's what he's saying. No pressure. I bring the guns online and target the house. I hate living dirtside, but this is the first time I've blown up a building over it. That thought is almost enough to make me laugh, despite the sitch.

Once he reaches sufficient altitude for us not to be caught in the shock wave, Vel gives the go-ahead, and I tap the panel. Beams of light arc toward the structure; impact offers both demolition and fire. I shoot several more times to make sure the destruction's catastrophic. Since it's not raining, the house should smolder until there's nothing left but wreckage.

"Sorry," I murmur to Vel.

"I have indemnity."

I cut him a look, but he's amused, not irritated. Which is excellent. I can only deal with one angry male at a time. It's a good rule of thumb.

"That was *epic*," Sasha says, watching the destruction down below.

March quiets him, but I'm glad the kid's not scared. If he was as timid as the turn before, I'd be swimming in guilt right now.

"Incoming." Vel wheels the shuttle.

"How many?" I ask.

"Six, fifty klicks out."

I ponder. "Are we fast enough to outrun them?"

"Aw," Sasha objects. "Blow them out of the sky!"

A few more comments like that, and I'll start liking this kid. I flash him a smile while Vel checks the intercept course. March's tension radiates until I feel it like a hot spot on the nape of my neck.

How mad are you? It's a test to see if he's still in my head.

Very. But not at you. I should've seen this coming. He's there, wrestling with frustration. *This is ten kinds of fragged up.*

I know you're scared for Sasha, but we'll keep him safe until we figure out a way—

There's not going to be *a way, Jax. We're stuck for the duration.*

Well, yeah. March told us how to wreak havoc in those strategy sessions. According to his advice, we chose our targets and bombed them simultaneously. We just didn't think he'd still be on world when the foolproof plan when into effect. *Oops.*

"Projected intercept in four minutes," Vel replies after he finishes analyzing the drone trajectory. "So no."

"Then let's hold here. I don't want them any closer to the base."

Moments pass in tense silence, then the six drones appear on my screen. I miss the gun-pit interface. I'm not as adept on the console, but I'll get better. I have to. I put the pressure from my mind. I can't think about how much is riding on me right now. But Mother Mary of Anabolic Grace, I've never fought with a *kid* on board.

Stop it. You can do this, I tell myself. *It's only a couple more than you took before.*

Relax, March says silently. *I trust you.*

His faith permits me to shoot the first one clean. *Five to go.*

The drones scramble, swinging up and away. I wish the shuttle had automated defenses. Next time, maybe I'll take Constance and download her into the nav panel. I bet she can shoot faster. More accurately, too. Vel swings us around, but he's not as experienced as March. We take a hit in the maneuver, glancing across the bow. The impact rattles us.

The shuttle doesn't have shields. Its armor will take a few more hits before we're crippled. Time's ticking while I fumble locking on the target. It's harder with March and Sasha aboard; the stakes are higher, and I feel like my hands are all thumbs. My head fills with fear that the shuttle will go down here, in the middle of nowhere, and we'll be stranded.

They'll find us.

I'm truly worried about March and Sasha. Now I understand how he felt about going into battle with me. Vel and I, we've fought together for turns. I trust he can handle his business. I know March can, too, but not with his kid in tow. He'll always protect him first, maybe sacrifice himself if push comes to shove.

This *sucks.*

Clumsy on the controls, I take out another one while Vel spins us away from the remaining four. More shots come in hard, and only a sharp altitude drop gets us away from the barrage. I'm tired, terrified, and not on top of my game.

Don't choke, Jax. Not now.

"I can help," Sasha says. "This will be easy. They're not big."

My hands are shaking. "Go for it, kid."

Leaning forward, he narrows his eyes on the drones, their lights showing him how to strike. Then he slams all four of them together; they explode like fireworks, bits of metal cascading down. He doesn't even have to gesture. The shuttle doesn't rock. That's some fragging impressive control. No wonder he took the blue ribbon.

"Way to go," I say, sitting back from the weapons console. Cold sweat trickles down my spine; that was closer than it should've been. "You saved us, Sasha."

March is ominously silent.

CHAPTER 14

"So are we part of the resistance now, like when I fight the evil overlords in Rebel Alliance XVI?" Sasha has chattered all the way to base. "This is like the mission where—"

"Can you sit in the cockpit and run a diagnostic for me?" Vel cuts in. "I must be sure the shuttle sustained no lasting damage."

"Sure. I mean, I can, can't I?" The kid glances at March for permission.

"Find me after you're done," he says tersely.

I offer Vel a nod of thanks. Sasha needs to be distracted while his uncle tears me a new asshole. I can tell he's furious; I'm just not sure why. At the house, he didn't seem this upset with me. He doesn't speak as he follows me from the hangar. Behind us, the doors have sealed, hiding our energy emissions once again. The next few hours will be crucial as it'll reveal whether Imperial troops detected our movements.

After a little thought, I lead the way to my quarters. Nobody else needs to hear this, and he requires privacy to yell at me. Sure, he could do it in my head, but it doesn't have the same impact for a thunderous scold. Once we reach my room,

I step in and seal the door behind us. I don't take a defensive posture, just brace and wait.

"What the hell were you thinking?" he demands.

"Which time?"

"When you let my kid take on the enemy!"

"I thought it was better than dying. I was choking on the guns." I don't explain why; it seems to me if he was in my head, he knows. I was too worried about their safety. For once, I couldn't compartmentalize.

"Then you should've given *me* the controls."

"That would've taken too long. By the time we swapped seats, the shuttle would've taken a hit to put us on the ground, and we'd have been stranded. How is that better?"

"You're not his mother, Jax, and you don't get to involve my son in war games."

"That's why you're mad?" I ask in reflexive surprise.

"What did you think?"

"Because you're stuck here with the shit hitting the fan."

He lifted his shoulders in a familiar shrug, dismissing that suggestion. "That was all Sasha. You had nothing to do with it . . . and I knew you were on a tight schedule. I'm worried about being stranded during wartime, but not angry."

"I'm sorry I used Sasha without your permission," I say. "But you could've said no."

"Then he'd think I didn't trust him to control his TK. He's made such strides that I don't want to undermine his confidence. He's just about a normal kid these days, and I . . ."

"You don't want to see him lose that." I get it now.

A bunker full of angry soldiers determined to rid their homeworld of the conquering force doesn't lend itself to normal childhood experiences. I sink down on the bed, full of remorse over . . . so many things. Mostly, what I feel bad about, though, is that I *don't* feel worse about March's being here with me. Regret should wrack me from head to toe, but the truth is, a kernel of happiness burns inside me. I want him, even if it's not by choice. That's how self-centered I am.

He puffs out a sigh and rakes a hand through his shaggy hair. "Are you going to make me fight another war for you, Jax?"

"I'd never force you to do anything," I say softly.

"That's true. That would devalue all the lessons you learned from St. Kai." Even after all this time, he sounds bitter . . . and jealous of the love I lost.

That makes me smile . . . because he's so imperfect and human and occasionally irrational. I push to my feet and cross to him, wrapping my arms about his waist. For a few seconds, he resists, then his arms come around me. He rests his chin atop my head.

"What do you want to do?" I ask.

"What I want and what can happen are two different things."

"You'd hop the next ship home," I guess.

"Obviously. Sasha needs to finish school."

"You can train him, though, right? It might not be as structured as the Psi Corp program, but—" I break off as a thought occurs to me. "Constance has training experience from Emry. I bet we could modify her programming for classroom-style teaching, and you can handle the Psi stuff."

March nods. "I'm familiar with the exercises. It's doable but not ideal."

Sadly, that describes most of my life. I could offer platitudes like *Things happen for a reason* or *It'll all work out for the best*, but March is relaxing in my arms. I don't want to piss him off again. It's a bit underhanded that I'm using proximity to defuse his anger, but what the hell, I'll bring whatever weapons I have to bear.

"That'll keep you busy," I say.

"You think I can be here and not get involved?" He laughs softly. "I'm still a soldier. It'll drive me nuts inside a week to know you're running missions without me."

"Would it have bothered you on Nicuan?"

"To some degree, but when you're so far away, it's less itchy."

"I'm sorry," I say again.

I know he didn't want this for Sasha. It's no way to raise a kid.

"Hey," he says. "You have nothing to apologize for."

"Except using your kid as a weapon."

"Don't remind me." He frowns. "It's a big game to him. I should've predicted how Sasha would react to all the hoorah and heroism. He loves strategy sims, playing hero. This turned out to be too much temptation. But I'm not sure he understands the stakes. In games, if things go bad, his avatar respawns."

"Not so much on the battlefield."

"Exactly. I don't want him to end up like me."

"You say that like it's a bad thing."

"To be me? I'm pretty fragged up, Jax. We live on my savings. I don't work because the only thing I know how to do, I *can't* do while I'm all Sasha has."

I'd never thought about how he might feel, living on Nicuan. I assumed he loved the kid so much that he didn't think of anything else. But it must be a constant reminder of his old life. It must be hard, at times. I hate thinking of him feeling alone and useless, nothing to distract him from missing me. He's not sorry for his commitment to Sasha, but I wonder if he ever feels trapped.

Yes. He doesn't say it aloud because that feels like betrayal of the boy he loves so much. *I can't do what I want. I have to think about what's best for somebody else.*

It's not forever, I assure him. *Kids grow up. That's kind of what they do.*

Sometimes, in the past few turns, that knowledge kept me going.

I add aloud, "You're not alone now. I can teach Sasha stuff. So can Vel, Constance, Loras, and Zeeka. It's not all on you anymore."

He rubs his cheek against my hair. "I shouldn't be so relieved to turn my kid over to three aliens and an AI, should I?"

"You need a break. It's hard to be everything to somebody, all the time."

"How would you know?" It's not meant to be a cruel question, but it lances straight through me all the same.

I step back then. "Are you saying I can't be counted on?"

"As long as it suits you."

"I thought you understood why I couldn't stay." Hurt lashes me.

His smile is beautiful and bittersweet. "I understood why you chose not to."

And he's right; it's an accurate distinction. I own this. But his comment makes it seem as if he's been nursing a grudge. This wasn't how I wanted to spend our unexpected additional time together; I will be shipping out soon on my first mission.

He goes on, "But I accept it. I never expected you to be different."

I fold my arms. "To be a martyr, you mean? Like you?"

His shoulders stiffen. "Jax—"

"Kids are adaptable. You stayed on Nicuan because you think you failed your sister. So you were determined you'd give Sasha anything he wanted, even if it made you unhappy. In fact, that was better, because then you could spend the time in penance. I'm not saying you don't love the kid, but you could've raised him in a place that didn't make you miserable."

"Like on a ship with you," he says roughly.

"Yes. Like that."

"It would've been too dangerous, Jax. Out in deep space, one tantrum from Sasha, and we're all dead in vacuum."

"So we use force fields. We teach him the dangers. It could've been viable . . . you just didn't try."

"I'd forgotten this about you."

"What?"

"That you don't hesitate to kick a guy in the nuts."

Is that what I did? I press on, ruthless. "I just want you to face the truth. It seems like you resent that I didn't don sackcloth and stay, even if it made me miserable."

"Maybe," he snaps. "Is that so wrong? That I want you to love me that much?"

"I *do* love you," I say. "But not more than myself."

"You don't love anyone more than yourself." As the words slip out, he looks horrified.

I still. While I've feared I was so selfish, nobody ever said it out loud before. The accusation hurts more than I could've imagined, coming from March; it's a surprise boot in the teeth. I exhale shakily. "I think you'd better go see how Sasha's doing."

"Jax—"

"Just go."

CHAPTER 15

The next day, I meet Loras in the detention area, as requested. Through the one-way mirror, I can see the two men. The short centurion, whom Vel will impersonate, is digging at his skin, desperate for another run; he's scratched deep, bloody runnels in his arms, until the dried flesh cakes under his nails. The other sits and rocks, his eyes glassy.

Loras clicks the sound on.

"Felt good. So good. Need it." The first turns bloodshot eyes to his catatonic cellmate. "Want more."

"The treatments are a little more addictive than we anticipated," Loras says. "I don't think he's fit even for manual labor."

"So it's not viable for recruitment," I say, swallowing my horror. "Did we get any useful information out of him?"

"A little. Mostly about the number of legates in the capital."

"That's something. What are you going to do with them?" As I ask the question, Zhan strides up.

He salutes Loras with two fingers, his bearing fierce and aggressive. "Reporting as ordered, sir."

"Kill them," Loras says.

Shock ripples through me. Somehow, I thought there would

be more fanfare. "Is Vel finished studying the short one's face?"

"It's a no-go," Loras answers, as Zhan keys in the code and enters the cell.

I can't say I was looking forward to the op, but it seemed our most likely way to gather information on the enemy. I don't understand what's changed. But before I gain clarity, Zhan executes both prisoners. It's as neat as I've ever seen, and the pleasure in Zhan's expression gives me a chill. So many centuries of enslavement—so many turns to hate and plot and dream of vengeance.

"What went wrong?"

"They were both declared dead," he replies. "Leviter saw their names on a PSA broadcast. The funerals are tomorrow."

"Oh, shit. So if Vel had turned up, days later, there would be questions."

"The centurions would likely assume that he had been collaborating, possibly held by the enemy, and had given up secrets."

"So they would've detained him. Possibly tortured him for information."

Loras nods. "They certainly would've uncovered his masquerade, and it wouldn't have taken long for them to link him to you, Tarn, and Leviter."

We had a close call.

I offer, "Leviter and Tarn will serve us well in the capital. They maintain ties to Nicuan, albeit distant ones."

"Are they willing to do some spying?" he asks.

"They're looking forward to it. Down the line, maybe we can figure out an alternative method to plant Vel in Nicuan territory."

Before he can reply, Zhan gets on the comm, ordering a cleanup crew. I turn away. These men would've shot us the night of the raid, but I'm already tired of killing. Too bad there's so much more of it in store; La'heng will run red with blood before we're through.

"Why did you want me here for the execution?" I ask at length.

"You're my second. The other La'hengrin must see that you'll follow my lead even when humans are put to death."

Nicuan nobles act inhuman sometimes, but in physiology, we share genetic stock. So I understand his point. "They're afraid when push comes to shove, I'll choose my own kind?"

He dodges the question. "They'll come to trust you, Jax."

Zhan steps out of the cell in time to hear those words. He nods. "You didn't protest. That will go a long way toward reassuring my comrades. It's one thing for them to see you filing petitions. It's another to kill for a people not your own."

"It's the right thing to do."

A team comes in a few moments to bag the bodies and haul them away. They'll be incinerated down in the deepest part of the base, no trace left behind. I can't help thinking of the tall centurion's wife; right now, she's grieving. She doesn't realize that her husband was alive until just now. She's not a centurion or a warrior . . . she's just a woman who loved a man.

Damn, I'm getting soft.

"Nobody has cared about what was right on La'heng since your people came and changed us," Loras bites out.

I'm used to his rage; it doesn't offend me. But it's nice when Zhan says, "Enough. Save your anger for our enemies."

Then Zhan sketches a half bow that reminds me of a *wa*. My chip seeks its meaning, but there is none. Or rather, it's gibberish. His fingers, hands, and elbows don't speak the silent language. They are only movements and angles, lacking all poetry.

"Don't worry about it," I tell the other La'hengrin.

Loras puts a hand on my arm, drawing me out of the prison area, down the corridor toward R&D. "Have you spoken to March?"

"About what?"

He offers a half smile. "Anything. There's a pool running on how long you stay mad at him. If you make up today, I win seven hundred credits."

I sigh. "But I'm still pissed off."

How come when a woman does what makes her happy, she's selfish? When I remember what he said, my head feels like it'll explode. It hurt each time he left, but I never thought he was *egotistical* for doing what he thought was right. That's a double standard, and I won't put up with it. I need to talk to him, but I've got to cool off first, or I'll throw words like knives. Those wounds don't heal because you can't unsay verbal cruelties; they linger in the memory like poison, and sometimes "sorry" isn't enough.

Loras shrugs, philosophical. "It was worth a shot."

For the next few hours, we go over some experimental tech that R&D has been working on under Constance's watchful eye. There's paint with microcircuitry that evokes a shifting camouflage effect, which can be applied to armor or vehicles. They're also developing a weapon that mounts on your forearm and strikes with the power of a ship laser. Perfect for the soldier on the move. Unfortunately, it overheats too fast, and there are still bugs to be excised.

After it nearly blows the arm off the dummy holding it during the tests, I say, "Maybe it's not quite ready."

The head tech nods. "But the camo paint is good to go."

"Thanks," Loras says. "I'll let them know in the docking bay. We'll get it on all our vehicles."

Two days later, I still haven't spoken to March. I told him to go, and he'll respect my need to cool down until I offer an olive branch. I appreciate his patience. Zhan says he's busy with Sasha's TK training, working with the soldiers on hand-to-hand combat and techniques for ambush, using the terrain to provide cover for an attack. Since the La'hengrin are newly restored to their ability to fight, they need the education. The recruits have excellent agility and natural reflexes to go along with their knack for languages. Most aren't as strong as a human, but their speed and natural ferocity make them devilish opponents. I can't think of anyone better suited than March for teaching them how to kick ass.

That day, I'm on my way to find Zeeka when Sasha stops me. "Whatever my dad did, he's sorry. Did you guys fight because of me? It probably *was* about me."

Mary, I remember being this positive the universe revolved around me. Sadly, I wasn't twelve at the time.

"Hi, Sasha, how are you?" I grin at him.

"Hi, fine, can we resolve this please?" He's getting some attitude, and he wears it well. I like cocky in a kid. Makes him seem less fragile.

"Are you acting as his emissary?"

"His what?" He frowns, which is kind of cute. "Do you mean, did he send me?"

"Yeah."

"No, he doesn't know I came looking for you. I'm supposed to be practicing."

"TK?"

"I'm so sick of it." He sounds bummed.

Not wanting to discuss my personal life with a kid, I try to change the subject. "Do you miss the kids at your school?"

"Some. Hey, don't distract me. You have to talk to my dad, okay? Please?"

Apparently, I'm a soft touch when a kid gazes at me with soulful eyes and offers the magic word. "Will you work on your exercises if I promise to find March?"

He puts out a hand. "Deal."

Stifling a sigh, I take it. Then Sasha runs off. I touch my comm. "Where's March?"

"In the barracks, Sirantha Jax." Constance still hasn't stopped calling me by my full name. I'm sure she does it just to screw with me. Some days, in fact, I suspect she downloaded special software that lets her approximate a sense of humor, messing with people using some kind of sophisticated algorithm.

"Thanks."

No time like the present. I jog toward the barracks, lifting a hand now and then to the La'hengrin. We have to increase our numbers—and that's the next step. There's no mass delivery system that permits personal choice, so it'll take a while. Fortunately, there's no deadline for saving the world.

I arrive outside the room where March is teaching. Before he spots me, I take cover in the doorway, watching him drill. He's broken them into pairs, as he did in the combat program he ran for the Conglomerate. Memories take me; I remember when I was a soldier under his command. But that's a bittersweet memory, like so many of them.

I wait until the class ends. He talks with a few La'hengrin, his harsh features radiating camaraderie. *This is good for him,* I think. *He needs a purpose.*

March spies me as he heads for the door, then draws up short. His features lose that easy air he had with the men, maybe because he doesn't know what to do with me. He's always sure around soldiers; he's got experience with them. From what he told me once, I'm the only woman he's ever loved. The rest, he paid for an hour of their time.

I open strong. "So Sasha bribed me to come talk to you."

"Oh?" Flicker of amusement. "What'd he offer?"

"To do his TK practice."

"You mean he wasn't? Dammit."

"Cut the kid a break. He was worried about you."

March sighs, running a hand through his tousled hair. "Yeah, he's been bugging me to talk to you. I kept telling him you'd come when you were ready."

"Thanks for not pushing," I say softly.

He takes a step toward me. "I didn't mean it like it sounded, Jax. It's not bad that you'll never lose yourself in someone else. It's part of what makes you strong."

He's said that about me before—that I'm the strongest person he's ever met. *I* tend to think I'm dumb. No matter how many times I get knocked down, I always stagger up again. If I had a brain in my head, sometimes after one of those hits, I'd just kiss dirt a little while. Save myself the pain. But I always find myself on my feet, swinging wide, no matter what.

"I get it. But here's the thing . . . it's not selfish to make the right choices for me, whatever they might be. If you want a woman who settles down, who'll work that rutabaga farm with you"—smiling, I mention the offer he made me so long ago—"well, I'm not her. I never will be. And I won't feel guilty over it, either."

"I don't expect you to. I *am* sorry, Jax."

I nod. "Forgiven. Let's spend our last few days together, okay?"

When March arches a brow, I realize he doesn't know. It's up to me to tell him. "I'm shipping out soon."

CHAPTER 16

March takes the news better than I expected . . . and we don't waste our remaining days. That's all I'm saying. Beyond the time we spend in my quarters, he trains the men and works with Sasha. He's prone to making the best of any situation, and I think, deep down, he's glad to be involved, even peripherally.

Zeeka teases me about our quiet nights on the way to the final briefing. "You're looking happy. Vermilion, even."

Mareq throats flush when they're excited, as I recall. So I think he's saying I have a satisfied glow . . . or something like that. I cast him a slantways look. "Please don't."

"I think it's awesome."

Mary, no. I can stand anything, today, but the sex-related speculation of my once-foster son who is also a sentient frog. *Some days* . . . By some miracle, Vel comes along to save me because Zeeka is still too awed by him to joke around in his presence. He thinks that Vel is the epitome of greatness . . . and well, he is.

The three of us walk to the hall, which is the only room in the base large enough for us to meet simultaneously. Even though our numbers will certainly increase, the body of the army will not be present here. They'll be in the field, assaulting various soft, lightly guarded installations. The plan of attack has been diagrammed to a decimal point. Now we just have to execute.

Which will be tougher.

"I haven't seen much of you lately." Not since we made the nocturnal run to extract March and Sasha from the house.

"It seemed best to give you some space."

That's enough unlike Vel that I frown. "Why?"

"You and March have been apart. There will be growing pains as you remember how to be a unit again."

"True enough. We've been fighting."

Vel inclines his head. "I am aware. But Sasha is excellent company for an unfinished human."

That makes me laugh. "Yeah, he's better than he was last time. Are you and I all right, though?"

"Why would we not be?" Genuine puzzlement flexes his mandible.

Once more, I've made the mistake of imbuing Vel with human motivations. He's not jealous of March or threatened, or anything that a human male might be, placed in his complicated relationship with me. But for him, it's not difficult at all. He's my friend . . . and he's content to wait. He's still mourning Adele; that will go on for turns, quietly and deeply.

I make up my mind not to worry about it again. There are enough real problems on the ground that I don't need to invent them. Zeeka, Vel, and I take seats near the back of the room. A few minutes later, Loras enters, with Constance beside him. Likely she's helped him organize this final presentation. He spends nearly an hour going over the plan, then he calls out the breakdown of personnel.

"Are we all clear on our assignments?" Loras asks.

My gaze roves the room, finding a few familiar faces, and then I nod. Others murmur their assent. We can't start a war with our small force holed up inside a mountain. Some of us have to take the fight to the enemy.

Therefore, we're splitting up. A small team—including Zhan, Constance, March, and Sasha—will remain at base, facilitating communication and ops. The rest of us will divide into cells comprised of ten soldiers. While it's possible that one of us might break and betray the base-camp location, that won't destroy the war effort because there will be so many of us in the field, and the rest won't know where we are or what we're planning.

Loras has been studying the most successful guerilla generals throughout the history of several species, and he's memorized the tenets as though they were the phonetics of a new language. He speaks of nothing but strategy and quotes ancient figures as dinner conversation: *The enemy advances, we retreat; the enemy camps, we harass; the enemy tires, we attack; the enemy retreats, we pursue.*

Over the hum of muted voices, he orders, "Break into your units."

Since I'm standing with two of my cell and we're easy to spot, I remain where I am. Loras comes over to join us; soon, the others find us. My cell consists of Vel, Zeeka, Loras, and six La'hengrin I don't know well. That'll change over the course of the assignment. I'm looking forward to some action, even if it's risky and against impossible odds. Maybe especially in that case because the danger makes it more interesting, more like jumping.

In addition to ops management and R&D, Constance will also tutor Sasha. He's not thrilled about hiding, but then, he's twelve. He doesn't get to fight. March will have his hands full, dealing with a disappointed kid with incredible TK power. Hopefully, he won't shake down the mountain while we're gone.

"That's all," Loras calls.

He was the first to receive—and survive—Carvati's Cure. This is *his* cause. I'm backing his play because he's my friend, I owe him, and this is the right thing to do: three compelling reasons to kick some ass. Once the squad members depart, heading to their missions in groups of ten, I turn to Loras.

"Are you ready?" I ask.

It's a big question for three words. He gets that . . . and takes his time replying. "I'm not sure anyone can ever be prepared for such an immense undertaking. But it's time."

"We're meeting the others in the docking bay at 20:30?"

He nods. "Vel is making some last-minute adjustments to the shuttle."

We're lucky; we get the ship with all the bells and whistles. The other cells all have transportation, but not like ours. While Vel and I have deep pockets, we don't possess unlimited resources. And there are other purchases to be made. Floating mines for the air lanes, weapons, armor, rations, field kits, and the list goes on. I'm tired just thinking about it.

And we've only just begun.

"I'd better get my bag and say my good-byes. We won't be back for a while."

If ever.

That part goes without saying. But Loras understands the stakes, just as I do. I've never fought a ground war before. The centurions have; they're all experienced mercs, having put in their time on Nicu Tertius. On the plus side, by the time they earn the right to serve on a cushy colony like La'heng, they're all getting on in turns, and they've been out of the field a while. So that's an asset; it'll be up to us to exploit it properly.

I head for my quarters, don my set of camo armor, and grab my kit. Next, I strap on my weapons: laser pistol on my hip, shock-stick on the other side, and a field knife strapped to my thigh. One last time, I check my equipment.

Constance is working in comms when I find her. Some might find it odd that I'd look for my PA, who—on the surface—is little more than a VI, but I don't think of her that way. However humble her beginnings, she's a person to me.

"Look after March and Sasha for me," I say softly.

She turns, her face set in solemn lines. "I will, Sirantha Jax. And you take care of yourself for me."

"I'm not the one you should worry about."

"Nevertheless, you will do as I instruct." She even *sounds* like a mom.

"I wouldn't dare do otherwise."

Then, to my surprise, she hugs me. Constance doesn't feel like a machine, all gears and rotors beneath the bioware. I huff out a choky breath and stand there imagining this is what it would be like to have a mother who worried instead of conducting illegal arms deals. Eventually, she steps back, hands on my shoulders.

"Did I do it correctly?"

I arch a brow. "What?"

"Display warmth and concern?"

It would be more effective if she hadn't questioned her mastery of the concepts, but I nod. "It was perfect. Thank you, Constance."

"You are welcome."

"Do you know where March is?"

She jacks into the computer with a touch of her fingertip, what a marvelous wireless interface. After a few seconds scanning the vid feeds, she replies, "In your quarters, Sirantha Jax. Shall I tell him to wait?"

"Please."

He must have come looking for me, and I just missed him as I headed to comms. This time, I don't run. In fact, I can barely put one foot after another, knowing what's waiting for me at the other end. I want him fighting beside me but he can't. He's all Sasha has. Being stuck here doesn't change that.

I don't know if I can say good-bye to March under these circumstances. He's never had to send me off to war like this; I don't know how he'll handle it. When battle looms, it's usually him leaving me. The time I took off during the Morgut War, I sneaked off while he was asleep.

"Jax." He steps into the hall to greet me as I arrive.

"I'm leaving soon."

March fills my head with warmth and aching regret. He wants to don armor and join the battle. The soldier in him is sick to his soul that he has to be a father instead of a warrior. I've never seen him in such desperate conflict with himself. Tears glisten in his hawk's eyes, shining molten gold. He blinks, so that the dampness tangles his long lashes. Not a single droplet falls. I can feel him swallow it back until it becomes a knot in his stomach to match the one in mine.

"I wish you weren't stuck here," I whisper.

"It's worse," he says, closing his eyes. "If I were far away, on Nicuan, I could pretend it wasn't happening. But here, I feel so helpless. I want to *come with you*."

"You can't."

"I know."

He hauls me into his arms so I can feel him shaking, or maybe that's me. We kiss; and it's salty, bittersweet, heat preceding the ice of separation. Our love is chased by endless farewells, like a sweet shot of liqueur with bitters at the bottom.

I don't say good-bye to him. Once we break apart, I just turn and move in the opposite direction. He's in my head until the distance grows too great. As he slips away, I hear, *Stay safe, my love.*

The scene in the hangar reminds me of when we all split up on Emry Station. So much has changed since then, so many lost. Dread twists my insides. This could be the last time I see some of these people. I no longer think about dying; instead, I fear being left behind. Even Vel, with his built-in chitin armor, though he's long-lived, can still die. And Loras, upon whom every hope is fixed, is merely flesh and bone.

CHAPTER 17

The shuttle puts down near a town too small to deserve the name. There's little Imperial presence because it's rural and remote, too far from the capital to offer any prestige as a post. Those centurions assigned here are atoning for some misdeed, like sleeping with a nobleman's wife or skimming from the legate's till. They're stationed at a mining outpost, as that's the industry that keeps this village going. The La'hengrin work the shafts, repairing equipment and doing hard labor.

It's a poor community; that much is obvious as I step off the ship. I've never seen such conditions on a world that wasn't class-P, which means it's too primitive to have developed spacefaring technology on its own. While the outpost manned by the centurions has every modern convenience, including a comm array on the roof, the houses down the mountain are humble, made of mud and stone, and they don't seem to have power: not solar, electric, or any other modern amenity. I cannot believe my eyes.

"Was it always like this?" I ask Loras.

Fury clenches his jaw, and he speaks through gritted teeth. "No."

Confronted with what my people have done to his, I feel sick to my stomach. It's not like this in the capital, although the La'heng are certainly subservient to the Imperial forces who protect them. But I didn't know it was like this in outlying areas.

"I don't see any Nicuan presence at all. How do the people survive?" Loras told me, long ago, that he required a protector—that the bond was necessary. Obviously, for traveling, he needed somebody to protect him physically, but I recall the way he spoke, as if it were a physiological imperative.

"There are protectors in the cities. They hold bonds in abeyance."

"Sort of like absentee landlords?" I ask, puzzled.

"Yes. It should be a personal thing of honor and promises, but it has dwindled to this, handled by proxies. Protectors hold massive rosters of those they 'safeguard.'"

"From the comfort of their palaces in the cities."

"Yes," he says through clenched teeth. "And then, when someone wishes to pick a pet for personal use, they apply to the protector to take the bond."

My head feels like it's going to explode. "That's *disgusting*."

"Let's go," Zeeka interrupts.

Just as well. I need to think about something else.

His armor has a special solar-heat feature since he's not warm-blooded, and the mountains get cold at night. According to all the treatises Loras has read, it's easiest to fight a superior force in such terrain. So that's where we begin.

The others fall in. As we get a few steps away from the ship, it blends with the rocky hillside, so that, from a distance, it's indistinguishable from the landscape. I'm really pleased with how R&D perfected the camo paint. As a unit, we close our helmets so that we fade in the same fashion. Movement gives us away, of course, but there's nobody on watch.

They're all inside drinking and watching vids, commiserating on drawing such a shit post. Loras chose our initial targets well. We fired the first salvo already, but we'll fight the war out here in the provinces. As with all great guerilla generals, he's determined we must win the hearts and minds of the people. Later, they will support us. They will hide us.

I've memorized the names of my new teammates, at least; we accomplished that much on the way out here. There are four males, two females, one of whom is breathtakingly beautiful—Farah, whom I met at the secret conclave in Jineba.

The other female is called Bannie. With brown hair and eyes, she's pretty, of course, but not awe-inspiring. She's capable, though, which is more important. I hear she did particularly well in the martial-arts portion of March's crash training course. It's impossible to tell the four La'heng males apart with their armor on, as they're all of a height. One of them is Farah's brother, Timmon, who resembles her somewhat. The other three are Rikir, Eller, and Xirol.

Loras leads the way up. The terrain won't permit a clean landing, so we come in on foot. Soon, over the next rise, I spot the mining station. It's all corrugated metal, ugly as hell, and hard to heat. Quickly, I skim the outpost for assets we can repurpose. *Aha.* The comm tower on the roof will prove useful once we take out the skeleton crew.

It's nearly dark; therefore, the workers have all gone home. Inside the fence, the compound is full of machinery and mining equipment in various states of disrepair. In a glance at Vel, who's easy to ID given the shape of his helmet, I ask a silent question. He inclines his head to confirm that he can do all kinds of interesting things with this stuff. Loras urges us toward the gate with a gesture.

"Stay low!" he orders.

The rest of us comply. It takes sixteen seconds to disable the simple analog lock; and then I follow the others through the compound toward the building. Using the machines as cover, though that's probably unnecessary, I climb the stairs behind Vel. Zeeka is behind me, weapon in hand, and Loras brings up the rear. Bannie has point, and I crouch as she kicks the door open, then drops. The first half of the team strides in.

Xirol nails the guy sitting before the comm before he has time to raise his hand. His head splatters. I drop to one knee to steady my aim and take out the man I gauge to be the commander. Chest shot, no fancy shooting for me. The burn forms immediately, the stink of charred meat in the air, and the surviving centurions dive for their weapons, but they're middle-aged and slow, plus they don't even keep their sidearms nearby. It's been that long since they had to fight.

The attack, if you could even call it that, doesn't take long. It's more like an execution. Afterward, Timmon and Rikir haul the bodies outside, so we have room to work. Zeeka's vocalizer has the mimic function, so he finds the comm, plays the log, then makes a call to central that will prevent them from sending a team.

"This is Montrose. We're having some trouble with the emitter array. I'm going to take it down while we make repairs."

It's a little eerie to hear a dead man's voice coming from Zeeka's helmet. The comm crackles. They've restored planetary communications since the bombing, but because Leviter's gambit has come to fruition, their messages won't be bounced off world via satellite. La'heng is now in lockdown, coded red. Nobody's coming to help them. The Imperials just don't realize how dire the situation is, yet.

"Acknowledged, Montrose, keep us posted. Central out." The centurion on the other end sounds bored.

And why wouldn't he be? There's no reason to fear that the La'hengrin may rise up. They're helpless and subservient, bound to follow orders.

Vel gets up on the roof to disconnect the array to keep the story consistent, which buys us some time. We'll plug it back in later to make regular bogus reports from Montrose. Old comm logs should give us a better idea what they expect from this station.

Afterward, I help the rest of the squad haul the other bodies beyond the gated perimeter. Mountain beasts should drag them off. If not, the elements will claim them. It's not like anybody is coming to look for them so long as Zeeka plays his part.

Then it's a forced march back to the shuttle. *So far, so good.* I swing into the back with the others while Loras runs up front with Vel. Xirol and Timmon are jokers, cracking wise about how soft the centurions are. Rikir is quiet, along with Farah. Bannie's talking to Zeeka about his implant.

I lean over, watching the ground rush toward us as Vel maneuvers the craft for a landing just outside the village.

From our preliminary intel, there's reason to believe they'll welcome us here. As I leap out of the shuttle—I'm the fifth to disembark—the La'hengrin come out of their houses to greet us. Despite the darkness, lit only by flickering torches, I'm not afraid.

Loras steps forward, pulling off his helmet so they can see his face. "Do any of you recognize me?"

One of the miners, still filthy from his shift, steps forward and lifts his hand in affirmation. "Your broadcast came on when I was in the rec room up at the mine. I told everyone . . . I'm not sure they believed me."

"What's your name?" Loras asks.

"I'm Deven."

"Loras." His clear gaze skims the crowd. "On the mountain above, your captors lie dead. Liberation starts here. If I must, I will go quietly, town by town, offering the cure. I won't lie to you. There's a chance you won't survive it. But for me, it was better to risk death than to continue living as a slave."

A chill ripples over me. In ten villages around the world, just like this one, cell leaders are speaking these exact same words. Maybe they don't all have Loras's charisma, but they do share his conviction. The crowd murmurs, then a woman whispers in Deven's ear.

"Tell us about this cure."

Loras glances over. "Vel?"

He's the most qualified, scientifically, to lay it out thoroughly yet in layman's terms. So in simple language, he explains how Dr. Carvati perfected the cure, using data found in the Maker records; they're ones who build the technology we use to navigate grimspace—and without our trip to the other 'verse, liberation wouldn't be possible now. Vel elaborates on how the treatment works, step by step, how long it takes, and, finally, the risks.

He concludes, "Currently, the failure rate is 5 percent. For every hundred who take the treatments, five will perish."

We're not trying to trick them. The audience rumbles more, confused, uncertain. In some ways, it must sound too good to be true but also terrifying. Because who wants to gamble with his life that way?

A woman raises her hand. "How will it affect our children? Will our babies be born free?" Clearly, this is a mother's concern in taking the risk.

Fortunately, Vel has the answer. "Yes, due to La'hengrin adaptive physiology."

That makes sense. Just as RC-12 caused their children to be enslaved, Carvati's Cure will undo the damage. If I had kids, I'd want this for them. Nobody should be forced to live as the La'hengrin do, devoid of agency and free will.

Finally, Deven says, "We'll hold a meeting in the morning and decide what's to be done. There's a cottage where you can stay tonight."

La'heng Liberation Army signal-jack ad: Profile Two

LORAS

[A man with navy eyes gazes at the camera with complete confidence.]

When I was seventeen, a stranger took me from my home. He sent me to school. He wasn't unkind. Eventually, he took me off Nicuan, and he lost me in a game of Charm to another stranger. This man, too, was kind enough, though he treated me like a tool to be used. He rarely asked me how I felt or thought about anything. I never received pay for my work, so anything I wanted, I had to ask for like a child.

Now most of you might think, this doesn't sound so bad. At least you weren't beaten or molested. But what person ought to hold that up as a measuring stick of what's acceptable? Eventually, the second old man died . . . and he left me to his great-nephew, again like property.

Do you sense a theme? But it gets worse.

My new owner didn't want me. He was embarrassed to take charge of me; he feared others would judge him—and rightly so. Consequently, he treated me even less like a person. It was . . . soul-crushing. That's a dramatic word, but it fits. In time, I ceased to consider myself a sentient being. I had no opinions. I merely did as I was told. My bond switched as it does, rarely, when my owner failed to protect me. The one who saved my life took possession. She was better than the others . . . and worse. She reminded me that I had desires of my own. She tried to treat me like a person. Eventually, I started to think I mattered to her, and I resented my life before. The injustice made me *angry*.

Then she left me to die, and an infamous pirate became responsible for my care. In his hands, I suffered the abuse others experience from the beginning. It was monstrous, and it did not end until I took the cure. Because I realized I would rather die a free man than live in chains.

Voice-over: And *that's* what you're fighting for. Contact the comm code at the bottom of your screen to find workers with the cure.

CHAPTER 18

The cottage is small and primitive. Fortunately, our field kits provide for bivouacking in less-than-ideal locales. I strip down to my thin uniform and wrap up. All around me, my squad-mates do the same. A night on the floor in a bedroll leaves me none the worse, and in the morning, I suck down a packet of paste; it doesn't taste any better than it ever did.

"This brings back memories," I say when I catch Vel looking at me.

He makes a noise my chip recognizes as laughter, no need to engage his vocalizer. I understand him just fine. "I was thinking the same thing."

For a moment, I drift in the incredible adventures we shared in the gate world, which I think is where the Makers originated. Other people will explore that possibility, however. It's enough that I've set the pendulum in motion. Someone else can follow each tick of the weighted ball.

Loras recalls me to the mission when he barks, "On your feet, people. Assemble in the square in five minutes."

After gearing up, I jog in lockstep with everyone else. Loras is a natural commander, a fact that surprises me. But when I knew him before, he existed in forced submission.

There was no chance for him to let his true personality shine then.

By daylight, the village seems even more humble, the poverty more shocking against the way the Imperials live in the capital. This planet has lush resources, and they're controlled by less than 2 percent of the population. La'hengrin aren't permitted to own property . . . ostensibly because they can't protect it. All the laws here are writ in this bullshit altruism, and it makes my stomach hurt.

The leader from last night, Deven, meets us with the rest of the population at his back. "We discussed what you told us last night."

"What did you decide?" Loras asks.

"A number of people want to volunteer. The rest of us would like to see how it works. You won't . . . force the cure on anyone?" He seems a little frightened today.

Sometimes too much change, too fast, can be overwhelming. It makes you want to put things back the way they were, even if the old situation sucked. I reckon we need to be careful how we handle these folks.

"Of course not." Xirol's ready smile soothes them.

"The centurions have been murdered," someone calls from the back.

"Not murdered," Loras replies coldly. "It is called rebellion."

"Are we supposed to go to the mines?" a La'hengrin woman asks timidly.

I can tell from her pallor that she must work there, along with at least half the village. None of them have a healthy glow to their skin. They all look a bit sick, anemic. If Doc were here, I'd ask him to run some panels and make sure they're strong enough for Carvati's Cure.

But he's gone, and nobody can take his place. Of us all, Farah has the most medical experience. She assisted an Imperial physician in the capital before she ran into Loras. But she's not a doctor. At best, she knows how to use medical equipment better than the rest of us. It's not enough for her to take blood and analyze the results with the equipment we have available. Our handhelds don't function as portable labs, and the village doesn't even have basic facilities.

"No," Loras says. "Even if you wish to remain neutral, I ask you not to produce any resources that will benefit the enemy."

"But where will our food come from?" a man demands.

So that's how it is. The centurions keep the village dependent on them for provisions and they pay them in subsistence coin. The climate might support some agriculture. Certainly, the soil here at the foot of the mountain seems rich enough. Yet the Imperials keep the La'hengrin on a leash.

"I will go over the records," Vel says quietly. He hasn't removed his helmet. Nor has Zeeka. This is probably wise, at least until the villagers aren't so spooked. "And I will determine how often they sent shipments to the central-processing facility. I'll find a way to keep your shipments coming while we sort things here."

The La'hengrin murmur en masse, discussing that offer, and Deven says, "So you'll take care of us . . . and we get to stay home with our families?"

"No more bluerot?" one of them asks.

Poor bastards. Bluerot and miner's lung are two of the worst and most antibiotic-resistant infections. Those spores thrive in tunnels, and once you're infected, it's almost impossible to cure. The best you can hope is a treatment that extends your life a little though toward the end, it's miserable. Worry plucks at me as I gaze through my tinted helmet at their pale faces. If we kill more than 5 percent due to weakness, I can't deal with it. There has to be a way to be sure. I wonder if there's a lab at the mining station.

Before Loras can speak, I whisper my request. He turns to me, obviously weighing, then nods. "That's smart, Jax. Good thinking."

Heh. This might be the first time I've ever been praised for foreseeing possible consequences. Who says I don't learn from my mistakes?

I tap Farah on the arm. "Let's run up to the mining station and see if there's a place where we can do some preliminary tests on our volunteers."

"You mean like a medical VI?"

"Basic diagnostic equipment would do. You know about the proper levels of blood cells and things, right?"

At this, she nods. "I memorized the normal ranges so I could handle the routine checkups Dr. Victus did to certify the centurions as fit for active duty."

"So you have some experience interpreting test results."

"Only normal versus abnormal. I wouldn't know what was wrong."

"That's good enough for our purposes."

"Wait, Sirantha. I will accompany you." As Farah and I head for the mountain pass, Vel falls into step.

He doesn't say it's in case we run into trouble, but Vel has been guarding my back so long that I don't think he'd let me go anywhere there's even a mild chance of combat without him. And I'm okay with that.

It's a fair hike, but there's no reason to fire up the shuttle when the La'hengrin make this trip every damn day of their lives. The mountain air is thin and crisp, even coming through the filtration in my helmet. I don't take it off because Vel hasn't, and I'm showing solidarity. Plus, it's fragging cold.

As we climb, I continue the conversation with Farah. "I think we should deny any volunteers who come back with any abnormal results."

"Agreed," Vel puts in. "It will not sway any to our cause if their loved ones die from a lack of care on our end."

Farah sighs. "That's assuming there's anything up here we can use."

"I also don't think we should make them march up here for testing. Vel, can you help me load the medical junk onto the shuttle and set it up properly in the village?"

"I could, but there will be a problem finding a power source."

"Dammit," I mutter.

"There will be solar panels on the roof," Farah says. "Stations this remote aren't wired into the thermodynamic grid."

"It would be a statement of our good intentions if we made some local improvements," I point out.

Farah laughs. "You've been talking to Loras, I take it? He goes on and on about the importance of winning the people to our cause. I don't know how many lectures I've endured about being polite and kind, never forcing our will on them, giving them freedom in all things, helping to make their daily lives easier—"

A chuckle escapes me. "Yes, he gave me a manifesto to read—123 riveting pages on my role as a guerilla warrior."

"Did you finish it?" she asks with a smile in her voice.

"I . . . skimmed." In truth, I got bored after fifteen pages and gave it to Constance, then asked her to make me a list of need-to-know info.

"I found the information helpful if not comprehensive," Vel says. "I now know how to construct a number of incendiary devices from base chemicals."

"That might come in handy," I say, grinning.

The conversation flows easily as we move up the mountain. At the top, the station remains still and quiet. The bodies are no longer where we left them.

"Animals got them," Farah guesses.

I suggest, "Or the La'hengrin who came up to investigate this morning pitched them down a mine shaft."

"Oh, I hope so." Bitterness rings in her tone before she straightens her shoulders, peering around the yard. "Where do you suppose medical would be in a place like this?"

"The buildings are numbered, not named." Vel strides toward one at random. "Some will contain barracks. Others will be the mess and the commissary if the station is designed on military principles."

None of the buildings are very large. It doesn't take us long to explore and discover that Vel's right about the layout. The fourth one we check has rudimentary medical equipment, including a diagnostic computer with sample analysis capabilities. It doesn't take a doctor to use it, just someone with Farah's experience. The centurions probably had a medic up here, not an MD.

"Will this be complicated to disassemble?" I ask Vel.

He's examining the various machines. The medical center isn't well equipped, as the centurions assigned here aren't in favor with the houses they serve. It's a bare-bones facility, but compared to what the La'heng have, which amounts to incense, prayers, and smoky bits of herb, it will offer tremendous value.

"I do not believe so. Let me head down the mountain to get the shuttle."

He has to since he's our pilot. Otherwise, I'd offer to save him the trek down the mountain. *Ah well.* At least he doesn't have to climb back up again.

"I can start taking everything down," Farah offers. "I'm familiar with this model."

"If you tell me what to do, I'll help."

CHAPTER 19

By the time Vel returns with the shuttle and a couple of our squad-mates, Farah and I have the equipment packed in shipping crates and ready for transport. With Xirol and Rikir helping out, it doesn't take long to make the transfer. I survey the station while we're moving stuff to see if there's anything else to help the La'hengrin. Most of it doesn't lend itself to communal use, however, and until we figure out a way to get power in every home, we can't give some people toys others lack.

Xirol decides they might like the vid equipment, so we pack that, too. The comm suite has to remain where the array's attached. It would take too long to move that, as the tower's pretty tall and intricately made. Soon enough, we're ready, and Vel flies us down. I'd be worried about detection, except he's perfected the stealth program to cloak our energy emissions . . . even if they do detect something, there's enough mining equipment that the Imperials can't be sure the shuttle doesn't belong here. They don't have our registry number for tracking purposes, and if we organize things properly, they won't ever get it.

The crowd has dispersed by now. They're less interested in

our comings and goings, as long as we're not hostile, we're not making them do anything, and we promise not to disrupt their way of life. The ones who have stuck around seem intrigued, however, by all the gear we're hauling out of the shuttle. Deven has cleaned up since last night, and he seems to be the spokesman for the village. That, or he's just the most vocal, regardless of whether they want him to be.

"What are you doing?" he asks.

"Setting up a clinic," Farah replies with a smile. "I thought we'd use that cottage you let us sleep in unless you have some objection?"

Unlike most males, Deven doesn't respond visibly to Farah's easy charm. Maybe he's spoken for. "That's fine. The owner died."

"That's an auspicious omen for a medical center," Xirol cracks.

Since he's rarely serious, I like his company. I get enough weighty business from Loras, who is all rebellion, all the time. Someone has to take responsibility if the war effort goes sideways, but I'm glad it's not me. My time on center stage is waning, and I yearn for the day when the spotlight swings away from me for good.

"Over here, Jax," Farah calls. "I need your help with the—" And then she says a bunch of letters and numbers, which I assume is the machine.

"Can I help?" Bannie asks.

I figure she can if I can. It's as simple as following directions. Before long, we're all working under Vel and Farah's supervision, putting pieces together and plugging things in. Rikir and Zeeka go up on the roof with the solar panels, and dust flakes down from above as they move around. I eye the slates warily, but they don't break, and neither male comes tumbling down on top of me, so I keep working.

When Vel clicks the final part in place, and the machines light up, I cheer along with everyone else. Power means that the guys have done their job up top. A thump says they've hopped down, then they haul another solar panel down to the church. Xirol thinks this is the best place to put the entertainment equipment since it's the only building big enough to house a large number of people. Though it seems a little odd to think of a religious building as entertaining, I see his point. There's no other fair way to set it up, and we don't want people fighting. It should go in a central location where everybody has a chance to check it out.

"Once we do a little cleaning, we'll be ready to start the exams," Farah says.

I nod, turning to Bannie. "Can you see if Deven can spare us some brooms and buckets and things?"

At least, I assume that's what we'll need. I can't recall that I've ever cleaned anything in my life. *Jax the janitor,* I think, as she moves to fulfill the request. Bannie comes back with a slim, shy-looking La'hengrin female in tow. The dark-haired woman holds out her hand hesitantly, as if she isn't sure I'll be polite.

I shake hands gently, not wanting to spook her. "I'm Jax."

"Darana. I'm Deven's wife. He said you need some help tidying up the place. I'm a good worker."

She doesn't need to sell me on her services. I nod. "Thanks. We really appreciate you pitching in."

Her smile lights up her thin, pale face, and I can see why Deven married her. "It's the least I can do."

Well, no, I think. *The least is nothing.*

Darana works like a champion, and she laughs when she realizes how little I know about this kind of endeavor. Cleaning is exhausting but rewarding work; a few hours later, we have the cottage ready for the grand opening. By now, it's close to nightfall, and I haven't had anything all day but that packet of paste.

"Dinner will be ready at the church by now," Darana says, packing up the supplies. "Nothing fancy, but I hope you'll come."

"Are you kidding?" Xirol grins at her. "My belly thinks my throat's been cut. I haven't worked this hard since I left my master in Jineba."

Farah makes a scoffing sound, as he's propped up the wall for the last half hour. Since Xirol came down from the roof, he's been watching Bannie, who pretends she hasn't noticed. This could be entertaining.

Darana puts a hand on Xirol's arm, staying him. "What's it like?"

"What?" he asks, clearly thinking about food.

"Being free."

"Indescribable." This is the first time I've ever seen Xirol dead serious. "It's like having your heart unchained because nobody can make you do anything ever again."

"How did you get up the courage to take those shots, knowing you could die? You started a whole new life . . ." Her voice trails off as she shakes her head in wonder. "I don't know if I could ever be that brave."

"You don't have to make up your mind right now," Farah says.

Darana nods. "Let's get something to eat before it's all gone."

When I leave the clinic, Loras is waiting outside. He's not wearing his helmet, and his cheeks are red with the cold, his eyes sharp and sad. I can tell there's something on his mind, so I wait until the others are out of earshot.

"These people need care, Jax. Some of them are really sick. There's a little girl, not more than nine, with such a terrible cough . . ."

Bluerot. For the first time in my life, I wish I weren't a jumper. Right now, I'd prefer to be a doctor. Or better yet, Doc should be here instead. If I could go back, if I could swap places, I would. Because he'd do so much good here.

"Don't." His azure eyes read my regret, and though he doesn't know the whole truth, I'm sure he senses my remorse.

I choke it down. "We'll do our best for them."

He nods, and I follow him to the church, where the La'hengrin have set up a small feast. The fact that it's their best, offered freely, when they have so little, chokes me up. I feel bad eating a bowl of the thin but delicious soup, mostly reconstituted vegetables with grain to add heartiness. The room is loud and crowded; so many bodies make for warmth, driving away the chill of the cold mountain night.

I wonder what March is doing right now, if he's thinking about me. He might be eating, too, joking with Sasha and talking about the day. Company will be scarce at base since the majority of the personnel shipped out in various cells.

After the meal ends, Xirol gets the entertainment center working. That means the church has power as well as the clinic. On the first day, we've made some improvements. Xirol finds a program on the memory core and turns it on. I shouldn't be surprised that it's all about the Imperials; they control everything else, so why wouldn't the vids be about them, too? This is some kind of drama that makes the life of a centurion look exciting and romantic. Before the show is half-over, the La'hengrin are booing, and Xirol switches it off.

"Is there anything about *us* on there?" a young girl asks.

The question is heartbreaking. This is their world, and yet they have been erased from it. Their culture has been undone, buried beneath wave after wave of invaders and occupations. For countless turns, the La'hengrin have served their various overlords.

Xirol says, "I'll check."

But he's seen more of the world than she has, and his mouth compresses, for once unable to find the humor. I share his consternation. Later, as everyone files out, I notice the girl who asked about La'hengrin vids can't take a step without coughing. Her lips are blue-tinged, and the cloth she holds to her mouth comes away tinged in red. She won't live to receive her first kiss or plan for her future. There's no limit to the number of things wrong with this scenario.

Since the cottage is too full of medical equipment to have room for ten of us, Loras asks permission for us to camp in the church. If we're sticking around a while, I see the need for a more permanent solution, but until we find one, this will do. The La'hengrin agree it's all right, so we bed down after everyone clears out. It's colder in the church than the cottage with the others gone, because our bodies aren't sufficient to warm the space.

I shiver as I remove my armor and crawl into the bedroll. So far, the rebellion has been different than I expected. Based on what I knew in the Morgut Wars, I thought we'd see more fighting early on. But I suppose if we did, then the effort would end before it began. They have far more centurions than we have free La'hengrin . . . but that will change, in time.

In the morning, I have more paste, bathe with cold water Vel supplies, then head to the clinic, where Farah is already set up.

"Would you like to help me?" she asks.

"I've never taken blood before."

"It's like using a hypo, only in reverse. Just press here and the device does the rest. And this is how you change the vial inside." She shows me how to pop the polymer tube out of the chamber.

It takes me a couple of tries, but I get the hang of it. "Yeah, I can do this."

She taps her comm. We use a short-range frequency that doesn't extend far enough for Nicuan forces to hear our chatter. "Loras, can you round up our volunteers, please?"

He replies, "Consider it done."

CHAPTER 20

The townsfolk come in for testing a few at a time, so Farah and I are never overwhelmed. I'm nervous the first time, but I watch Farah smooth an antiseptic pad over the phlebotomy site, so I do the same. Then the gizmo does the work, and it's quick. Afterward, I fumble only a little in getting the new vial in place.

All told, it takes an hour to take the genetic material we need. Farah feeds the samples into the machine one by one, as this isn't a sophisticated piece of equipment. In hospitals, they have the capacity to analyze in batches. There was no call for that at the mining station. At least it's fast, however. Five minutes later, the first result appears on screen.

She skims it, then turns to me. "Everything looks good. Some readings are in the low range, but nothing that makes me think she's a poor candidate."

We work side by side for a couple more hours. At the end of the session, she's disqualified seven people, due to irregular white-blood-cell counts, anemia, and a couple of problems that might indicate something more serious.

Farah gnaws her lip. "I wish I was qualified for diagnosis and treatment. I feel so *useless*. Did you know that La'hengrin aren't allowed to go to university unless it's to study languages or communications?"

I hadn't, though I did wonder why so many served as translators or communication specialists aboard ships. It seemed that was the only way to get off world, and even then, they could only travel under someone else's aegis.

"Otherwise, you're stuck on La'heng."

"Living like this." Her mouth firms into a taut, white line.

This must be hell. If they don't travel with their *shinai*, then most La'heng don't even know the rest of the world is like this. They only see what they're shown.

"I had a friend who could've helped," I say softly.

"What happened?" Evidently, she can tell by my tone that he's gone, not just far away.

"He died in the bombing of Venice Minor."

"You were there, I hear?" It's not a prying question though it is a leading one.

I nod.

"Loras said it was bad. I guess you've had some adventures."

"I'll tell you about them sometime." We'll have ample opportunity as we go village to village and liberate the La'hengrin.

"I'd like that." She pauses, her expression becoming shy. "Women don't usually like me, you know."

"How come?"

She shrugs, by which I infer she doesn't want to talk about it. Fair enough.

Farah's not just lovely; she's also a nice person. But maybe other females don't take the time to get to know her. They just look at her face and decide she must be a bitch and treat her accordingly. That would be lonely.

I change the subject. "Do you think we have time to start the treatments?"

After checking the time, she nods and calls Loras. "These folks don't seem healthy enough to withstand the cure." She reads the names. "You get to break the news, boss man. Can you send the rest of the volunteers in groups of ten? It should take us about fifteen minutes to handle them, so send them at regular intervals."

He cocks a brow, leaning toward her just enough that I'm intrigued by what his body language communicates. "Anything else, your majesty?"

She laughs, and genuine delight adds a sparkle to her green eyes. *Loras and Farah?* I've never seen Loras interested in a woman before, but he's spent most of his life off La'hengrin. It's possible that other species don't appeal.

"That should suffice for now, but I'll keep you posted."

"Do that." There's a hint of a tease in his voice, a small smile playing at the edges of his mouth. For those seconds, I'm sure he's forgotten I exist.

Once he heads out, I ask, "So what's the deal with you two?"

Hot color washes her cheeks, the shade of tropical flowers that grew in my mother's garden on Venice Minor. "What makes you think—"

"I know what I saw."

She gives up the pretense. "We're just flirting now, but I really like him. He's . . . different than most La'hengrin males. More confident."

I'm curious about something, but I can't think of a tactful way to ask this. If I want to know, I suppose I just need to come out with it. "Would you ever consider hooking up with someone who wasn't La'hengrin?"

Farah arches her brows. "Where are you going with this, Jax?"

A laugh escapes me. "Not why I'm asking. I just wondered because I've never seen a mixed couple—"

"Ah," she says. "Prurient curiosity. There's no taboo against it precisely, but it's impossible for love to flourish in an unequal partnership."

"Loras said that about friendship."

She nods. "He was right. Servitude aside, our physiology makes it impossible for us to crossbreed with other species."

"I didn't know that."

"Why would you? The first conquerors tried to dilute us with their offspring, but our bodies look on alien material as viruses, and our immune systems react accordingly."

"So to start a family, you need another La'hengrin."

"Yes. I suppose someone with a sophisticated lab might

manage to combine genetic materials, but no one has cared enough to try."

"If you want Loras, I hope you get him. He deserves to be happy."

Before Farah can respond, the first volunteers enter the clinic. They break into groups of five, forming lines before us. I'm ready with my hypo for the first shot.

"There will be seven injections," I say, loud enough for everyone to hear me. "On the last day, we'll find out if the treatment worked."

"What if it doesn't?" the woman before me asks, rubbing her arm.

I glance at Farah. Surely the news will sound better coming from her. She has an indefinable quality, along with her rare beauty, that combines to make her captivating. Add those to her kindness, and she's damn near irresistible.

"When the cure fails," Farah says gently, "all our repressed rage rushes in at once. It drives us mad."

"Can it be fixed?"

She shakes her head gravely. "No. There is actual damage to higher neural functions. All that remains is the urge to kill."

"So you'll put us down," a man says.

It's the cleanest solution. Adaptive physiology makes it difficult to devise treatments for the La'heng, and since they're not a wealthy people, medical companies have no motivation to help them. Which is *wrong*, but it's how the universe operates.

The resistance lacks the resources to run an insane asylum. Volunteers in the clinic seem to realize as much, and they fall quiet, waiting. No more hard questions. As I work, I try not to remember that one or two of these people will die a week from today. They all wear somber looks as they move in and out of the line, as if they're aware of the same thing.

As Farah requested, Loras sends them in waves. Two hours later, we finish the first round of injections. Only six more days until we find out who lives and dies. That leaves me feeling grim. So I murmur something to Farah and head out into the crisp dusk. Sunset in the mountains is dramatic; the light drops away with little notice. One moment the sky is bright, then the ground drowns in shadows.

I find Vel working on a roof, not installing a solar panel, but mending it. Since I've known him, he has ever been a fixer of that which was broken. Even me. Maybe especially me. It might be wrong for my heart to be so cleanly divided, but I don't hurt as much with March gone as long as Vel's here. He only left that one time under the most dire circumstance—with my blessing—to serve his people. Like me, he resigned at the first opportunity. He is my true north, my compass for what's right. If ever I chart a course, and he will not follow, then I'll know it's wrong and turn back.

"Are you done for the day?" I call.

"Nearly. It is becoming difficult to see." He leaps nimbly from the roof and comes toward me. "Did you enjoy playing doctor?"

"Not really. They need more help than I can give. And I keep thinking about day seven."

"It is a terrible choice," he says.

"What would you do if you knew you only had a week left to live?"

"There is no way to avoid my fate?" he asks, canting his head. Generally speaking, he's not given to hypothetical speculation.

"None."

"Then I suppose I would get my affairs in order and spend my remaining moments with those most dear to me." It's a prosaic response but perfectly Vel.

Xirol comes up behind me, joining the conversation. "I'd find a girl and spend the week drunk and naked. If I was lucky, I'd die before I sobered up."

The old Jax would've approved of that plan heartily. I'm not sure what I'd do in the La'hengrin's position. What an awful blade to carry on your shoulders.

Soon, the rest of the squad has assembled on the green, a humble place to start a revolution. Until this moment, I don't think it occurred to me how much downtime there would be, how much waiting. But we can't do anything until this time tomorrow—at least that's what I'm thinking when Loras says:

"Listen up. We're going to start teaching these people how to fight."

"We can't," Rikir protests.

Farah is nodding, a smile widening on her lovely face. "We can if they don't hit anyone, if we drill it as exercise and repetitive motion."

An admiring light glimmers in Loras's eyes. "Precisely as I intended."

Bannie follows the thought to its conclusion. "So by the time they all take the full course of treatments, they'll know something about self-defense."

"Do you think they'll all step up?" Timmon asks.

Loras shrugs. "It must be their choice. I won't force my will on anyone else, or that makes me no better than"—he cuts me an apologetic look—"the humans."

At that moment, I realize I'm a minority of one. I mean, I *knew* I was the only human in the cell, but it doesn't register until I have nine pairs of alien eyes trained on me. I manage a smile, but I'm feeling like there's a target on my back at the moment.

"Yeah, sorry. I can't help my genetics. Take your frustration out on me if it'll make you feel better, but don't mess up my pretty face."

That makes Rikir laugh because, on a good day, I'm *not* pretty. Strong-featured, sure, striking, maybe, in the right light, but I've never been "pretty." That breaks the tension, and I stride away before they decide they'd like to play pound the human.

CHAPTER 21

The next week passes quickly.

On the final day of treatments, false bravado pervades the village. It's especially tense and hellish as Farah and I finish the treatments one by one. Then comes the waiting with our squad-mates standing by in case something goes wrong. Mary, it'll be so traumatic if—

And then we're done.

Not a single loss. I close my eyes in thanks while the La'hengrin cheer. Fights break out immediately, and one of the women drops to her knees, weeping. She rubs a splayed palm back and forth across her chest, like she can feel the loosening of the tethers that keep her subservient to the Imperial government.

Loras clasps my shoulder. "Your idea about the screenings helped. I'm guessing we would've lost some of them."

"That's not a wholly accurate predictor," Farah points out. "We lost a few before, and I had their health records. They were good, strong candidates."

They go off together, arguing, while the men around me stand down. Bannie discreetly wipes away a tear, watching the volunteers react to their first moments of freedom. Xirol's mock fighting with one of the men, and Rikir is explaining that if the centurions come back for any reason, the villagers can't reveal their new liberty.

I second that. "True. It has to seem like nothing has changed. Or they'll come down on you. That can't happen."

"Understood." Deven stands in the clinic doorway. "Is it possible for me to get into the next group?"

His wife, Darana, steps out from behind him. "Me too?"

"Sure," I say. "It would be a big help if you could take this handheld and enter all the names of those who want to join you. We'll proceed in the same way, doing screenings first, then another week."

Deven nods. "In a month, you'll have treated everyone here, except those who have health problems."

"That's the plan. Then you'll all be free to join the resistance. If you're interested, we supply room and board . . . no pay at the moment, and you'll be sent out to do for others what we've done here."

At first, this will be a quiet, sneaky sort of war. We must build our army before we engage on a larger scale. The key will be doing enough damage to keep the planet on lockdown without permitting them to run us to ground. That'll be a challenge.

"I don't have any skills. I can't fight—"

"We'll teach you if you want to learn."

Later that night, Xirol finds a period vid set in the days before humans came to La'heng. It's bloody, sexy, barbaric, and way over the top, probably of dubious cultural accuracy, but the people love it, especially those who survived the cure. Because now they *can* smash someone in the head with a rock. Not that I support violence as a solution to every situation, but if you can't even defend yourself, and you need a keeper like a child, then it starts looking pretty appealing.

While Farah and I do medical screenings, the guys teach the combat classes for the La'heng. The first crop of cured volunteers can spar while the second group practices the movements purely as exercise. The days are routine, but I stay sharp, with an eye on the sky, just in case. *So far, so good.*

But that just makes me nervous.

In the end, when trouble comes, it's not from above.

On the fifteenth day, I'm sitting beside Farah, finishing the treatments, when the first patient runs amok. I wasn't around during the trials when Carvati first described the damage, and when Loras quietly did his recruiting in the capital, I was working with Tarn, Leviter, and Vel to handle the bureaucratic end.

So this is my first time, close up, to see the eyes run red. Blood fills the sclera, until the woman's eyes are like marbles on a bed of red silk. It's horrifying—and then she lunges at me, her teeth bared. Rikir grabs her from behind, preventing her from tearing out my throat in two bites.

"Darana, no!" It's Deven, who just graduated as a free La'heng.

Xirol restrains him, too, but he's not insane, just . . . heartbroken. She's his wife, and she's dying of bloodlust. His face a mask of pain, Loras holds out his hand for the hypo we keep ready, just in case. It's a kind death, a chemical cocktail that stops the heart. Loras sinks it into her arm while Deven screams her name over and over again. He's just about strong enough in his grief to kick Xirol's ass, so Zeeka and Vel step between him and his wife.

Darana collapses; Rikir lowers her gently to the ground. With her eyes closed, she doesn't reveal the madness. Her face is calm and quiet when she breathes her last. Nobody moves. I can't stop shaking. It was *my* hand holding the hypo that drove her mad.

"You killed her!" Deven shouts at me.

"No." Loras meets his gaze. "I did. I realize it's no comfort. You loved her. But don't blame Jax. Blame me. And save your anger for the centurions. They've earned your wrath."

"Let me go. I must . . . see to her." When they're sure Deven won't attack, Vel, Xirol, and Zeeka step out of the way.

With heartrending tenderness, he gathers Darana's body into his arms and strides from the clinic. He isn't the same timid man we met a few weeks ago. From such tragic moments are heroes made. I just wish the price hadn't been so high.

Farah beckons her next patient forward. Not surprisingly, the man hesitates. There are five more volunteers in the second group, and none of them look sure anymore. I sit quiet.

I'm not talking anyone into anything. They know the risks; they know the potential rewards.

The silence stretches like a taut wire, gradually thinning, until a woman steps forward bravely, offers her arm to Farah, and closes her eyes. I hold my breath as she receives the injection, but she's all right. And then all the others gather their resolve. There are no more deaths today, but I don't kid myself that this is over. The last round of treatment will be complicated, now that we've had our first casualty.

It's been days since I've seen Vel for more than a few moments, and we're always surrounded by other squad-mates. I go looking for him through the village, which is in much better repair than when we arrived. Lots of supplies have made their way down the mountain, appropriated by people who no longer fear Imperial reprisal. They trust us enough to keep the boot off their necks at least.

I stop Zeeka, and ask, "Have you seen Vel?"

"He's up at the mining station."

A walk won't hurt me. I don my helmet and start off at a jog, but soon the altitude forces me to slow my steps. The air is thinner. I'm mostly used to it now, except during vigorous activity. When I reach the top, the gate stands open, and some of the metal has been scavenged for use down below. It makes me happy to see this place being repurposed.

I find Vel in the office where the fight took place. The bloodstains remain on the floor, but it's been long enough that the smell has faded. He's listening to logs and making notes on his handheld when I walk in; I remove my helmet so he can see my face.

He glances up with a welcoming cant of his head and greets me in Ithtorian. "Sirantha. Did you finish?"

Mentally, I tell my chip to switch, and when I speak, it's with my vocalizer. The clicks and chitters make it easier to confide, "We had a casualty."

She won't be the last, but seeing Deven, hearing his raw anguish, well, I feel pretty shaken. I need . . . I need *Vel.*

And he knows. Before I take a step, he's out of his chair and has taken four. Then he's right there with me, chitin to armor. He rubs his face against the side of mine, such a comforting gesture. My chip processes the Ithtorian, and I know he's murmuring to me, *Shh, brown bird. Still your wings.* From anyone else, brown bird as an endearment would insult me, but with him, it's perfect.

"I do not care for your armor," he says eventually.

I gaze up at him in surprise. That's the first time he's commented on how I feel: good, bad, or otherwise. It seems so personal. Our connection has always been more about kindred spirits than the state of our bodies. Things are complicated between us already, and the comment startles me.

Apparently, he reads my confusion, explaining, "It makes you feel Ithtorian. Combined with hearing you speak so, it is . . . disconcerting."

Yeah, I can see how it would be. "Do you want me to take it off?"

CHAPTER 22

The question comes out more suggestive than it sounded in my head. For a moment, I freeze, but this is Vel. He's never going to assume a meaning I don't intend or look for the lascivious angle. That's outside his nature. With a human male, I'd have to worry about stupid jokes. His sense of humor doesn't extend to the ribald, at least not so far as I've seen.

"Yes," he replies. "You do not feel like yourself."

So I strip out of my armor to the uniform beneath. I'm wrinkled, but it doesn't matter. I'm not here to win any prizes for my appearance. Since it's my only set, I pile the gear carefully on a chair, then Vel reaches for me. His arms are long, oddly jointed, and they end in razor-sharp talons. I should be afraid of his solace as it can rip me to shreds, but his natural weapons make his care all the more remarkable.

The shards of pain and regret in my chest settle somewhat when he draws me against him. I lean my head against his thorax, marveling that this seems so natural. When I first saw him out of his camouflage, he was hunting me . . . and I was terrified. So many turns have passed between then and now. Everything has changed.

"Tell me about the woman we lost," he invites.

As I speak, he moves us toward the small sofa the centurions spent most of their lives sprawled on. It's ratty and threadbare, but at least we have some privacy here. I'm tired of being quartered in the church, surrounded by snoring soldiers. Vel guides me to a seat as I relate meeting her, how it came to pass, her husband's reaction, and the way I feel about being the one who gave her the shot that led to her death. Speaking of it leaves my throat raw from the tears I can't let go because I don't have the right. I didn't know her. I only hurt her. Sometimes, good intentions don't matter at all.

"Everyone chooses, Sirantha. I doubt she regrets her decision."

"Do you ever wonder where people go? If there's anything to Mary, the Iglogth, or whatever people call their gods?"

"So many things remind me of Adele that . . ." Here, he hesitates, studying me with his side-set eyes as if gauging my reaction. ". . . I feel that she is with me still. So perhaps I *want* it to be true more than I believe it must be."

I smile. "I hope you're right."

"I miss her." The chip translates his meaning simply, yet there comes a more literal echo in my head, as if he's said, *My home is gone from me*. Ithtorian is a beautiful language, full of poetry and nuance.

"I do, too."

He draws me against his side then because he will offer me comfort where he can't ask for it himself. Because I know he grieves for longer than some species live, I curl into his side. His claws find my hair, surprisingly soothing when he draws them through in long strokes. It's an absent caress like you'd give a pet, but I don't mind.

"Did I ever tell you she asked me to marry her?" he asks.

Surprise rockets through me. "No."

He told me a lovely story about how they met, how she came to find the truth about him, and, eventually, why he left. But I've not heard this.

I have to ask, "Was this before or after she found out—"

"Before."

"Ah. Do you want to tell me about it?"

"If you like."

"Only if it doesn't hurt to talk about her."

"Remembering feels better," he says. "Because you knew her, too."

"Then go for it." I love the way Vel tells stories.

"Adele came to my residence for a meal, that night. And she asked, 'Vel, do you love me?' I had heard the word before, but I had no reference for its meaning. I was new to the idea of feeling anything but pride, ambition, duty, obligation . . . those are Ithtorian precepts."

"What did you say?"

"I said yes because I could see the answer she wanted. She kissed me. Then she said, 'Marry me.' "

"Why didn't you?"

"I could not marry her without telling her the truth. And I feared honesty would cost me her companionship."

"So you thought about it."

"Yes," he says softly. "I wanted a tangible bond. But it did not seem fair to her."

"How did you get out of it without hurting her?"

"I said I did not believe in the custom."

"She was all right with that?"

He nods. "She never mentioned it again after that. And a few turns later, she discovered the truth."

"Thank you for telling me."

"I have shared with you things that no one else knows, Sirantha."

That prompts a smile, lessening the ache in my chest. I only mean to close my eyes for a few seconds, but the next thing I know, it's morning. We haven't slept together since we came back from the other world, through the gate, where we lost five turns. You'd think it would be uncomfortable, but as I shift, I notice the pillow he tucked beneath my head. He's still out, with an arm curved about me, his talons in my hair. There are weapons on the floor beside him on the other side within easy reach. If anything tripped his perimeter alarms, he'd have been up and shooting before I could unstick my eyes.

I watch him for a while, knowing Loras must be wondering why the hell we spent the night at the mining station. Zeeka probably told him I was looking for Vel, so hopefully, he thinks we were working. Which we should've been. There's still the matter of the shipments to sort out. Maybe Vel can hack a warehouse to show the cargo received, then diverted elsewhere. It'd be funny if this phantom ore was just constantly bouncing around the planet.

As I ponder the problem, feeling a little stronger than yesterday, he stirs. I can't remember ever watching Vel wake up before. Through the gate, I relied on him and vice versa, but I sprang up tense as a knife blade. There was no opportunity for stillness and intimate observation. That's the word. "Intimate." I shy away from it a little, but not from Vel.

His eyes flicker open. I consider how many Jaxes are there, greeting the day.

"I did not mean to sleep," he clicks. Irritation colors the glottal stop at the end.

I lift a shoulder. "We needed a break. I'm not a good soldier. I hate the makeshift accommodations and the uncertainty and—"

"Precisely so." His irritation with himself melts into amusement.

In response to that display of humor, I touch the spot just above the curve of his mandible. I know he can feel it. Before, he told me about places where there are gaps in the chitin, spots Adele touched because she knew he enjoyed the contact.

He stills, startled. It's not something I've done often, and never after a night like this one. "Sirantha."

But that's all, just my name. I don't know what to make of that, so I take refuge in a joke, ignoring the complexities. "Do you think we've been reported AWOL?"

Vel cants his head, mandible flaring in silent laughter. "An excellent question. How do you suppose Loras punishes deserters?"

"By making them plant a victory garden for the villagers," I mutter.

"I would agree with you, but it is not the season. And we have no seeds."

"Be thankful for small blessings."

"We should move, Sirantha. Don your armor." Though he doesn't intend it unkindly, it means the barriers need to come up between us, so we can do our jobs.

I slide out from under his arm, but I must have revealed a

flicker of reluctance because he catches my shoulder gently. His claws prick but don't break the skin. "It is not my desire, you understand, but my duty that beckons."

"Yes," I say softly. "Mine, too."

"I am glad you looked for me, Sirantha."

So am I. But it's time to get back to business. Since he's been analyzing the shipment patterns, I hope he's sorted out how we can screw with the Nicuan nobles as well as keep them out of the village.

"Have you figured out a solution to the shipment yet?"

For obvious reasons, we don't want the Imperials to get the ore. Anything we can do to disrupt their society will benefit the resistance down the line. I put on my armor while he does the same. The weapons go on last thing, with him contemplating the problem.

"I might have, but it is risky."

"That seems to be our mantra these days. Tell me what you have in mind?"

"The La'hengrin simply turn the ore over to us. Then Leviter seeds the Imperial bounce with stories about shipments being stolen."

"Are there any drawbacks?"

"The possibility that additional centurions will be sent to secure the mines."

"They can call us in to deal with it, if need be?"

He nods. "Should I advise Loras?"

I've learned my lesson about going outside the chain of command. "Probably. It won't do to piss him off if things go wrong."

In the rebellion, there's no risk of a trial or a court-martial, but it might be difficult to serve if Loras thinks Vel's undermining his command. The La'hengrin need to know that Loras is the strong one, and that it's possible for him to lead after turns of taking orders. They need that confidence in their own self-reliance.

He taps the comm, but there's no response. The short-range frequency we use doesn't extend up here. So I say, "I'm heading down. I'll send him to talk to you."

"Thank you, Sirantha."

"Thanks for making me feel better."

In reply, he offers a *wa*, and the sight gladdens my heart. *Fair winds carry you from my side and back again, brown bird.* Instinctively I know this is both a gentle farewell and a wish for my safe return. It's Vel's way of saying, *I wish you didn't have to go.* But we both have work to do.

Farah will be expecting me to begin the final round of treatments. Soon enough, we'll take what volunteers we can muster, give them rudimentary training, then move on to do it all over again. Without March beside me and with such work ahead, it will be a long turn.

INTERNAL COMMUNIQUÉ
FROM: THE OFFICE OF THE GOVERNOR
TO: LEGATE FLAVIUS
SUBJECT: YOUR GROSS INCOMPETENCE

What the hell is going on? We're missing five shipments of ore now, and it's getting dicey. Manufacturing has slowed down. People are starting to notice the scarcity of goods. You promised me you could resolve the problem with a minimum of public attention. You said you'd keep the media out of it.

Yet I'm not noticing measurable progress. Instead, from what my nephew tells me, you spend all your time chasing La'hengrin tail. If you're unable to get the job done, sir, I'm happy to promote someone in your stead. My centurions will gut you and put your head on a pike if you don't solve this mess immediately.

INTERNAL COMMUNIQUÉ
FROM: LEGATE FLAVIUS
TO: GOVERNOR SEXTUS VARRO
SUBJECT: MY ABJECT APOLOGIES

Governor,

First let me apologize in the most abject fashion. The LLA is responsible for hijacking the shipments, but they are gifted at finding boltholes in the provinces. I will root out their leaders and retrieve the empire's lost property. You have my word on it.

CHAPTER 23

My prediction turns out to be more accurate than I ex-pected.

Over the next six months, I repeat the pattern with Farah until I have enough experience to work as a medical assistant. The death toll rises, but so does the number of free La'heng. Occasionally, I catch the news on vid, usually days old, but other cells keep the Imperials hopping in the capital, where most legates believe the resistance is centered.

I'd like to harry the establishment, but there's more important work for us to do right now. The task seems daunting, utterly time-consuming, but there's no easy fix. We can't send out a comm message inviting all enslaved La'heng to turn up for treatments. So it has to be this way: slow, secretive, and steady. My one consolation is that we're gaining momentum.

Not every village empties out as a result of our work there, but the numbers definitely thin. For every hundred and fifty we set free, forty of them join us. Loras divides them into teams and sends them to base for orders and equipment. That way, like everyone else, they know only one fact that could be revealed during capture. I suspect most La'hengrin would die rather than yield anything that could help their oppressors.

At last, Loras tells us our orders have changed. "There are now enough other La'hengrin in the field to free us up for other duties."

A ragged cheer goes up from the whole squad. None of us are happy about the lack of action. What we've done might be necessary, but it also had tragic moments. I get the shakes now when I pick a hypo to give that last treatment because ten of my patients have been put down. Loras always does it. Like he told Deven months ago, he takes that failure seriously.

"First, we're going back to base for some R&R," he goes on, pitching his voice to carry above the celebratory hoots. This time, the noise gets so loud he can't talk over it, so he folds his arms and waits. Eventually, his pointed look sinks in, and we all shut up.

"Afterward, we're heading to the capital to wreak some havoc."

The outcry becomes deafening, with the La'hengrin chanting some cry they heard in one of Xirol's period vids: *Ah-ooh, ah-ooh, ah-ooh! Ah ah ah! Ah-ooh, ah-ooh!* To me, they sound like higher primates who have lost their words, but they've earned the right to sound that way. Nobody can tell them to shut up and get back to work. Well . . . Loras *can*, but that doesn't mean they have to listen.

"How long before we move out?" I ask Loras.

"A couple of hours. We're packing up here and heading to secure transport for our volunteers."

"How many are joining up?"

His smile reveals pure pride. "Half the village. The more the story grows, the more the centurions seem disturbed by the scope of the LLA's reach, the more people believe."

I nod. "It's kind of a self-fulfilling prophecy. You tell them we can do it, something impressive happens, the Imperials react, the ones we haven't cured yet hear about it, and they think we're some massive planetary invasion force."

"We're getting there," Loras says.

As a commander, he keeps a tight schedule. Everyone is ready to go at the appointed hour, waving good-bye from the shuttle. It seems like forever since I've slept in the same bed more than one night. Shit, half the time on this assignment,

I've had a bedroll on the ground. Considering how much I hate dirt, that really sucks.

I'm looking forward to a hot meal, programmed however I choose from the kitchen-mate, a hot shower, and a kiss from March. Not necessarily in that order though he may demand I take care of the second thing before I get the third.

My heart soars right along with the shuttle, firing as the thrusters do. I burn hot and fierce, knowing this is an interlude in a long and brutal war. But if I lose my ability to appreciate the little things, there's no way I can bear the big shit. Behind me, the rest of the guys chatter about the first thing they're gonna do, curiosity about how much the base has changed since we left, who might be around . . . a lot of questions that have no answers, really, but I share their excitement.

"How are the readings?" Loras asks Vel.

"Stealth field holding, sir. No emission leakage that I can detect."

"Good. There aren't supposed to be any ships in this area."

Vel flies is in low through the mountains. After dark, the ranges all look the same to me. Even though I've been here multiple times I doubt I'd be able to repeat the flight pattern without exact coordinates. I skim the ground for signs of trouble, but it looks like, so far, the base has gone undetected. That's a lucky break; otherwise, we'd be fighting for our lives with no place to go.

Instead, the shuttle zooms into the lit cavern, and the door shuts behind us. It's quiet in the hangar, missing the hum of activity that characterized the place before everyone deployed. There's only one other skimmer present, so the facility will be *really* empty inside.

After climbing out, I stretch my legs; and then, without waiting for the others, I head toward the main corridor at a dead run. Logically speaking, I know if they've been holed up in here, March and Sasha may be testy, but they should be safe. But I won't believe it until I see it with my own eyes. Compartmentalization has permitted me to do my job without obsessing, but now that I'm back—

I run faster.

March meets me in the hallway and grabs me around the

waist. He spins me until I'm dizzy. I wrap my arms about his neck and get the kiss I thought I might have to shower for. When I draw back, I note his pallor. The vitamin D in the bulbs can't compensate for pigmentation.

"It's been a long eight months," he mutters against the curve between my neck and shoulder. "And I can't say I care for being a military spouse."

I laugh. "Hey, it's not too late to join up. See the world, kill some guys."

"Can we?" Sasha demands.

Turning, I spot the kid lounging behind us. He's taller than he was last time though maybe if you were with him every day, you wouldn't notice. He's going to be tall, like March, but built on lankier lines. Puberty might dump a ton of heavy muscles on him, though.

"How've you been?" I ask.

"Bored. This place sucks." But he sounds grouchy, not traumatized, so that's something. "In some cultures, they consider a kid a man when he turns twelve. So I'm more than old enough to enlist."

Loras has recruited La'hengrin who are thirteen and fourteen, but I keep that information to myself as March levels a warning look at me. *Got it, this is father-son business. I'll keep quiet.*

"We've had this conversation," March says patiently.

Sasha flashes a roguish grin. "I keep hoping I'll wear you down."

"You're young. Hope springs eternal."

"Eventually, he'll forget his original objection," I assure Sasha with a teasing grin at March. "He's getting older every minute."

March narrows his hawkish gaze on me. "Is that right?"

Sasha spreads his hands, disassociating. "*She* said it . . . not me."

"I don't notice you springing to my defense," March points out.

The kid smirks. "You look great . . . for an old man."

I laugh. I love the cockiness. It was just starting to peek out when I left. It looks like he's been developing the 'tude. The girls are going to love it—should he ever meet any. Inside the base, that's not likely.

"Listen, I can't stand myself, so I bet you'd both thank me for cleaning up. Afterward, you two want to get some dinner?" I'm surprised how natural that feels. I'm not one to raise a kid, but now that he's of an age where reason and humor work on him, it seems less terrifying and awkward. I can talk to him like he's a person who might become a friend someday.

"Sure," Sasha says. "It's not like I had anything else to do. Connie's checked my lessons for the day, and I've put in my TK hours, right, boss?"

"I'll meet you in the mess in half—" *Make it an hour,* I hear in my head. The side of my neck tingles as if he's kissed it, but March never moves. My breath hitches. "In an hour."

Nodding, Sasha says, "Sounds good."

"I'll go with you." March sets his hand lightly in the small of my back, and though I can't feel it through my armor, my whole body reacts.

CHAPTER 24

As soon as we step into my old quarters, which March has put his stamp on in my absence, he hauls me into his arms. Hunger radiates from him, and I kiss him back. Long moments later, as he unfastens my armor, I back off.

"A fast shower, first, seriously."

"Too bad it's not bigger," he mutters.

Shower sex? Yes, please. But the facilities here weren't designed for pleasure. It's a military installation, and we had to shave credits until they bled in building it. That was part of Loras's recruitment plan, in fact. He quietly approached La'hengrin in the capital who had skills he needed and offered the cure.

"Agreed. Just . . . get naked and wait for me."

I pull off my gear and drop it on the chair in the corner. Naked, I walk into the lavatory and take the quickest shower of my life. If March weren't waiting for me—and if I weren't cognizant that we have less than an hour to meet Sasha—I'd spend longer in here. It feels like forever since I had a hot bath.

Skin still steamy from the hot mist, I step out, and March pounces me. Sweeping me into his arms, he lowers me onto the bunk. It's narrow, but when he pulls me on top of him, it's big enough for two. I lean down, dusting kisses over the curve of his lower lip, his firm chin and strong jaw, then the bump of his broken nose. His lashes flutter against his cheeks as his breath catches.

"I get the feeling you missed me," he whispers.

"It sucks without you."

"Here, too." He wraps his arms around me, nuzzling my damp skin.

Pleasure spills through me, bright as sunrise and equally irresistible. I feel like I can't get close enough to him. I'm a miser hoarding sensations and memories because I don't know how long Loras intends us to stay—or how long it'll be between our mission in the capital and the next time I see March.

"I hate long-distance relationships," I murmur into his ear.

"I'm right here."

For now. I don't say it, but he hears because he's always in my head, if he's close enough to be. And he sees all my doubts and private griefs, all my hopes and unlikely expectations. There are no secrets between March and me.

"Don't, Jax."

"I'll do this instead, shall I? Or this . . ." By the time I finish teasing him, his whole body is taut, and his breath comes in ragged gasps.

He frames my hips in his hands and draws me over him. I don't need more foreplay because his pleasure, steamy hot in my head, gives me more than enough. His thoughts become random, chaotic; memories of other times chase through my mind. March's fantasies are all of me in various poses, but I catch a glimpse of a scene he keeps hidden away like a shameful secret.

So I make it come true this time; I don't stay where he puts me. I slide down. He catches my shoulders. "What are you—"

"I'm in charge. Lay back."

His eyes widen, but he does. Faint color touches his strong cheekbones as I fulfill the desire he couldn't articulate. He knots his fingers in the sheet, knees coming up to give me better access. With lips and fingers, I give him what he needs. There's no shame between us. Nothing he wants is wrong.

"Jax," he groans.

Love you. I love you. The words become a drumbeat in my head, and he loses control completely. To my surprise, I come when he does, and the orgasm sweeps through me like a leveling wave. As I quiver against his thigh, I realize it's probably an adjunct of his strong Psi. He hauls me up into his arms, between the cradle of his thighs, and I settle in with my head on his chest.

"I can't believe you did that."

I give a lazy grin. "You wanted it."

"Like you give me everything I want."

"I try," I say seriously. "Sometimes it's just not possible because it conflicts with what I need. But I'm never looking to deny you anything."

March checks the time. "We have twenty-two minutes."

"You think you can go again, old man?" I arch a brow, mocking him.

"Is that supposed to be funny?"

Belatedly, I realize I shouldn't tease him. He lost five turns while I was in the other world, and I'm not aging like I did.

"A little?" I try.

"Let's see who's old." He rolls me under him, and that's the last coherent thought I have for a while.

Eventually, I end up on top.

"Yes," he growls, as I sink down.

I want this to last, but because it's been so long, it can't. Like a summer's day, it burns bright and hot, showering me in ephemeral heat. I move on him faster and forget to consider his pleasure. But March enjoys it when I take charge, when I use him to take what I need, because it gives him the freedom to be passive. I peak first, squeezing my eyes shut when the tremors hit. He arches up with a cry, thighs tense.

Afterward, he trembles beneath me, all lazy satiation. My muscles lax, I collapse in his arms and relish the stroke of his rough fingers on my spine.

"I'd like to kiss you all over," I say, dragging my nails down his chest. "But we don't have time."

"That seems to be a theme with us."

"Someday," I promise.

"I'll hold you to that."

I take a quick, two-minute shower to wash the sex smell

off, then March follows suit. As I open the wardrobe, I notice he's left all my clothes here, like we're living together . . . something we've never really done. For the first time, I let myself imagine it. Not on the ground, of course, but on a ship—a master suite with a big bed and plenty of storage, something sleek and fast that lets us see the universe together.

This isn't the time to make plans, however. The war still has a long way to go. I can't think about the future until I keep my promise to Loras.

"Do you think he'll know what we've been doing?" I ask.

"Of course."

Oh, Mary. "Will he say anything?"

March grins. "Probably. Do you care?"

After considering it, I say, "Not so much."

When I arrive in the mess, there are few people here. March follows me, scanning for Sasha, then he spots him. The kid brightens a little and raises his hand to beckon us over. He's already eating.

"I figured you two wouldn't come out for a day. I owe Zeeka ten credits."

I glance at March to see how he's taking this. But he's smiling. "That'll teach you not to bet on a sure thing. I wouldn't make dinner plans, then break them."

Changing the subject, I ask them, "So is it weird to be the only humans here?"

"You'd know," Sasha points out.

I think about my own question. "Sometimes. And other times I forget . . . until somebody reminds me."

"That's about how it is here," March puts in.

Sasha nods. "The La'hengrin don't *look* that much different than us."

"High metabolism and adaptive physiology," I offer.

"Does that mean it's impossible for the La'hengrin to get fat?" Sasha wonders.

Now that he's brought it up, I can't recall seeing any who are, but so many live in abject poverty, where there's not enough food, there's no way to evaluate at a glance. So I shrug, not wanting to think about their plight right now.

"I'll get the food," I say to March. "What do you want?"

He gives his order, and I head to the kitchen-mate to input

our orders; once it produces the meals, I take the plates to the table. As I'm serving, Vel and Zeeka come in. I beckon them over. Soon, all the guys from the squad arrive, and our table's packed.

Xirol sits down next to Sasha. "When are they gonna spring you, kid?"

"You should talk to my dad. Explain all the reasons I'm needed."

March tenses.

"You'd be useful," Loras says quietly.

Which won't go over well, as he's in charge, and March knows that. So does Sasha, who says, "Does this mean you'll take me with you this time?"

"So what's everybody having?" I cut in.

Vel takes the cue and describes his meal, but I know he intends for the La'hengrin to recoil and rib him about how disgusting his food is. The tense moment passes. I bob my head in thanks, and he offers a discreet *wa*, just a fold over his plate with elbows tucked.

Though an argument's been averted for now, it's not the end of the issue. The tension will get worse.

CHAPTER 25

I'm in the fitness room the next day when Sasha corners me. From the kid's expression, he means business. He wants to talk about the subject that March shut down last night. But I'm not sure why he's trying to drag me into it. Maybe he thinks I have some influence over his parental unit?

Sorry, kid. Not that *much.*

But I smile in greeting as he climbs on the machine next to me. I've already done fifty reps, but I keep going slowly, so he can bridge the subject and get it out of the way. To my surprise, he works for a little while before glancing at me.

"Do you think I'm too young to help?"

Yeah, this is a potential minefield. In fact, I don't. I feel like once kids are old enough to have opinions, they should be *allowed* to have them. But I'm not his guardian. I can't give permission for him to sign on with the LLA in any capacity.

I also refuse to lie because that would be easier for March.

"No."

"Help me convince him," Sasha says. "I talked to Loras. He's got an idea for a Special Forces unit. There are a few La'hengrin like my dad and me. They can do stuff, too, and

Loras thinks it makes sense to put us in a squad together because we could handle missions no other team can."

"It's not a game. People die. I'm not sure if you get that . . . and I'm positive that's the doubt your dad has. He doesn't think you understand the reality . . . and he wants a better future for you, one that *doesn't* involve killing people."

Sasha puffs out a breath, driving the machine with his frustration. "So he's putting his baggage on me? How is that fair?"

"Life's not fair, kid." I want to smack my head against the wall as soon as the words come out of my mouth. I've officially become an old person.

"I'm going nuts here. I feel useless, like I kept us here for nothing. I know what it's like out there, I could help, and nobody will let me. Plus . . . I'm lonely. The only person who talks to me these days is an AI."

I'm sure that's not true; what he means is, he's feeling neglected because his uncle is often busy, and he wants to fight. Being thirteen, he's prone to exaggeration.

Before I can reply, he goes on, "But I guess none of that matters because I'm not old enough to be taken seriously." He slams out of the room without looking back.

"It's not my call," I say aloud, but Sasha is gone.

With a heavy heart, I decide to broach the subject to March. He may not want to talk about it, but ignoring the subject isn't going to make it better. Sasha will only get angrier, cooped up at the base as his hormones kick in. It sounds like March hasn't been spending the time with Sasha that he used to, or Sasha wouldn't have made the crack about Constance. Whatever's going on, I'll end up in the middle of it. It seems like I always do, regardless of my intentions.

With a faint sigh, I shower, then go in search of March. When I locate him, he's closeted with Loras, going over the information Tarn and Leviter have sent back to base. Obviously, March is working on strategy and deployment while he's here. He might even be helping Constance coordinate individual maneuvers in the field. I can't back up enough to see the big picture, but I'm sure it's diabolical and effective. This must be what March is doing while Sasha feels worthless. Lessons with an AI, then practice with a power you're never permitted to use must feel pretty pointless. March is so focused on the kid's physical safety that he's not thinking about his mental and emotional health.

Mary, I don't want to have this conversation.

As I step into the room, Loras looks up with a smile. "Ah, Jax. We're almost finished here. I collect you're here to take March away?"

I laugh at that. "I don't *own* him, so that's his choice. But if you're at a stopping point, I could use a word."

"Farah's commed me twice anyway. She wants to talk about . . ." At my skeptical expression, he flushes. "Oh, never mind."

"Right. She wants to *talk*."

March seems puzzled, but he doesn't ask. Instead, he falls into step with me as I leave the briefing room. "What's up?"

"It'd be faster if you just look." There's the number one perk of a Psi lover.

Frowning, he complies, and within a minute, he's glaring at me. "This isn't your concern, Jax."

"Sasha made it my business," I say, folding my arms. "If you don't stop coddling him, you'll lose him. He's not a baby anymore."

"He's *thirteen*."

"How old were you when you killed your first man?"

He turns, running a hand through his dark hair. "I don't want him to turn out like me."

"From where I'm standing, that's not a bad thing." I put my hand on his shoulders, feeling his tension. "This war will go on a long time. I know you don't want to hear it, but he'll be grown by the time it ends, most likely. And if you pen him up without regard for how he feels, he's going to run like hell when he gets free. You might never see him again."

"The idea is ridiculous," he snarls. "He's a child."

"Not as much as you want him to be."

He levels a gaze on me that's all icy amber light. "Do me a favor, Jax. Stay out of my business."

Hurt spikes through me. "I thought you were my business."

"Sasha isn't. You walked away from any right to interfere where he's concerned. I understood why. But you don't get to step in now and make a big, fragging, Jax-style mess out of a kid I've done a decent job with."

That's what he thinks? I wish I could argue, but history shows otherwise, so I can't even say he's wrong. I never seem to make anything better without screwing it up first. It's my MO, and I'm doing it again right now.

"Then why are you with me?" I ask. "Why do you wait for someone like me? Especially when you already made it clear you think I'm selfish for wanting my own life."

"I can't leave, can I?"

Shock pushes me back a step, away from him. "I didn't make you wait five turns for me. You could've moved on. And you wouldn't be stuck here."

"Jax . . ." He seems to realize belatedly how much he's hurt me. "I waited because I love you."

There's a prickle in my mind, like sharing headspace will make it better. Instead, it just shows him how bad I'm wounded. But he can't wipe these feelings away—and even if he can, I don't want him to. So I bring my walls up and force him out. I learned to do that during the Morgut War, when we were partners in the cockpit, but nowhere else. The force of it drives the color from his cheeks; I've never done that before.

I take another step backward. "Bullshit. You waited because you like being a martyr. But you know what? I've done some bad, fragged-up things in my life. And I'm sorry for them. But I *do not* believe I deserve to be unhappy. I refuse to be with someone who's using me like a hair coat."

"It's not like that," he says.

"Really? You act like you're the only one who's been lonely. I'm waiting, too."

"Yeah," he snaps. "I'm sure you are . . . with Vel around."

"You're jealous of him?"

"He put his *mark* on you, Jax. Of course I hate it . . . but then, I'm a primitive male. Obviously, I don't get your 'special connection' that transcends sex." Anger radiates from him. "You know how that makes me feel? Like you get all your emotional needs met somewhere else, and you just come to me for a good, hard—"

"Seriously?" My jaw drops. "You've been inside my head repeatedly. You know that isn't true."

"All I know is that you love someone who isn't me. You'll go *anywhere* with him . . . but you never stay with me."

I shake my head. "It's more accurate to say he'll go anywhere with me. So maybe you're jealous of that . . . because you can't right now."

"While we're clearing the air, Jax, what about the colors Vel wears? Tell me that's nothing to do with you. I looked up that symbol, and it means 'grimspace' in Ithtorian. So while you were with him—and I was waiting—you gave him some kind of commitment? That's more than I ever got from you. I just hear bullshit about how Kai said desire means more than promises."

Okay, maybe I screwed up. I should have said something to him, but when? As I was leaving Nicuan, or during one of the vid messages? *By the way, March, I gave Vel my colors. It doesn't mean we're married. I love you, bye!*

"You said you accept me . . . that you get me. You let me think you understood. Now you're telling me that was all a lie?"

His shoulders slump. "I thought I'd lose you if I told the truth."

"You'd only lose me if you forced a choice . . . because love shouldn't be like that." I sigh softly. "And I have a feeling you're only bringing it up now because you don't want to talk about Sasha."

"I don't," he says miserably.

I go on as if he hasn't spoken. "And now I'm not allowed to have opinions on this aspect of your life that I'm not a part of? Whatever, March. I know exactly how Sasha feels . . . and if you keep it up, you'll lose both of us."

I turn then because I'm damned if I'm spending my limited R&R fighting with him. He can go back to looking at charts with Loras, or maybe he should talk to his kid. Either way, I'm done. When he dragged Vel into it, he went too far.

CHAPTER 26

There's another day of leave, at best.

But I'm not in the mood to join my squad-mates in blowing off steam. I brood, work out, and take my meals at off-hours, so I don't have to see anyone. Eventually, I need to apologize to March for interfering; I don't blame him for being angry. In retrospect, it's crazy to discuss letting a kid fight. For the La'hengrin, it makes sense because it's their world, but for March, it was the ultimate red flag, and I should've known better. I was thinking of Sasha as a fully developed person, not a minor who needs to be guided. That was my mistake. But he made some, too, not least was misleading me about his level of understanding of our situation—and the things he said about Vel . . .

If Dina were here, she'd tell me to get over myself already. But she's not, so I wallow for a good long while before Vel finds me. It's the middle of the night on the surface, but I'm not sleeping. Doubtless, I'll be sorry for this move when we ship out in the morning, but for now, I keep drinking, so long as the kitchen-mate will keep processing my requests. The shitty part is, the nanites kick in the minute I get a good buzz on. They process the alcohol that's poisoning me and restore me to sobriety faster than I like.

"I had an . . . interesting conversation with March earlier."

I glance up as Vel sits down opposite me. The mess is totally empty at this hour, so there's ample privacy. Though I don't feel like talking to anyone, not even him, I say, "About what?"

"You."

"That's fantastic," I mutter.

"He asked about my intentions, Sirantha."

For a few seconds, I think the nanites have stopped working—which means I'm normal—and drunk . . . and that I can't have heard him right. "What?"

"He seems to be laboring under the impression that he stands in the way of our grand passion." By the rapid twitch of his mandible, Vel is hideously amused.

"I'm going to kill him."

"No need for violence when our passionate love has been acknowledged at last."

"So you suffer the agonies of the damned due to our fierce, unconsummated devotion?" I eye him, wondering how far he'll take this. "Well, I'm in the mood for revenge sex, and I might be drunk enough to do unspeakable things to you."

"Perhaps not quite the agonies of the damned." He's still wearing the Ithtorian equivalent of a smirk.

"Yeah, I thought that might make you backpedal."

Somehow, he musters a sober mien. "I am sorry. I should not find so much entertainment in your interpersonal difficulties."

"You're just afraid I'll make you sleep with me."

"I fear no such thing," he replies. "You have slept with me many times."

Not what I mean, but it's just as well there are no witnesses. March's head would explode. Maybe he fears this bond more because it's not about sex. I sigh and put my head on the table. This isn't the time to ponder such things. I need to stay sharp. Personal issues can wait . . . or they should, at least. Unfortunately, people don't preserve neatly in plastic, frozen in place until you're ready to deal with them again.

Vel rests a claw lightly on my hair. "He offered to step aside to make way for me."

Oh really? How enlightened of him. It's not like *I* can choose. Obviously, the males need to settle it between themselves and save me the burden of thinking.

"What did you say?" I quirk a brow.

"That I needed to talk with you first." Here comes the mandible twitch again.

This time, humor overwhelms the aggravation and chagrin. "You knew that would drive him crazy, didn't you?"

"I . . . suspected."

"Are you ready to beg me to be yours alone?"

From the flash in his side-set eyes and the way he draws back, Vel looks genuinely horrified. "No."

"I didn't think so." I prop my chin on my hands and sigh. Yeah, I'm screwing with him a little, but he deserves it.

His claws grow restless now that I've put him on the spot. They click out a nervous message of apology against the tabletop. "I do care for you, Sirantha. You are . . . the most important person in my life. But . . . that is . . . I cannot—"

I let him off the hook, listing the reasons why it's not going to happen. "You're not ready for a romantic relationship. You remember what it was like with Adele. Then you lost her. And you don't want to feel like that again. Plus, you're still healing."

I understand this about Vel. It's too bad March doesn't. And then I realize . . . he *doesn't know.* He sees only our closeness without understanding the context.

"Why do I love such an idiot?" I mumble.

"I imagine he asks himself the same question."

I sit up. "*Ouch.* Are you pissed off at me?"

"No. But neither of you is perfect."

"True enough. Would you mind if I told him about Adele?" It's his story, but it will go a long way toward easing March's mind and helping him understand that Vel's not a threat to him . . . at least, not during his lifetime.

It could take eighty turns before Vel is ready to move on. I might be grieving myself by that point, and he'll be there to help me through it. Then there will be an endless future together, so long as my nanites are still working, and who knows what will happen that far down the road? Not me. I can't even wrap my head around it. Most days, it's all I can do to handle the here and now.

"I do not mind if you reveal the bones," he answers at length. "But some of the story, I spoke for your ears alone, Sirantha."

"Understood. I'll just tell him the basics, and that you need a friend. Which I am."

"I have never known one dearer," he says.

"I should go wake him up. There won't be time to talk in the morning, and I don't think he'd get over it if we left things like this, and something happened to me."

Despite my ability to heal wounds that would end anyone else, I'm not immortal or indestructible. The nanites can't grow me a new head or rebuild me if I'm charred to ash. I can still die; it just takes more to kill me.

"He would not." He runs a claw down my cheek. "Nor would I. And who knows, perhaps someday—"

"You don't have to make me any promises. Just be there. That's all."

"I will be."

"I'm sorry you got dragged into this. It's . . ." I shake my head. Words fail me.

"It was . . . diverting, to say the least. I have never been the seductive third in a love triangle." And he's smirking again. "It is not a role I have played before."

"I imagine not."

"Tell me, Sirantha, what is it about me that you find irresistible? Is it my gleaming chitin? My eyes? My mandible? No, I have it. My talons drive you wild."

"You're never going to let me live this down, are you?"

"Probably not. It is possible, however, that in five hundred turns, neural decay will set in, and I will no longer recall how hilarious this is."

"You're an evil, evil Bug."

"Occasionally. Off you go now."

I shoot him a dirty look as I head out. At this hour, I encounter only Constance, who's walking toward comms. She never sleeps for obvious reasons; she just plugs in now and then to recharge.

"How's Sasha doing?"

"At his lessons, brilliantly. In other regards, I am concerned." Her words match her grandmotherly façade. Maybe she really *does* worry.

"He wants to fight."

"I know. We've talked about it. He's fascinated by the children's brigade. Not that he sees himself as a child."

"What do you think?"

"It is not without precedent . . . yet as Commander March says, Sasha is young. I am not qualified to render psychological analysis in this scenario."

"You must have an opinion, though." I tilt my head, inviting the truth.

"I do. In your service, Sirantha Jax, I have learned to respect free will. You let me choose whether I wanted to be in the sphere, part of a ship, or in a physical body. You never told me I was wrong for using the resources and processes available to me to make that choice. You gave me freedom." She meets my gaze in a most un-AI fashion, as if she's a real person inside those circuits and wires. "I think it is wrong to deny Sasha his own choices even if he is but a young sentient being. His mistakes should be his own."

"Even if they prove costly?" I ask.

"Commander March should not deny the boy out of his own fear."

"Thanks for the opinion. I'm on my way to talk to him now." I realize the AI can't make decisions as a human would; her thought processes are alien, and they're morally gray as applied to this particular situation. Yet I think it pleased her that I asked.

She taps a few panels in the comm suite, and informs me, "The commander is watching vids in his quarters."

"You can tell that?"

"Yes, from the energy consumption."

I point out, "He might've fallen asleep with the console playing."

"A possibility. But I don't imagine you'll let that dissuade you."

"No. This can't wait."

In wartime, there's no guarantee of tomorrow, so it's best not to leave things unsaid.

CHAPTER 27

He's not asleep, but despite what I told Constance, I didn't think he would be. March answers the door, looking haggard. "I wasn't sure if I'd see you before you left."

"Did you want to?"

"Of course."

"There are some things we need to talk about."

He steps back, inviting me into my old quarters with a gesture. "By all means."

"I need to tell you a story."

His brow furrows. "Now?"

"There's no better time."

In as few words as possible, I explain that Vel had a human lover—that they were happy together on Gehenna for many turns, until she made him leave her so he wouldn't have to watch her age. Then I tell March how she died, not so long ago, and that Ithtorians mourn for a long time. When I come to the end of my recitation, I ask, "Do you understand why I'm telling you this?"

"Because she remains at the center of his heart . . . and I'm jealous for nothing."

"Pretty much."

"I gather he told you that we talked?" A hot flush steals over his cheeks, making him look feverish, as well as weary and heartsick.

"Yeah."

"I shouldn't have interfered like that. I don't know why I did. I just . . . I don't know. I went a little crazy or something. I could only see that I'm not making you happy. We fight a lot. I thought maybe—"

"See, that's your mistake . . . thinking you need to make me happy. I'm in charge of my own moods. Yes, we're fighting more, but it's because we're talking. There are no secrets with you in my head, but before now, you haven't told me how you feel about what you see there. And I don't have your facility at poking around in people's minds. That said, I haven't been good about sharing, either. It's something we both need to work on." I take a breath before continuing, "I do apologize for interfering about Sasha. I wasn't thinking like a parent at the time . . . because I'm not one, so I get why you went ballistic."

He nods, stepping toward me as if he's afraid of being rebuffed. There's no prickle in my brain. He won't intrude since I forced him out. "I have a bad habit of only bringing things up when I'm already mad about something else. So I put my fears in the worst possible way, and I hurt you."

"Words are weapons," I say softly.

"I'm so sorry for what I said. I don't think you break everything you touch."

"Thanks."

"I already told Sasha, but you should hear it as well. If his feelings on joining the resistance haven't changed in a turn or two, then I won't stand in his way."

"Is he content with that?" It's a huge step for March, hating the idea as he does, fearing for his nephew's safety. I know he wanted a future devoid of violence for Sasha; he doesn't want the kid going down his road.

March nods. "He thinks it's a fair compromise."

"And meanwhile, you'll train him? Loras has some plan for a Special Forces unit. Maybe you can—"

"I already volunteered to put it together."

Pleasure but not surprise rolls through me. He always

wants to be in the vanguard, but life doesn't always permit our dreams to come true. So we cling to them in tatters and threads, until the colors fade beyond all recognition.

"I wish you were coming with me," I say softly.

His smile layers exhaustion, tension, and desire. "As do I. You've no idea how weary I am of being left behind."

"It isn't always me, leaving . . . or it hasn't been." I figure I might as well get it all out in the open.

"Are you talking about when I stayed to fight on Lachion?"

I nod. "And then when you went to look for Sasha while I sat in prison."

He flinches as if I've stabbed him. "I thought you understood."

I recall speaking those precise words to him about why I couldn't stay on Nicu Tertius and play at motherhood. By his pallor, he recalls it, too. This exchange is less raw, less heated, but no less candid. March squares his shoulders.

"I did, but that doesn't take away the sting. You know that."

"I hurt you," he says, as if this is a revelation.

"Yeah, but that's fair. I've been breaking your heart since the day you met me."

March sits down heavily on the bunk. "It's why you don't trust me. All this time, I've told myself that's just the way you are . . . you don't lean on people. But you do rely on Vel . . . and that's why I envy him so much."

"I thought I explained—"

He goes on as if I haven't spoken, "You just don't lean when you're unsure."

"I do love you," I say.

"But you doubt that you can depend on me. Because at the start of things, I put duty first. I chose Lachion . . . and then my sister's child."

"I didn't ask you to put me ahead of honor or family obligation."

"But I have to, don't I? If I want your trust, that's how it has to be."

I can't lie to him. "Yes. Right now, we have love, but we don't have faith. One of us is always keeping an eye on the horizon."

"Because I left you, when the time came, you chose not to stay with me."

"No, that's not why. Even if you had been perfectly steadfast, I wouldn't have stayed on Nicu Tertius. That's not the life for me."

"I was steadfast," he protests. "I waited."

"Waiting isn't the same as being there," I bite out.

"Isn't it?"

For the first time, the bitterness boils out; there's no stemming it. "You could have hired someone to start the search for Sasha. Stayed for my trial. Once it was over, we could've gone together. You chose to *leave me* while I was locked up.

"I said all the right things, but the truth is, I blame you. Once again, you chose somebody else over me. It was my fault I wound up there, I get it . . . and you wanted to disassociate if the worst came to pass—"

"That's not true. I didn't lie when I said I couldn't bear it, Jax. The whole time, I remembered how it was when I thought you were dead. Remember how I wired Farwan headquarters to blow?"

I nod, eyes fixed on his taut features.

"That's how it was. I had the monster on a thin chain on New Terra. The longer I stayed, the more it strained. I stopped caring about due process. I only cared that somebody was keeping you from me, and I wanted to kill them all." He takes a deep, shuddering breath, and the beast gazes out from his eyes. "If I'd stayed, I *would* have."

"I thought Mair cured you."

He laughs, and it's a wild, hopeless sound. "She put barriers in place. She roused my empathy. But there is no cure for what I was, Jax. I fell into the pit again, after Lachion, after so much death and darkness. It's always, always in me. I thought you sensed it. Thought that was the reason you never committed to me—because you recognize the bomb in my head."

"But Sasha . . . raising him has changed you."

"I've got more rope for the creature now to keep it bound, more boxes and chains to force it down. But it is never gone."

"Why did you stay on Lachion?" I ask then. "Was it as simple as you claimed? You owed Mair a debt for saving you?"

He forces out a shaky breath, and I see that his fingers, when he runs them through his disheveled hair, are unsteady. "I'd like to say yes, unequivocally. But now, viewed through the lens of hindsight, I think it was partly that and partly fear. I was afraid you were dying . . . and you turned aside so easily. You shut me out."

"So that's where it started," I whisper.

The problems between us began with me. I feared being helpless, dependent on him—needing him too much. Here we are, so many turns later, afraid of needing each other at all. My skittish nature broke so many things, and I didn't even know it at the time. But I'd just lost a lover, and I was afraid of taking another wound.

"I'm sorry. That came from fear and insecurity. I suspect . . . we fell in love too soon."

I don't say what he's doubtless thinking—that I wasn't over Kai completely—and our timing sucks. It always has.

He laces his hands together. I can tell it's an effort for March to stay out of my head, not to check what's on my mind. It's hard for him not to reach for me. I'd feel better in his arms, but physical contact can't solve our underlying problems. Without communication, our relationship will become what he fears it already has—just two compatible sexual partners who know how to push each other's buttons.

He sighs. "I shouldn't have pushed. I should've shown I'd be there for you, no matter what. Instead, your rejection on Emry was in my head when I decided to stay on Lachion."

"It doesn't matter anymore." I've aired my grievances. So has he. Beyond that, there's no benefit in dissecting past mistakes. Our course has carried us to this point. It only remains to be seen where we go from here.

"Is there anything left between us?" he asks. "Anything but sex? You love someone else now. I feel it."

"I already told you—"

"Vel doesn't want to be the center of your world. Yet that doesn't change how you feel about him."

"Yes, I love him. But he's not my lover."

"Do you wish he was?"

It should be a ridiculous question, but with the gravity of his face, I can't laugh. I shake my head. "No. March, if there were nothing between us, I wouldn't hurt so much. I wouldn't cry over you or wonder how it's gone so wrong."

"This is the worst possible time with the war and all, but . . . can we start over? I want to be the man you need. I can't change the choices I've made—"

"Neither can I."

"But we can decide to let the past go. Begin again."

Can we? I don't know if it's that easy. How do you forget the wounds that burn in your heart like hot coals? I don't have a choice, though. I agree to wipe the slate clean, or it ends between us, here and now. Am I ready for that? Can I bear it?

CHAPTER 28

The answer, when it comes to me, offers immense com-fort. "I can if you can."

I'm *not* the woman who loves the one she's with. I'm also not one who gives up because things aren't perfect. You fight for what you love. You commit to making the relationship better. I don't believe in the perfect match. There's the one you love enough to stay with; there's the one who puts up with your shit. It's not romantic in the standard sense, but to me, it feels better. It feels real.

March moves then. He brings me into his arms as if I'm made of crystal. In my hair, he whispers, "I don't deserve a fresh start, but I'm glad you're giving me one. I won't let you down, Jax. This time, I'll stay 'til the end."

"I don't either," I mumble. "I'm a screwup. Fortunately, life is arranged so that people *don't* get what they deserve."

He laughs shakily, crowning my temple with kisses. "That's true enough."

"Do you have any other grievances? This is your last chance."

"No. I just have a request."

I hold my breath, afraid it will be difficult or complicated, especially with me leaving at dawn. "What's that?"

"Be honest with me."

Relief flickers to life like a gentle flame. "I promise. No more withholding. Will you do the same?"

March nods.

We spend the remainder of the night talking. Mad as it sounds, it all feels brand-new again even though he is familiar as my own face. He doesn't suggest making love, and that's just as well. Odd as it might sound, I fear that sex would destroy this fragile rapport.

When I leave him, I am superstitiously afraid this will be the last time. Because there's none of the raw anguish, just a fearful, nascent hope for the future. And hope is a butterfly, so easily crushed by careless hands.

Yet duty calls. Exhausted from twenty hours of argument—and thinking about the conflict—I hastily shower and gather my things. The rest of my unit is already waiting in the hangar. To my surprise, Sasha's there, too.

He salutes Loras and hesitates when he spots me. "Can I hug you?"

"Do you want to?" I ask, startled.

"Kinda. I know you talked to my dad. Pissed him off, too. I guess you wouldn't have done that if you didn't care about me a little."

"I do." I'm surprised at how true that is. He's March's kid, not mine, but now that he's older, he's grown on me. "I suspect I was wrong to intervene, but I went to bat for you."

"Thanks for that. He sees me as a baby, but I'm not."

"I don't think it's that so much as he wants to protect you."

Sasha narrows puzzled blue-green eyes. "But he can't. Not forever."

"True."

"Sirantha!" That's Vel, telling me politely that everyone is waiting.

"Let's have the hug, kid."

He delivers it awkwardly, as if he doesn't know whether to hug me like a girl or with the backslapping camaraderie of a male he wants to impress. In the end, I get a little of both, then I step away. This time I don't look back as I vault into the shuttle. The others are already inside; they look rested and ready to wreak havoc.

"Is it safe for us to head for the capital?" I ask Loras, as Vel powers up.

He shakes his head. "But we're doing it anyway."

Xirol laughs. "Now that's what I'm talking about. I hope we see some action."

For me, the word "action" brings back inescapable memories of Venice Minor. Of the bombardment and Doc's death. I hold those moments close; they remind me of mistakes I don't mean to make again.

"We will," Loras says.

Eller breaks his long silence to say, "Be careful, people. Things will get worse before they get better."

Even Xirol can't make a joke out of that. I nod to show I take his warning to heart. In truth, the same dread burns in my bones, as if every last bridge has been burned. From this point on, there's no way out but through. Then again, that's the only path I've ever had.

It's still dark, of course, when we slip out of the base. There are no other ships up here, and night cloaks our movement. We won't put down in the city proper. The shuttle has to be hidden where we can reach it yet beyond the range of our enemies. That means a precise set of calculations.

"How is the war shaping up?" Vel asks.

Loras shakes his head, visible from the front only because I've half shifted in my seat. "In small pockets of resistance, just enough to keep them unsettled. The Imperials are looking for conspirators in the palace at the moment."

"Courtesy of Leviter and Tarn?" I guess.

He laughs softly. "But of course."

"Can they help us at all in the city?" I ask.

Loras angles his head, donning his commander's air. "Shouldn't you wait until you learn your assignment?"

"As long as it's not more treatments," Farah mutters.

I'm glad she said it, not me. But it's so true. I'm tired of playing that role.

"No, we've moved into the next phase of the plan," Loras replies.

Low-key whooping fills the shuttle, and Loras doesn't

shush us. The conversation becomes general, though I take some ribbing from my squad-mates. Xirol nudges me.

"You made yourself scarce, Jax. What did you do?"

"Or should we ask who?" A joke from Eller? The world must be ending.

"Very funny." I pause for best comic effect. "You know who I did." More hoots follow, but they're good-natured. I add, "I don't mind you speculating about my sex life. At least I have one."

Zeeka laughs the loudest, but I detect a note of false cheer. Maybe he's realized he'll never find a mate out on the star roads since his people are all on Marakeq. In that, he's like Vel. But then, Vel found somebody to love him on Gehenna; two, if you count me—and I do. So there might be a woman who doesn't mind if Z's different.

"Eller, she's talking to you," Xirol cracks.

The silent La'hengrin laughs. "Still waters and all that."

"We're nearly to the drop point," Vel interjects.

Loras scrutinizes the landing site, an estate that's fallen into disrepair upon the death of the legate who owned it. His heirs are all off world, and the man promoted to the position doesn't receive personally owned property as part of the promotion. Which means nobody ever comes around here. There's no staff, no witnesses, but there's always the risk of being detected on Imperial scans.

"Bring it in. Drop to single thruster and kill it before we hit the ground."

Vel complies even as he objects, "That will interfere with the stabilizers."

"I have faith in you, Ithtorian." Loras has steel in his voice. He expects the impossible, and people deliver it.

Me, among them.

The shuttle spins a little, but Vel lands in accordance with Loras's requirements. Tonight, it's dark and still, no moon, clouds obscuring the stars. It's ominously quiet for a modern world. No ships overhead. No lights in the countryside to reveal civilization.

Apart from the major cities, the invading "protectors" have broken La'hengrin society down into pockets of isolated slave camps they call villages. It has been so long that most of them can't remember what it's like to have power and running water. They've been forced into medieval conditions without adequate housing or medical care, and they couldn't even fight the changes that came down, law after law, for their own "protection," preventing them from striking back.

Grimly, I swallow my disgust and outrage. I'm doing what I can to make it right. That's all anyone can do.

Vel guides the shuttle into an outbuilding, where we'll hide it until further notice. From this point, our cell devotes itself to dismantling the infrastructure in the capital. From what I heard while on leave, it's already unsteady without an influx of reinforcements and supplies from Nicu Tertius. The Imperials stationed here aren't the best of the best, bright-eyed and full of ambition. So without backup, they don't know what the hell to make of our little rebellion; they also have no idea how big it will eventually become.

Vel is telling Loras, "It is not invisible. A dedicated search will—"

"Erase all the destinations in the nav com," Loras interrupts. "If they find the shuttle, I don't want them uncovering any clue where we've been. Can you do that?"

"Assuredly," Vel replies.

"The rest of you, grab your gear and huddle up. I have some last-minute instructions."

I obey; my pack is light compared to what I carried on Conglomerate missions. But we had better gear then. Better odds, too, despite the bullshit I feed myself on a regular basis. I'm sure the others do the same. Well, except for Zeeka. He still thinks the good guys always win; it comes from getting most of his culture from old vids.

"We go in on foot. From there, we'll be splitting into four teams."

"Two, two, three, three?" Bannie asks.

She's questioning how we'll divide up. I don't blame her for being nervous. We've worked together for a while; even if it wasn't thrilling, we're used to each other. It'll be different inside the city, all of us possessing separate missions.

"That's correct," Loras answers.

"Will you give us the breakdown now?" Zeeka asks.

Loras sighs. "If it will relieve your minds. Farah, you're with me."

That announcement draws some ribbing, but the others shut up when Farah crosses her arms. Sometimes, she's scary.

Loras continues, "Zeeka and Rikir. Vel, Jax, and Xirol. Bannie, Eller, and Timmon. I'll give your individual assignments as we march."

It's forty klicks to the city. No telling what we'll run into between here and there.

CHAPTER 29

The march should take seven hours, tops, but things get interesting ten klicks in. Loras signals, and I scramble off the road. I crouch behind a wild, thorny hedge, waiting for whatever he heard. The others have their heads cocked, listening; and then comes the rumble of an engine.

"Imperial," Rikir whispers.

Xirol nods.

By the sound of the vehicle, it's an aircar, not a shuttle, and it's zooming at a pretty low altitude, skimming what used to be roads, long before the Nicuan came. Now, they don't maintain them, so they're just dark, frayed ribbons threading through a green wilderness. Some La'hengrin exist in remote poverty their whole lives, fearing their protector will sell their *shinai*-bond.

"It's probably a legate," Loras says. "On the way to his country estate. They're the only ones who own property in this region."

Like the dead one whose place we're using to hide the shuttle.

"If we can stop the vehicle, we can use him." Zeeka tilts his head, tracking the lights. I can see them now.

"How?" Xirol asks.

Z seems a little nervous, but he outlines his plan: "Remember how you meant to send Vel in as a centurion to gather intel on Imperial installations?"

I nod, along with everyone else.

Encouraged, Z goes on, "It seems like a legate would be much more valuable, and this is a prime opportunity to snatch him for the infiltration."

Holy shit, he can supplant this legate in the capital. This is *so much* better than the original plan. It will be risky, certainly, but the rewards could be immeasurable.

Loras nods. "Good thinking." He turns to Vel. "Can you do it?"

"With sufficient time for study."

"I'll get them to stop," Farah says.

She doesn't look at Loras. Instead, she drops her pack and strips down to her black tank top and matching panties. The La'hengrin males freeze; they can't stop staring at her. Loras growls low in his throat, but she doesn't turn toward him. He lunges at her, but Rikir catches his arms.

"Let her work, man."

I hear his teeth grinding as she pushes through the bushes. The thorns tear at her skin, so her distress will be real when the aircar lights skim over her. The blood, too, is real. It's hard to get my breath as she slumps onto her knees, beautiful even in misery. Overhead, the purr of the engine rumbles louder, closer, until I can't hear anything but that sound.

As I watch in disbelief, the aircar cruises by. I didn't think anyone could resist Farah. Beside me, Xirol mutters, "I'd have bet fifty credits against that."

"Me too," Rikir replies.

Loras snarls, "Shut it, both of you."

Then the lights overhead swerve, spiking back in our direction. The aircar hovers, yellow beams skimming the ground all around. The constant uncertainty has taught them to be wary, if nothing else. It's smart.

"Be still," Vel whispers.

"Beautiful girl alone in the wilderness . . ." Eller says. "Of course they think it's a trap."

Loras gestures for silence. "We have a minute, maybe less,

to take that aircar. I need you to flank quick and quiet. Farah will buy us that much time."

"Yes, sir," I say, along with everyone else.

I check my weapons. No guns. He wants a silent kill.

It should be easy. Aircars aren't big enough to hold a whole squad of soldiers. The aircar's passengers apparently decide there's no trouble on the ground, just a helpless La'hengrin female. This must seem like a gift from the gods because slaves this beautiful ordinarily cost a fortune. The legate probably imagines her *shinai* has been killed in one of the raids, leaving her helpless. They don't wonder why the resistance abandoned her . . . because that's the kind of thing the centurions would do without a second thought.

The car whines as it lands. Then a falsely commiserating voice asks, "Are you hurt?"

"A little," Farah breathes.

Though her back is turned, I can imagine her tremulous look. I count four men, one legate, three centurions, and I glance at Loras for the order. He gives it in a curt hand gesture, his face white and livid in the moonlight. As I break cover, I understand why. The legate has his hands on Farah—and if I had any doubts about her relationship with Loras, they've been put to rest.

Knife drawn, I move in smoothly along with Vel, Timmon, and Xirol. For all his levity, he's a skilled killer. Vel and I, odd as it sounds, are veterans—and Timmon, well, he doesn't like seeing bastards touch his sister. I can't blame him.

Timmon kills the legate with a jab to the kidney; no armor blocks his blade. It enters cleanly, and as the Imperial falls back, he slices his throat. The rest of us work as efficiently. Xirol goes for a clean break, twisting the centurion's head to the side whereas Vel crushes the larynx with his talons, then finishes the job. I take my foe with an initial stun to the stellate ganglia. Quick downward strike with the handle of my knife, and I follow the stun with a vertical stab into the subclavian artery. Five seconds later, he's on the ground, dead. It should bother me how good I am at this. Before, I could say with sincerity that I was just a jumper. I can't anymore.

Farah pushes to her feet, smiling. "Good work. Does someone have my clothes?"

Sometimes I think she's as much Loras's second-in-command as I am. But I'm not interested in debating that at the moment. After Timmon hands them to her, she dresses quickly. It's cold enough that I can see my breath, so she must be freezing. The clouds threaten rain; we're far enough south, away from the mountains, that precipitation falls in drops rather than flurries.

"Get the centurions off the road," Loras orders.

Nobody drives on them, but there's a small chance another aircar could spot them. Best to shove the bodies into the thornbushes and leave them for the animals, as we did in the first village. Xirol, Rikir, and Eller get busy while Loras studies the vehicle.

"This isn't going to work," Bannie says. "It won't hold all of us."

Farah nods. "We might cram everyone inside, but there's no way the engine has enough lift to carry everyone."

"What's the new plan?" Xirol asks.

Timmon starts to grab the legate, but Loras throws up a hand. "No, he comes with us so Vel can replicate his features."

I assess the aircar, then say, "It'll carry six, tops. Five if you're taking the corpse."

Loras makes a swift command decision. "We'll rendezvous at the legate's country estate. There may be resistance, but my team can handle it."

"There probably won't be many centurions," Zeeka says.

Vel nods. He's tapping on his handheld, using the aircar as a wireless router to piggyback connection to Imperial databases. Hopefully, they won't be able to tell his interface from the legate's data stream. This war effort has crippled his usefulness because he can't access information like he does on other worlds. He finds it frustrating.

Now he's in his element, at least. "This Legate Flavius is a minor official. Twenty centurions serve him. Ten are reported to guard his residence in the capital. And we just killed three."

Flavius? I lean in, hardly daring to hope. "Shine a light on his face, will you?"

Xirol does; there's a lot of blood, but I have no doubt this is the same asshole who taunted me over lunch so long ago, when I was still filing petitions. I smirk. Who *got his just desserts, huh, Flavius?* It's delightful that he'll serve the cause postmortem.

"Is this the same Flavius?" Vel asks, familiar with my frustrations.

"Yep."

"If he left ten guarding his home in the city, then seven Imperials will be waiting for us," Loras muses. "I'll draw lots for the four who'll accompany me in the aircar."

"Shouldn't you pick the crew who are best at hand-to-hand?" Zeeka asks. "In case you run into trouble."

It's a logical question, but Loras doesn't want to rank us. I can see by his expression that he fears creating resentment in the squad. So he narrows his gaze on the young Mareq, and snaps, "Don't question me, boy."

Z brings his long arms forward in a shamed hunch. "Sorry, sir."

Loras turns to Vel. "Can you randomize all ten names and have four come up on your handheld screen?"

Vel's insulted by the question; his mandible flares, and *not* in the friendly fashion. "Certainly. Let me finish downloading the dossier on Legate Flavius, and I will attend to it."

A few clicks, and the screen lights up with each word, one by one. *Bannie. Timmon. Rikir. Eller.* The rest of us will be hiking. Farah squares her shoulders, and Loras takes a half step toward her. A nearly imperceptible shake of her head stops him. For a few seconds, his face is naked with regret; he wishes he could disregard the lottery. But she doesn't go to him. Right now, she's a soldier, and she can't give him what he wants . . . or it will damage morale.

Mary, do I know how she feels.

"Vel, you have bravo group," Loras says.

"See you on the other side," Xirol calls, as the aircar powers up.

Then it's just the five of us in the dark.

La'heng Liberation Army signal-jack ad: Profile Three

ORIANA

[A girl gazes off-screen at something the viewer cannot see. Then the interviewer speaks.]

Male voice, off-screen: Can you tell us your story, Oriana?

Oriana: Of course. [She faces the camera.] Unlike most of my people, I don't remember my family.

Male voice: Is that unusual?

Oriana: A bit. Most of us are born in the provinces, where we're sworn to a protector. If we're lucky, he visits once to make sure we're still breathing; then he returns to his life in the city. I was born in the capital to two La'hengrin servants already bound to one of the noble houses.

Male voice: But you said you don't remember your parents.

Oriana: The master of the house traded me. I don't know why. He gave my bond to a powerful legate when I was an infant, and I never knew any life other than obedience and servitude. I thought it was natural that I shouldn't think too much—that I didn't need an education because the legate had no intention of seeing me trained as a translator, which is the only cerebral work my people are permitted on world. I have heard stories since that others who escaped La'heng have taken other training, always with their masters' permission—and those masters are never Nicuan.

Male voice: Have you met your parents?

Oriana: They died in service. There was an assassination attempt, and they gave their lives so their master could escape.

Male voice: The La'hengrin cannot defend themselves. How could they help during a fight?

[Her face falls into deep, sad lines.]

Oriana: They cannot. But they can die. Sometimes, a few seconds is all a coward needs to flee.

Voice-over: And *that's* who you're fighting for. Contact the comm code at the bottom of your screen to find workers with the cure.

CHAPTER 30

As I move out, the sky opens up. The promised rain spills down over us in a liquid-silver curtain, cold enough that I feel it through my insulated armor.

I glance over at Zeeka. "Your gear holding up?"

I fret about him more than I should. Most days I tell myself it's because he's cold-blooded, so climates like this one can screw with his physiology. He'd be better off on a tropical world, far away from this war.

But Z nods, his eyes shining. "Warm as my bunk. I'm good, Jax. You don't have to worry about me."

"Everyone needs a hobby," I mutter. Mine used to be wondering how I'd die.

It's a mystery to me how Z isn't crazy from grimspace deprivation, but unlike Argus, he took the training without any hint of addiction. That might mean Doc was right all along; the Mareq have the perfect ability to tolerate—and navigate—grimspace. If the Makers had anything to do with their engineering, that makes sense. If the Mareq are a servile race, created by the Makers, then they *would* have all the genetic markers necessary to make them useful.

As for me, I'm suffering, as always. Sometimes, when the

need gets too much, I consider eating some pills or powder, maybe a shot, but chem won't solve my problem. It'll just give me another addiction. So I strangle the feeling until it's bearable, and I go on, because that's my job. I lock the pain and the longing up with everything else I want and can't have right now.

Like March.

"The estate is twenty-five klicks that way," Vel says, pointing.

"Just a hop in the aircar." But there's no rancor in Xirol's tone.

Loras chose his companions fairly, even when he wanted to take Farah with him. I have no complaints about the process though it left me marching in the rain. Farah pulls up her hood to keep out the damp, and the rest of us follow suit. Vel takes point with the rest of us in twos. Z ends up beside me, Xirol with Farah.

In this weather, I estimate four hours, but Vel sets a bruising clip. He's almost running, like he knows something bad's waiting for us, as if Loras and the others flew into a trap. I want to ask if his instincts have told him something, but I don't want the others to overhear. Instead, I resolve to be ready.

My boots slip and slide over the cold, muddy ground. *This is what it was like for March on Nicuan,* I think, *except it was hot . . . and it went on for turns, until he snapped. No wonder he's got a monster inside him.*

Under Vel's aegis, it only takes us three hours and change to make those klicks, and I'm exhausted when lights glimmer out of the darkness. They shouldn't have had trouble with the number of centurions present. All should be well. But when Vel raises a hand to motion us to stillness, I press forward, trying to see what he does.

"What's the holdup?" Xirol asks. "I'm ready to get out of the rain."

In answer, Vel points to the number of aircars parked before the manor. There are five, one of which Loras arrived in, but I don't see any sign of him. There are no sentries posted outside since it's a miserable night, but they're inside.

"It looks like a house party," Farah says softly.

I nod. "Assuming four people per vehicle, that's an extra sixteen men."

"Plus the seven centurions," Zeeka adds.

"Loras gave you command, Vel." Xirol says. "What are our orders?"

He crouches beyond the range of the lights that illuminate the manor exterior, tapping his handheld. Then he shakes his head. "I cannot get a clear reading. There are devices inside, interfering with the energy emissions."

"So we don't know where they are," Farah says, her voice taut.

For her, this must be doubly terrifying. Both her brother and lover have vanished this rainy night. They might be hostages; there might be more centurions on the way. If we're caught here, it destroys the plan to sub Vel for the legate and makes this detour pointless.

Plus, we could all die; I'm glad I'm not in charge.

"If they were outside, they'd have spotted us," I point out.

"We must do some recon," Vel says. "I am the most qualified for the task. Remain here until I return. Stay out of sight."

"Shit," Xirol whispers.

I feel exactly the same way as Vel slips into the shadows. Intellectually, I know he's a better hunter than any of us. He knows how to go unseen, how to snag his target, from all those turns as a bounty hunter. But it doesn't help a lot when you're squatting in the mud, rain pouring down, and you don't know what's going on.

"What if he doesn't come back?" Zeeka asks.

Pain twists through me, nearly making me cry out. Even the idea is devastating. Unthinkable. Somehow, I manage to reply, "Then we move out. We have our orders for the capital. We'll divide up as directed and carry on."

I'm not stupid. If Loras and the others are lost, if Vel doesn't make it out, then the four of us have no hope of taking out all the centurions inside. Without Loras to drive the war effort—he's the face of the revolution—I don't know how it can go forward, but it has to. I won't let all this work be for nothing. If I can't do it with my friend, I'll finish it *for* him.

"I have his contacts," Farah says softly. "I can step in."

Those words must feel like razors in her throat. Yet her

face remains set and determined, her delicate jaw firm. This woman is worthy of Loras. Mary, I hope he's all right. This isn't how it's supposed to end; he shouldn't die a martyr for the cause.

I curl my hands into fists within my gloves. The minutes tick away slowly, feeling more like hours. At last Vel slips back into position, and I fight the urge to hug him. *Not appropriate, Jax.*

"I suspect the others arrived after our men," he reports. "I could find no sign of anything amiss, however, so I do not believe they have been detected."

Farah exhales slowly. "So they're hiding, trapped inside."

"We don't dare use the comm," I whisper.

Vel nods, indicating it might give away their hiding spot and get them killed. I made that mistake once. It won't happen again. *Sorry, Doc.*

"We need a diversion," Zeeka says.

"Good plan." Xirol studies the aircars parked before the manor. "One of those would make a nice, big boom."

If Sasha were here, we wouldn't have to lay charges. But he's just a kid. And when he's old enough, when March gives him permission to fight, he won't be on my team anyway. He's going into the Special Forces unit.

"I'll do it," Zeeka offers.

Z feels about explosives as I do grimspace; for him, jumping is a job, an exciting one, but not an addiction. He's lucky in that regard.

"Allow time for us to get out of sight before you trigger it," Vel orders. "Set the charges to take out as many of the other vehicles as you can. Then meet us around back. We will enter through the kitchens as they come out to investigate."

"What's our priority inside?" Xirol asks. "Find our people or kill the enemy?"

As I knew he would, Vel says, "Rescue first. Once we reunite, and our numbers are restored, we can engage."

"Yes, sir." I speak in unison with Z, Farah, and Xirol.

"Move out."

Z splits from the rest of us, running across the yard in his bounding style, but he avoids the lights deftly, until I can no longer see him. Staying low, behind Xirol, I move down the box hedges toward the side of the house. Vel leads; every now and then, he pauses to listen, then presses forward again. Tension tightens my shoulders, but he's good at what he does. Despite the rain and low visibility, we make it to the back door fast.

Still quiet.

Three minutes later, I'm starting to get worried. Z should be here by now—

And then he is. Breathless, he falls in behind Farah, big eyes looking to Vel for confirmation. The Ithtorian inclines his head. Zeeka presses a button on the remote in his hand, and the subsequent explosion rocks us. Inside, immediate commotion results; and then comes the sound of running footsteps and shouted questions.

"Our cue," Vel says.

Because he'd never ask us to do anything he wouldn't, he opens the back door and steps into the kitchens. Our camo can't blend in a room that's all white and silver; the paint isn't formulated for interior environments. It matches rocks or trees, and it works best when we're not moving. The pattern on our armor swirls, making me dizzy, so I look away.

And focus on the terrified La'heng servant opening her mouth to scream.

CHAPTER 31

Xirol's on her in a blink, hand across her mouth. He whispers, "We're resistance. Nod if you've heard of us."

She's plain, fine-featured but unexceptional. Her hair is a muddy brown, eyes hazel. The girl ducks her head just a little. I gather that means she's heard of us, but since she works for a legate, none of it is good. She still looks terrified. I wonder what propaganda they've been spinning.

"We're not going to hurt you," Farah whispers. "In fact, we can set you free, just as I am. Do you see my weapons? I was a slave once, too, just like you."

"I'm going to take my hand away, if you promise not to scream. Do you?"

Another nod.

Xirol lowers his hand cautiously, but she doesn't cry out. The girl eyes Farah with an equal measure of fear and fascination. "How can I be free? Who will take care of me?"

"I care for myself," Farah answers. "And sometimes my friends, too."

"Is there really a cure? Legate Flavius says it's all lies."

He won't be saying anything, anymore. This doesn't seem like the time to break the news to her. I wonder how much of the *shinai*-bond stems from turns of psychological dependence. They've been told, repeatedly, that they'll die without protection. Is it possible for the mind to control physiological response when belief becomes so ingrained?

"Who do you think is fighting in the mountains?" Xirol asks.

"The legate says there are no free La'hengrin. That it's all the work of foreign devils who want to steal us for themselves."

My heart sinks at this news. Sadly, this *has* happened. The Conglomerate handed management of La'heng to Nicuan, as one of the tier worlds equipped to deal with slavery on such a scale; but prior to that, during Farwan's reign, the Corp sold La'heng to the highest bidder, and disgruntled, defeated factions then used the planet as a staging ground for their grievances. They tried to take what they couldn't buy—with varying degrees of success. The result was complete destruction of local infrastructure, and the conquerors determined what was rebuilt. Each time it occurred, things got worse and worse for the La'hengrin.

"Do you like working for the legate?" Zeeka asks.

If she's loyal to her master, then we must tie her up and gag her. I hate the thought of treating a helpless female that way, but we can't have her raising the alarm. Xirol gives me a look that says this is worse for him; he can't bear it when one of his people has come to love the boot on her throat.

"No," she says softly. "He hurts me."

Those three short, simple words possess incredible power. Beside me, Vel curls his gloved claws, and I sense he wants to rip out the legate's throat himself. If Xirol's and Farah's expressions are any clue to their feelings, he can get in line.

Z puts a gentle hand on her shoulder. "If you help us, we can free you."

"It's true then?" Her small face shines.

Farah nods. "I have the treatment in my bag."

I catch her eyes, brows raised, asking silently, *I thought we were done?*

But she doesn't respond. Apparently, she and Loras have some hidden agenda. And that's fine. A leader isn't expected to share everything with his troops. I just need to shut up and follow orders. It sucks that I'm so bad at it.

"You'll take me with you?" the girl asks.

Only Loras can make that promise, but Farah agrees. "Certainly. You can join the resistance in the capital."

The girl takes a step back. "But I can't fight. I only know how to clean and run the kitchen-mate."

"Shhh," Xirol says gently. "Easy, *carenna*. We'll find a job for you."

"Soldiers need to eat," she murmurs, as if reassuring herself. "And a clean place to stay. It can't be worse than here." Visibly gathering her courage, she asks, "What do you need of me?"

Vel tells her, "Hide. Do not emerge until you hear us call the all clear."

"What's your name?" Farah asks.

"Tiana. You're going to kill them, aren't you?"

I'm a little afraid of how she'll respond to the truth, but Xirol meets her gaze. "He deserves it. They all do."

To my surprise, her brows come down in a fierce look. "I know."

"Quickly now, we don't have much time before they come back," I say. "How many men are here?"

Tiana gives us an accurate count, a few less than I feared since some of the vehicles only carried two or three passengers, not the full four I'd estimated. And then she runs, scrambling for a hiding place.

"Move," Vel orders.

He's not being an ass. There's no time to stand around chatting. The exchange with Tiana cost us precious moments from the distraction. Soon the centurions will figure out that it was a deliberate detonation, not a mechanical malfunction, and they'll storm in looking for trouble. Before that happens, we must locate Loras and the rest of the squad.

We step out of the kitchen to search. Fortunately, they must've heard the explosion, so I spot Loras coming down the stairs. Before he can do more than offer an appreciative smile, the front door slams. Booted feet tromp across expensive natural flooring, and a high-pitched male voice whines about the destruction of his vehicles outside. This legate sure brought a lot of guards.

"Sorry, Legate," a deeper tone replies.

"They're here," the legate says, growing more shrill. "I know they are."

"We did a perimeter check after the explosion, Your Excellency. The rain makes it impossible to track, but as soon as it clears up, we'll hunt the bastards down." The centurion sounds so positive.

"Legate Flavius should have arrived already," the other legate says fretfully. "He knows how great a risk I took in making the journey at all, especially now."

That means they haven't found the corpse, wherever Loras stashed it. Good news. But two legates at this gathering? How . . . interesting. Before we go, I need to poke around and see what conspiracies are brewing here. From March, I knew well that Nicuan nobles are never happy unless they're intriguing—and it's a bad idea to split focus when there's a war on. That will work to our advantage.

Setting that aside for now, I glance at Loras for orders. *Do we attack or wait for them to disperse?* They clearly don't know we're inside the house. They think this is one of the resistance's famous hit-and-runs, where we blow up property and disappear. Since that's been the mainstay of the rebellion, I don't blame them for leaping to that conclusion.

But the game's about to change.

The odds aren't great for a pitched battle; apart from Vel, none of us are commandos. We managed on the road because the centurions were distracted, staring at Farah's half-naked body. Here, there are two of them for every one of us. It's a tough call.

After an agonized moment of indecision, Loras signals. "Up the stairs. On my mark, we draw them."

"Bottleneck," Vel says. "And it is always good to fight on the high ground."

What he doesn't mention is that we might be screwed if any of them survive the initial run. The landing up above is narrow; it doesn't provide much room for a melee. Yet maybe that's an asset, too, since the centurions have turns of combat experience over us.

"Ready?" Loras asks.

The squad nods.

"Bring 'em, Jax."

I scream at my utmost volume, infusing the sound with ululating terror. Centurions spring into motion while barking questions at each other. Their boots ring on the wood floor, announcing their approach. I bring up my weapon and drop to my knee. I can fire through the railing; I'm small enough. The angle is such that I'll catch them before they hit the stairwell.

The first enemy pops into sight, but my hands are steady on the pistol. March and Sasha aren't here to fill me with fear, so using the sight, I make a clean shot. Red light streaks toward him, and he tries to dodge, but the laser strikes his armor. *Dammit.* It didn't get through. I fire again as he presses up, and this time, the chest plate explodes to expose the raw burn on his chest. Farah and Bannie, both shorter, drop so they can focus fire beside me. One more hit, and the centurion staggers, drops. Over us, the men lay down such a fierce line of fire that the centurions fear to cross. It's insta-death right now, but we can't keep it up. Our weapons click, the power packs overheating. We continue; somebody loses a hand. Or a face.

Finally, Loras says, "Rotate your shots, let your guns cool down."

My unit in the Armada ran tighter than this with March at the helm, but he had turns of command experience. Loras is doing his best, but this is new to him, just like it's new to so many La'hengrin. They're not used to handling weapons. We should've planned better, but what the hell, we're in it now.

CHAPTER 32

One of the centurions decides the quiet means it's time to charge.

"Don't," another shouts. "It's a trap."

I didn't know it was, but Vel did. He wasn't firing along with the rest of us, so he nails the enemy with enough force to split his helmet. It's not a kill shot, but the next one is. The enemy's head explodes in a charred stew of splattering brain and bone.

"Hold," the deep voice thunders. "They want you to charge, idiots. Don't, unless you have a death wish."

Shit. It sounds like the voice of experience is taking their strategy in hand. Soft and spoiled these centurions might be, now, but they didn't survive ten turns on Nicuan by being terrible at their jobs. This will get a lot harder.

"Can they call for reinforcements?" I whisper.

Loras shakes his head. "I cut the comm connection. I doubt any of them know how to repair it."

"Nice," Xirol murmurs. "They can't call for help without calling someone to help them call for help."

Despite the grave situation, I grin. My muscles tense as I

hear the low voices below us talking, beyond my hearing range, though. I turn to Zeeka. "Can you make it out?"

Z silences me with a gloved hand on his mouth and everyone else falls quiet. Our weapons are cool now, but the centurions below have something else planned. They're not running up the stairs one or two at a time; that would be idiotic. Too bad only two of them failed the test. We still have eighteen down there to kill.

"What do you mean the comms are down?" the legate screams. "My aircar's a smoldering pile. We can't call out? Someone get me out of here! I'm too important to—"

Then there's a thud, followed by a thump, like somebody hit him. Are centurions *allowed* to do that? What the hell is going on? I wonder if we stumbled into an internal coup.

"Something is not right," Vel says.

The rest of us nod. Doesn't change our mandate, however. We still have to kill everyone in the house, then blow it up. I hope Vel can convince everyone that Legate Flavius survived the attack. Tiana will help sell the story; that's the best way she can serve the resistance, I realize. Keep doing her job, lending credence to Vel's disguise.

Zeeka leans in. "I know what they're planning. Take cover!"

That's the only warning we get before a centurion aims a heat-sensing smart grenade at us. I scramble; the Smartie won't go off until it locks onto a large heat source. It won't sit still long enough for anyone to disarm it—if it gets that close, it blows. In that way, it's like a mobile proximity mine.

A few of my squad-mates fall in behind me, and I slam the door. Other slams echo nearby. I hope everybody's safe. The centurions haven't solved their problem. They can't get to us with the grenade in play. They can only hope it will soften us up.

Then an explosion rocks the whole upper story. *Shit. No, no, no.* The door I'm hiding behind smokes. From my position, I can't reach the handle, but Loras can. For the first time I notice who's with me: Xirol, Loras, and Zeeka. Anyone else might be dead. *Vel* might be. Somewhere ahead of me—on the other side of the door—a woman screams, and then the sound dwindles into broken sobbing.

"The stairwell's open. Go, go, go!" the deep voice commands.

"They're coming," I say, pulling myself together through sheer will.

As they press, they fire, keeping us from taking up our former positions for best defense of the high ground. Laser strikes bombard the area, all light and heat, burning an already damaged floor. The smoke in the air stings my eyes, but if I lower my helmet visor, I'll lose some peripheral vision. In close quarters like this, outnumbered, I can't afford to be less than my best.

I draw my gun and ease forward. Though I know Loras is just as worried, he whips out his weapon and kicks the door wide. The centurions respond with a barrage of shots until I see light through the thick synth flooring. Using it for cover, Loras stays low and shoots as the enemy breaches the top of the stairs. Zeeka and Xirol follow suit, but our concentration isn't tight enough to keep them from pushing.

Behind me, down the hall, Farah kneels with her back to the battle. It's a total breach of training, but I can't blame her . . . because she's cradling her brother's head in her hands. Oh, Timmon. His blood stains her armor, her arms, and she rubs her cheek against his, her eyes wild with grief. We have to protect her until she comes back to her right mind.

Where's Vel? I wonder desperately.

The centurions don't give a shit about those we've lost, however. They've lost brothers tonight, too. If Mary's willing, I'll kill more. I injure one who falls back, but it's not a fatal shot. His armor sizzles, and it must burn like hell, but he's a professional. The centurion levels his gun on me, and I slide forward. His shot hits where I used to be, but now I'm out of cover. They all train their pistols on me, which was exactly what I hoped they'd do. That gives the others a few seconds to recover. Instead of freezing, I keep rolling, past the broken banister, then I fall. On the way down, they hit me twice; one shot burns through to my arm. The pain's excruciating in the first few seconds, then it's like the nerves are cauterized, so I can't feel the damage. That might be typical, or maybe I can thank my nanites.

I hit the ground with a thunk. The armor takes some of the

impact, though I think I might've broken a rib. Sharp, stabbing agony lances through me as I push upright to stare at a pale, ferret-faced man. His sharp features match the legate's voice, and he seems groggy as hell, like he can't figure out who I am or what he's doing on the floor next to me. He also has a deep bruise forming on his jaw from where his own men knocked him out.

Before he can shout, I crack him across the face with my good arm. He sways, then falls over. I shouldn't hesitate. He needs to die. Whether he has a family or a wife who loves him, it doesn't matter. He's the enemy. Yet I fumble my knife for a few seconds, then I sink it into his subclavian artery for a clean kill.

Overhead, combat continues. More smoke and laser fire. I don't know how my squad's faring, but I'm not out of the action; a little fall won't stop me from kicking some more ass. True, I can't fight with my left hand, and I think I dislocated my shoulder, but I can still work the right side. Good enough.

I whip my shock-stick out because my laser pistol requires a steadiness I can't bring to bear. Between my fear of who died in the explosion, reaction to killing a helpless man, even if he's an asshole, and my injuries, I'm as likely to take out my comrades with friendly fire. I should be able to create some confusion behind the lines, though.

Moving gingerly, I creep up the staircase, mostly empty now. They're fighting in the hallway, in the bedrooms, but they left a sentry at the top of the stairs. Because of the noise, he doesn't hear me coming, so I whack him on the back of the neck. The neural shock does the work, so he falls into convulsions. It feels like a stab wound in my side when I bend to cut his throat, ending the spasms.

Sparks pop before my eyes when I straighten. Okay, maybe I hurt myself more in the fall than I realized. But I just have to push through the pain. The nanites will fix me up. Unlike most people, I don't need a doctor unless I've lost body parts or major organs. This quality makes me special . . . and creepy.

The dizziness increases. All right, so maybe I overestimated what I have in reserve. I'm not strong enough to fight, but I can still help. I get my gun like I'm not trembling too much to aim it. Farther down the hall, I see a couple of centurions hunkered down, exchanging fire with my squad.

I shout, "Assholes! Can't you kill somebody even when they're half-dead?"

Reflexively, they wheel and switch targets.

Someone yells, "Get down, Jax!"

I pitch sideways, not a dodge so much as a fall, but at least this time I land on my good side. Still, impact hurts like a bitch, and I close my eyes, fighting hard not to pass out. I really need not to get up for a minute. If those centurions have their way, I never will. There's no coming back from a missing head, even with nanites.

Hm. Maybe I need to sign a DNR order. Or would that be a Do Not Grow a New Head order? I might be hurt worse than I realized.

Laser fire spatters the ground perilously close to my face, close enough that I breathe in ashes from the seared wood, but the two centurions drop. Distracted, they make easier targets for my squad, however many of them are left.

I close my eyes just for a few seconds. I'll fight on in a minute.

CHAPTER 33

I wake to movement.

There's a fire in the sky behind me, darkness ahead. I shift to see who's carrying me and gaze up at Vel through blurry eyes. A stone I didn't realize I held drops away.

"I would appreciate it if you did not frighten me again in that fashion." He's speaking Ithtorian.

Which means he wants privacy, or he's so upset that he forgot to ask his vocalizer to kick in. Either way, the others can't follow this conversation; nor do I want them to. My relationship with Vel is more intimate than what I share with the rest of the squad.

I exhale, testing my side. *Can't tell if it hurts as much as it did earlier. Speak Ithtorian,* I tell my chip. "Sorry. I was worried about you, too, you know."

"I did not offer myself as a sacrifice when I could barely stand," he bites out.

Shaking my head, my vision clears enough for me to count the figures moving ahead of us. Six. Not eight. *We lost two.*

"Who?" I demand hoarsely.

I've become friends with Farah and Bannie. I like Xirol, too. Please don't let it be Zeeka. And we need *Loras—*

"Eller," he replies. "And Timmon."

Relief suffuses me, followed immediately by contrition, because Eller was a good man; I remember how he said it would get worse before it got better, and it seems those were prophetic words. Timmon was Farah's twin. Recollection swamps my foggy brain. In my mind's eye, I see Farah out of her mind with anguish, Timmon's head in her hands.

I should be ashamed for being glad, even for a second, that we lost them instead of someone who's important to me. As I've learned—and it was hard—I'm not the center of the universe.

Guilt silences me.

I sense his fierce rage; I don't remember when Vel was this angry at me, if ever. His faceplate is open, so I touch the hinge of his mandible. Few know that it offers pleasurable contact, a hint of familiarity.

He pulls my hand away, clicking sharply, "You will not charm me, Sirantha. Nor will you soften my censure."

Stung, I chatter back, "I was *comforting* you."

"Call it what you will. You will not stroke away my wrath." Strong word, but it fits what he's feeling.

I want to get down; he shouldn't have to haul me around when he's so furious, but I'd only slow us, and we've lost enough already. Now that Vel isn't talking, I hear quiet, hitching gasps from Farah. She's choking back her tears, so she doesn't make everyone else uncomfortable. I wish she could sob her heart out, but that luxury has to wait.

Then I notice a small figure beside Loras, no armor. No shoes. In this weather, she must be freezing. "Tiana's with us?"

"Yes." One word, and he sounds like he'd rather chew glass than talk to me.

How do I fix this?

"I didn't mean to be a sacrifice. I was just trying to help."

"Do you have any notion how I felt, Sirantha?" He continues without letting me guess, not that I was going to. "When the grenade went off, and you were not with me, I feared the worst. And then . . . you fell. Twice, I lost hope."

"Then the next time you saw me, I was yelling at the centurions like an idiot." I try a smile. "But in my defense, this isn't the first time. Remember the Silverfish?"

Back when I first met Vel, when he was still hunting me, I

wound up on a ship with him and a bunch of Morgut. He was using them as muscle before the war. I cut myself and drove them into a frenzy, forcing him to save me.

"I recall. But I did not love you then." His casual use of the word underscores the bond between us, echoed in his colors on my throat, mine on his thorax.

"You still saved me. You always do." And that's why I'm never afraid to leap, no matter how stupid the risk seems. He'll catch me; he has my back.

"And if I do not?" he rages in staccato clicks. "What if I fail? Then you leave me responsible for your death. If you cared for me as much as you claim, Sirantha, you would not place such a burden upon me."

He's right.

Remorse buries me. "I'm sorry, white wave." The endearment comes easily in Ithtorian." I won't do anything like that again. I swear."

He goes on, more gently, "When you gave me your colors, you promised to be my companion. That will not occur, should you perish. There are some wounds, Sirantha, that even you cannot heal."

"I know."

These clicks come even fainter, soft like a human whisper. "Some wounds, I could not recover from, either."

Like losing me.

"What happened after I passed out?"

"I will explain everything when we reach the safe house. It is not far, now."

"Safe house?"

"Tiana said she knows a place. The legate had it built in case of treachery."

I smile, despite the lingering pain in my shoulder. The dislocation hurts more than my ribs at the moment. "Good thing for us he was paranoid."

"Here," Tiana says in her small, piping voice.

From the outside, it looks like a ramshackle outbuilding, similar to La'hengrin homes, but inside, it's high-tech. The house *questions* us. "Where is Legate Flavius?"

"Here," Vel replies in a voice I last heard in an expensive restaurant.

He must have found comm records; those are mission critical. It also contents the VI.

"Voice print confirmed."

I'm glad the legate cheaped out on security and didn't include biometric scans, but doubtless he couldn't imagine there would ever be a real enemy on his property. The most he expected to face is treachery in terms of some political alliance, not outright war.

Loras sends Xirol to scout the place. When he returns, he says, "It's clear."

"This is a small cottage he used for . . . various purposes." By Tiana's hesitation, I figure the legate brought women here, ones he didn't want inside his primary residence.

"I must remove your armor before I can fix your shoulder," Vel says.

Since I don't have the range of movement to do it myself, I nod. "Go for it."

"I do not wish to hurt you."

"Sometimes it can't be helped."

As Vel carries me up the stairs, Tiana asks Loras, "Should I fix something for the men to eat?"

His measured reply hides a charnel house of pain. Men died on his watch. "If you wish. You don't serve us. You're an ally, not our slave."

"It would please me to repay you for my freedom."

Vel chooses a bedroom at random and steps inside, kicking the door shut behind us. Pain jolts through me as he sets me on my feet. I sway but don't fall though the agony that spikes through me when he unstraps my chest piece creates black spots in my vision. I strangle a low moan.

"I am sorry," he clicks in Ithtorian.

"Don't worry about it."

With quick efficiency, he removes the rest, leaving it in a careful pile on the chair by the window. Then he asks, "Do you want to lie down?"

"Moving would hurt more, I think. Just finish."

He steps in behind me, positions my elbow, and then rotates my shoulder outward. It hurts like a bitch, but on the second attempt, it pops back into the socket, offering immediate relief. There's still soreness, of course, but not like before.

I moan a little, tears starting in my eyes. The nanites will fix the damage soon, but this helps. I can bear it.

"Better?"

"Much."

"You need medical attention." He examines the two places where I've been shot; the flesh is black right now, with a hint of red beneath.

"Why bother?" I say with a touch of bitterness. "I'm not going to die."

"That does not mean you do not suffer." He's still behind me, one hand on my elbow, the other on my shoulder. It's an intimate pose. If I turned, I'd be in his arms.

I change the subject. "You said you'd fill me in after we got here?"

"Indeed. We interrupted a scheme to overthrow their prince. The two legates had hatched a plot together, but our arrival made the other believe that Legate Flavius had betrayed him."

"Lured him there to die, you mean?" That explained the legate's shrill terror.

"Precisely."

"How does that help us?"

"In the morning, after I have a chance to complete the camouflage, I will signal for rescue. In the capital, I will show proof of the other legate's treachery."

"Which will endear you to the prince."

This is far better than anything we could've planned using the centurion. Though Legate Flavius was a minor official before, Vel can parlay this opportunity into greater power. With him on the inside, we'll have access to all kinds of information, such as weapon caches and troop movements, just what the resistance needs to break the Imperial war machine; like all invaders, they'll lose the will to continue sooner or later.

"That is the plan," he agrees.

"Did we blow the house?"

"Zeeka took great pleasure in it."

A pang goes through me; we left our fallen behind.

CHAPTER 34

I step away. "You'd better get to it, then. It will take most of the night to perfect your disguise, so you can slide into the legate's life."

But he doesn't let me. His talons close gently on my upper arms. "When I thought you had died, Sirantha, I realized I had not been completely honest with you. Or myself."

"What do you mean?"

"Before, I said I was not ready to put myself at the center of your world and become responsible for your happiness."

"I remember."

"But it seems you are already at the center of mine. I laughed at the idea that I would demand March step aside for me . . . because I do not see associations as humans do. And I do not seek to interfere in your other relationships. That much is true . . . but tonight made it clear how important you are . . . and how horrifying my future appears without you."

This doesn't seem like that much of a revelation. "I already knew I matter to you, Vel. You wouldn't have taken my colors if I didn't."

"I am not making myself clear."

"Not really, no."

"Imagine my death." The clicks are curt, merciless, and they summon an instant mental picture.

Desperately, I dive for the far side and catch hold of the stone lip, dangling with one hand as Vel disappears. The torch-tube bounces away into the darkness, leaving me alone with my ragged breathing and the fear of falling.

Oh, Mary, so am I. Get to solid ground, Jax, and then look for Vel. He can't be dead. Not Vel. Oh, please, don't leave me alone.

Each movement tears at the wound in my side, but I pull myself up, conscious of fresh blood dripping down my hip. Blindly, I feel for his pack and locate another torch-tube. Our last. I crack it without hesitation and shine it into the pit. At first, I see only the razor-sharp spikes that line the bottom. The Makers hated grave robbers. And then I spot Vel, clinging to the side about halfway down, his claws dug into the soft, crumbling stone.

On the Maker homeworld, I almost lost him, and I glimpsed the future without him. A hole opened up inside me that could never be filled, no matter who else I met or loved. Is that what he faced tonight?

"I understand," I say. "I went through this when you fell in the catacombs."

"How do you bear it? I feel as if fear will paralyze me."

"Didn't you worry about Adele?" This can't be wholly new to him.

"Not in the same fashion. She lived a quiet life, full of normal hazards. You court danger like it is your lover."

I offer a wry smile. "Yeah, if you wanted someone safe, you picked the wrong person to bond with."

"You say that as if I had a choice."

Maybe I should be insulted, but I totally get it. Sometimes, people matter, and you don't even notice it happening until they're inside your emotional perimeter. "How can I make it better?"

"Stop being so reckless. Show a little self-preservation." He pauses, his clicks slowing. "Come here, Sirantha."

Vel draws me close, rubbing the side of his face against my cheek, a tender gesture. This time, when I touch the hinge of his mandible, he doesn't snarl at me. For long moments, we stand like this while he adapts his worldview. For once, *I* knew something before Vel.

"I already promised I'll dial it down. You're right . . . it's not fair of me to expect you to be everywhere."

"However, I am touched you have that much faith in me," he clicks quietly.

"You're incredible, you know. It's hard *not* to believe you have superpowers."

"Only compared to everyone else." The cant of his head and the flare of his mandible reveal his amusement, so I laugh.

"I'm glad you're not getting cocky on me."

"It is no more than reasonable confidence."

At the sound of boots on the stairs, I pull back and head for the door. The movement jars residual pain from shoulder and ribs, but the nanites are already hard at work. Duty calls. "I'll let you get to work."

"If it would not repulse you, I prefer you to stay."

I turn, surprised pleasure curling through me. Though he's done this in front of me before, in the jungle on the Maker homeworld, it wasn't like I could give him privacy; we *had* to stay close. This feels like a milestone, an unlocking of the last door between us, more secret than sex.

"Why would it?"

He spreads his talons in an uncertain gesture. "I am not a good judge of what humans find repellent."

"I've seen you do this before."

"Not by choice," he replies.

It was cold, as I recall, and he needed the camouflage for warmth. Vel settles in the chair by the window. Thin fingers of light press in through the glass, illuminating his work. The gaps between the chitin—the seams where he can feel a lover's touch—fill with the material he uses for the faux-skin. He shapes with artist's hands. The substance is fluid, but thick, and it sets quickly, so he has to work fast.

It takes a couple of hours for him to finish. I'm fascinated by how he creates the eyes and hair, a sort of biological programming that humans aren't evolved enough to emulate. Otherwise, we'd be able to change our hair and eye color by willing it so. Perhaps someday, a few more rungs up the ladder.

I study his handheld, displaying an image of Legate Flavius, then compare it to Vel's new face. He's got a lean look with an aquiline nose and a strong jaw. It's a cruel mien, set in the lines of a man who thinks only of his own pleasure and his own advancement. Legate Flavius looks like the bastard he was.

Vel is also a dead ringer for him.

"You nailed it," I say. "How long did you study him?"

"Loras permitted me to examine the corpse extensively while he searched the comm for clues about what we'd interrupted."

Most people would probably find that disgusting. Instead, I ask, "Did you make a note of all the birthmarks?"

"Of course."

"I'm guessing Flavius is single?"

"Correct."

Vel has been stealing other people's lives for turns. He's experienced at it, and it's for the best he's going in alone. I just wish it didn't tie me up in knots.

A knock sounds, then Loras asks, "Vel, are you ready?"

"Yes," he calls in universal.

Not his voice. Legate Flavius. His vocalizer is a wondrous thing.

I open the door. Loras has some clothes, probably from a master bedroom down the hall. This one isn't grand enough to be used for his various assignations. For Vel's sake, I hope Flavius wasn't too much of a degenerate. He'll hate debauching countless women as part of his cover.

"Get dressed," Loras orders. "The rest of us will move out shortly. We can't be in the vicinity when you call for rescue. Between Tiana's help and the comm logs I forwarded, you should be able to pass."

"So the girl goes with me?" Vel asks.

"She can smooth any rough patches, give clues while you settle into his life."

That's why he wanted me to stay. This is good-bye, at least for a little while. I can't read the legate's face though I know Vel watches me from behind those eyes. I've often wondered how he makes the connection between his eyes and the human ones, or whether it's like a mirrored window, so we see color on this side, but it's all clear—the same view as he always has from behind them. This isn't the time to ask.

Loras turns his eyes on me, blasted in their blueness like a sky in the mountains just before nightfall, arid and untouchable. "Are you fit to march?"

"Yeah, I'm fine." In fact, my injuries are the least of my worries.

"You have five minutes to wrap up," Loras says in parting.

Vel dresses efficiently; he is experienced in human attire. He's slid in and out of so many lives. How many does this make?

"I don't know what to say," I whisper.

This feels like when he went off to command the Ithtorian fleet, only a thousand times worse, because he won't have warships at his fingertips. This time, he only has his own ingenuity and the help of a frightened servant. How I wish I could slip into a new skin as easily he does, but even if I could, that wouldn't help him. He needs Tiana's inside knowledge of how the legate's household functions.

"How about 'I will see you soon'?"

"But is that true?"

"I intend for it to be so. How much would you give to be with me, Sirantha?"

For a few startled seconds, I'm not sure what he means, what he's asking. I leap to the human interpretation of *be with me*, but this is Vel. Not March. Therefore, he's talking about the mission.

"I'd feel a lot better if I could watch your back."

"From what I have gleaned from his private correspondence—and a few formal reprimands—the legate spread his attentions far and wide. That will be . . . awkward for me to maintain, at length."

"So you want me to play significant other, once you have a chance to sell the story that he's met someone? I don't think that would work. My face is too well-known—"

"Yes," he says. "Your face. Are you willing to give it up?"

The question sends a shock through me. I'm not beautiful, but I am comfortable in this skin. Changing my face would leave me with a stranger in the mirror. I hesitate, considering all the factors in play. Part of me is loath to sacrifice my identity even for Vel, but another half thinks this might be a fresh start. There would be no more paparazzi, no more people on news net following my every move. For the first time in ten turns, it would mean privacy.

"Would cosmetic surgery even work on me?" I wonder aloud.

"The nanites repair damage . . . they are not programmed to safeguard your appearance. So theoretically, they should speed your recovery, not impede superficial changes."

"Theoretically," I repeat wryly.

A new face would change everything . . . but if I'm offered the choice between helping Vel and wondering if he's all right, then I'll do whatever it takes to back him up. Even this. Mary knows how March will feel, but it's not like I can ask him, and I wouldn't even if I could. This is my decision, my body. I hope he can adapt to the change; but if he loves *me*, not my skin and bone, then it shouldn't matter. He'll adjust. No matter what I look like, I'll be the same person.

"You discussed this with Loras?" I ask.

Vel inclines his head. "He knows someone in the city willing to do the work."

"What's involved? I mean, how long will it take, how much will it hurt . . . ?" I grin, but the truth is, doctors give me the shivers these days. I'm always afraid they'll lock me up and run experiments.

"Everything is done with sonic shapers, some minimal laser work. There will be some pain and swelling, but you could expect to resume a normal routine within forty-eight hours. Perhaps less, depending on how your nanites respond."

Taking a deep breath, I make the decision. "Of course. If you need me, I'm there, whatever face I have to wear."

"Thank you, Sirantha. Loras will explain further."

I back out of the room, taking care with my injuries, and navigate the steps with utmost caution. Everyone else has assembled downstairs. Farah sits on a chair with her hands folded in her lap, eyes still red and swollen. The squad seems subdued, each dealing with loss in his or her own fashion.

Xirol glances up at my approach. "Glad we didn't lose you, Jax."

I'm about to make some smart-ass remark to break the tension, but I think better of it. Some things can't be dissolved with a joke. So I just incline my head. I don't sit down because it would hurt getting back up again. My pack will sting going over my shoulders, but it can't be helped. I'll march out of here along with everyone else even if it kills me.

FROM: E_L
TO: [RECIPIENT_ENCRYPTED]
COMM CODE 18.255.91.23.88

I have the information you requested; it should permit you to plan with greater efficiency. Things progress well in the capital. I have planted several rumors that I expect to bear fruit within the next two months. The resulting scandals will weaken the nobility's faith in one another. It is most amusing to watch them chase their tails, seeking traitors and conspirators among their most loyal. Sometimes, conversely, the legates take the most steadfast refusal to break as indication of certain guilt.

How are things at base? For obvious reason, I will not be returning before the cessation of hostilities. You must be feeling trapped, given your history and current custodial obligations. Feel free to disregard the question if it is too personal. I'm possessed of inveterate curiosity, my partner would say, and sometimes I don't know when to mind my own business.

Of course, that's how I ended up in a relationship, too, so maybe he wouldn't object.

I'll be in touch.

E. L.

FROM: M
TO: [RECIPIENT_ENCRYPTED]
COMM CODE [MESSAGE BOUNCING; MULTIPLE RELAYS. ULTIMATE DESTINATION UNKNOWN]

Thanks for the intel. I've scheduled four new strikes. For obvious reasons, I'm not putting any information about our targets on the bounce. But if you're as good as people say you are, then you already know what I intend to do and how I'll deploy our troops. If I ever get out of the base, I'll look for hints of your handiwork on the bounce. It's frustrating because we're completely off the grid, dependent on information you feed us, then I'm responsible for disseminating it to the men in the field. I have help, of course, so I'm not carrying the weight alone, but still, it's more than I wanted. I came here for a vacation, for Mary's sake.

As far as my custodial obligation, he's a pain in the ass. The kid's determined to make my life hell because I wouldn't let him ship out with everyone else. And yeah, I'm feeling trapped. The work helps. I feel guilty because I'm looking forward to the kid's birthday, as I promised to let him join up, then. It also means I can get out in the field again. I probably shouldn't be so relieved to start killing again, as that never leads me anywhere good. But I'm also worried about our mutual acquaintance. She has a way of finding trouble, doesn't she? If it's not too much of a security risk, maybe you could update me on how she's doing the next time you send a report my way?

Thanks in advance.

M.

P.S. I don't mind your curiosity.

CHAPTER 35

Six days later, I'm sitting with Xirol in a black-market medical facility. The place is clean, though not fancy. Plain block walls have been painted institutional gray, and the equipment, a bit battered and scarred, has seen better days. The doctor is a nondescript man with shorn hair and a quiet manner.

My injuries have healed, so far as I can tell. Even the twinges are gone. In a few seconds, the equipment validates this expert self-diagnosis. I do have scars where I was shot, but the nanites will take care of those in time. They don't tolerate imperfections in the body they're maintaining, which makes it pretty ironic that they ended up inside someone as flawed as me.

"You're in top shape," the doctor says.

"That's not what I heard," Xirol jokes.

"Are they passing around naked pictures of me again?"

The doctor looks marginally interested in Xirol's reply. "Nah, just topless ones."

I laugh. Then the doc gets down to business. He doesn't call me by name because he doesn't know it. I have no idea who he is, either, except he's willing to turn me into somebody else. I can tell he's not native from his features. My best guess is, he's disgruntled Nicuan, looking for payback on those who cast him in disfavor over some petty politicking. Whatever. He's taking my money through a complex circuit of intermediaries. Officially, it'll look like I donated these credits to charity.

"I've examined the stills," the doc says. "And created a composite of the ideal feminine face, based on the accumulated data of the target's preferences."

"This should be good," Xirol mutters.

"Let's see it."

The doctor activates a screen built into the wall, and the image appears. I stare at her, thinking, *This will be me.* Nothing about her says Jax. Her features are fine and delicate, with a small, pert nose and pointed chin. Her eyes are almond-shaped and slightly tilted at the corners, giving her a feline air. Only her lips have anything in common with mine, full and long, but shaped into a kissable bow.

"She's beautiful," I say.

Xirol stares at the screen. "That'll take some getting used to."

"Why, because I'll be so different?"

"No, because you'll look La'hengrin."

He's right, I realize. The fine features and the shape of the eyes are right, but since the doc's created a composite, I'll look even more native, the epitome of all feminine La'hengrin qualities. Yet she's not me. It shouldn't matter, giving up this so-recognizable face, yet it does, a little. Since Vel needs me to explain the change in the legate's behavior, I'll do it, no question. Odd. I didn't expect it to bother me at all. But I've been Jax so long that I clutch over giving up my identity, even for Vel. Then I set aside my reservations.

"Will that be a problem for you?"

Xirol shakes his head. "Look, I know you have a thing for me, but you're just gonna have to accept that it can never be."

"Alas, I know. You and Bannie, right?"

To my surprise, color washes his handsome face. "Shut up."

The doctor isn't interested in wasting time. "You have the choice between red hair and blond." With a few taps on his handheld, the screen responds, splits, showing me what the woman looks like with both colors.

"What do you think?" I ask Xirol.

"If I say I like redheads better, will you tell Loras I'm after Farah?"

"What would Bannie say? She's a brunette."

"Brunette isn't a choice on the table," he points out.

"True." I glance at the surgeon. "Break it down for me. I've always had dark hair."

"Well, 45 percent of the legate's companions have been redheads; 55 percent were blondes."

"So he likes both. No brunettes?"

The doctor shakes his head.

"Asshole."

"Quite. He likes them young, too, so you'll need a course of Rejuvenex along with the procedure."

Dammit. Anger sparks through me. These days, I don't age much, or at least, not like other people. *Now* I have to reverse the turns I've already earned? I like my laugh lines and little crow's-feet. They give me character. When I get this new face, this smooth, young face, nobody will ever take me seriously again.

And March? He'll hate this *so much.* I already look fifteen turns younger. People will think he's a dirty old man. Granted, in this day and age, it can be hard to tell how old someone truly is. I knew a couple with a seventy-turn age difference between them, and it truly wasn't noticeable.

Xirol grins. "This must be a dream come true for a withered old thing like you."

"Fine," I mutter, realizing they're waiting for a reply.

The doc arches a brow. "You seem displeased. Most women would love a fresh start. The Rejuvenex will perk everything up, tighten your skin—"

"I know how it works."

Obviously, he doesn't understand my complaint, so he asks, "What about your hair? I don't handle that aspect myself, but I can have an esthetician come in. There is one I trust."

Frankly, I don't give a rat's ass. I want to keep *my* hair. I haven't been this upset since I had to shave it all off. But that won't work. My coarse, curly hair doesn't suit this face. But otherwise, I don't know what I'm talking about; let's be honest.

Aloud, I wonder, "Maybe I could combine the two. Red with pale streaks? Strawberry blond?"

"Red with pale streaks would be hot." Clearly, Xirol's expert opinion will make all the difference to the success of the mission.

But the doc agrees. "Yes, deep auburn with highlights would be most pleasing."

"Bring your friend in and add it to the bill." I pause. "Can I keep my eyes?"

"They're gray . . ." A few taps for analytical comparison, then he nods. "Not as common as blue or green, but not so remarkable that you need new irises."

"I was thinking more about *lenses*," I say, horrified.

Xirol shakes his head. "That's disturbing. You've seen how we live . . . so before a couple of turns ago, I didn't even know people could get new faces. New eyes. It's kind of . . . creepy." He's unusually serious, but I nod my agreement.

It is *creepy.*

"No need for either." The doc doesn't notice my reaction. "I'll also need to remove those scars. They're unmistakable. Memorable."

The nanites nibble at them, slowly. Doc suspected in time they would heal; but I can't wait for nature to take its course. People have told me before that it's a simple laser treatment to take them away, make my skin perfect and unblemished. I always resisted because I felt like it would be a betrayal, erasing Kai from my body. I carry him in my flaws just as I do in my memory. It's time to let him go. He wouldn't want me to wear his death in my skin. He'd want me to remember his life; that's the sort of man he was.

Despite my tight throat, I answer, "That's fine."

"Do you want me to remove the tattoos? They're fairly recognizable as well."

"No," I say. "Leave them. I'll wear something to cover them." I glance at Xirol. "Is that a thing here? Do the Nicuan ever collar their La'hengrin to show possession?"

A flash of pure pain washes over his features. "Yes. When a Nicuan male takes a particularly beautiful female La'hengrin in a sexual *shinai*-bond, sometimes he dresses her in a jeweled collar that reflects his ownership. It discourages other nobles from making offers."

"You sound like that's personal for you." Hard to explain, but his tone isn't just general offense. It's old pain.

"My sister," he says softly.

He doesn't need to say more. I picture a beautiful girl who looks like Xirol, collared by some bastard who uses her as a sex toy. And she has no recourse at all.

"Can she take the cure?" I ask.

"She died."

No wonder he hates them. So many La'hengrin have stories like this. Each one hurts me, diminishes me. I won't rest until they're free. I can't.

"I'm sorry to hear that," the doctor says quietly. "My countrymen can be pigs."

I wonder if he's ashamed of his heritage.

"They can be," I agree.

"I'm doing what I can to help the La'hengrin. Speaking of which . . . I need you to lie back. The procedure, for obvious reasons, will take several hours. Even modern technology can't peel your face off and instantly replace it with a new one."

"I'll be here, Jax, just in case he gets any ideas." From Xirol's expression, he thinks the doc is a little dodgy, and I appreciate his protective stance. He's a good guy; Bannie is lucky to have him.

"Thanks, I appreciate you looking out for me." The chair I'm sitting in angles back, flattening to become a surgical table. "How long's the recovery period?"

"Twenty-four to forty-eight hours," the doc replies. "It depends on your healing rate, of course, but I'll provide medication for pain and cream to reduce swelling."

I nod. "Let's get this over with."

"Not words a man ever likes to hear," the doctor says, smiling.

His expression makes me laugh, as he intended, and I remember Doc. I miss him, as I always do. "Sorry."

"Don't worry," Xirol says. "I won't let anything happen to you."

I want to say I appreciate it, and I'll do the same for him

sometime, but the hypo pricks me. Drugs flood my system, and I'm out.

When I wake, I'm somebody else. Of course, I can't see the other woman yet. My face is still swathed in bandages, so I peer at the world through a narrow white framework. I'm numb, too, which is a blessing. This will hurt when the anesthesia wears off . . . though not as much as it would for a normal human. The nanites will have a field day, restoring me from the surgical procedure.

"Are you with me?" the doctor asks.

"Yep, I'm awake."

"Good. I'd ask you some personal questions to be sure I didn't scramble your brains with the laser scalpel, but I don't know anything about you."

Funny. Maybe the Nicuan nobles didn't like his sense of humor. He didn't take their consequence seriously enough, so he fell out of fashion, and now he's doing full makeovers for the rebellion. He was focused and purposeful at first, but once he had all the info he needed, his bedside manner relaxed. That's good for me.

"It's safer that way."

He nods. "There was an interesting anomaly during the procedure . . . I had to keep giving you anesthesia because your system shook off the drugs much faster than I've ever seen, even in species two or three times your size. Is there something I should know?"

Xirol steps forward into my line of sight, then. "As long as she's healthy, Doc, you don't need to know more than you already do. How you feeling, Jax?"

"Like I had my face cut off." My words are slightly muffled, but Xirol laughs.

The doc accepts the rebuff. "Fine. I need to keep you overnight. Tomorrow, I'll call an aircab . . . and you can program the destination yourself."

Loras gave me Legate Flavius's address before we split up, so I'm ready to catch up with Vel, find out what I missed, and do some recon. My head is fuzzy, though, so I'm barely coherent as the surgeon goes on, "I did the Rejuvenex treatment as well. I think you'll like the results."

Dammit. I don't want to turn into my mother. I can't stay focused; my head swims, and I wink out again.

In the morning, the doctor removes my bandages, and he stares at me, mouth half-open. Finally, he says, "You're not human."

It's the kind of remark I'd expect from anyone who knew I'd been shot in the heart . . . and survived on an artificial pump until they could clone me a new one. The nanites don't want to let me die. This physician is just going by my recovery rate, though, and the way I reacted to the anesthetic. And that doesn't make me feel better about the tiny biotech running amok in my veins.

"I am," I reply. "Mostly. The *slightly not* part doesn't concern you. Destroy all my blood samples and medical records, any tests you might've done before you operated."

Xirol steps toward the doctor; he doesn't speak, just lends his presence to the request. "She's La'hengrin, Doc. Adaptive physiology, accelerated metabolism. Can't you tell by looking at her?"

Curiosity wars with compliance as the man considers. Xirol moves his hand to his weapon, flicks the strap away from his knife. The surgeon must know that Xirol will kill him before he can summon help.

Hoping to defuse the situation, I add, "If you don't, you'll have the resistance after you, as well as Nicuan nobles."

"No," Xirol says softly. "The resistance is right here. And I'll take care of business if he doesn't want to work with us again. Tie up loose ends, so to speak." Until this moment, I didn't know Xirol could be terrifying as well as funny, but a shiver runs down my spine.

"Very well," the doc snaps.

I say, "Do it now, while we're here."

Under my watchful gaze, the surgeon follows my instructions. "Happy now?"

"I'm not *un*happy. Call the aircab and have it meet us out front."

The clinic is housed in an unassuming structure, five kilometers from the Imperial palace. Nicu Quintus doesn't merit its own emperor, but they do have a ruling governor who takes precedence over everyone else, even princes of noble houses.

With a wave to the annoyed doctor, I draw my coat on. No uniform, just plain black shirt and trousers that could come out of any wardrober in the city. My hair feels odd, silky, on the back of my neck. I give my head an experimental toss, and I'm astonished at how it floats. The esthetician must've given me a treatment that straightened and changed its texture.

I don't like it at all. It's not me.

But I'll deal.

Xirol follows me out. The lift is fast; it gives a view of the whole street as I zoom down. By the time I reach the ground floor, the aircar hovers at the platform out front.

He pauses. "This is where we part ways, Jax. I have my assignment waiting."

"Thanks again for staying with me."

"You'd do the same for me."

Absolutely, I would. Because good-byes are hard, even when you expect to see the person again, I run toward the aircar without looking back. Inside, there's no driver, just a bot built into the front to give the impression that you're not trusting your life to a VI . . . though you totally are.

I input the address. I'm committed now. No going back.

CHAPTER 36

Legate Flavius lives well.

His home is three stories, enclosed by a tall stone fence capped with metal spikes. He has top-notch security, drone cameras flying to survey the property and report back to his centurions. This man has people, friends. For the first time, I come near to panic. As a bounty hunter, Vel did this often, but always with more prep time. He spent months learning his prey, discerning the best way to slide into their lives.

I made one stop before coming here. Fortunately, the merchant needed the sale bad enough not to ask for identification when I presented my credit spike. Now I'm wearing a jeweled collar like Xirol described. It's beautiful, and it covers my tat, but it also makes me feel servile, like someone could hook a ring and leash to it. Which is fine for people who do that sort of thing for fun, less so for those who don't have a choice in the matter.

Tiana opens the door when I ring. She shows no hint of recognition; but then, why would she? In the days since I saw her last, I have discarded everything that made me Jax.

"I'm here to see the legate."

"Do you have an appointment?"

I shake my head. "He'll want to see me."

Her mouth firms into a white line, and I see her judging the latest acquisition, hating the subservient La'hengrin female she thinks I am, now that she's free. I've found we hate most in others what we can't stand about ourselves. She received the cure from Farah while I was having the procedure done, and she's agreed to stay on to help Vel. Though she might disagree, Tiana is already a warrior, fighting for her people in the best way she can.

"I'll announce you."

Maybe it would expedite matters, but I don't tell her who I am. If this goes wrong, she can't betray what she doesn't know. Such a pragmatic dispensation of secrets and lies, but it's the mantra of the resistance. Yet I don't want her to despise me, so I whisper, "I'm resistance. Here to help."

Tiana cuts me a quick look, then smiles. I can tell she assumes I'm a free La'hengrin, recruited for reasons unknown to her, but it's more comforting than thinking I'm a slave. More cheerful now, she escorts me to an enormous room with a vaulted ceiling, decorated in antiques and expensive touches. Reminds me of my mother's formal salon, before we left New Terra for that extended vacation when I was thirteen. My father hardly ever ventured in there; he said it made him nervous. That's how I feel right now though not because of the décor. The wait feels interminable before she returns.

"He'll be with you presently. Would you care for refreshments?" She's polite even if she despises seeing her sisters in this condition.

"Thank you, no."

While I wait, I examine various paintings and objets d'art. The legate had good taste in home interiors if he furnished the place himself. If not, he had the sense to hire someone who does.

At last, I hear footsteps in the tile hallway. I turn with a smile that doesn't feel natural, as if my skin belongs to someone else, and draw up short. The centurion standing in the doorway is most definitely *not* Vel. He's short and stocky with broad shoulders and a chest thickened through physical conflict. Pocked skin, a smashed nose, and a thin-lipped mouth give him a sinister aspect.

"You have some nerve coming to the legate's house uninvited." I can't place the accent, but it's not as refined as most Nicuan voices. This one fought his way up. That makes him tenacious—and a pain in the ass.

Vel needs to get rid of him.

I arch a brow. "Pardon me?"

"You heard me. But since you don't seem to grasp the obvious, I'll spell it out. Whores aren't welcome in the residence during the day." His muddy gaze rakes me from head to toe, and it's so intrusive, I feel like covering up. "I can see why you think he'd make an exception for you, though. You're a pretty, pretty piece."

I'm fragging exquisite. This face was expensive. But that's not the point.

He takes my silence for an admission of guilt. "What's wrong, darling? Did you really think you'd get away with this?"

"The legate is expecting me," I tell him.

"Of *course* he is. Don't worry. If you make me happy, I won't tell anyone."

I can't kick his ass. I mean, I probably can, but I shouldn't. The legate wouldn't be interested in a woman with mad ass-kicking skills. By the images the doctor showed me, he went for fragile, helpless types. They likely made him feel less an abject failure as a man. So physical conflict is out unless I kill the centurion, and having a member of the legate's household go missing so shortly after an attack on his country estate, well, that wouldn't sell anybody on Vel's cover.

Think, Jax.

"I don't think the legate would like that," I say humbly.

"As if you truly know him, despite that pretty collar around your throat."

"I can't fight you," I say, because that's how a La'hengrin female would respond. "But you do not have permission to touch me."

Not that those words have ever done any good.

His face hardens. "Then I'll have you taken up for trespass. And they'll be rough on a beauty like you in the penal stations. I can be sweet. Gentle, even."

I draw in a shallow breath, like I'm scared. And this bastard responds. He *likes* women to be frightened. It's disgusting; he preys on the La'hengrin females in his care. I wonder how many times he's pestered Tiana.

Before I decide what to do, more steps ring out, and the centurion shakes his head. "You're in it now. Too late to keep this between you and me."

Vel steps into the doorway, clad in legate skin. He leans with careless disdain, arms folded across his chest. How did he perfect the mannerisms? Maybe there were vids for him to watch, here. The legate strikes me as the sort of man who would document his achievements, however small.

"What's the meaning of this, Cato?"

"Nothing to worry about," the centurion replies. "I have the problem in hand."

"It sounded to me as if you were importuning one of my guests."

The centurion pales. "I thought—"

"That is the trouble. You did *not* think. I heard you blackmailing this woman for sexual favors. If you come within three meters of her, I *will* kill you. Is that perfectly clear?"

"Yes, Excellency."

"Get out of my sight."

I swear, the centurion almost pisses himself in fleeing the room. Vel shuts the door behind him, then crosses to me; he looks perfectly at home in the legate's skin. It's a gift he has, emulating mannerisms, and his sophisticated vocalizer does the rest.

He moves to embrace me; as he leans in, he whispers, "Glad you're here, Sirantha."

I hug him back. "Even if I'm not myself?"

"That will take some getting used to."

I cock my head, realizing his speech patterns are different. He sounds less like himself, more . . . human. When he impersonated Doc, his only mistake was calling me Sirantha, as nobody else does. To this day, Vel's still the only one who uses my first name. With him, I don't even mind, though it's a sore point with others because it reminds me of my mother and the way she dropped my full name whenever I pissed her off.

"I hate it," I mutter. "One look, and your guard assumed I'm helpless."

"That may come in handy."

Staying close to him because I don't know what the situation is, I murmur into his ear, "Is the house secure? Have you swept for spyware?"

He shakes his head, then nods, answering my questions in sequence. *Great.* That means someone is spying on us already. Well, on the *old* legate.

"Have you presented your evidence to the prince?" That question I can ask in normal tones. It doesn't break cover.

"Not yet. It took me several days to get an appointment, but he's agreed to see me at the end of the week."

"I'm sure he'll be fascinated."

I need to decide what kind of character I'm playing. La'hengrin females aren't all the same, despite their shared circumstance. So is she quiet, meek, demure, silly? Given what I know of the late legate's predilections, she'd likely be all of the above—or at least capable of pretending in order to keep him happy. Belatedly, I realize I don't have a name.

"I hope to earn new rank and prestige with this revelation."

I hope we learn about weapons caches, troop movements, and planned strikes against the resistance. But that won't happen overnight. First, Vel has to ingratiate himself with the prince and get appointed to the Imperial War Council. Then we'll have access to all kinds of data that we can forward to our people—and in time, bring this struggle to an end.

Nicuan forces aren't numerous, but they control the credits and tech. Once the cure circulates fully, we'll outnumber the enemy. Sufficiently demoralized, they'll surrender and withdraw. But not without some bloody battles, first.

All in due time.

I raise my brows at Vel. "You didn't introduce me to your centurion."

It would help if I had a mental connection with him, but we can't do the silent talking. Fortunately, he's skilled at reading subtext. He makes a flourishing gesture toward the door.

"He didn't deserve the honor. Let's go where we can be more private."

Hopefully, he means to a room that's not bugged. He escorts me to his bedchamber, which is enormous. Like the rest of the house, it looks expensive but tasteful, but the red-and-gold color scheme doesn't suit Vel. Not that it matters.

Once he shuts the door, I ask, "We're clear?"

"Yes. We can speak freely in here. Flavius has a white-noise generator installed in the walls, running continuously."

"Which interferes with any spyware?"

"Precisely."

"I guess he wasn't an exhibitionist."

Vel smiles with Legate Flavius's face; and that's just *so weird* that I have no words. The man annoyed the shit out of me, then I saw his corpse on a rainy night in the provinces. "No, the legate had other perversions."

"Do I want to know?"

"No."

"It's not important anyway. What I was driving at downstairs . . . have you told anyone about me yet? Come up with a backstory or a name?"

He shakes his head. "I thought it would be better to leave that in your hands."

"Yeah, it will be easier for me to remember details I invent."

"I suspected as much. Are you ready to begin, Sirantha?"

I nod. It's time to start the next phase of the war.

CHAPTER 37

Moving into the town house proves painless.

The legate has many servants, but Vel promotes Tiana to the head of the household. Such a move would make everyone think he'd selected a new sex toy, except my presence scotches that gossip. Cato leads the surviving centurions, but they bunk in separate quarters behind the main residence. He passes me in the hall with dark looks that promise trouble.

While waiting for Vel to return, I use the wardrober to design exotic outfits. It's hard to think about fashion when I know my squad is fighting without me, but I can serve best here, now. Plus, ex-Flavius's accounts can stand the strain; it's not like he needs credits anymore. The time I spend waiting I use to write my character background. Mishani was taken into service when she was a child, and her *shinai*-bond has passed three times. Legate Flavius took one look at her and fell into a deviant sort of love that permits no distance, requires total ownership.

Pretty clothes can only take me so far. Once I have enough dresses, I sprawl on Vel's bed, pretending I'm not nervous. Mishani would be worried about his safety due to what it meant for her *shinai*-bond. The La'hengrin don't enjoy riding the winds of fate, tossed wherever whimsy dictates. I'm anxious for different reasons. *Hope the meeting goes well.*

I couldn't accompany him, of course. I'm eye candy and not privy to important political business. Nicuan nobility is patriarchal to the point of aggravation, especially for those of us who were born peen-free. So I wait in the legate's bedroom, where I'm sure nobody's spying on me. My room adjoins through the shared bath, but I don't have white-noise generators in my walls.

I flick on the vid to see what local news has to say about the rebellion. A pretty, dark-haired Nicuan presenter is speaking when I tune in. "There has been trouble in the provinces, but the governor's office reports there is no cause for concern. The so-called LLA, or La'heng Liberation Army, is 'a passel of shepherds who lack both equipment and leadership. The centurions will put an end to this resistance, which is nothing more than a call to anarchy.' "

"That's what you think," I tell her.

I switch the feed to a film already in progress. Ironically, it's the one I watched in the mountains with my squad. The images on screen bring with them a host of bittersweet memories. Timmon and Eller have already fallen; how many more brave men will we lose before this war ends?

The bedroom door bangs open, startling me. Cato looms in the doorway, his eyes threaded red. Even from here I smell the stench of whatever he's been drinking. "Something's not right," he snarls. "The legate's changed too much. He and I used to go out, taking the choicest La'hengrin whores, and now I'm supposed to believe you're enough to sate him? I don't. There's something wrong."

Shit. The mission could unravel here. I roll off the bed, putting it between us, and look surreptitiously for a weapon. He slams the door behind him. *Good.* That means privacy.

"Don't run. I want to talk to you."

Talk. Yeah. I'm sure that's what he has in mind.

Cato lunges toward me, but I wheel around behind him. The minute I fight back, he'll know I'm either not La'hengrin, despite my appearance, or that I've taken the cure. Either way, it means he can't be allowed to leave this room alive. He'll tell anyone who'll listen about the spy in the legate's household. I have to take care of this problem before it escalates.

The centurion throws a sloppy punch. If he weren't drunk, it would have connected. As it is, I feel the breeze in the near miss. Nearby, there's a slender crystal lamp. I smash it into shards so glass litters the ground between us.

"Wrecking the place won't save you, love. Nobody will come to your aid. I'm in charge here, whatever the legate told you. He's forgotten, but I'll remind him."

What the hell. Something in his tone suggests Cato has some hold over Flavius, blackmail material maybe. He's ready to beat the shit out of me; I see the glint of anticipation in his gaze. I'm to pay for the humiliation he's suffered.

I don't think so.

Under the pretext of self-abasement, I drop to my knees and palm a pointed shard. He makes a fist and draws back his arm just as I slice his hamstring. His scream of pain is lost in the white-noise generator. He was right when he said nobody will come, no matter what goes on in the legate's chamber. He lands a glancing blow on my cheek, and even injured he's strong enough that my head snaps back. I roll into the fall and grab his ankle, then tug with all my might. His injured leg buckles; the centurion drops hard on his side, and I press my advantage, diving across his thrashing body with all my strength. With a slash of the razor-sharp shard, I finish him quickly though there's a bloody mess by the time I'm done. Mary, what am I supposed to do with the body? Shaken, I cover the corpse with a sheet and wait for Vel. He'll help me dispose of it.

I shower, desperate to get the red off myself. The next two hours are incredibly unnerving; by the time Vel returns, I'm mad with impatience. He approaches with a spring in his step, which makes me think the meeting went well. Rising, I greet him at the door as Mishani would. He brushes my cheek with his lips, and they feel real enough, if cool and dry. I imagine how it was for him, living a lie for so many turns on Gehenna. I don't think I could do it.

Before we can talk about how it went with the prince, we have a crisis to resolve.

"Buried any bodies lately?" I ask.

He tenses, noticing the disarray in the room beyond. "What happened?"

I summarize, and he mutters a curse. "I'm sorry. I thought he was sufficiently cowed."

"Apparently they had subtext in their relationship. Nothing we could've known."

"Let's get him out of here. Tiana can serve as the lookout." Without delay, he calls for the housekeeper, who smiles when she realizes who's dead.

Tiana beams at Vel. "You can plant him in the garden out back. He'll do more good fertilizing the flowers than he ever did in life."

It takes another hour to do as she suggests, then clean up the evidence.

Back in his room, I ask, "What will you tell the other centurions?"

"That he got a better offer."

"Good enough. How did it go?" I feel odd being so calm about what we've just done.

"See for yourself." Vel fiddles with the comm suite, and then queues up a vid, taken from his ocular cam.

Fantastic. Though I knew he planned to try, I wasn't sure if it would work through the camouflage; the picture looks relatively clear, just a thin veil that blurs the image. The sound is a bit muffled, as the mic is implanted in his skull, but with a few taps on the control panel, he renders it audible. I settle in to watch the log.

There are a few wasted moments, where Vel's forced to cool his heels in the antechamber while somebody, probably a secretary or personal assistant, stares at him with a superior smirk. Then, at last, he's escorted to the great one's presence. Prince Marcus is a small man with a receding hairline and a weak chin. He's a little overfed, smug, and he wears too much brown, along with an impatient expression. From his reaction, he's not thrilled to see Legate Flavius. Vel is correct in his manners; he's been studying protocol while I got a new face.

"What do you want, Flavius?" The noble's tone says, *This better be important.*

"As you may know, my country estate was attacked some days ago."

"Rebels?" the prince asks without real interest.

"I wish it were that cut-and-dried. It was Legate Arterius."

The other man's attention sharpens; he steeples his hands. "Those are serious allegations. I hope this isn't some posthumous power play."

"I have evidence of a plot to discredit both of us and commence Arterius's ascent to your title. May I forward them to your handheld?"

Marcus nods, but I can see he doesn't believe this story . . . until he starts reading. Wisely, Vel edited out all the damning information that shows how the ex-Flavius colluded with his boy Arterius to see Marcus executed for treason against the empire. On La'heng, that takes some pretty serious disloyalty, as the current emperor, happily wallowing in his own importance on Nicu Tertius, doesn't give a rat's ass what goes on here.

"This is . . . unconscionable." When the prince glances up from the documents, he's shaking with rage. "What transpired at your estate? I want every detail."

Vel outlines the situation with judicious excision. The firefight rages between his house guards and the enemy centurions, no resistance involvement. In the end, only Flavius and his faithful servant Tiana make it out of the inferno alive. The way he tells the story, it's riveting, and by the halfway mark, Marcus is leaning forward for the next revelation.

"So many brave centurions must be commemorated," he declares after the finale. "In light of their sacrifice, it would be my privilege to host a party in their memory. You will be my honored guest, of course."

"You do me too much courtesy, Your Highness."

Marcus shakes his head. "You have not sought to profit by this in any measurable way. I erred in my judgment of you, Flavius. Any other man would have been on my doorstep, the moment this occurred, demanding restitution. Not you."

I glance at Vel, who pauses the vid. "Restitution?"

"The prince employed Legate Arterius, which means he bears some responsibility for his actions. There is legal precedent for Flavius to require his country estate to be rebuilt, for the prince to pay the cost of new centurions."

"But you didn't do that."

Vel grins at me, an actual grin, starting the footage again. "Watch and learn, Mishani."

"*Don't* call me that."

"I had to put my house in order, Your Highness. There were families to be notified, regrets to be expressed."

Prince Marcus reacts with tangible surprise that Flavius did the proper thing first, so the guy must've been a right bastard. "One never knows how another will react to adversity," he says, shaking his head.

I understand the con, now. If Vel hadn't fended off the attack at such high cost, Marcus would have been next. Because he asked for nothing, the prince feels like he owes him something. The repayment will come in favors, not in credits, but that serves our purpose far better.

"I wish I had never been tested," Vel replies gravely.

The prince inclines his head. "As do I. But history is ever littered with tales of men whose reach exceeded their grasp."

"I shouldn't keep you further, Your Highness. Thank you for making time for me today."

"It was my pleasure, Flavius." His body language has changed over the course of the conversation. Irritation has yielded to gratitude and genuine regard. "I'll be in touch regarding the banquet, invitation by courier forthwith."

"Thank you." In a subtle touch of flattery, he backs out of the room. It's a nicety expected only in the presence of the emperor, so Prince Marcus rarely sees it, I bet.

Then the recording ends, bringing static to the screen. Vel cuts it off. "And now you're up to speed."

"You're still talking like Flavius."

"Does it bother you? I find it's best to stay in character. Reduces the chances I'll make a mistake later."

"Not really. It's just . . . odd. You're a bit of an actor, aren't you?"

He ducks his head, as if embarrassed. "Maybe a little."

"You're good at so many things. I just have grimspace." Saying the word sends an ache curling through me.

"It's a result of a long life span. You'll pick up lots of skills as we rub along. You've already trained in combat, weapons, and gunnery."

I pause, realizing he's right. The days when I was only fit

for jumping have passed. Now when I return to the star roads, it will be out of love, not necessity.

Tiana taps on the door. She still doesn't know who I am, but she's a kind person who deserves better than she's gotten out of life so far.

"Do you want supper at the usual time?" she asks.

"Please."

Tiana dips at the knees, then hurries away. Household chores don't require backbreaking labor in the city as they do in the outlying villages, but I hate that she doesn't have other options.

Once she's gone, I ask, "Do you think Cato bothered her?"

"Not anymore," he observes. "In other news, apparently everyone is talking about my reform. The other nobles are dying to meet you."

"I can't wait," I mutter.

CHAPTER 38

"How do I look?" I ask, twirling.

"Like someone else," Vel replies.

It's an accurate answer. I didn't expect flattery from Vel, who has no taste for human beauty. The day of the party has dawned at last, and I'm wearing a deep blue gown with sparkles affixed to it. I don't know when I ever dressed up this much. The old Jax partied a lot, but she didn't circulate among high society. I was a staple of the midnight bounce for misbehavior in various bars across the galaxy. This is outside my experience. Fortunately, my stint as a diplomat taught me some refinement. I should pass as Vel's arm candy.

"Good enough. Ready?"

He offers his escort out to the waiting aircar. This one isn't available for public hire, and it's larger than most, with a capacious backseat and a driver. He's a servant under Tiana's dominion, but they don't know about our masquerade. I have mixed feelings about that; I want to tell every La'hengrin I meet about the cure and how they can join the resistance, but some of them might be indoctrinated loyal drones; they could expose us to our enemies. It's a tough call. But then, there's never any guarantee about who you can trust.

I slide into the back, careful to arrange myself like a lady. Vel hands me his handheld. "Study these four men. I need you to charm them."

This isn't the first time I've read dossiers, but I can use a refresher on Prince Marcus, his nephew Gaius, Drusus . . . the Imperator of the Guard, and Sextus Varro, the governor himself. Tonight, I'll be rubbing elbows with the brightest lights on Nicu Quintus. *Assholes.* As the aircar pulls away, I skim what Vel knows about my targets. This mission will be tricky, as I need to captivate them without making them think I intend to cheat on Legate Flavius, my lord and master.

"Any advice?"

"Start with Gaius. He should be the most accessible."

Still reading, I nod. "It looks like he landed a courtesy position in the governor's office, thanks to his uncle. Nepotism is the best."

"Isn't it, though? I'll keep an eye on you, but I'll try not to get in your way."

I can't get used to how different he sounds, how thoroughly he's analyzed Flavius's speech patterns and adopted them as his own. I don't mention it, however, because the aircar isn't certified surveillance-free. This conversation, the legate's enemies would ascribe to the political scheming natural to Nicuan nobility.

"Noted."

For the rest of the trip, I refresh my memory on what each man is interested in and how I can use that knowledge. I've never played the femme fatale before, never had the sort of beauty that made it feasible. This should be . . . interesting. The driver hovers beside the balcony on the second story designated for VIP arrivals. A waiting servant in black formalwear swings the gate open to secure against the side of the car.

When the ramp clicks into place, I step out, skirt in hand. With a deliberate mental reminder, I take delicate steps, skirt raised a bare centimeter above my sparkly, ridiculous shoes. Vel alights behind me, one hand on the small of my bare back, and it's easy to forget that his skin isn't real—that there are claws beneath the surface. He gives no sign of hesitation; he specializes in slipping into someone else's life.

I skim the gathering beyond the wide archway. This level of the governor's mansion has been designed like a garden—with no expense spared to keep the illusion in place. Out-of-season flowers have been nurtured in glasshouses, beneath costly vita-bulbs. The red blooms sit in ornate vases, cut for this occasion, perfuming the air with a sickly sweetness. All around me, everyone is well fed and richly dressed. One woman wears enough jewels to build everyone new cottages with solar panels in the first village we visited. Then I swallow my anger because Mishani would be impressed, awestruck even. She's a humble La'hengrin mistress, elevated by the legate's desire. I widen my eyes, skimming the colorful gowns and the men in suits that speak of their rank.

"There's Gaius," I murmur. "Introduce me?"

Vel wraps an arm around me. "We must pay our respects to the prince first, my sweet."

It's a gentle correction, but my cheeks flame, just as Mishani's would. Disappointing him means the difference between a pampered life and abject poverty. If he sells her *shinai*-bond, all this comfort and security goes away. The girl I'm pretending to be would never forget it, so I need to seem anxious, eager to please. Nicuan men seem to like a whiff of desperation wafting about their women.

"Yes, of course," I say softly.

The crowd parts for Vel as I can't imagine it ever did for the real legate. Perhaps it's as a result of his new standing. Farther in, I spot the prince chatting with three beautiful women, all of whom are taller than he is. Not that he appears to mind. Prince Marcus lifts a hand when he sees Vel, beckoning him over.

"Ah, here is our guest of honor. Flavius, have you met—" Marcus supplies the women's names, but I don't bother to memorize them.

"A pleasure." Vel bows over each hand in turn, with distance in his manner.

The prince favors me with a warm, slightly disturbing smile. "And this must be your lovely Mishani. There is talk, you know, Flavius."

"Is there, Your Highness?" He affects surprise.

"The rumor is making the rounds that you intend to give

this girl your name." Though the prince's tone is playful, his manner is guarded.

"Stories always proliferate," Vel says dismissively. "Take a knee, little one."

On cue, I offer an obeisance similar to the one I learned for the Grand Administrator on Ithiss-Tor, adapted for the different state occasion, of course. By the prince's expression, he approves. When I straighten, he's beaming.

"Oh, she *is* lovely. No wonder you can't bear to let her out of your sight."

"That's an exaggeration, I fear."

"But I've heard she shares your quarters," the prince says archly.

Heard from whom? With some effort, I keep my face blank. Mishani wouldn't respond unless addressed directly though I hate being talked about as if I'm a piece of furniture. This is what Loras dealt with all those turns. No wonder he's so angry.

Cato, I decide. The centurion wasn't loyal to his legate; power games go on at all levels of Nicuan society. He did some damage before he died, but we can control the fallout.

"A man likes certain comforts close at hand," Vel answers lightly.

The prince nods. "So true. And it's less expensive than renting a house for her. If you had a wife, it wouldn't work, but I admire your ingenuity, Flavius. I wish I still had such autonomy." His avid gaze lingers on my smooth skin.

I fight the urge to cover up.

"Yes, marital alliances do curtail a man's freedom, but from what I hear, you profited handsomely from your union."

Prince Marcus brightens, doubtless reflecting on the number of credits in his bank account, brought by the wife who doesn't seem to be present. "This is true."

"If you don't mind, Your Highness, we'll pay our respects elsewhere and stop monopolizing your attention."

That sounds like heavy flattery for me, but the prince only nods: *Yes, of course, everyone in the room is waiting for five minutes with me.*

What a jackass.

Vel leans in to whisper, "Well done."

"I didn't *say* anything."

"Exactly. The prince's wife is a harridan, never stops nagging. They moved into separate houses after six months."

"Why don't they terminate the union?"

"Too many political ramifications and potential financial complications."

"So a pretty girl who does whatever he wants and doesn't talk back probably constitutes his fondest dream."

Vel smiles. "I suspect he envies me right now." He pauses, drawing me to the side, so a couple of party guests can sweep past us, glittering and laughing too loud.

The music is soft, more background than sharp focus, but there are a few dancers. I spy Gaius among them. He's young, perhaps twenty-five turns, and taller than his uncle. He has a round face that makes him look younger and a little extra flesh around the middle. He might even be attractive if he didn't seem so nervous. As he maneuvers his partner on the floor, his forehead beads with sweat, and he stumbles twice, just while I'm watching him.

"The kid's a mess," I whisper.

"Local gossip has it that his mother sent him away from Nicu Tertius in disgrace. He wanted to marry a maid, or something shocking like that." Irony in the last sentence. "She hoped his uncle could cure his democratic notions."

He's not the lazy young wolf I expected. I thought he'd be the easiest mark, but with this new information, I must reconsider my approach.

Then an idea strikes. "Go look for Drusus or the governor. I've got Gaius."

CHAPTER 39

When the dance ends, I'm standing on the edge of the floor, wearing my best *I'm alone and frightened* look. The face the doctor gave is lovely enough to draw Gaius's gaze—and when nobody comes to claim me, he pauses, hesitant. My gaze meets his, equally timid, then skims away, because clearly I'm not worthy to look upon the prince's nephew.

Naturally, he joins me. "Are you here with someone?" His voice is a pleasing tenor, soft enough that I can barely hear him over the music.

"The legate said he would be back directly . . ." I trail off with uncertainty that invites him to be decisive.

"Would you like to dance with me then?" It's an invitation, not a demand.

Maybe Gaius isn't a Nicuan noble at all. If he was switched at birth, it would explain so many things. I incline my head and offer my hand, which he takes. He seems surprised, like even submissive females regularly reject him.

The music commences; the dance is more graceful and ceremonial than anything I ever did in a spaceport bar, but I follow his lead without trouble. At this moment, my body feels younger than it has in turns, and that's disconcerting.

That little twinge in my knee has gone away entirely, and I can't feel where I dislocated my shoulder. The doctor was probably referring more to taut skin and perky breasts when he said I would like the Rejuvenex results, but it's nice not to have those little aches. It also feels like I'm living in someone else's skin, and for the first time, I think, *This is what it's like for Vel.*

For a few moments, there's silence between us. He's counting steps, I think, and I'm playing the shy ingénue. But to get anywhere, I can't be mute, so I murmur, "Thank you for asking me. I don't know anyone."

"Your escort shouldn't have left you. These parties can get a bit . . ." He trails off as if at a loss for a word that won't shock me.

Which is rather hilarious, considering that Mishani sleeps with Legate Flavius in return for her room and board. So it's not like the sweet young thing doesn't know the score; unfortunate necessity dictates her actions within the confines of the *shinai*-bond. Yet I play along. Gaius needs to feel like a hero. At a glance, I can tell he's rather broken, sad, and feeling worthless. I might be able to use that.

"You're kind."

"Not really." But he's smiling now, maybe because I've been nice to him. "I'm Gaius, by the way."

"Mishani."

"Which legate . . . ?" Awkward, leading question.

"Flavius." It's not hard to let a little trepidation slip into my eyes. "I don't know where he went."

"If he's looking for you, I'll explain how you came to be with me." Evidently, Gaius understands that nobles can be irrational and hotheaded. He doesn't want to see me beaten for an imaginary infraction.

"You might get in trouble," I say softly, because Mishani doesn't know about Gaius's connections. He likes that because he thinks she danced with him on the strength of his smile.

"No, I'll handle it, don't worry."

"What do you do?" A harmless question, and I'm curious how he'll answer.

"I work in the governor's office."

Truth, then, but not all of it—there's no mention of his

uncle, the prince. Which means Gaius wants to be liked for himself.

"You must do important work." Mary, I'm already tired of this girl, with her wide eyes and breathy voice.

"Not as much as you'd think," he mutters.

So he's discontent. I file that away as potentially useful information and cock my head as if bewildered.

He smiles down at me. "Never mind."

"Have you been here long?" I ask.

He won't tell me about the scandal or why he ended up here during this dance, but he needs a confidante. With skillful management of our encounters, I can become that person.

"Since just before the troubles."

That's what Nicuan nobility calls the growing insurrection that will end with nothing short of complete expulsion of enemy forces. They don't realize how serious the situation is despite the planetary lockdown. Because there are glittering rooms full of expensive art and purchased women with painted faces, they think everything can continue as it always has. Most have no idea what's going on in the provinces.

"You can't go home then," I say with real sympathy.

He shrugs. "I couldn't anyway."

"Oh." Mishani wouldn't pry, so I finish the dance in silence.

When he escorts me to the edge of the dance floor, Vel is waiting with arched brows. "I told you I would be right back, Mishani."

Oh, he's good.

Gaius steps up, as promised. "It's my fault. I implored her to favor me with a dance."

Only then does Vel pretend to recognize him. "Of course. Anything for Marcus's nephew."

"The prince is your uncle?" I shrink back toward Vel, like I'm unworthy to be in the presence of such greatness. Maybe I have a bit of theatrical talent, too.

"Yes," Gaius admits.

"It was a pleasure." Vel steers me away.

I cast a quiet look over one bare shoulder. Gaius stands gazing after me with flattering intensity. Young men can be so tiresome in that respect. They fall in and out of love on the weight of a shared glance or a touch on the arm, constant as the wind.

"How did you pass the time while I danced?" I'm careful to keep my questions innocuous, in character for the girl I'm pretending to be.

"I spoke at length with the Imperator."

"I don't know him. Is he important?"

Vel smiles, the indulgent expression of a man who thinks the woman beside him is an adorable idiot. "Very. Dance with me." Not a question. He owns Mishani, after all, and her compliance is a given.

Yet I'm surprised as he leads me out. I figured we'd go after the governor next, but on second thought, this makes more sense. He can't make a beeline for all the important men in the room. The machinations will be noticed instead of taken as normal social interaction.

He draws me against his shoulder with an expertise I shouldn't find surprising, and yet I do. "I didn't know you danced."

"You've barely scratched the surface of my skills, my sweet." It's a reminder to be Mishani, not Jax.

I school my features into starry amazement, and he chokes a laugh. *Aha, the perfect infiltrator has a weakness.* Maybe I shouldn't be amused right now, but I've discovered I don't mind being undercover. At least, not all of it. I wouldn't want to do it forever, but for now it's an adventure, and I've never been able to pass one up.

Vel whirls me, attracting admiring glances from those sharing the floor with us. He moves like all men want to—with bold confidence, like he doesn't give a damn about the staring. That's the sort who gets noticed.

By the time we stop, I'm breathless, and some of the shiny-eyed stuff is real. I try to picture March doing any of this and fail utterly. He's a warrior, not a spy.

Me? I'm a bit of both. I guess that's why they're both in my heart. I miss March, but I'm experienced in sealing off the sorrow and not letting it interfere with my mission.

"Attention," Prince Marcus calls, as I catch my breath. "As you all know, we've gathered to honor Legate Flavius, who did me a great service at vast personal cost. He has not asked for restitution, yet my conscience will not permit his heroism to go unrewarded. So it is my pleasure to announce his new rank tonight. Welcome your new primus."

The crowd applauds, some with sincerity, others with daggered looks. A congratulatory mob surrounds us, and I press up against his side. Beyond the inner circle, I spot Gaius watching us with a return of his sorrowful stare. I guess he's remembered how much his life sucks. *Poor kid. Yeah, right.* At least he's better off than the La'hengrin.

From what I know of the convoluted ranking system, a primus is higher than a legate, serving the prince directly. Which means all the legates now glaring at Vel fall under his command. The governor is above the prince because there are so many princes from various houses, and somebody has to be in charge. The Imperator ranks higher than a primus, but only in matters of national security. It's all kind of confusing, but fortunately, Mishani doesn't need to know shit about politics; that's the upside to all my doe-eyed silence.

"Speech!" someone calls.

Soon the cry is taken up and echoes through the room, until Vel steps forward with a smile, ready to meet their demand. "I'm honored that His Highness thinks me worthy of this title. I'll do my best to live up to the standard of the primus who came before me."

Prince Marcus raises his glass. "To the new primus!"

Not everyone in the room is thrilled. Even as they toast, I feel the anger and envy burning across the distance. And all the while, Gaius watches in silence.

Afterward, Suni Tarn catches my eye from across the room. He holds the look long enough for me to gather he wants to speak with me. I guess that means Loras brought him in on the op. So I run my hand down Vel's arm to catch his hand in mine. He doesn't resist when I twine our fingers together, though this is a bold move for Mishani; it's a public claim on the new primus, and it doesn't go unnoticed. Most men of rank would disassociate at once from a presumptuous La'hengrin, but he permits the move, thus stating that he returns my regard. I haven't enjoyed subtext so much since we left Ithiss-Tor. Pity the Nicuan nobles don't know how to execute a proper *wa*.

Vel lets me lead him on a meandering course toward the former chancellor and his partner, Edun Leviter. The two men are handsome in their black formalwear. Leviter wears touches of silver at his cuffs, and it's an elegant echo of his hair. By the time I reach them, they've gotten rid of the few guests who wanted to make conversation. Leviter has a way with a brow raise and a sardonic look that makes you want to crawl under the nearest rock.

"Good evening," I say.

Tarn says, "It's a pleasure to see you again."

Since I haven't met him as Mishani, he's affirming my suspicion that he knows. Loras must have anticipated our need for aid and provided intel. That's helpful. Now we can arrange a meeting with no awkward fumbling.

"I understand you have quite an art collection," Vel replies.

Leviter nods. "Suni is the connoisseur, but I appreciate beautiful things."

"If it wouldn't be too forward, perhaps Mishani and I could come to see your Durand? It is rumored to be exquisite."

"Edun and I will be leaving the city next month for an extended holiday," Tarn says, and the words sound like a warning. "So it would be best to arrange the appointment soon."

"The day after tomorrow?" Vel suggests.

"Perfect. Do you have your handheld? What's the code?" After Vel's reply, Tarn pulls his out and beams his address to the device.

"I look forward to it," I say.

"We should mingle." When we move off, Vel leaves his hand in mine, telling everyone that he won't tolerate slights to me.

It's a bold maneuver. Enemies will reveal themselves faster over my unseemly rise. They won't be able to bear that a female like Mishani has so much power over the new primus. In time, after listening to enough vitriolic whispers, Prince Marcus may come to regret his generosity, but we're not trying to build a lasting political career, only obtain access to classified information while creating dissent in the Imperial government.

This should work like a charm.

FROM: E_L
TO: [RECIPIENT_ENCRYPTED]
COMM CODE 18.255.91.23.88

Our mutual acquaintance is well, but . . . not herself. Certain permanent alterations have been made; you should be prepared for that. She's serving the cause in the best possible capacity at the moment, and due to her work—and that of another changeable individual—we hope to have eyes and ears inside very soon. That will obviously help your efforts in the field. How is the campaign going? I saw in your report that the war effort is going well in the provinces, and that five more villages should be liberated by the end of the month.

Enemy forces are suppressing our ads at every opportunity, but I find ways to get them on the air. The private comm codes are busier than ever, with La'hengrin seeking information on ways to help the resistance. The centurions have come near to taking out our broadcast centers a few times, but we've scrambled, moved the equipment just in time.

Numbers are up in terms of recruitment, especially with the last three victories. I'll forward you a list of casualties and assets once I finish the final assessment. Though it's a quiet war, and Nicuan does its best to silence all signs of trouble in the provinces, the conflict will not be won via inaction. It's only a matter of time now. I've seen countless wars, and I believe that. The people have caught fire, and they will not stop.

E. L.

P.S. I haven't been blessed with offspring, but I hear they can be trying. As I understand it, the trouble is worth it.

FROM: M
TO: [RECIPIENT_ENCRYPTED]
COMM CODE [MESSAGE BOUNCING; MULTIPLE RELAYS. ULTIMATE DESTINATION UNKNOWN]

I'm afraid to ask what you mean by "certain permanent alterations." But I suppose I'll find out. Great work with the ads. As more people get access to modern comms, they're helping immeasurably. I had a class of a hundred turn up here. Spent two weeks training them, and now they're all on assignment in the field. After the recruits leave, it feels so quiet. Empty. I'm not alone in wishing I could get out. The kid's going stir-crazy; and yeah, he's totally worth the trouble. I was just venting.

We're running short on gear. If you could get me locations on supply caches—food, weapons, anything the military may have hidden away—we need it desperately. And a number of the villages in the provinces have been cut off. The measures we took to keep the shipments running have broken down. The Nicuan are now too afraid of hijackings to risk sending the food as they used to. They'd rather let people starve than see the resources end up in enemy hands. And I understand the tactic. It's classic, as armies march on their stomachs.

I'm looking forward to that report you promised me.

M.

CHAPTER 40

Tarn and Leviter live in a sleek high-rise with excellent security.

For obvious reasons, they don't require us to pass through the scanners. That would alert the system that Vel and I aren't who we claim to be. So Tarn comes down to meet us, obviating the need for such measures. I follow him to their private lift; they have the entire top floor of the building, and the view is breathtaking, one of the best I've seen on La'heng.

He motions us to silence until we step into the apartment, then says, "You can speak freely here."

"White-noise generator?" I guess.

He shakes his head. "Edun has hacked all the spyware so it logs a variety of incredibly mundane conversations. Those tasked with keeping watch over us must think we're the dullest dogs in the world."

As Tarn mentions him, Leviter comes down the hallway into the common room. The place is furnished in minimalist design; it's not warm, but it is elegant. It suits both of them, and they appear more relaxed—for obvious reasons—than they were at the prince's bash. I take a seat before anyone else because I don't have to be Mishani right now, and it's a relief.

"You've heard from Loras?" I ask.

Leviter nods. "Yes, he gave us a full report of activity in the capital, so we can facilitate. I must admit, this has been unexpectedly entertaining."

Tarn grins at him. "You already had your hand in when I arrived." He turns to me with an amused look. "He was bored, you see. Thought it would be diverting to see what trouble he could stir up here."

"You destabilize governments for fun?" Vel asks.

Leviter shrugs. "Sometimes. If there's no paying work to be had."

That makes me wonder what crises he's perpetuated. "Who have you worked for? Or is that an *if I tell you, I'll have to kill you* question."

Tarn and Leviter exchange a look, then the former chancellor replies, "He worked for me during the war."

Even Vel seems intrigued. "Is that how you met?"

"Virtually." Tarn puts a hand on Leviter's knee. "I couldn't get involved with him openly while I was chancellor."

I raise a brow. "Why not?"

"Because I worked for Farwan." Leviter's curt response explains everything.

"You were one of their cleanup men, weren't you?" I know the type.

A frown pulls Leviter's brows together. "I was the best."

"So I put you out of work. Sorry about that." I wonder if that means he hates me. So far, he hasn't acted like he does.

He shrugs. "I always maintained diversified interests."

"I appreciate your help." I change the subject, seeing his reluctance to discuss his past further. "What news do you have?"

Tarn accepts the need to get down to business. "Loras says his mission is going well. He'd like you to be ready to move in two months."

That seems like a short time to get appointed to the war council and obtain the classified data we need. "Do they have databases?"

Leviter shakes his head. "The nobility here cling to outmoded fashions, and that includes information storage."

"So we'll need physical access." I sigh. "That makes it harder, if it's even possible at all."

"It should be, skillfully played." Leviter sits across from me, all predatory grace. It's impossible to tell how old he is, but I read no mercy or scruple in that gaze. "You've made a good start, shaken the foundations a bit."

"How would you suggest we proceed?" Vel sounds more like himself, and I'm glad for it. I've gotten used to his manners and his courtly, formal air.

Thus invited, Leviter outlines a plan of action that's Machiavellian and diabolical in its ruthless sophistication. At first, I hesitate. Gaius seems like a decent guy—for a noble—and I hate the thought of screwing his life up worse than it already is. If he's caught, or if I fail to turn him, it means the end of the whole scheme.

But the resistance needs us.

"All right," I say at last. "I'll do it."

"You're a true patriot," Leviter responds with gentle irony.

Because this isn't my home. These aren't my people. Yet I fight as if they are.

Vel pushes to his feet. "Let us look at the Durand since that is why we came."

The painting *is* exquisite. It's perfectly centered in the midst of gentle lights that reveal its beauty without damaging the aged masterpiece. It is a young man, alone in a wood. The trees around him are dark and threatening, yet, from the foliage, it seems to be springtime. There's no reason for the sense of foreboding the artist has managed to convey in subtle shadows. The subject is handsome, certainly, but he also radiates a slightly helpless air. A blanket is spread on the ground before him, with the rudiments of a meal arrayed; there is enough for two. His hand is out, extended to some person beyond the edge of the canvas. From his expression, I assume he's meeting his lover, but those gathering shadows make me think something terrible is about to happen. That's the genius of *Man, Waiting.*

"It's worth whatever you paid for it," I say softly.

Leviter chuckles. "That presumes a great deal."

"Did you steal it?" That would be a hell of a heist. A piece like this would have been in a museum, certainly, or a private collector's vault.

But the silver fox won't be drawn. "If you learn only one thing from me, let it be this. Admit nothing."

"I'll get a message to you if I hear from Loras again," Tarn puts in. "He feels it's best if I serve as intermediary. Less risk."

He's right. A meeting with Tarn and Leviter can be written off as mutual art appreciation. There's no stigma. But if anyone catches us with the head of the resistance, it's over. And despite Nicuan antipathy to technology, they still monitor the wireless bounce. Better not to take the chance.

I never thought I'd be reliant on Tarn in this fashion.

Vel and I head out, becoming Mishani and Flavius as soon as the lift touches the ground. His private car—with driver—returns us home. I don't speak, turning over the meeting in my head. Reluctance plucks at me with nervous fingers; Leviter's plan for Gaius is further than I intended to go.

He surprises me with a kiss, but I roll with it. Surprising how real his lips feel against mine, how natural the hair between my fingers. He is a good mimic; his mouth presses with authority. It's not a deep kiss, but convincing enough for our purposes. The driver is watching through the small gap in the security panel. When the vehicle stops, we break apart.

Vel guides me out of the aircar. "Come, my sweet."

Right. The chauffeur will tell the rest of the household that we couldn't keep our hands off each other on the way back. The staff has to think he's insatiable since we're in his bedroom *all* the time. But there's nowhere else to talk, here.

"Is the kissing weird for you?" I ask, once the door closes and locks behind us.

"In what regard?"

"Does it feel abnormal?"

"It is not natural to my people, so in that respect, yes."

"On Gehenna, you said when you kissed Adele, you felt nothing but pressure."

He nods. "There are no nerve endings in the faux-skin."

This isn't relevant, so I shut down my curiosity and move on. "What did you want to talk about?"

"What Leviter proposed . . . can you do it?"

"I think he was into Mishani at the party. It's not a question of whether I can."

"But you don't want to."

"It just . . . it seems wrong to make him fall in love with

me, then beg him to save me from you. The kid's here because he fell for the wrong person once already."

"For Leviter's plan to work, he must believe joining the resistance is the only way to keep you safe," Vel says. "And he must be willing to do anything for you."

"Yeah, that's the part that bothers me."

Vel may be able to get access to the information on his own. In time. But using Gaius as my cat's-paw will get the job done more efficiently. Leviter is known for such strategies. He isn't overly burdened with human empathy though his relationship with Tarn attests to the fact that he's not without emotion entirely.

Vel studies me. "Your call."

He won't make me do this. If I ruin this kid's life and break his heart, it's on me. Then I recall the La'hengrin starving in the provinces, "protected" by those who haven't lifted a finger for their welfare in fifty turns. My resolve firms. Yes, I'll sacrifice one for many.

This is war.

CHAPTER 41

It's easy to fall into a routine.

To forget the people you haven't seen for a while.

A month after my transformation, I realize I have no idea what the squad is doing, if they're safe, or if the mission—whatever it is—has been successful. That makes me feel like a traitor to the cause. I'm here in this fine house, plenty to eat, while they suffer. I've forgotten that Timmon is dead. Eller is gone as well, and the memory hits me like a punch to the gut. Surely it's not normal to adapt as fast as I do. But frag, when did I ever claim to be? Whatever, I have a job to do. If there's guilt to be dealt with, I'll ball it up and look at it later.

Today, I have my fifth meeting with Gaius. I ran into him by "coincidence" at a restaurant a few weeks back, after extensive research on his habits. I was careful not to offer too much or commit to anything. He has to believe that I'm being systematically abused . . . and that I'm too downtrodden to orchestrate my own rescue. If the boy has any chivalrous instincts, they'll go crazy this afternoon.

I close my eyes, so I don't accidentally dodge the blow. But it doesn't come. "Go on, hit me."

"I don't think I can."

"It's part of the job description. Believe me, I can tell the difference. It's the legate, hitting Mishani."

When the blow lands, I'm glad I've never pissed Vel off. Not that he ever punched me . . . not even when he was *hunting* me. Still, my ears ring, and I see stars. I taste blood. My lip is already swelling, broken against my teeth. He had to do it right before the meeting, or my nanites will obviate the damage. Gaius needs to see that my situation is getting worse—that the legate's violence has escalated.

"Thanks," I say with a distinct lisp. "I'm on my way, then."

This time, I "sneak" out of the town house, avoiding the legate's aircar. Public transport carries me to the plaza, where I meet Gaius. En route, another young man watches me with a furrow of concern. He wears a uniform, which makes him a centurion, but he doesn't look old enough to have served ten turns on Nicu Tertius. That means he's a legacy, somebody's child born on La'heng, and his father is sufficiently well connected to get him hired on without any test of skill.

There's not a lot he can do without my permission, so he sits back. I disembark a short time later, and by the time I reach the rendezvous point, the blow looks a day old; my lip has scabbed over, and the soreness dissipates somewhat. Shit, if he's late, I'll miss my—

"Mishani." There he is, right on time. He's taken care with his appearance; freshly shaved, dark hair waving down to his collar, he looks every inch the important young nobleman. When I turn, his breath catches. He takes my hands with an impetuosity he's restrained to this point.

After a moment of silent observation, he asks, "Are you all right?"

"Yes, fine." I don't meet his gaze.

"What happened?"

I offer an uncertain smile. "Things are not going as well as he wishes."

"What does that have to do with you?" he demands.

"When he's in a bad mood, I annoy him. It's not his fault."

"No man worth the name should ever treat a woman thus." He's quietly furious. With gentle hands, he touches my swollen mouth.

I can see in his boyish features that he's totally enamored

of the beautiful victim Mishani appears to be. She's everything a nascent hero needs to feel worthwhile.

"I can't leave," I whisper miserably.

"This is wrong. He's supposed to *protect* you."

Yeah, I think. *Welcome to the La'hengrin reality, Gaius.*

"He's not so bad. Let's speak of something else."

"Each time I watch you walk away, it gets harder. Knowing you're going home to someone who hurts you . . . I can't bear it." He speaks with the fierce, heedless passion of the very young.

Makes me feel ancient.

"There's nothing you can do. Can't we just enjoy—"

"If something happened to him . . . and I saved your life, then your bond would default to me, wouldn't it?"

I nod. *It would, if I were La'hengrin.*

That's where Gaius is supposed to be, emotionally. He had to come to that conclusion by himself, and it took him four weeks to get there. Vel is making progress independently, but he hasn't been appointed to the war council yet. He doesn't have the clearance he needs to get this information. I'll guide the kid, subtly.

"Come." He takes my arm, guiding me out of the plaza to the café.

We don't eat on the street, as that would offer too many opportunities for discovery. Instead, Gaius takes a private dining room, where nobody can see him romancing Legate Flavius's pet. There are no humanoid workers here, just servo-bots, which facilitates secrecy. Forbidden things offer a unique enticement.

I sit down and let him order for me, playing skittish. "I can't stay long . . ."

"Don't go," he pleads. "I'll find a way, I promise. You should be with someone who cherishes you."

At least the kid hasn't promised to marry me. He learned that much from his exile. I'm sure he thinks I'll be so grateful to have a kind master that I'll adore him until the end of our days, even after he takes a wife, gets bored with me, and treats me like an old pair of shoes. *Fragging nobles.*

"This is wrong," I say with conviction, and move as if to rise.

He stops me with a gentle hand on my arm. "I need to discredit him with an offense that merits execution. Then I'll step forward and offer you my protection."

Damn. The kid has more steel than I thought.

Hesitantly, I say, "The legate doesn't know I overheard him, but . . ."

"Tell me."

"He planted the evidence that made the prince promote him. The other legate didn't do anything wrong."

"So Flavius falsified the data trail and killed him?" Gaius's brows shoot up, and for a few seconds, I think I've overplayed my hand. "Do you have any evidence to support this?"

I shake my head sadly. "No. He's good at hiding his true face."

"What a monster."

"Maybe . . . you could do something to him . . . and blame the resistance?" That's as bold a suggestion as I dare offer.

"No, the prince wouldn't believe—unless . . ."

"Have you thought of something?"

Gaius grins. "Maybe. I could do to him what he's done to his rivals."

Good boy.

Mishani pretends to misunderstand. "You're going to invite him over, have your centurions kill him, and claim he invaded your home?"

"No, that's brutish. I'll plant sensitive information on his comm suite, then turn him in as a traitor."

My eyes widen. "So the prince will think he's working for the resistance?"

It's also ironic for obvious reasons. Once we have that "sensitive information," our mission ends, and we disappear. Gaius will be crushed.

Color touches the tops of his cheekbones. "It's only what he deserves for what he did to the other legate. And you."

I lift a shoulder in a graceful half shrug. "I am La'hengrin. Nobody cares about us."

"I do," he says. "It's not right how you're treated."

Dare I hope he means more than just me? It would be a stroke of luck to find a sympathizer in Gaius. "You could get in trouble, talking like that."

"I trust you." He lowers his voice. "Older nobles disagree, but the resistance may be more organized, more of a threat than others believe. The cure is real . . . so you might be free to choose, soon."

"Choose what?"

"How you live . . . and with whom."

"I can't even imagine." Surely that's how a young La'hengrin would respond.

"It won't happen overnight, but change is coming." All right, that *does* sound like he supports the resistance.

So I ask the question with artless candor. "Gaius, are you working with the rebels?"

"No. They wouldn't trust me. I'm part of the problem." The fact that he knows as much speaks well of him.

This revelation leaves me with an interesting dilemma. If I clue him in, he might help us without the need for subterfuge. It's also possible that he'll feel bitter and betrayed due to the emotional manipulation. Weighing both, I decide to continue with the original plan. If he steals the data, there won't be a trail linking back to him, and when the legate and Mishani perish, Gaius won't mention any confidential information packets on the man's comm suite.

However, knowing his opinions might prove helpful down the line.

"I should go," I say softly.

"But you haven't eaten anything."

"I'm not hungry. And it's hard . . ." Let him make of that what he will.

"I know," he whispers. "But trust me, Mishani. This will be over soon."

Famous last words.

CHAPTER 42

"How did you do?" I ask.

Vel had a meeting today, where he was supposed to reap the benefits of being a primus. To date, the privileges have been largely symbolic. But he radiates self-satisfaction, so I suspect it went well.

"I've been appointed to the war council. They're forwarding information regarding their fortifications and strategies."

I fly at him, and he catches me around the waist. Vel whirls me until the room spins. Tapping his shoulders, I make him stop. "I'm thrilled, but dizzy. Put me down."

"Nearly there," he says softly.

"This feels like the longest job ever."

He nods. "Time drags when you're wearing a false skin. How did your meeting go with Gaius?"

Quickly, I fill him in. He makes the connection quickly. "Between the two of us, Loras will have the information he needs to take the war to the next level."

"That's what I'm hoping. I doubt you'll get access right away to the kind of data Gaius intends to plant on you."

"Then I will glean what I can and ready preparations for our deaths."

"That sounds . . . a little disturbing."

He smiles. "Does it not? Thank you for coming with me. I never worked with a partner like this before. It is most agreeable."

"Are you kidding? I wouldn't leave you hanging."

"No," he says. "You would not."

I smile. "What should we do to celebrate?"

"Blow up the governor's palace?" He cants his head, inviting me to smile.

I do. "We have some loose ends to wrap up first."

"It is almost time. I had word from a compatriot today—"

"From the resistance?" I demand. "Tell me."

"I *am* trying."

"Sorry." I have the grace to look embarrassed.

"The cure is on course to be complete in the next six months."

"You mean all the provinces have been covered? I didn't know there were that many teams working."

"That was the plan. If we kept it quiet, the treatments would spread without interference. The Imperials pay little attention to what transpires outside the cities, so long as it does not impact their personal comforts."

"Then all of those La'hengrin will be ready to fight soon."

"Precisely."

I take a deep breath. "I'm a little scared, you know? We've been planning this for so long. What if we fail?"

"The resistance has superb strategists. The Imperials have relics of an outmoded system."

"When you put it like that . . ."

That's the last chance I have for a tête-à-tête with Vel for a while thereafter. Events accelerate, conspiring to keep us playing our roles. Social obligations keep me meek while I hope that Gaius is doing his part. I'm frustrated at my present lack of ass-kicking, but if everything aligns, I'll be on the front lines soon.

Vel plays me logs of the war council meetings. They're long and boring, mostly. As the new primus, he has to listen to all the opinions before volunteering one himself. He discovers what the enemy knows about the resistance . . . and it's terrifying. We have to find some way to keep them from acting on this intel.

I also fear we have a leak, somewhere. Fortunately, the cells are designed to minimize collateral damage. While we might lose one cell . . . and the base, the rest of us will be unharmed. Hindered, certainly, by the loss of headquarters, but the movement won't die. We can rebuild.

"We have to warn them," I say, heart in my throat. "Sasha and March are at the base."

"Already sent word to Loras through an intermediary."

"Not the incipient threat?"

"No, the means of contact do not permit such specific information. I asked for a meeting as soon as he can manage it . . . but I do not even know whether he is in the city right now. I hear things are tight in the provinces. More centurions."

"Are they fighting?"

Vel nods. I *hate* that we're not around to help. Hate it. There's nothing worse than being helpless to prevent harm from coming to those you care about.

The situation comes to a head ten days later.

"It's time," Vel tells me.

"You have the data?" I can't believe it.

"Gaius planted it in my subaccounts this morning."

"You had alarms to warn you of the intrusion?"

"Of course."

"Have you gotten everything you needed from the war council?"

"I have. Troop movements, plans. If we delay any longer, the intel will become useless."

"Time to die then." I shouldn't sound so cheerful about that, but I'm so ready to leave this life. "How does it happen?"

I spare a moment's regret for Gaius, who's going to be crushed, but if the legate's murder of his beloved Mishani makes him hate other nobles, so much the better for the cause. He might even work on our behalf, going forward.

"Murder/suicide. Tiana will help."

"She'll tearfully reveal what happened, just before the house went up in flames." I nod. "But what about an inquiry?"

"The prince will want it covered up. He will not want it revealed that he promoted a man so unbalanced that he murdered his La'hengrin lover for infidelity, then killed himself."

Mary, the guilt's going to break Gaius's head. I steel myself against that knowledge since just because this isn't true right now, it doesn't mean something similar hasn't happened, probably more than once. Better if Gaius believes—sees the corruption in the system—and acts. He needs to grow up anyway.

"We don't have much time," I say then. "I know he plans to report you at the earliest opportunity. He's desperate to be with Mishani."

"I will get ready. You collect the things we cannot leave behind."

"Do you intend to warn the centurions?"

He offers a level look. "Do you want me to?"

After the way Cato treated me? No way. His men haven't bothered me since the legate "discharged" their leader, but I have no warm feelings for them. I don't reply; instead I grab a bag and start packing. Electronics and data equipment go with us. The clothes? They can burn. Jax doesn't need pretty dresses. She's ready to put her uniform back on.

Vel moves like a ghost through the house, deploying chemicals that will make the fire look like arson, not a bomb. The containers have timers and can be released once we're out of here. I dress in dark, nondescript clothing and pull a hood over my distinctive hair. Nobody can see us walking away. It would be better if we could wait until nightfall, but Gaius won't hold his report.

Sometimes you just have to roll the dice.

Vel joins me on the sidewalk, and we move away before he clicks the button. Tiana is already waiting for us at a nearby hotel. Once the place goes up, her mission begins. I hope she's strong enough.

The smoke rises swiftly; I cast a glance over my shoulder and am astonished to see the house already engulfed in flames. There are two bodies inside, but they'll be burned so badly that not even the best scanners will be able to tell they don't belong to Legate Flavius and his lover, Mishani. At least, that's what the supplier who sold us the chemicals for the house fire claimed. It's popular among those looking to fake their own deaths.

Tiana steps out of the hotel room, looking anxious. "Are you all right?"

"We're great for dead people," I reply.

She still doesn't know it's me, but she's come to respect Mishani. Her mouth smiles, but her eyes are worried. "Did you evacuate the other servants?"

Vel nods. "They joined their assigned units. Everyone is safe."

That much is true. We got the La'hengrin out. The centurions are another story, but I doubt Tiana cares about them anyway.

"I don't know if I can do this," she says, stepping back into the room.

The door swishes shut behind us. This is a cheap place by Imperial standards, not much used except by tourists, and since the borders have been closed for so long, it's hurting for custom. Nobles looking for a quick-and-dirty afternoon use the place most. The hotel also has shitty security, which Vel can wipe and alter to fit our needs, which is why we're here.

Or more accurately, why we never were.

"We need you," I say to Tiana.

She's come a long way from the woman we met at Flavius's country estate. She took over the household, recruited the other servants, and now she's about to take on the most important mission of her life. I suspect she knows that; hence the nerves.

I go on, "There's no way this story flies without your eyewitness testimony."

"Yes, you are crucial to the plan, Tiana. To the resistance. If you would see your people free, you must act."

She draws in a deep breath, and her face loses some of the green cast. "All right. I'll go now, before I lose my nerve entirely."

I remind her, "It's natural for you to be scared. The prince will expect it. So if you're stammering, trembling, it won't matter."

"Got it," she says. "If it goes well, you won't see me until the war's over."

"I know. Thank you for everything."

"Do you have the device?" Vel asks.

She nods, and then goes forth to strike a blow for freedom.

CHAPTER 43

"Will she be all right?" I ask.

"There is a small chance that she will undergo a security scan on her way to see the prince. If so, the dormant spyware she carries may be discovered . . . and she will be executed."

My heart surges into my throat. "You knew that before?"

"Of course. It changes nothing, Sirantha. It is a risk we must take. If they do not believe that Legate Flavius is dead, if they think there is even a minuscule chance their operation has been compromised, they will change all their plans, rendering months of work useless."

"Still, we should have warned her."

"To what end?" It's a question that has no answer.

Deep down, I know he's right. And I've made the decision to sacrifice one for many already in this war. It just seems especially wrong where Tiana is concerned. She survived captivity. She lived through the cure, and now she's working for the resistance—and we're using her blind willingness . . . like the Nicuan nobles do. The comparison leaves a sour taste in my mouth.

Just then, the device crackles to life. "She must be getting close. I instructed her not to initiate it until she passed security if there was a checkpoint."

"Oh. So the scans won't detect a dormant bug?"

"They shouldn't. It will read as a small token. The electronic components are shielded, inert, until she activates it."

And by the noises I'm hearing, she has. No vid, obviously, but I hear footfalls, the rustle of fabric, and Tiana's breathing. This is good tech.

"Wait here," someone tells her curtly.

She sounds like she's trying not to cry. Good. That will sell the story.

"What is amiss?" the prince asks at length.

"Your Highness . . . the most dreadful thing . . . fire . . ." In nearly incoherent fits and starts, she babbles out the story we need the Imperials to believe: Mishani's secret lover and Flavius's insane rage.

Tiana spins the fight into a thing of tragic proportions, complete with Mishani's dying of a broken neck, then how Flavius went on a mad rampage. He set all the fires and nearly killed Tiana as well, but she ran as the flames spread, and a centurion pulled her to safety. Now he owns her *shinai*-bond, and the town house stands in ruins. She thought the prince should know immediately.

At last, she falls silent.

Does he believe her? Shit, I wish I could see his face.

"This is . . . astonishing," he says at last. "Appalling. I do appreciate your coming to tell me. I do need to handle certain . . . realities in a situation such as this. You said a centurion saved you? So you're protected? Good . . . good." He repeats the last word in a tone that makes it clear he doesn't give a rat's ass about Tiana's fate.

"He's waiting for me, Your Highness. I'm to join him at the barracks." Which is where all centurions who find themselves without a patron end up.

"Thank you. You may go." No words of sympathy for her loss or concern that she might be hurt or frightened.

She's La'hengrin, less than nothing in his eyes.

"Yes, Your Highness."

If he had been less distracted, less worried about spin control, he might've demanded corroboration from the centurion, but it's unthinkable that a La'hengrin could be wandering around telling stories without the express permission of her protector. For once, their rules serve us well.

A shushing noise tells me that Tiana has gone, and she's left the device behind, just as promised. Her part is over; she's safe. Thank Mary.

Seconds later, Prince Marcus makes a call. "It appears I have an opening in my office. Quite unexpected."

I recognize the governor's voice in the reply. "Oh? What's happened?"

Marcus repeats the story, though without the emotion or the excellent flourishes. I find his version quite plebeian, in fact, but what matters is that he bought it. Flavius and Mishani are dead.

"Gaius seems to be coming along nicely," the governor observes. "I've seen no sign of democratic bias since he came to work for me. So promote one of your other legates to primus and give Gaius an official title with my blessing. He's been my aide long enough."

That's a lucky break although not entirely unforeseen. With Gaius on the inside, there's a chance he'll hinder their movements. That is, if he didn't lie to Mishani in the hope of getting on her good side. Men sometimes do that when they're trying to impress a woman. Given a taste of power, he might forget all his scruples.

But I hope not. He's one noble I'd like to save.

Prince Marcus sounds suitably grateful. "I didn't dare hope—"

"Spare me the false coin," the governor snaps. "The wheels turn just so, and we both know it. Remember your family owes me when it comes time to reconsider my appointment."

"Of course. How shall I handle the press?"

"Accidental fire. Death by misadventure."

Marcus laughs. "The usual, then."

"Indeed."

They disconnect shortly thereafter, and the prince leaves his office. It was risky of Tiana to carry it in, but we needed confirmation that the cover story was effective. The bug will decay into splinters of metal dust, so by the time anyone encounters it, there will be no clue as to its original purpose. And that's our cue to scramble.

Vel sheds his skin and feeds the material into the recycler. He can leave no trace of what's happened in this room. To avoid attention, he rebuilds his composite average-guy face; otherwise, people would remember an Ithtorian coming out of the hotel. He's not associated openly with the resistance, but we must avoid scrutiny. I wish I could permanently change my looks with such facility, but I'll have to made do with a cloak. I'll be careful not to show my face to anyone on the way to the rendezvous.

Mary, I can't wait to see the rest of my unit.

It takes him two hours to complete the transformation—with my help. This time, he gives me a flat-edged knife, and says, "We must hurry, Sirantha."

Yeah, every minute we spend here increases the risk of discovery. Though it seems Tiana got away clean, it's better not to risk capture. She knows where she left us, after all. First rule of guerilla warfare is to camp only where your enemies cannot reach you. This hotel doesn't qualify.

At last, he's someone else, and I'm wearing a maid's attire. "You ready to hit the security room?" I ask.

He pats his pack. "Set."

I lead the way, glad to be active again. There are no words for how sick I am of playing the submissive, obedient female.

A sole Pretty Robotics worker occupies the security room. Helpful. Vel disables it with an EMP and wipes the short-term data drive while I search the security cameras for the footage that shows our arrival. Since we weren't publicly dead yet, there was no outcry; we were just another couple here for some afternoon delight. That's not shocking, completely in character with what the VI sees every day.

"Here," I say. "And there's a backup."

Quickly, efficiently, Vel corrupts the footage so it's impossible to tell who we are. This is better than deletion, which might make someone think there was a secret being kept—and credits to be had for exposing it. This? It's technical failure, and it happens often in places where the hardware isn't top-of-the-line.

"Done," Vel says.

"Let's roll."

My heart pounds frantically as I step onto the moving walk. Only the poor—of whom there are a few—and the La'hengrin use the ground transports. The moving walk takes us to the hub, where we catch an enormous land ferry to the provinces. They don't go all the way to the villages, mind. Once you hit the pastoral hub, then you walk . . . or if you're lucky, someone picks you up.

Vel uses his body as a shield, keeping everyone away from me, as I'm the weak link as we make our getaway. This run is terrifying . . . and exhilarating. I'm smiling by the time I climb onto the ferry, which rumbles and puffs like the outdated tech it is. I can't believe these beasts are still running. They're part combustion engine, part solar-powered, and they have great tires that flatten the foliage as they go. There are no roads, per se, but in a vehicle like this one, they aren't required. No pilots, either. Just a VI who knows the route by heart and will not accept deviations, regardless of rationale or request.

I take a seat at the back, and Vel slides in beside me. There are few people on the transport—just an older La'hengrin male, who has probably outlived his usefulness to his protector. Nobody goes out to the provinces if they have a choice; the cities have all the work, all the opportunity. But that's the whole problem with this system. The La'hengrin *don't* have any choice.

CHAPTER 44

When we reach the camp after hours of hiking, I'm tired. It's located in a sheltered valley that we find by virtue of coordinates on Vel's handheld. At first glance, it doesn't look like much, but as I draw closer, I see bodies and tents—it's a fully mobile encampment, nothing big or heavy. Everything can be folded and squared away in field kits.

There's a sentry. The light is behind him, dying behind the mountains in a sienna halo, blinding me to everything but his shape. He calls out, "Password?" And then levels the gun on us, just in case we don't know it.

They're taking no chances. It's unlikely Imperials could find this place without capturing one of us, but better not to risk compromising the operation. I haven't communicated with Loras in weeks, but he set up this rendezvous via Suni Tarn.

"Vector 7845," Vel responds.

"Welcome back!" The sentry turns out to be Xirol. "That you, Jax?" He peers at me; he's the only one who's seen my new face.

I nod. "Sorry, I know it's weird for you."

His face has gained lines, and he's lost his easy smile.

Which means something terrible has happened. Dread grows like a fungus in my gut.

"Go on. Loras is waiting for you."

I trudge past the picket into a small knot of tents. There are no fires burning. Instead, there are a couple of small chemical stoves that emit no rads, no smoke.

Something is cooking in a primitive-looking pot, and it smells fantastic. I realize I don't remember when last I ate.

Glancing around, I take stock further, doing a head count. This isn't just our cell . . . and I wonder what's up. I find the guerilla warlord himself sitting at a camp table with charts and maps spread before him. It's shockingly low-tech, but they can't track us through the bounce, either. This is less efficient but more secure. Once he's made all the plans, committed them to memory, the paper burns.

He looks up with a distracted smile. "Jax?"

"Yes, it's me. Brief us?" While the war rages in the provinces, our unit is now positioned close enough to strike at the capital.

He hesitates. "Our squad required augmentation. There were . . . losses."

"Who?" Vel asks.

"They caught Bannie two weeks ago. Rikir disregarded my orders and tried to save her. The Imperials executed them both quietly."

That explains Xirol's expression. "What happened, exactly?"

Loras studies me. "Xirol tried to go. Rikir restrained him physically, and we sedated X for his own protection. I didn't think anyone else was close enough to Bannie to require it. In the morning, Rik was gone. He left a note."

"What did it say?" I ask.

"That he was doing this for Xirol, who was like a brother to him. He knew Xirol would never rest until he got her back or died trying."

"Shit."

"I am so sorry," Vel says.

So who's left? I saw the sad, broken version of Xirol coming in. Zeeka waves at me from across the camp, and there's Farah, frowning at the med kit. So there are only six of us now. It hits me hard; I'll never see Bannie, Eller, Rikir, or Timmon again, and for a while, we were inseparable. We were a unit. Maybe if I'd been there, I could've done something . . . but that's survivor's guilt talking. I ought to know. I've felt it before.

But there are certain practical implications. "Does this mean the base has been compromised?"

Loras spreads his hands in a gesture of uncertainty. "I've got an ear on Imperial comms. So far, no chatter has surfaced on whether they got critical intel from the captives. We'll proceed with caution. The base is crucial to ops and deployment. I can't give up the resources unless we're sure the hammer's coming down."

Oh, Mary. March and Sasha . . . Every second we gamble, they're in danger. I can't lose March. Not when I sacrificed Doc to save him. It has to mean something, or I won't be able to stand myself.

Like a good soldier, however, I hide my feelings. "What's going on here?"

"I'm building a small Special Forces unit," Loras explains, addressing my initial question. "For missions that require unique skills. They'll remain with us, permitting greater control in their deployment."

Across the camp, I study the new soldiers. With a shock, I recognize Sasha. The man next to him can only be March. He turns, as if sensing me, skims the camp, and frowns. He shakes his head, the puzzled expression deepening into a full scowl.

Thank Mary. They're safe. At this moment, I don't even care why they're here. It's enough that they are.

"Will you excuse me?" I say to Vel and Loras.

They follow my gaze, then Loras nods. "Certainly. I'll go over the new mission with you later."

I'm nervous as I cross to him. He looks like he thinks he's going crazy, feeling me nearby, but he doesn't *see* me. I pause in front of him until he glances down at me without a hint of recognition. If he came into my head, he'd know, but March doesn't do that with random strangers; it took him forever to learn to block.

"Can I help you?" His amber eyes are cool, assessing, and

disinterested. If I ever wondered how March looks at other women, this shows me.

"I guess I have some explaining to do." My voice hasn't changed.

But he doesn't give me a chance. He pulls me into his arms, and he's in my head in the same motion, all glowing warmth. *I thought I'd lost my mind. I sensed you, but . . . okay, this is different. I can't say it's entirely unexpected, though. Leviter gave me a heads-up in his communiqué.* His gift comes in handy because I can transmit information quickly . . . while he kisses me senseless. Before the time we break apart, he knows everything that's happened since I saw him last.

March leans back, studying my new face. He tips up my new chin and sighs. "You're beautiful. But not Jax."

"Vel needed backup."

"Was it hard, giving yourself up for him?" By his expression, he wants to hear it was.

I nod. "I didn't like the assignment, and I hate this new look. I may have it tweaked later though I don't know if I'll go back to old Jax entirely. I like people not knowing who I am. It may be an advantage later. But you said Leviter—"

"He hinted, obliquely, in one of his messages that you had undergone certain changes and 'were not yourself.' Now I see what he meant."

Which explains why he's not more taken aback. His presence in my head says he's just relieved I'm alive, more than anything. I share the feeling.

"Was the mission a success?" March adds.

"Yeah."

He gives me another visual inspection, this time head to toe. "This will take some getting used to. You look so young . . . and La'hengrin."

I fear that might prove a sticking point. "I know. But people will think you're irresistible."

"They'll think I'm a pervert." But he kisses me again, drawing me against his chest, so I can hear his heart beat.

"I guess Sasha had his birthday, and he didn't change his mind?"

"You guess right."

"So you came with him."

"Like I'd let him fight alone."

Yeah, that's not in character. It had to grate on him, hiding in the base all this time, even for Sasha's sake. He's a soldier to his core.

"Have you assessed Loras's battle plans?"

"Yeah, I consult with him. He's hammered out a sound strategy. If he can keep up the pressure on multiple fronts, I don't see this taking long, relatively speaking, not with the numbers we can now bring to bear."

"Relatively speaking?"

"Less than five turns."

I make a mental note. "The campaign in the provinces has been successful then?"

March nods. "The more teams we put in the field, the faster it goes. So long as they're just quietly roaming village to village, it doesn't alert the Imperials."

"The final phase has been a long time coming," I say softly.

"But it's in sight at last." He keeps an arm around me, anchoring me against his side. "All the preparations are in place."

Coming from March, that means a lot. On Nicuan, he received his share of bad orders and fought more than one lost cause. If he thinks we can do this, then it's a matter of time.

"Who's this? Jax is gonna *kill* you." Sasha joins us, striding toward his uncle with a purposeful glare. I find his outrage rather endearing.

So I have to laugh. "It's me."

He recognizes me then, peering at my eyes. "They're the same, but everything else is different."

"Yeah, it's a long story." And I'm not telling it just now. "How long before we move out? And what's the scoop on your new unit?"

"SpecForce," Sasha says proudly. "I'm the strongest with TK 9. Dad's never been tested, but he's near TP 7. Others in the unit are PRE, CL-Aud, and Pyro."

I'm guessing that's precog, clairaudient, and pyrokinetic. "You've been training together?"

"Yep. We kick some ass, too. Shelby tells us what's coming, my dad confirms, Ceepak can hear it from ten klicks away, then Hammond and I destroy it."

"Where do the rest of us come in?" The remainder of my unit.

Guilt surges again.

March replies, "Loras has it all worked out. We have a list of high-priority targets. We're launching a number of simultaneous strikes.

"Excellent. Let me suit up."

With a quiet kiss because he's not my commander and I don't give a shit what Loras thinks of fraternization in the rank and file, I head off to the tent where Farah's waving to me. "It's good to see you." Unlike most, she isn't surprised.

So she knew about the undercover stuff.

She goes on, "I have your uniforms here. Most of what you left behind, in fact."

"Thanks. Let me get changed."

There's no time for socializing, though. When I come out, Loras commandeers me to go over his master plan, which has three stages and multiple targets, factoring for retaliation, escalation, and so many variables. When he's finished, I have to admit it's genius.

"We have the numbers to support this?" I ask.

He nods. "Absolutely."

I glance over at Sasha, who's the youngest of the Special Forces team. But none of them is over thirty turns. "Are you sure about this?"

Loras studies his splayed fingers for a few seconds and lifts his head. "Honestly? No. But the alternative is not to try, and I find that unacceptable."

"Fair enough."

Raising his voice, he calls to the rest of the camp. "We move out in the morning. Get some sleep. You're all on leave tonight, so to speak."

"But don't go anywhere," Zeeka calls.

Loras grins. "Exactly. I expect you all to be sharp at 0400."

The whole crew groans, but it's a good-natured sound. Excitement thrums beneath the surface because we all know the time is coming. No more hiding. No more secret schemes or sneaking around. It's time to fight.

CHAPTER 45

First, we go after their big ordnance.

"Target acquired," Ceepak says.

It's crazy, but the guy can hear a pin drop from ten klicks off, just like Sasha said. Or rather, he can sense it, even though he's so far away, not with his ears, but his mind. I don't know how this shit works; it only matters that it does.

Loras glances at the precog. "How does it look, Shelby?"

"Outlook's good," he replies. "No outside interference on my radar."

"Move, move, move!"

Weapon in hand, I drive forward along with the others. When I get close, a rumble shakes the earth beneath my feet. Ceepak shouts, "Multiple mechs powering up. Some subterranean. All weapons arming."

"Take cover!" Loras shouts. "Sasha, I want you on the heavy weapons."

That makes sense, but March won't love it. Yet he's beside me behind this rise, hunkering down with gun in hand. Drones burst out into sight and I nail one with a clean shot. It sizzles, then slams into the ground in an orange arc. March takes another, and from all around me, shots come down. Then the ground opens—a subterranean lift—and two Peacemaker units ascend.

Like all such mechs, they boom a warning. "Civil disobedience in progress. Vacate the area, or you will be pacified."

Which means blown the frag up. Nobody moves.

"Draw their fire," Loras calls. "So Sasha can work."

Yeah, we don't want our young TK-9 to be splattered. I pop out of cover and fire a volley that sparks on the ground before them. If they were smarter, they'd realize I'm not even aiming properly, but Peacemaker units are not blessed with sophisticated processors. Not like Constance. They don't even have a proper VI chip.

The one on the left fires up its chest-mounted cannon until it's whirring blue-white, then it unloads on my position. Before me, the ground craters and March pulls me back against him. Though I'm hard to kill, one hit from a Peacemaker unit would do it. I'd be nothing but chunky meat. I feel sick with the risk but also reassured by it. I'm *not* indestructible.

"Let someone else take a turn," he murmurs.

"Roger that."

I stay down while listening to laser fire. Then there's an interesting sound, like the Peacemaker is shooting wild. Sticking my head up, I see that Sasha's got one of the mechs airborne and he's lifting it high enough for gravity to do the damage. The kid's face shows bright red, his brow gleaming with sweat. The chest cannon is pointed straight up with no target; energy goes up and dissipates, until he spins the unit, then it nails the Peacemaker below it, and Sasha slams them together with enough force to pop them into metal fragments. I cheer along with everyone else.

One of the Special Forces guys—Hammond, I think—yells, "Good job, kid!"

That's funny, considering he's, at most, three turns older than Sasha. But before we get too cocky, smaller mechs and more drones come out of the sublevel. These lack the armor plating the Peacemaker units have, so I can take them out, one by one, with careful shooting. They're not ranked for hardcore combat. I'm sure the Imperials thought their cache was secure enough not to require a rugged armored force to defend it.

Once we blow up all the moving targets, Loras demands, "Recon."

The man closes his eyes, listening. "No movement down below, sir."

"Scout it. Vel and March, make sure it's clear."

Since they have the most experience sneaking around, that makes sense. But I don't like being left aboveground while they go off into danger without me. March flashes me a smile because he's in my head. I hear silent laughter. *Serves you right, after all you've put us through.*

Us. He's aligned himself with Vel? That seems like an interesting mental shift, but I don't pursue the ramifications. Instead I move over to join Sasha and the rest of the Special Forces guys. "You did great today. Was it hard?"

"A little. But this is better than any control exercise. Pretty soon I'll be able to make stuff do exactly what I want."

Scary power for a kid so young, but Sasha seems like he has his head screwed on right. March gets the credit for that; he's done a great job. I listen with half an ear to their ribbing while I worry about what's going on down below. I don't relax fully until March and Vel emerge on the lift.

"Area secure," March tells Loras.

Vel's mandible flares in satisfaction. "You will not credit what we found."

"Let's have a look." Loras signals to the rest of us, and we get on the platform, which is broad enough to hold us.

He toes the panel to activate our descent. The lift goes down farther than I expect, a good fifty meters belowground. They've excavated a proper bunker here. The platform deposits us in a simple open room. This isn't designed to sustain human life or offer shelter against some unthinkable war; it's storage, plain and simple. And there's barely room for all of us to stand. I nose around, finding high-powered laser rifles, antipersonnel cannons, disruptors, splicers, and tech so dangerous that it's outlawed on tier worlds. And that's just the gear for one soldier. There's more. In the corner stands a strange device. It doesn't look like much, at first, but by the way Loras and Vel are whispering, I know it must be epic.

"What is it?" I ask March.

"MO," he replies. "Massive ordnance with ground launching platform."

The device is the height of a man, with a barrel-shaped cylinder atop a small stand. Three men could haul it, though not easily; Sasha can take it anywhere we need to go, however. Several soldiers cluster around the MO, and someone else counts the shells nearby.

"There are enough for five strikes," Farah replies.

Loras nods. "Vel, can you crack the targeting computer?"

"In time, I believe so." The Ithtorian kneels beside the machine, examining it.

"Excellent."

To March, I murmur, "I'm not clear on what kind of damage this thing does. I mean, I know it's a big gun—"

He levels a somber gaze on me. "To level a city, that's what you use it for."

"Holy shit."

He nods, seeing I understand. "If Loras uses it, I don't know how he'll live with himself. It's not like bombing a building. He can't get all his people out of the affected area."

A whole city. I can't wrap my head around it.

"He wouldn't do that," I say.

"I would." Loras comes up beside me. "It will not be my first choice, but if it is the only way to drive these bastards from my world, then I will prove to them by any means necessary that the cost of staying is too high."

"But what about the La'hengrin in the city?" I ask.

"They will be remembered as martyrs to the cause."

Mary, I hope it doesn't come to that. But it's his call, not mine. He's the leader, the face of the resistance. There's a bounty of 4 million credits on his head at this point, still rising each time he hits a new target. When the Imperials find out about this, I can't even imagine how much it will be.

March touches my cheek. "War is never clean. It never comes down to heroes and villains. Everyone does terrible things, and the scars stay with you always, even if they don't show on your skin."

I run a self-conscious hand down my arms. "I don't feel like myself anymore."

"I miss your face," he admits. "And I was used to the feel of your skin. But you're still the same person."

How funny. He's comforting me because I'm more attractive. Only March would understand why that bothers me.

Because you feel like you've lost part of your character.

Yes, that's why. Articulately expressed, too.

"I can always have it fixed later."

He arches a brow. "You'd ask a cosmetic surgeon to scar you?"

Hm. When he puts it that way, I can't imagine any doctor worth his salt agreeing. The ones who would, I probably don't want working on me. Besides, it might be better this way. With Jax's face, Jax's scars, I'll never be free of my past. The paparazzi will always have records of what I've done, and there will always be a chance they could find me. Hound me. It might be best if I start over.

"Can you get used to it?" I ask.

He shrugs. "You were beautiful before. You are now. Just different. Still you. I do mind a bit how young you look, but that's a separate issue."

"Yeah, sorry about that. You could take a course of Rejuvenex?"

"Ordinarily, I'd scoff, but maybe I need to. Just this once. I don't want to live to be two hundred."

With regular treatments, the human life span can be extended. With Rejuvenex, people live to be a hundred and fifty, sometimes two hundred if they have the credits for the best doctors. I've heard they're working on tech to transfer brain patterns into Pretty Robotics frames, but so far as I know, that's experimental. And March wouldn't want that.

"I wouldn't mind if you did."

This is the first time we've talked about the difference in our life spans. March exhales softly, like the thought hurts him. While the others discuss how to transport the weapons, he wraps his arms around me and sets his cheek on my hair. I put my arms around his waist, silently aching.

"Don't worry," he says softly. "It won't be easy. I know that. There will come a time when I hate my body for breaking down. I may be cranky. Resentful. But I wouldn't miss a moment of any of it as long as I'm with you."

"You know Vel's always going to be around? I hope you'll never make me choose." I hate saying it, but it *must* be said. Few things have ever scared me more. March is jealous of Vel, and I don't know if he can handle this. I'm not asking him to share me in the sense that I want to add another lover to our relationship, but it's definitely unconventional. Yet *if* he cares about me as much as he claims, he won't ask me to give up someone else I love. He won't want me to be unhappy.

March tenses, his face set in quiet, unhappy lines.

"Sorry to interrupt," Ceepak says urgently. "But we've got a shuttle incoming, sir. I'm guessing we triggered a perimeter alarm at the nearest outpost."

"How far out?" Loras asks.

"Eighty klicks and coming fast."

"Everybody grab the heaviest weapon you can handle and get to the surface. There's no room to dance down here."

Plus, there are tons of explosives that he doesn't want going off during the fight. I grab a laser rifle with military scope and a disruptor. I swore I'd never use one of these again, but under the circumstances, I hope the shock and agony teaches the centurions a lesson.

"Zeeka, grab some of those proximity mines. Can you trap the approach in less than ten minutes?"

"Yes, sir!" The young Mareq salutes. He's the best at demolitions now, even better than Vel, who's competent at many tasks.

"Everyone got their gear?" Loras asks.

We all nod, and then get back on the lift. Ceepak listens to the shuttle drawing closer. His brows pull together. "I think there's another inbound behind it. The echo masked the approach."

"How many men will a ship that size hold?" I ask.

Ceepak sighs. "I can't tell how big it is."

Shit. Well, I don't know how his gift works.

"We should expect between twenty-five and fifty men," Vel says.

Loras doesn't let that report daunt him. "All right, people. This is it. We've got five minutes to set up. Make them count."

INTERNAL MEMORANDUM
FROM: THE OFFICE OF THE GOVERNOR

KIA 10,189

MIA 5,276

Turned 102

Cured Unknown, estimated 2,000,000 or more

Resources Lost

4 Weapon caches

5 Food storage facilities

3 Shuttles modified with weaponry

12 provinces

At this time, I have no choice but to declare a state of emergency. Martial law is effective immediately. All rights of lower-class citizens are hereby revoked. Only nobles may be on the streets after 8:00 p.m. All violators of this curfew will be treated as enemies of the empire. Much as I hate to admit it, gentlemen, we are losing this war, a centimeter at a time. We must strike back. Hard.

CHAPTER 46

Zeeka lays the mines.

The rest of us are in position. Two shuttles land in the center of the valley, as Loras predicted. He said the strike team would put down as close to the cache as possible to verify whether it was secure. March seconded that guess.

Centurions pour out of the ships. I lose count after twenty, but there are a lot of them, around forty, I think. They fan out, cautiously. Ten meters from the cache, the first mine goes off, taking out the four guys in range of the explosion. The others scramble back, hands on their weapons. Their leader yells orders, but he knows they have nowhere to go. They can't progress unless they disable the mines; we've got them pinned down.

As one centurion gets out a kit for detection, Loras says, "Now!"

I open fire.

There's no cover for them except the shuttles, and they use it. They're wearing good armor, so it takes more than one shot with the laser rifle to kill. So I switch to the disruptor. It doesn't have good range or accuracy, but this weapon requires neither. My stomach churns the first time I fire. The centurion screams; there's blood all over his back, and now he's got armor inside his spine. I fire again; he falls. Shock will finish him.

I take aim at another, and it's more gruesome. I nail him in the head, scrambling his flesh so that his skull turns inside out, with bits of brain and bone coating the surface. He dies instantly. Beside me, March uses his rifle with expert proficiency. He shoots in bursts: one hit to break the armor, the second to injure, third to slay. I never noticed how efficient a killer he is before. It also keeps his weapon from overheating.

Sasha calls, "Permission to destroy the shuttle, sir?"

"Granted," Loras yells back.

This time, Sasha doesn't pick it up or slam it. I suspect this is the most difficult feat I've seen him perform yet. Instead, he applies pure force, crushing the metal until the bolts and rivets give, and he keeps pressing, until there's nothing to hide behind. As soon as the centurions realize what's happening, they scramble toward the other one, but they have fifteen meters to cover. During that time, it's a shooting gallery. I take down four more with the disruptor, and their screams unnerve their comrades. Bodies line the ground. Twenty-two dead. If my estimate was correct, there are eighteen to go.

"Go large," Loras yells at Sasha.

Yeah, it's time. We're burning daylight here. They might be trying to stall us, keep us from emptying the cache and taking the MO while reinforcements arrive. Sasha creeps along the perimeter, avoiding the mines, until he has line of sight on the remaining centurions. Then he flings them into the air. I take aim along with everyone else. They fire wildly, sometimes shooting each other in their terror. Since they're falling, not flying, I know how scared they must be. But they don't live in terror long. Eighteen corpses hit the ground, some smoking with laser wounds, others turned inside out. Others are ballistic kills because they have rounds designed to pierce armor. There were all kinds of weapons in the bunker.

"This shuttle's still functional," Ceepak says. "Do we steal it?"

"Might come in handy for transporting the MO," Xirol adds.

It's a risk. They can track it. They know the serial number and the emission signature. But maybe we can use that to our advantage. By Loras's thoughtful expression, he thinks the same thing. There are only twelve of us, so it should hold the whole squad, plus the weapons.

Then he nods. "Let's do it. We'll draw them into ambush. The more we kill out here, the less there will be to face us in the capital."

"Good plan," March says.

Loras turns to Zeeka. "Collect the undetonated mines. We'll use them again."

"Yes, sir."

"Jax, take the rest of the men down to finish cleaning out the cache."

"Roger that."

There are dollies down below that make my job easier. With help, I soon have the remaining gear ready for transport. I glance around one more time, seeing only bare walls and dusty floors. There's no telling when the Imperials built this installation. And there are others out there, waiting for us to plunder them.

"Take it up," I say.

Vel checks that we don't exceed the lift's weight limit, then he hits the button. The platform jolts into motion, slow as anything. On the surface, the men are edgy, and Ceepak has his eyes closed, listening in his head for more incoming. I help with loading the shuttle, then swing aboard.

Loras is saying, "We have two pilots . . . who wants the helm?"

"March can fly," Vel says, sitting beside me.

I strap in because the harness reminds me of a proper ship, and my repressed longing for grimspace hits me like a foot in the ribs. Several long, deep breaths restore my equilibrium, then the comm crackles. We all freeze.

"Bravo unit, respond. Did you encounter hostiles? I need a sit-rep."

This has to be the base that deployed these men. March glances at Loras in the cockpit beside him. "How do you want to play this?"

He turns the options over in his head while the rest of us

wait in tense silence. Ambush or full-frontal assault? The problem is, if we don't respond, they'll know they're walking into a trap when they come looking for the shuttle. So they'll armor up and bring more ordnance and centurions.

"Answer," Loras says. "We take the fight to them."

There's no way to know how many soldiers will be there or what kind of equipment they'll have. Our one advantage is that they won't be ready for battle when we land. They'll be drinking, screwing off, and watching porn.

March taps the comm. "Threat neutralized. We're on our way back, but the shuttle's comm was damaged in the firefight. I can barely read you."

Obligingly, Loras screws with the settings so base camp gets nothing but static and feedback from us. They don't have a chance to ask for passwords before the feed goes out. Mary, the centurions will be surprised when we arrive.

March examines the controls for a few seconds, then says, "I've found them on the nav log. We just need to follow this course back the way they came."

"Get us in the air," Loras orders.

Other ships shouldn't bother us because we have the necessary permissions and registrations. The proper crew just doesn't man the ship anymore. Other shuttles in the air won't be able to tell that from a distance. And La'heng has precious little air traffic, pretty much just VIPs en route from one city to the next. Imperials won't be caught dead in the provinces if they have a choice.

March complies with an easy grace that makes me wonder if he's missed flying the way I miss grimspace. A warm little ping in my head says he's here, as well as flying the ship, and he responds, *Of course. I only ever wanted to fly. Everything I did, all the mistakes I made, were because I wanted my own ship.*

You do seem to have trouble keeping them, I tease.

Not the next one, he promises. *The next ship I get, I'm keeping. No more drama. No more explosions.*

You sure you can guarantee that? We seem to lead interesting lives.

He pokes back, *Well, you don't look like Sirantha Jax anymore. That should greatly reduce our risk.*

Are you saying I bring the chaos?

Maybe.

You might have a point. I laugh, drawing looks from the guys around me. I just shrug.

Sasha explains, "She's talking to my dad."

Among this crew, that's enough. We have enough special skills among our number that they don't blink at mental conversations. Ceepak is doing his *shut up, don't bother me* thing, checking for possible problems heading our way, and Shelby examines the immediate future, eyeballs rolling behind his lids like he's in REM sleep. He'd warn us if it looked like this attacked ended in our bloody destruction. Well, if he could see it, he would. Precog's imperfect, as I understand it. He can only get glimpses of possible futures, as they're always in motion, and each little choice ripples the water a little more, changing course from what it was a few seconds before.

"What kind of weapons are we packing?" Xirol asks. "On the ship I mean."

"Standard-issue guns," March replies.

"We need to talk strategy," Loras says. "Is it better to open fire and take out as many buildings as we can, go for big collateral damage, or should we aim for a surgical strike?"

Most of us don't have enough experience to consult in this regard, maybe only March and Vel. The rest of the team is La'hengrin, with no prior military history, and many of them are specialists as well. I keep quiet, along with everyone else.

After a thoughtful pause, Vel answers, "It is impossible to know until I see the fortifications. Some structures may prove impervious to the shuttle's guns."

Loras glances at March. "Thoughts, Commander?"

"Don't call me that. You're in charge."

"But I'm asking for your expert opinion."

If Vel's unwilling to guess without more data, then it will come down to March's best judgment. Mary grant he's right, whatever he decides.

CHAPTER 47

The ship comes in with guns hot.

March decided the base probably doesn't have heavy fortifications, so we'll do more damage quick and hard with the onboard guns. From above, they look like insects running around, mowed down by the barrage of incoming fire. It's hard enough to buckle buildings, and Sasha has the power to bring the death from above, too. With a nod from Loras, he joins his uncle in wreaking havoc.

First, we take out the comm tower, then the rail guns mounted at either side of the base. Next, Loras disables the other ships. They're all dead metal, no engines, by the time we put down. There are only a few survivors after the initial assault, and they're bloody, soot-stained, wild-eyed. Most aren't even geared up; their armor's half on, weapons discarded in their flight for cover. As I think we've annihilated them without their firing a shot, forty more centurions break from a building across the field. They're locked and loaded, sober and ready for combat. From the colors on their armor, they are elite, and we're in serious trouble.

"How come you didn't warn us?" Loras shouts at Shelby as I dive.

"Frag me, I told you it's not perfect!" the soldier yells back.

"They specialize in hand-to-hand," March says in my ear. "They usually work as bodyguards to high-ranking nobles."

"Are you good enough to be elite?"

He nods. "If I were crazy enough to serve the same house for ten turns."

"There is that," I mutter.

"My point is, we can't let them close. Only Vel and I have the necessary skill to hold our own one-on-one, and they outnumber us."

I don't take offense. Though I have melee training, I'm not the strongest, certainly not enough to disable a man who's wearing such thick armor. My only hope is to nail them on bare skin and short out their nervous system with my shock-stick. But the armor covers everything but their cheekbones, and the elite have their helmets sealed. Unlike most centurions, these men look like bona fide badasses.

"Cover fire!" Loras calls. "Shift work, you know the drill."

I lay it down, quick and tight, so there's a bright barrage sizzling against the churned ground. Not enough to kill an armored foe if he stumbles, but the elite are canny, not committing to the battle until they assess our ability. Their commander watches for a moment, then he signals his men.

I cup my hands to carry over the weapons. "They're flanking! Watch the rear."

"Dammit," March swears. "There's too much ground to cover. We can't—"

"I got it," Sasha shouts.

He slams the corrugated metal from a few ruined buildings into place behind us, creating a field picket and walling off our vulnerable flank. I wonder why he doesn't just kill them all when March answers in my head. *He's already used his gift a lot today. The more he uses it, the more it takes out of him. There's an energy exchange, and he could go into cardiac arrest if he pushes too hard.*

That makes sense. Otherwise, he could just smash and kill everything without need for rest or recovery. The human body does have limits.

He frowns at Sasha. *Even as a TK-9, he probably shouldn't*

have done that . . . but inanimate objects are easier to move than people. They don't thrash or resist.

On closer examination, I see that Sasha looks pale, almost green, and he's sweating like mad. Yeah, no more TK for him. He catches his uncle's eye, nods, then grins. I can read the visual exchange.

March: *Cut it out.*

Sasha: *Fine. I won't be a hero anymore.* Grin. *Today.*

"Get out there, Z. Hurry!"

In reply, the Mareq springs forward, mines in hand. His webbed fingers are a blur as he sets them. "I need you all at least five meters back, or you'll get caught in the blast radius."

Then he bounds back to us, arms flapping as he urges us back toward the makeshift wall. At least my weapon has cooled down while the enemy commander leads his men back around the way they came. With the path blocked, they have to come straight at us, and we'll make them earn every step. As they burst into sight, charging, Loras gives the order.

A few of the elite fire as they run, wild shots, because it's hard to aim on the move. It's an acquired skill, in fact. Some soldiers I know have taken multiple training courses to perfect the knack; it's not something I can do. Though I'm competent, shooting's not in my blood like grimspace. I work with March, and we take the same target, using penetration fire to burn through the armor. His next shot kills. It's a sweetly hypnotic bob and weave. Vel unleashes an EMP burst, taken from the cache earlier, and fries the computer components on their laser rifles.

Their guns spark in their hands, then go inert. No electronic firing mechanisms, no computer-aided targeting. But since they specialize in hand-to-hand, they don't seem overly troubled. Firing in pairs, we take out ten before they cross the yard. And then they're on us, thirty to twelve.

I vault into a fighting crouch, discarding my gun. Knife and shock-stick in hand, I brace for the charge. Adrenaline pounds through me like a second pulse in my ears. Vel is nearby; so is March. They've flanked me to keep the bigger centurions from surrounding me. I appreciate that, even as I swing into the fight.

The shock-stick hums in my hand, but it's not going to be

sufficient. I can't kill them on my own. Fortunately, Vel's hand-knives are sharp enough to tear chunks out of their armor, and he's strong enough to knock them the hell away from me. I want to help, but I don't mean to be stupid about it. So I defend as best I can, a distraction if not an ass-kicker of men in armor.

I wait for opportunities. When March cracks a centurion's helmet off, I slip into the opening and lay my shock-stick upside his head. When he drops in convulsions, I take a knee, ducking a blow aimed at my head, and cut his throat. There's a centurion running at me while the melee rages, and I wheel low, taking his legs out from under him. What I know about combat amounts to making my size and speed work for me. When he hits the ground, he loses sight of me because helmets limit your peripheral vision. I jam my knife into the gap between armor and helmet. Twist, and the sharp stink of copper scents the air.

Another down.

Xirol cries out. He's got three on him, and he's La'heng, not a former merc or a bounty hunter. I hurdle a corpse without thinking. Then another. The SpecForce Pyro tries to help him, but his control isn't the best, and he sometimes cooks things he isn't trying to, so he doesn't dare light everything up, or we might all go boom.

Xirol's uniform is already bloodstained when I get there. He falls, but I can't tell how badly he's injured. The three elite turn on me, thinking I'm more of a threat than I am. Just out of range, I stop and beckon them on. *Come on, you bastards. Leave him alone.* Through the visors, I can see they're amused at my challenge. Compared to three hardened veterans, I look laughable, wearing Mishani's pretty face with her doe eyes.

"I think I'll keep this one," the first growls. "For a little while at least."

"Until you break her," another laughs.

The Pyro lays down a line of fire between us. I cut a glance at him, half-impressed, half-worried. Like Sasha, his face is clammy-pale, and sickness swirls in his eyes. Mary, I'm glad I have the grimspace gene. It would suck to be Psi.

"Come get me," I yell, backing off.

As long as I get them away from Xirol, it'll be—

Deliberately, the biggest one turns, grabs his knife, and jabs it into Xirol's chest. I scream because the flames are now my enemy. If he wasn't dead before, he is now, and I want to kill these bastards with my bare hands, to peel their skin from their muscles, and break their bones. It was such an evil, calculated cruelty.

Part of me says, *It's no different than what you do with your knife, finishing those you drop with the shock-stick*, but I don't want to think about all the ways I'm like these centurions. They are the enemy. They are the monsters. They have to be, or I can't do what I must. By the time the centurions skirt the flames, Vel and March are beside me again.

Working together, we kill them. I play my part with mechanical confidence. Thrust, parry, retreat, block, dodge, see the opening—destroy. Around us, the battle rages, but I can't hear the cries anymore. I'm lost in my own head, where the sobs sound louder than a ship engine, rising and falling like the sea.

CHAPTER 48

"Are you certain?" Loras asks hoarsely, a few days later.

I can't move. Can't breathe. Can't think. March rubs my back, as we all listen for the crackle of the comm. We're parked at the edge of range, so the connection's tetchy at best. Then it comes.

"Affirmative. They brought the whole mountain down."

The base is gone. *Damn the fragging Imperials.* They have MOs, too, but unlike us, they don't hesitate to use them.

"How did they find it?" Zeeka asks.

"It must have been Bannie," Loras says heavily. "They broke her."

Which is precisely why the cells run as they do, independently, so the only thing members can betray is the location of the base. And now it's gone. I can't get my head around it. I rub my temples.

We abandoned the Imperial shuttle a few days back, filling our own cache with the stolen weapons. The MO can be transported on our stealth craft or deployed from here. Loras's grim expression indicates he favors immediate retaliation.

Farah puts a hand on his arm. "Take a day. Reflect. Decide if this is the best strategy or if it's revenge."

He nods curtly.

"How many did we lose?" I ask.

There was the skeleton crew, of course, and anybody who might've been on layover for R&R, gear, or training protocols. *Constance. Constance is always there. Oh, Mary.* Maybe it's stupid to cry because by other people's standards, she wasn't a real person. To me? To me, she was. Tears well up, and I knuckle them away, not wanting to distract the others. Zhan, too, was permanently assigned to base. I remember how committed he was to the cause, how passionately he cared about freeing the La'hengrin.

Vel spreads his claws in an *impossible to know* gesture. "There is no way to determine how many were inside at the time of the attack."

"Pull up the bounce," Loras orders. "Local news should be covering this. This is a huge Imperial victory."

Since we're in the field, there's no entertainment suite, just Vel's handheld, but it's top-of-the-line. With some tinkering, he tunes in, and the vid comes up. The Nicuan presenter rambles about some upcoming party, who's wearing what this season, and who was spotted on whose arm last night. Just as I'm about to click it off in disgust, Vel stops me. Different music plays, heralding a shift in the tone of the broadcast.

"Yesterday evening, the first cohort deployed massive ordnance against a hidden base filled with terrorists. They encountered little resistance, and the operation went off without a hitch, demonstrating the bravery and skill of our military. They have since released footage . . ." She discusses the location of the base and how things went before cutting to the canned feed.

It's grainy, low-quality, but I recognize the landscape. I've flown over that ground many times. The drone-cam hovers well out of the blast radius, waiting. I hear the missile before I see it, a rumble-whine that zings past, arrowing toward its target. Death should be more dramatic; there should be a rush of flames, but when it hits, the mountain trembles, then collapses inward. I can't *see* the force that killed so many of our brave soldiers, most of whom hardly had a taste of hard-won freedom.

"Is there a chance anybody survived?" Zeeka asks.

Farah answers, "Unlikely. I'm sorry."

The Special Forces guys huddle up, whispering. They're making plans for revenge, whatever Loras decides. This won't go unanswered. Sasha might kill himself teaching the Imperials a lesson, and March would never forgive me for that.

"Take a breath." I put a hand on Sasha's shoulder.

Over the turns, I've come to care about this kid. I don't want him to go out in a blaze of glory. His gift could kill him if he doesn't manage it, and I fight the impulse to lecture him. But then, he's *not* a child anymore. This life has seen to that.

"It's not right," he chokes out. "Those people, they never saw it coming. You should have a chance, you know? You should be able to fight."

And what the hell do I say to that? Because he's *right*. The shine to his eyes makes mine worse, and I open my arms, because I'm here, and he could use a hug. I figure he might tell me to frag off because he doesn't want to look soft in front of his buddies. Instead, he takes a couple of steps toward me and hugs me hard, digging his face into my shoulder. Sasha pats my back and makes comforting noises, like he's doing this for me. I don't dispute it because maybe he is. Maybe I *do* need him.

I can't see for Sasha's shoulder; he's taller than I am. But I hear other soldiers fighting back their own tears. This is so fragging hard because we don't know who to mark MIA. There are no records. No names on a list. I wish there were.

A few minutes later, Sasha asks, "Are you feeling better?"

"Yeah. Thanks."

When I step back, he's got his grief under control. So do I. March watches with his customary stoicism. He's lost men before, sometimes his whole company. Now I understand on a visceral level why he hates Nicuan nobles, and I admire him all the more because he put aside that loathing to do what was best for Sasha.

"What's the plan?" I ask.

We've been camped here, outside the city, waiting for word, but Loras plays his cards close to the vest. When he hears whatever he needs to, then we move. And then maybe he'll confide his strategy.

"Let's eat and get some sleep," Farah says.

"Excellent," Hammond mutters. "More paste."

Angrily, his squad-mates remind him he has nothing to bitch about, especially compared to those who were inside the base. That does shut him up, and he subsides into a low simmer while we all suck down packets of tasteless goo. But it'll keep us alive until something better comes along.

Who knows how long that will be?

Warmth in my head signals March's arrival. I glance at him sitting quietly beside me. *You all right?*

I nod. *We have to retaliate, don't we?*

Sooner or later. There's no way to win this without proving the resistance is willing to do whatever it takes.

That includes merciless slaughter. It's not a question.

It does. Nicuan has never been known for its compassion or restraint. Their vendettas are legendary.

I'll kill your family, friends, and anybody who ever had kaf *with you?*

Pretty much.

Dull pain throbs behind my ears. *I hate this. We were just starting to get to a place where they had to take us seriously. Now the cities will be buzzing with how the centurions are kicking resistance ass.*

March lifts a shoulder. *It's all propaganda, love. This isn't a permanent victory. It's a setback.*

A setback, he calls it. This is fragging catastrophic. Now we have no way to coordinate troop movements, no central intelligence. The best we can do is pass messages on the short-range bounce and hope they reach the intended parties. This is a crippling blow.

Do you even care that Constance is gone? I'm sorry as soon as I think it. I expect him to withdraw from the sharpness of it, but he doesn't.

I do. She was special. We wouldn't have survived the Morgut War without her.

Yeah. People would think it's weird to mourn an AI, wouldn't they?

He brushes a gentle hand across my hair. *Who gives a shit what people think?*

At that, I turn into his arms, and I don't move away until first light.

In the morning, there are hard decisions to be made. Farah and Loras argue in low tones until he summons the rest of us. I guess she was opposed to whatever he intends to do, but there's a new hardness in his eyes now, like he's stepped out onto this ledge with both feet, and he will do whatever it takes to win this war—to free his people—even if it means drowning this world in blood. Unlike the rest of us, his grief hasn't hit him as pain; in Loras, it has become undiluted rage. The force burns in his blue gaze like twin, white-hot flames.

"There's only one way we can prove they haven't broken us," he says. "We take out a high-profile target in immediate retaliation. Farah has convinced me not to use the MO, for now, but I'm afraid the day will come when it's unavoidable. For now, this is the new mission."

"What?" Zeeka asks.

"The governor of Jineba must die."

CHAPTER 49

This op is risky, and Vel took all the chances.

He crafted a new face and slipped into Jineba to get within short-range wireless bounce so we could coordinate with Tarn for our escape, once the mission's done. It felt like I couldn't breathe, the whole time Vel was gone. Even with scramblers, there's no guarantee of privacy. I hope Tarn and Leviter have been boring enough not to draw suspicion.

They're our only hope of getting out of this alive.

Now March and I are on a rooftop, preparing to assassinate the governor.

I peer through the scope and check the calibrations. It looks fine to me, but this isn't my area of expertise. Then I step back, smiling my thanks for the glimpse at a skill set I don't possess. It's so odd to stare at someone who's so far away, but I can see the lines in his lips, the size of his pores, and the hair in his nose. There's no clear shot at this point, however. The governor is half standing behind one of his aides, chatting with some well-built brunette.

Of us all, March has the most experience with the silent kill. He's equally proficient at distance or close-up. This time, it must be the former. Silently, I back away; today, I'm guarding roof access. Nobody can slide in behind him, screwing up this day's work, because I'm here to kill them if they try.

At camp, we argued over who was best qualified, but in the end, Vel conceded he has more experience capturing men. He seemed a little worried about sending me off with March, as he and I haven't worked together as much as Vel and I. But then, March took him aside and asked him to keep an eye on Sasha. That gave me an odd, warm twinge, as if we're truly a family, a strange one, to be sure, but we're learning to function as a unit.

This mission has to be foolproof. In armor, with my helmet on, there's not enough of my face showing for anyone to recognize me. And besides, if they see me, I kill them. That's my mandate.

So I station myself beside the door while March studies his angle and compensates for other factors, such as wind speed. The irony is that this rifle came from the cache we stole earlier. Down below, the people scurry like insects. It's cold enough that I can see my breath, but I don't shift to warm up. The crowd's already assembling for the governor's speech. At precisely noon, he intends to tell them in ringing evangelical tones how the rebellion will soon be over, because of their decisive victory in destroying our hidden base.

Really, there should be centurions guarding every possible sniper's nest, and I spot a few of them on distant rooftops. I guess it's been so long since they left active service that they've forgotten how to spot the best vantage. Their rusty observational skills work in our favor, so I'm not complaining. I check my weapons. No pistol, just knife and shock-stick. If I kill somebody up here, it'll be quiet.

Music strikes up below us. The strains sound like a muffled ping of a child's music box at this altitude, but it means the program is about to commence. I face away from the edge, watching the door with full attention. March doesn't need my scrutiny to perform.

The floor rumbles, which means the lift is arriving. *Damn.* I dismissed the centurions as careless too soon. They're not total idiots; they're just running late. I fall into a fighting crouch, hoping there aren't too many. March can't miss his shot.

There are four of them when the door swings open. Surprise on my side, I take one quickly, a result of the live shock-stick. While he spasms, the others go for their comms. Shit, no, I can't have that. I lunge and knock the tech out of their hands and then stomp them for good measure. But the maneuver gives them time to regroup. Their hands edge toward their guns. I'm armored, but if the three of them concentrate fire, I'm done.

March's shot rings out. A single burst, clean and true, I hope. My hope bears fruit when the crowd below shrieks. Pandemonium breaks out, audible even up here.

I glance around for cover; there's a ventilation unit I can use. As they shoot, I dive. This is a problem because I don't have a gun. Laser shots slam into the metal, sparking and sizzling; the scent of hot steel scents the air. Fortunately, they can't get at March for the unit that's keeping me from certain death. The chaos below covers the noise as they loose a second volley. But I hear one of them moving as the other two lay down cover fire.

March slips up beside me, and I've never been gladder to see him. "How many?"

"Four total. One won't be getting up for a while."

"Shock-stick?"

I nod. "So three to deal with before we can use the maintenance stairs."

"Small arms?"

"Yeah, just pistols. We've got one incoming to our position, but I don't think he knows I've got company back here."

"You kept them from reporting in?"

"That was the one thing I did accomplish."

"Good work, Jax." As he says that, the centurion swings around the ventilation hub.

I swing the shock-stick as March slams the butt of the rifle into the man's helmet. The timing is spot on, as the headgear bounces up enough for me to make contact with bare skin. Immediately, neural shock sets in, and he convulses on the ground. His comrades don't slow their fire, however.

One of them calls out, "Report! Hostile terminated?"

March replies, "All clear."

If they're dumb enough to come check it out, they deserve to die. On the one hand, I understand why they haven't retreated to request backup. They saw what appeared to be one small La'hengrin female. They have no reason to think four armed centurions can't handle the situation, and I've smashed their comms, so they don't know we just shot the governor. For all they know, the furor down below is because of a parade.

Yet when the next one comes to "take me into custody," I choke off a laugh. March lashes out with a field knife. Clean, cut throat. He's good at that, it gives me chills, because I know how many people he's killed. And how much it hurt him. I hate that I've brought him to that place again, but please, Mary, let this be the last time.

After La'heng, grant us peace.

That leaves us one.

March and I charge him, through a barrage of fire. I take a couple of hits. One doesn't breach my armor; the other does. I've been shot so often at this point that the agony, followed by the cauterized numbness, is familiar to me. I stumble, but I don't fall. I lay into the final centurion with my shock-stick, as March does the same. He fights with such brutal power that he cracks the man's chest piece, and then he's mine. Seizures set in. Ruthlessly, we finish off the ones who are in spasm, leaving no witnesses. This is how it has to be.

Quickly, March packs his gear. Then we step over the corpses and make for the maintenance stairs. They'll lock the lift down once they pinpoint the trajectory of the shot that killed the governor.

Now we just have to get out of here—and that's the hard part.

A full-out sprint carries me down forty flights of stairs. Fortunately, I'm in top shape, and it doesn't leave me winded because we still have a lot of work to do. I check the exit, but the centurions haven't locked it down yet. Their response times are sluggish, even now, when they should be on high alert.

Four streets from the assassination site, Tarn picks us up in an aircar, as agreed. He's crucial to the next step. He doesn't make conversation until we're well away from the plaza. Seconds matter because, closer to the crime scene, they're impounding all the vehicles.

"Good to see you," Tarn says, when it becomes clear we made it.

I nod. "Even under these circumstances. Did you get the equipment we need?"

"It wasn't easy, but yes. Edun is waiting to bounce the feed as you requested."

"Thanks. We need to lie low for a day or two, until the search slacks off."

"Understood. And I've prepared suitable quarters for you. Don't worry, our flat is bigger than it looks."

Since I've never gotten the full tour, I can't argue that. I just nod, glad I can't feel how bad I'm wounded. Shock would've killed anyone else. I can't get the centurion's astonishment out of my head. I saw his utter horror at how inhuman I've become. Normal people fall down and don't get up when they're shot in the gut.

Fragging nanites.

Since Tarn and Leviter pay top dollar for their flat, they have a landing pad on the roof. It eliminates questions about what—or who—they're bringing into the building. On the way to their apartment, we pass nobody, and Tarn takes care of the security with a few taps on the panel outside; and then he escorts us in.

March says softly, "I'll tend your wound, Jax."

He knows he doesn't need to. The nanites will fix me. They'll fight infection. I don't demur because it's something tangible he can offer as an apology for my pain. Not that I need one. The tiny tech is why Loras chose me to guard March's back. I'm not the best fighter, but I am the most durable; I can take the most damage without dying.

Tarn finds a med kit, then greets Leviter with a kiss. The other man seems distracted, fiddling with a wide array of chips and wires hooked into his comm system, but he pauses to cup Tarn's cheek, before returning to his work.

"Can they trace the bounce back here?" I ask, while March coats the charred flesh on my stomach with antibacterial gel.

Leviter replies, "Minimal risk. It's worth it."

As I understand it, he's creating a necessary link for Loras to hijack the local news feeds, as he's done regularly for the recruitment profiles, always on a different channel, so they can't track him. This message will be different, however.

The vid screen flickers, and the presenter disappears. Loras fills the screen, his jaw set, eyes burning with ferocious rage. "Your governors are pretenders. They *will* die. Appoint another . . . I'll have him killed. And his sons. His wife. His friends. Kill one of us, Imperial Pigs, and ten shall take his place. The enemy is all around you. We are 1 billion strong. Heed me, your days are numbered."

Then the message ends in a black screen filled with the LLA logo. *Damn.* That's powerful stuff. Even *I* have chills.

CHAPTER 50

Later that night, March and I are in Tarn and Leviter's guest suite, not just a room, as it has a kitchen-mate and full san facilities. The room is lavishly appointed in neutral natural fabrics, no cheap synth, which means they have money. Guests could closet themselves in here for days—and maybe that's the point. The convenience reduces the disruption to the household; such efficiency rings of Leviter to me.

When I mention it to March, he agrees. "In the gospel according to Leviter, visitors should be neither seen nor heard."

I nod. "It's probably best if we aren't roaming around the penthouse. I hear the centurions are doing spot checks."

"True. They're looking for rebels under rocks these days. Fortunately, they don't have the manpower to cover all the territory in the provinces."

They have technology, though. And they're doing terrible things with it. I can't count the nights I've gone to sleep listening to bombs detonate in the distance. Nicuan has unleashed a bloody countercampaign, and the results haunt me. The grimmest aspect comes in knowing it will get worse.

This luxurious room doesn't feel real. It's odd to have a bed waiting; I wonder how the surviving members of my squad are doing, if SpecForce has run ops while we were on mission elsewhere. I'm afraid of what news awaits us on our return. It seems the situation just keeps getting darker; I tell myself the horizon seems most grim just before first light, but in truth, I don't know how much more of this I can take. Sometimes, the war seems endless.

"Can we really win by persuading Nicuan that La'heng is too costly to keep?" I ask.

March nods. "It's a sound principle, proven effective in past conflicts. The insurgents just need the resolve to stick it out, no matter what it takes."

In my present frame of mind, that's a scary thought. How much worse will get it get? "Loras won't stop. He can't. Otherwise, all this has been for nothing. He's sacrificed so many lives already—"

He touches my mouth to stop the desperate flow of words. "I don't know if you've noticed yet, Jax, but . . . he's changed. The time you were gone with Vel, we took some hard losses. Not just the base though that was a factor."

"Changed how?"

"Just . . . don't be surprised at any decision he makes, going forward. He's a lot harder than the man who came to La'heng with you."

I don't want to think about how the war has changed Loras—or any of us, for that matter. "We haven't talked in a while . . . about us. Last time, we left things up in the air. I shipped out, and you never had a chance to answer me about Vel." I gesture at my face. "Now there's this, too. I feel like there's a lot to say and not enough time."

"You haven't pressed me . . . and I appreciate it." He pauses to study my features. "Would I have chosen this? No. But it doesn't matter. You're still you."

"I might get some tweaks later, so I don't look so La'hengrin." But it's low-priority. I don't think I'll ever want my old face back; I'm ready to cut ties and disappear.

"Your looks are the least of my concerns," he says, opening his arms.

I curl into him, fighting the urge to demand an answer. He was jealous of Vel before . . . and I'm afraid one day, he'll feel like, *Enough's enough.* I prefer to have some forewarning if he's approaching maximum density on that head.

"Did you make up your mind?" It's been hard as hell to live in the moment and just be with him, as happy as we can manage under the circumstances. It's offered freedom, certainly. We have little experience just being together, but this time, neither of us is in charge; there's no imbalance of power. Just March and me, learning how to be a unit. If I'm honest, we never have been. Our timing has sucked, all the way through, but I think this round, we might get it right.

He nods. "I did some thinking while you were on assignment. I realized I can't ask you to forsake all others. I won't always be around . . . and you'll need somebody to help you through after I'm gone."

I don't want to think about that, but clearly March has. He's considering what's best for me, long-term, not what's easiest or most comfortable for him. Which means he loves me a crazy amount. But then, I already knew that. He's the one who waited, even long after a sane, reasonable man would've given up on me and moved on.

"Thank you for that. I know it can't have been easy to come to that conclusion . . . and I promise that Vel and I, we're not—"

"He's your best friend. I get it. It was just . . . when we were fighting so much, it was hard to see how easily he relates to you. It's always been tougher for us."

"We were both pretty broken," I say honestly. "We had to get our heads in order before we could make a go of this. Then we had old grudges and insecurities eating at us."

He nods. "Love is the start, but it's not everything. Tell me, do you trust me now, Jax? Could you lean on me?"

Given that my head's on his chest, it might seem like a silly question, but I understand where he's coming from. "See for yourself."

He's kept out of my head during this conversation, not taking what I haven't shared, but at my invitation, he slips in, and

I bask in the resultant warmth. I hope he sees what I mean to show him—that I have no doubts about us. I believe in him. March rubs his cheek against the top of my head.

"I miss your hair the most," he confesses. "It had such personality."

Which is an odd description, but I get it. "When this is over, I'll see what I can do."

Jax . . . The fact that he whispers in my head alerts me this is important; he must not feel comfortable saying it out loud.

Yeah?

I want something from you.

Anything, I promise instantly.

He's been so patient and understanding, even when the situation got complicated. Another man would have walked ages ago. So whatever he needs, I'll make it happen.

A sheepish feeling accompanies his request. *I'd like us to get matching tatts.*

Everything clicks into focus. In order to feel on even footing with Vel, he requires an equivalent symbol of my commitment. Kai whispers in my ear that such gestures are meaningless, but for the first time, I dismiss his ghost; I loved him with all my heart when we were together, but he's gone. I will cherish his memory, but all my relationships will not be driven by his tenets. I am not his Jax anymore.

If you want, we'll go to Gehenna to the same shop where Vel had his done.

March shakes his head. *I'd prefer for us to find somewhere new.*

On a symbolic level, that makes sense. And it's more of a promise than I've ever given him. The fact that I'm willing comforts him; the last of his tension drains away. Our immediate future may be uncertain, but if we survive, we'll be together. He sees that certainty in my head.

"That works for me," I say aloud. "Since I'll never settle down or have offspring, a few centimeters of my skin seem like a fair trade."

"Centimeters? I'm having my face tattooed across your back."

I grin because a playful March is irresistible. "But you said you wanted us to get matching tatts. You really want your mug back there?"

"I won't have to look at it." He winks, as if I didn't already know he was teasing.

"On me, you will," I point out.

"True enough. We'll figure out the design when the time comes." He sobers. "Right now, we should probably get some sleep. No telling how long it will be until we see a bed again, after we leave."

For two days, we're hiding with Leviter and Tarn, as it doesn't make sense to try to slip out of Jineba at the height of the manhunt. We have orders to rejoin our squad after the furor dies down, at a given time and place. If our luck holds, we'll slip out of the city on foot, as public transport has been locked down. There are checkpoints all around the city; and if you're stopped, you need a foolproof identity kit. Nicuan masters have chipped all the La'hengrin in the cities, a particularly disgusting measure that proves ownership. Obviously, I don't have one, so if we're stopped, it will mean combat.

But I won't contemplate possible pitfalls tonight. March and I have forty-eight hours of enforced R&R, and I intend to make the most of them.

La'heng Liberation Army signal-jack ad: Final Profile

DEVEN

[A man with sunburnt skin and dark eyes gazes at the camera, his expression flat.]

Female interviewer, off-screen: Are you ready, Deven? If this is too hard—

[He makes a curt gesture, silencing her.]

Deven: It was difficult to live it. Words are nothing.

Female interviewer: Then proceed when you're ready. We're rolling.

Deven: I was born in a small mountain village north of Jineba. We had little . . . the whole town economy was driven by the mines. We worked them to survive, providing ore for Nicuan factories closer to the city, but they also killed us. I had three sons once. At ten turns, the youngest died, coughing blood. Bluerot. He died in my arms. I sent him to the mine to work because if I had not, the Nicuan governors would have reduced the amount of rations my family received, as it is Imperial law for all La'hengrin to "engage in productive labor for the good of the empire" after the age of eight.

Female voice, gentle: I'm sorry for your loss.

Deven: Save your pity. The worst is yet to come.

Female voice, subdued: Please continue.

Deven: My wife, Darana, was crushed. I was heartbroken. But we pressed on. We all worked in the mines that killed my boy until the LLA arrived in our village.

Female voice: What happened then?

Deven: I took the cure. Survived it. So did my oldest sons, then fourteen and sixteen. My wife was not so fortunate. She, too, died in my arms.

Female voice, obviously moved: Are you sure—

Deven, ignoring her: My sons and I joined the LLA, determined to fight for La'hengrin freedom. They're both dead now.

Female voice: Do you regret your choices?

Deven: I regret that my family is gone and that my people are still enslaved.

Female voice: Will you fight on?

Deven: Only death can stop us. La'heng *will* be free. I have nothing now but the cause and what remains of my unit. I will see my world liberated or die in the attempt.

Voice-over: And *that's* the LLA, fighting for you. Contact the comm code at the bottom of your screen to find workers with the cure or to join the resistance.

CHAPTER 51

Two days later, there are a couple of dicey moments as we sneak out of Jineba, but good timing and March's reflexes drive us into hiding until we find a path around the checkpoints. Occasionally it means backtracking or circling around the long way, but eventually, we clear the last obstacle and emerge into the countryside. It's not as peaceful as one might hope, though.

I hear detonations in the distance, and it's not our forces since Loras hasn't given the order to strike the cities yet. We're entrenched in the provinces, building troops and supplies, before we commit to the final phase. Which means the Nicuan are responsible. My stomach feels leaden as I fall in behind March. The rendezvous point is a day's hike, and we'll be crossing dangerous terrain alone. Drones do low buzzes overhead, scanning for hostiles, and some of them carry ordnance. If Sasha were with us, he could take them out, but that would also report our position. So long as we don't assault their tech, the drones won't register us. We're not carrying any weapons it would detect, nothing with a power source. That leaves us with primitive methods of self-defense, however, until we rejoin our squad.

Over the next rise, I learn the source of the noise, and I freeze with shock. Then, instinctively, I start forward, as if I can save them. March catches me, draws me back against him. I want to fight him, but there's no point. I can only watch, helpless with pain and rage, as Nicuan bombards a civilian target. The town is full of elderly La'hengrin who have been retired from public service. Their protectors don't want them anymore because they've committed the ultimate sin; they've aged and are no longer beautiful. So they're banished to this village to live out their remaining days in loneliness and squalor.

"We don't have any forces there," I protest.

"Doesn't matter. This is supposed to break our will to carry on."

No screams are audible, but I imagine them. March and I crouch, unable to pass, until the Nicuan drones cease the onslaught. The machines gun down survivors below; anyone who runs, dies, and I can't look away from the carnage. I don't know when I've felt more helpless or more horrified.

This is the longest hour of my life.

Eventually, the drones complete their programming and veer away, off to another target, probably to rain more destruction on innocents. I've never hated like this before, but as I run down to the hillside to check for survivors, it boils in me like lava. March follows me, more cautious in his approach, but I have to know.

Bodies are everywhere. One old couple died wrapped in each other's arms. His face is lined; so is hers, and they cling to love even in death. His legs are gone. As I stumble through the wreckage, I see more and more death. Nobody's breathing. I stagger away from the broken buildings and lose my field rations. This is worse than Venice Minor—and I thought nothing could ever be so bad. But I didn't see Doc and Evie's corpses, afterward. The Morgut missiles burned everything to ash. This ordnance is different, leaving carnage calculated to dishearten the most determined foe.

"We have to move, Jax. We can't save them."

"All right." I pull myself together with some effort, but I can't compartmentalize. Not this. It's too big. I have no secret spaces in my head large enough to hold it. So the horror sits in the front of my mind as I walk, replaying constantly.

"Don't," March says softly. "It'll drive you crazy."

"You must've seen that before. How do you stand it?"

"Similar atrocities. War is never clean." He doesn't stop, even to comfort me.

I understand why. That hour cost us; if we don't reach the rendezvous point in time, we'll be alone behind enemy lines. And we can't get the job done that way. It has become more critical than ever to remove Nicuan from this world. The crimes they've perpetrated against the La'hengrin will cease—and they will be punished. I'll see to it. Now I understand what March meant when he said Loras had changed; I feel like I have ice in my veins. What do the Nicuan care about some old people? Maybe it'll teach the slaves their place.

Six hours later, we arrive at the agreed location. It appears to be deserted. At first, I think they've gone without us, and my heart drops. Then I spot movement; Loras, Vel, Zeeka, and the others are wearing armor with camo paint, perfected when Constance was head of R&D. I can't believe she's gone. Never got to thank her . . . or say good-bye.

"Glad you could make it," Z says cheerfully.

Vel greets me with a particularly eloquent *wa*. *Now white wave can rest. The tides were restless while brown bird flew.* His way of telling me he was worried about me.

I don't have the patience for pleasantries, however. This time I don't return the *wa*. Once he hears, Vel will understand. Immediately, I corner Loras and give him the intel on the devastation; his jaw clenches as he listens to my report.

Then he circles his hands in the air, signaling Farah. "Get our gear packed. We need to clear the area."

"That's all?" I demand.

"We don't want to be here when they come back for round two," he tells me. "It serves no one if we die before we're through. I'll send a comm out, advising civilians to get to one of our fortifications if at all possible. That's all I can do right now."

"But . . ." It seems wrong to walk away from this, yet I know he's right.

We have to bide our time until our forces are ready. The guerilla war will continue in the provinces. We'll keep stealing supplies and shipments while holding the ground we've taken. If we could get some defense towers up, drones would have no way to assault us. But at the moment, our resources are insufficient to protect civilian targets. There are strongholds in the north and west, where Nicuan hasn't been able to penetrate our airspace in a while, but those safe zones are few and far between.

Over the next six months, I learn that the hard way. We run missions constantly, high-risk scenarios on various targets: raiding, stealing, and harrying the enemy. This particular day, I'm riding high, as the factory burns in the distance—Zeeka's handiwork—and the squad is cheerful. We just cost the Nicuan nobility a billion credits in ruined drones. Ceepak is cracking wise, promising even more destruction, and we echo his cockiness with an approving rumble. These days, there's no base, but Tarn is coordinating strikes. When we lost the ops center, he stepped up, offering his experience during the Morgut War to keep each individual cell harassing the Nicuan giant.

But then everyone falls quiet. Because . . . there's a smell in the air, one I've grown too familiar with over the turns. Death. Death on a grand scale. I've seen some terrible things, and the bombing of that village was among the worst, but this? I have no words.

There's a gaping hole in the earth, purposefully dug, but the enemy didn't have the decency to bury the dead. And the madness has method. The sign posted near the pit reads: DEATH TO THE CHILDREN OF INSURGENTS. THE FAMILIES OF ALL TRAITORS TO THE EMPIRE WILL BE EXECUTED.

This mass grave is full of children. I can tell that by their size though they've been dead for days. So many of them, I lose count in those first ghastly seconds, but each small face imprints in my head. I squeeze my eyes shut, but I can't stop seeing this. Shakes overtake me, and I drop into a squat, breathing too fast through my nose.

Someone's hands are on me, soothing, and I slap them away. There's no solace for this. Sasha, who isn't much older than the kids in the hole, is here. He shouldn't be exposed to this. Part of me wishes he and March had never come to La'heng, despite what they've given to the cause. I wish *I* weren't here; I long for the fierce colors and the scintillant beauty found only in grimspace.

"It doesn't matter what their families did or didn't do. They were *children*. How do you fight an enemy who will do this?" I ask of nobody in particular.

"You become the sort of person who will do worse," Loras answers coolly.

"I can't."

The leader of the LLA stares down into the mass grave, as if memorizing each face. "I can. I will. I must."

I see the steel hardening in him, tempered by multiple Nicuan atrocities. Each time they raise the bar for what's too horrible to contemplate . . . and Loras's retaliation will be devastating. He's been saving it up for turns, witnessing horror after horror.

When Farah unleashes him, the Nicuan will burn.

CHAPTER 52

The months roll on with inexorable sameness. We don't get downtime. Push, push, push. That's all Loras says. But he's not wrong. The resistance is gathering momentum; in the city, there's a youth movement dedicated to making the centurions' lives miserable. They don't wear uniforms, so it's impossible for the Nicuan to tell who belongs to the resistance without a wholesale execution of slaves. It's not that I think the nobles wouldn't do it; but they're fundamentally selfish beasts. If they kill all their slaves, they'll have to work.

The next op will be a joint effort between my squad and Deven's cell. Our target is the munitions supply depot that's arming centurions to take the war to more helpless villages in the provinces. We can't let that happen.

My whole body aches with exhaustion, accumulated through months of little sleep, constant movement, and battle readiness. For the first time, I'm glad of the Rejuvenex treatment because I might not have been able to keep up. I don't know how March is doing it, as he's still got his same body, already battered from prior turns on Nicu Tertius. Yet he doesn't complain; he's coordinating with Deven at the moment.

Then it's deployment time.

After a series of successful strikes, the Nicuan are on high alert. They've stationed a ton of centurions here, guarding the munitions. Our manpower is on the low end for this objective, but we've got La'hengrin determination and SpecForce. I hope it's enough to carry the day.

The camo paint on our armor doesn't work as we move, but when we settle into position on the rise above, it helps. Gazing through binocs, I scope out the scene below. Multiple guard towers, heavy hardware. If we intended a frontal ground assault here, we'd be doomed. Fortunately, we have other options.

Loras orders, "Ceepak and Shelby, you're on watch. Look after Sasha and Hammond while they do their thing. Z, I want you ready to roll with Beta Squad." That's Deven's team. "How fast can you wire the place to blow?"

"Depends," Zeeka answers. "On a lot of factors. But I'll work as quick as I can."

The LLA commander nods. "Good enough, it's all I can ask. The rest of you will bunker down over there." He points across to the other side of the hill. "Lay down enough fire to make the centurions think there are more of you. Vel, you're in charge of scrambling their hardware, so they can't get an accurate scan of life signs in the area. That means you're with Beta Squad as well."

We'll draw them away from SpecForce, so they can complete their mission. So much weight rests on Sasha's young shoulders. Talk about getting your Psi training in a crucible.

"There's no margin for error here, people. This is the last objective before we can begin the final offensive and take the battle to the last Nicuan stronghold, the cities."

I get the importance. We have to pull some teeth out of the beast's mouth before we dare stick our hand in, but it doesn't lessen how scared I am. This war has taken so much already. When Vel leaves my sight without looking back, nausea roils in my gut. Thank Mary March is geared up and bunkered down beside me.

What's left of our team moves along the hillside slowly, getting in position to open fire on Loras's signal. Which will be low-tech, as well. We've fought under incredible disadvantages, limited by lack of communications since the base went down and dwindling resources. The Nicuan destroy things rather than let our people use them. They're mining farmland, so the La'hengrin are starving while the nobles get fatter in Jineba and Kayro. I've come across so many fields with the bodies of helpless farmers littered across them, blown to bits when they tended their crops.

This nightmare feels endless. Turns ago, when I agreed to this, I didn't realize what it would mean. I was naïve. I've been so many women in my past, played various roles, but it will be a different Jax entirely who leaves La'heng.

If I do.

Right now, I feel none too sure.

As one, our unit waits until Loras sends up the flare from across the way, where he's guarding SpecForce. Farah is here with me, and she raises her weapon. We open fire as one, scattering the centurions crossing down below. March is beside me, raining death, as SpecForce goes to work. Sasha takes out two piles of crates himself; those are weapons that will never be used against us. Hammond is starting fires all over the place. There's some risk as we have Beta Squad, along with Vel and Zeeka, down there, but I trust they can look after themselves. They'll avoid the towering infernos Hammond lays down and do the rest of the job while the centurions deal with our distractions.

That's exactly what they are, too: sound and fury, covering the real target—the warehouses. Zeeka will slip inside them, one by one, while we keep the enemy busy. Mary grant they don't catch on and turn their attention inward. Vel screwing with their comms will help; if they can't readily compare notes or issue orders, they'll be crippled, as centurions aren't known for being quick thinkers—too many turns of blindly following orders.

Sometimes I get lucky and kill a centurion. Secretly, this thrills me. In my head, they all wear Cato's face. That's probably wrong; some might be more like Gaius, but it permits me to unload without mercy, until my rifle beeps a warning. Then I drop down and let March cover the gap in the pattern.

"How's it look down there?" I ask him.

He peers through the scope. "Burning. Explosions. Men dying."

"Their men?"

"I think so. It's pretty hard to tell. We won't get word from Beta Squad until the mission's complete."

"We'll know if Z succeeded when he detonates."

"True enough."

I raise up to fill in when March's gun goes hot. Around me, the others are doing the same, switching fire. We learned from the mess at Legate Flavius's estate, at least. Lately, our raids have been surgical; turns of teamwork are paying off.

Five minutes later, a boom rocks the ground. Even from here, I can see the fireball spiraling up from the building down below. Another follows immediately, then another, and another, until all five warehouses have been leveled, leaving only smoking craters. A ragged cheer rings out from our crew.

Farah says, "Z really knows his explosions."

Elsewhere, it's pandemonium, with a few crazed centurions staggering around, hands over their ears. I feel almost guilty about gunning them down.

Almost.

By the time my team and SpecForce finishes mopping up, there's nothing moving down below. I should feel . . . something at this colossal loss of human life, but I'm happy. Triumphant, even. I don't like what this war is turning me into; before, I worried I was becoming a monster because I had so much technology inside me, but that's not what determines your humanity. It's the capacity for empathy, caring about other people.

And I'm losing mine, millimeters at a time.

I can't fret about it now, however, as I'm worried about Vel and Z. No celebration until I see them clear the rise, weary but whole. I run to him, and March is right behind me. To my surprise, we end up in a kind of group hug. Vel seems taken aback by this new development, but he doesn't recoil.

"It went well?" I ask.

"A few close calls, but we handled them." Which means there was fighting.

I check him out visually, but I detect no damage. Then I make my way over to Z, who is surrounded by a congratulatory mob. "You did it. How does it feel?"

"Wonderful," he answers gravely. "And terrible."

I know exactly what he means.

We can't celebrate long, however. This victory is critical, but there's more work to be done. So we join up with Loras and SpecForce, then march ten klicks before the commander stops us. Over a quick meal, he has some new orders for us.

Loras stands in the center of the makeshift camp, arms folded. "I won't lie to you. I never have. There's still a long campaign ahead, but we're winning. I've laid out some new targets. As we head for Jineba, we'll be taking out key Nicuan personnel." He outlines the strategy—where but not who or why.

"Legates?" I guess.

"And their families," Loras answers. "Does anyone have a problem with that?"

I remember that pit full of children . . . and say nothing. Beside me, Deven shakes his head; his pain is oceanic, hidden behind his devotion to the cause. "I lost three children to the Nicuan, two in this war. Why should theirs get to live?"

There's no answer to that. I pack my things and fall in with the others. There's a long way to go before our next op.

CHAPTER 53

Revenge is a dish best served cold.

It's been a long turn full of skirmishes, near misses, hunger, exhaustion, dirt, and bivouacking in hostile environments. We're buying time. Keeping them after us while the medical teams circulate wider and wider, deploying the cure. The waiting game feels like it has no end, but as long as we keep the Imperials snapping at us in the provinces, they won't notice that the cities are slowly attaining their freedom. They won't realize how few La'hengrin are required to obey, as they'll continue to serve until they receive orders to rise up.

Today, though, Loras has decided to do something terrible; he's waited a full turn for his retaliation for the destruction of the base. Kayro is a smaller city, sparsely populated with La'hengrin. There's no way to evacuate all of them. Loras is unconcerned; he says if they knew what was coming, they would gladly give their lives for the cause. But he's taking the choice away from them.

It doesn't matter what I think. He programs the coordinates into the targeting array, then he launches the MO himself. It streaks away, deceptively small for the devastation that will ensue when it detonates. We have four more bombs like this, enough to strike terror into Imperials' hearts. And that's the point.

I walk away. Out of camp and into the quiet silence of the surrounding forest. A dangerous risk, but I need some distance. I'm tempted to keep walking. Loras has become someone I don't recognize, like the push for freedom is burning away his compassion. But I'm not his moral compass. If Farah couldn't talk him out of this—I don't even know if she tried . . . because she's changed, too; the war has made her cold, occasionally cruel—and, well, I need to stop thinking about it.

Feels like forever since I've been clean.

We're nomads.

Hunting and killing on the move. We've raided so many estates in the provinces. Executed nobles and centurions alike. Each life we take weakens their resolve, wears at their certainty that this is a winnable conflict. The strikes also damage Nicuan hierarchy and infrastructure. But it doesn't feel good when you burst into someone's home.

At night, Loras pores over field reports, assets seized, casualty lists. As time wears on, we've become more organized, perfecting a coded system of passing messages cell to cell. It's simple to decode if you have the key, and it's always changing. I know the Imperials are frustrated because they can't crack the cryptography. *Why won't they leave?*

La'heng doesn't belong to you. Admit defeat and go home.

I hope Loras doesn't make us watch the news, reporting on how many died in Kayro. I don't need to see the number to know it's millions, many of them La'hengrin. In any city, they outnumber those they serve. Not all Nicuan on world are combatants; there are office workers and domestics, traveling in the nobles' entourages. They die just like everyone else.

I'm tired of bloodshed, tired of ruthless destruction. I'm afraid Loras is becoming as much a monster as the Nicuan. When, early on, he said he would do anything to free his people, I couldn't have credited this.

Footfalls sound behind me, then I hear Vel's voice. "It is horrendous."

"Yes," I choke out.

Annihilation on that scale cannot help but offend the soul unless you're dead inside. He draws me to him in patient motions, stroking his talons through my hair. I listen to him breathe, counting the differences between us. The exercise is soothing; it calms me.

"The Nicuan nobles cannot last against such opposition," Vel says eventually. "The La'hengrin have no comparable targets for escalation. The legates could strike another city, but if they evacuated their own people beforehand, word would certainly get out."

"You don't think the Imperator would sacrifice nobles for victory?"

Vel cants his head, pensive. "He might. But the moment he did so, the surviving princes would remove him from office. He would triumph only at the cost of his career."

"Most Nicuan are too selfish for that."

"Precisely. So they have no means to match Loras, no way to hurt him as greatly. Though it was a regrettable decision, it will end the war."

"You know more about this stuff than I do." It's not comforting, exactly, but if he's right, then I'll live with my participation in this, as I do everything else. By blocking it off and refusing to feel it.

"Jax," Zeeka calls. "We're moving out."

"Roger that."

When Vel and I get back to camp, the stealth shuttle's already loaded. Since we travel with the MO and launching platform, we can't move like the other cells do. I guess this is a benefit of traveling with the commander in chief of La'hengrin forces. I'm the last to board, after Vel. March is already waiting, strapped in and looking worried. He comes into my head with a sweet familiarity.

I let Vel take this one. It's a big step for him, bigger than it sounds, but after our conversation in Tarn and Leviter's flat, I'm not wholly surprised; this is March's way of showing me he means what he says. *You okay?*

Not really. But I'll deal. There's no choice.

It was the right call at the right time. It's been long enough since they took out the base that they can't mistake this for wrath. It was a calculated maneuver, and that will scare them even more. Anyone can push a button in anger. It takes particular strength to do so when your head is cool.

I'm not sure I'd call it strength.

Resolve, then.

Hearing validation of the strike from both March and Vel doesn't erase my pain at the loss of life. I glance over at Zeeka, wondering how he keeps his spirits high. The Mareq seems cheerful all the time—happy to be here, happy to be included, happy to be fighting, learning—pretty much anything that's going on, he's glad about it. His people were like that, as I recall. When we landed on Marakeq to bring back Baby-Z2, instead of responding to the unknown with fear, hostility, and aggression, they acted like we were a joyous surprise.

Finally, I ask Z what I've wondered for turns. "Why doesn't anything get you down? After what we just did, so many people died—"

His wide mouth falls into amused lines. "Everything dies. There's no way to stop that tide. In the end, all we have is the pleasure we take from life. For my people, it's not long. I can spend my time crying or I can *live.* I can seek wonder. Haven't you ever noticed that people tend to find what they're looking for, my friend?"

The truth of his words takes my breath away. How unexpectedly profound. I suspect I'll learn so much from him in the thirty turns he has left. I suspect they won't be nearly long enough. Tears prickle in my eyes, but I don't let them fall. I don't want Z to think I misunderstood.

"Thank you," I whisper. "I don't know when I ever needed a lesson more."

He's puzzled, but glad. He turns to speak with Ceepak, not realizing what an impact he's had on me, this Mareq who once took nourishment from my bare skin.

"He is wise," Vel observes. "I lived a great many turns before I internalized that particular lesson."

"I wonder if the Mareq have genetic memory, so they remember things their ancestors learned. To make up for such short lives?"

Vel says, "It would explain much."

Before I can reply, the shuttle puts down three klicks from our next target. It's another estate raid. You'd think the nobles would stay out of the provinces, but even in wartime, they think they're above commonsense precautions. Who would dare attack Legate Whoever in his own home, right?

We would, obviously.

"Ceepak, stay with the shuttle," Loras orders.

That makes sense because he'll hear anybody coming. He has to guard the MO at all costs. Without it, we become toothless hounds.

He adds, "The rest of you, move out."

Another battle, another scar. He was right, the one who first said *War is hell.*

Imperial News Bulletin

[The presenter on screen is an older male, losing his hair in the subtle pushback of hairline toward his temples. He wears a dark suit and there are shadows beneath his eyes.]

I will now read a prepared statement from the governor of Jineba.

At this time, I must report with a heavy heart that the terrorist group known as the LLA has detonated a weapon of mass destruction in Kayro. There were no survivors. All travel to the region has been discontinued; no public transport or private air travel will be permitted because of the complete irradiation. Groundwater will be contaminated for turns to come.

If nothing else, this attack should convince you that these people are monsters. They murder their own without regard. They have no care for those who have done their best to shepherd this planet. The LLA is full of bloodthirsty extremists who care only for the abstract tenet of freedom and nothing at all for the welfare of this world.

The empire will retaliate. We have destroyed important LLA installations, and we will continue to fight until this threat has been contained. Even now, your legates are planning a counterattack. This tragedy will not stand.

Grieve for your loved ones. Hate those responsible. And have faith in your government. We will not fail you. Justice will be served, and the guilty will pay.

CHAPTER 54

The battles blur together.

Death. Blood. Dirt. Mud. Pain.

Last night, Deven executed an entire noble family on Loras's orders. The commander was adamant that we send a message to Imperial forces. And so it went out on our next signal-jack broadcast. They must believe we have the will to do what is necessary, and nothing frightens civilians more than the death of children.

In truth, I'm losing heart. It's been two turns since we left Jineba, two turns of wearing the wrong face and living a life I loathe.

When will it end?

The provinces are battlefields, but we must take the cities if we hope to dig the Nicuan out of here. Otherwise, this war never ends. Loras is prepared to bomb four more cities; we have the capacity, which would severely cripple Nicuan nobility. It would also significantly reduce the La'hengrin population. I don't want him to do that; once was enough. There has to be another way.

"This is the shittiest sixteenth birthday ever," Sasha says, breaking into my thoughts.

He's been fighting for an eighth of his life. That's so wrong. But no question, he's strong and brave, a credit to March. Few young men his age have the same grasp of suffering and sacrifice. I'm just not sure that's a good thing.

"Hey," Ceepak protests. "This is the finest mudhole credits can buy."

The kid has a point, I admit. We're entrenched fifty klicks outside the city. Other cells have joined us. Since the Imperials have lost all their heavy installations, they can't target us. The fighting is limited to waves of centurions who push, then fall back, trying to keep us out of the capital. It doesn't matter, though.

The enemy's already behind the lines. By my calculations, the cure has just about saturated the populace. Everyone has had a chance to take it . . . or decline. Some have; they fear freedom and self-reliance, or else they fear death. They'll wait for a version of the vaccine that's one hundred percent effective. But those La'hengrin are the minority.

"I made you a cake," Farah says.

Sasha brightens, his expression hopeful even through the rain. His face has become less elfin and delicate over the turns. Now he needs to shave, and he has March's stubborn jaw though still his mother's fair hair and sea-hued eyes.

Farah grins; she can be evil as hell. "Not really. But I did steal you one at the last estate we raided. It's probably stale and smashed by now."

"Let's have it," Sasha demands.

So, between booms of thunder, Farah portions out the treat, giving Sasha the biggest chunk. He stuffs it into his mouth with both hands, and his eyes close. I can't remember the last time I had something sweet. No choclaste, no *kaf*. For months, we've been living on paste, what we scavenge from the estates, and sometimes fresh meat, which grosses me out.

"You're a man now," March says, deadpan. "I need to find you a joy girl."

Even Loras hoots at this, and Sasha covers his face in mock-embarrassment. He mumbles through his hands, "You know I can crush your skull, right?"

March grins. "And I can make you not want to anymore."

"I hate you." Sasha makes a rude gesture, which I'm pretty

sure he learned from Ceepak, as it's a La'hengrin move. "You're such an ass."

"We've got incoming," Shelby shouts.

He must've glimpsed them with his gift. At this point, they're far enough away that Ceepak can't hear them, so that means we have a little time.

Hammond grouses, "I might as well go back to my bunk in this rain. I'm useless." It's kind of a cliché, since he's Pyro, but he's the unit hothead.

"Use your weapon," Vel reminds him. "Some of us kill without any powers at all."

Shelby laughs, and Hammond slugs him. Sometimes, I see very clearly how young the SpecForce team is. Sometimes, they remind me of boys on a field trip, and yet they're tough, dedicated, and disciplined, all of them.

"Wrong," Z says. "You do have a power."

"I do?" Vel's mandible flares in surprise.

"The power of being awesome!" Z's thrilled with his translator, I can tell. He pulls off the slang and bumps chests with Ceepak, who's been teaching him this shit.

Thunder booms overhead; lightning cracks the sky. And I hand Sasha my soggy cake. "Here. You only turn sixteen once."

He grins at me. "Or you're doing it wrong."

"Have you thought about the future at all?"

"A little, I guess. Before, back on Nicuan, Dad and I talked about me going to the engineering academy on New Terra."

"Is that what you want to do?"

"I think so. I definitely don't want to be a soldier. I'm glad I helped . . . I still think it was the right move, but doing this forever would seriously screw you up."

"No shit." He's seen things no kid should see. And I wonder if he can possibly be as healthy as he seems. "Your dad's got some issues."

"He'll be all right. He's got you." That's the nicest thing Sasha has ever said about my relationship with March. Mostly, he ignores the intimate aspect of it.

"You're okay with us? You hated me at first."

He scoffs. "I was ten, what did I know? I was also scared of the dark, and I collected little army men."

"Heh, when you put it like that . . ."

"The weirdest part of it, to be honest, is now you look like somebody *I* should be dating. That's gotta freak the old man out some."

I laugh. "When the war's over, I'll change it up a little."

At the moment, that's the least of my concerns. I've been wearing this uniform for days. I can't remember the last time I bathed. Oh, wait, yes, I can. It was after the estate raid, a month ago. I jumped in the san-shower and steam-cleaned everything, clothes and all. At night, when bunking on the cold ground, I dream of a dry bed and hot food. I dream of grimspace and the rumble of a ship engine lulling me to sleep. They're not big dreams, but they're mine. They get me through.

"I hear them," Ceepak says, sobering us. "Fifty, coming in quiet."

March nods. "They're using the storm as cover. Not a bad move. I've used it myself a time or two."

Zeeka's already trapped the whole perimeter. A number of centurions will go sky high, but some will break through. Loras organizes us in lines, and I end up in the trench between Sasha and Vel. He wants March up front, helping with tactics.

"Did you hear?" Z asks, raising his rifle.

The cold rain sluices down his armor. Because I can't help it, I wonder for the thousandth time if he's warm enough.

I shake my head. "What's up?"

"Tomorrow's the day of reckoning. We march to the city, and Loras is calling all the free La'heng to active service."

So in a few days, it ends. No more dodging. No more war games. Terror and elation battle for supremacy within me. In the end, it's easier for me to focus on the movement along the ridge. My distance shooting isn't good enough, but Vel drops one as the centurions push through the mud, through driving rain and wind to fight for nobles who don't care if they live or die. Their pay cannot possibly be sufficient for the odds they face, and yet they don't back down. They follow these orders to their deaths. Is that bravery or stupidity?

The enemy hits our mines and explodes in a bright orange ball. Meat that used to be men splatters everywhere. And still they come on. I raise my rifle. Fire. Again.

I am saturated in death, so dirty I may never get clean, and yet I, too, fight on. I take target after target, covering the men ahead of me. I follow orders like the centurions. Because there's no way out but through—it's especially true now.

Some famous guy who was about to be executed said this: *Give me liberty or give me death.* That's how the La'hengrin feel.

Me, I've lost some of my passion but none of my commitment. I'm in this until the end. I *will* keep my promises.

CHAPTER 55

The camp is hardly worth the name, just a place where we've pitched our tents. No fortifications, no precautions, but since we're marching on the capital, it doesn't matter. The cells will unite outside Jineba, but until then, the units are small and mobile. Hard to track. It's worked like a charm so far.

"If I say I might die tomorrow, would that get me some rack time with you?" March has come up behind me, wraps his arms around my waist.

Tomorrow, along with everyone else, we move on Jineba. I should be terrified, or at least worried, but my soul is calm. This feels right. Inevitable. This is where I'm supposed to be. It is a night of perfect synchronicity, where the stars that shine overhead are the ones I'm supposed to see at precisely this moment.

"You don't have to bargain for it," I say, facing him. "I'm yours for the taking. Have been for turns. Though so many other things have, that hasn't changed."

"Then come on, Jax. Celebrate life with me tonight."

"Eat, drink, and be merry, for tomorrow we may die?"

"Something like that. I'll settle for the merry part." He

sweeps me into his arms, ignoring the hoots from our unit. Zeeka calls out a teasing remark, and I salute him over March's shoulder.

He crouches and crawls into his tent, with me still cradled in his arms, a feat not for the weak or uncoordinated. There isn't much room, and I'm conscious of how our bodies show as shadow shapes. Then he kisses me, and I don't care if the whole company watches from start to finish. His mouth has always made me feel like that, and it doesn't matter that extra lines frame it now, or that more silver peppers his dark hair at the temples. He's not perfect; he's hurt me. But neither am I, and I've wounded him, too. When all the columns are tallied, emotional profit and loss reckoned, I will always, always love him.

I'm glad to hear that.

More kisses, sweet and soft. On the night before battle, I expect him to be fierce and fast, but instead he loves me with a slow, inexorable sweetness that brings tears to my eyes. Not a centimeter of skin is revealed that he doesn't caress with gentle hands made rough through turns of work. The rasp against my unexpectedly smooth skin surprises me, every time. I don't know if I'll ever be used to it. This moment, this spun-crystal starburst of a moment, feels brand-new, like the first time I touched him, only this time, I appreciate what I hold in my hands.

"If I say you're beautiful, will you get mad?"

I pull back a little. "Why would I?"

"Because you don't look like yourself. But I don't mean that anyway."

"What do you mean?"

"You." He touches the skin over my heart, the temple where my hair sweeps away from my face. "The Jax part. Not your body. It feels like I've loved you forever even when I had no hope of you feeling the same way. Then, later, when I fought despair that I'd ever see you again. I'd wait longer than five turns. I'll never give up."

I kiss him, unable to find words for a few seconds. And then I whisper, "That's my favorite part about you. I can't decide whether that makes you devoted or crazy."

"Crazy-devoted?" he offers.

"Mmm. That."

The talking stops for a while, gives way to hot touches and slow friction. There's no room for femme dominant when the time comes, but he works extra hard to make it good for me. In the end, he has to kiss me to keep me from screaming. I always thought sex might grow stale, predictable, over long turns with the same person. How could you not get bored? But the truth is, the longer you love the same person, the more mysterious they become. March is like a pocket universe, full of stars, and I will never learn all his light.

Afterward, he holds me, stroking my back with confident hands. He knows how to touch me. Tonight, I won't consider what's ahead and how difficult it may become. There's only the magic of this moment.

"How do you think it will go tomorrow?" I ask.

"Loras is ruthless enough to get the job done. He learned that from Hon."

"Do you think everything happens for a reason? If I hadn't abandoned him, he wouldn't have acquired the steel necessary to free his people."

March considers, dusting a kiss against my brow. "I'd like to believe Mary has a master plan, but I'm not sure of it. I think we can only do our best, learn from our mistakes, and hope it's enough."

"Are you ever sorry for how you treated him?"

He doesn't need to ask who I mean. Before I saved Loras, March held his *shinai*-bond, inherited him from his great-uncle. "I could claim it was just the way I was raised, the way I saw people treat the La'hengrin. But it doesn't excuse my behavior. It only explains it. Wrong is wrong. I didn't even realize how bad it was until you pointed it out, then it was like my blinders fell off, and yes, I was ashamed. I regret it still, the way I treated him."

"Have you talked to him about it?"

"Once. He said, 'You were only worse than other masters in your eagerness to rid yourself of me.' I made him feel like a burden."

I nod. "It's like you said, I guess. About doing our best and learning from our mistakes. You've spent turns fighting for him, following his leadership without question. I think we've both made up for those old wrongs."

"Does your conscience feel clean now, Jax? Will you be ready to move on when the time comes?"

I examine my inner landscape. There will always be scars, of course. I carry regret over Doc and Evie. For those six hundred Armada soldiers. For the squad-mates who died on the way. Some of them, like Xirol, I tried to save and failed. I'll live with that. But pain isn't the same as guilt, and most of that has melted away.

At length, I nod. "I'm more than ready. I miss grimspace."

"I'm amazed you've been on the ground so long without losing your mind."

This is the longest stretch, no question. It feels like penance, and I've achieved expiation at last. Kept my promises.

"Sometimes, when I'm alone, I close my eyes, and I go flying. I build the colors in grimspace in my mind's eye until I can feel it. That echo is enough to keep me from losing it. But I need to fly soon."

"We will," he promises.

"You, me, Vel, and Zeeka. Quite a crew, huh?"

"The best."

Then there's more kissing and little sleep. In the morning, it's time to take the fight to Jineba. No more fragging around. No more skirmishes in the provinces against targets that don't matter as much. This war needs to end.

I am Sirantha Jax, and I have had enough.

CHAPTER 56

The city swarms with combatants. The cured La'heng aren't in uniform, so the centurions don't know whether they should attack until it's too late. If they were complete monsters, they would be gunning down even those who cannot fight, but they can't make themselves do it. After so many turns of benign neglect cloaked as protection, they can't turn on their charges so easily. It speaks well of them even as they die screaming.

I spot Deven fighting in the distance. His squad is one of the most effective in terms of successful strikes, and I credit his leadership for that. Loss drives him. Unless we free La'heng, his family's sacrifices mean nothing.

Fire rages in the wealthy quarter. Buildings crumble. I hear Sasha's work in the heavy thud of toppling skyscrapers. It doesn't require as much force as you'd think; he only has to destroy the supports low to the ground, and whole structures fall.

Across the courtyard, a centurion falls with his head splattered. Half his skull winds up in the street. The air stinks of burnt meat and ozone, and the constant weapons fire makes the very air feel charged, as if the particles are too heavy with lightning not to tingle against my skin. The survivors of my cell gather round for their last set of orders. Today's the day. Win or lose it all, we take the palace.

"Let's see how much steel the Imperator has," Loras growls. "On my mark, we push. Stay to cover, but don't let them drive you back."

"Yes, sir," we say in unison.

I lose track of how many times I fire my rifle. There's no close combat yet, but March and Vel are ready. Centurions die as we push, leading the charge. Thousands of La'hengrin press in behind us. This ragtag army makes up in determination what it lacks in skill and training. They will not stop. Nicuan must understand that by now. It will be freedom or death.

Loras leads the charge. In terms of distance, we're not far from the palace. There is no governor anymore, just officials trying to keep a dead system running. The high-ranking ones are holed up here. Shit, they've set up artillery at the top. Heavy weapons, coming in hot.

"Stay low," March shouts, as a missile hits the wall behind us. "And move!"

I scramble, but the blast still throws me forward, out of a cover. I'm shot before Vel drags me back. This time the armor soaks the damage, though I have an impressive hole in the back of the suit.

"Are you well, Sirantha?"

I nod. "I'm fine. Let's catch up with the others."

Ahead, March goes down in the barrage. He's not moving. I grab Vel's arm. This can't happen now when we're on the verge of a new life together. We're almost to the happily ever after.

"Do something!"

"On it." Vel hunkers down, peers through the scope, and finds the face of the man working the launcher. With admirable efficiency, he shoots the centurion between the eyes.

Then he does it three more times, until they stop stepping up to the artillery to man it. Their commander screams orders, indistinct over the rest of the battle, but nobody's listening anymore. The spirit has been ground out of these men over turns of combat, over uncertainty and the fact that they're *not* fighting for their homes. They all know they can choose to leave—to end this. And they're ready.

Then I sprint into the chaos, desperate to reach March. He still hasn't gotten up. Sasha will never forgive me if his uncle is—no, I won't even think it. I won't. To cover me, Zeeka uses an invention of Vel's to give his grenades better accuracy. He twirls it and then slings one toward the missile launcher. It explodes on impact, throwing shards of metal and polymer in the air. The boom's big enough to take out two centurions huddled nearby, using the stately, soot-stained pillars as cover.

I roll March over. His face is bloody, black with soot, and I can't tell if he's breathing. "Can I get a medic over here?" I shout. "Medic!"

The rest of Jineba can go to hell. I've sacrificed enough to this war; I won't give up March, too. Farah hurries over, dodging barrages of intermittent fire. For now, Z is keeping them busy, but it could get scary any second.

She runs the scan, then says, "Concussion. Broken ribs. He should live, but he won't be fighting on. Can you and Vel get him out of here?"

"Roger that." I'm grateful for her orders, as I would've done it anyway. But this way, I have official sanction for my actions; after Venice Minor, I learned that lesson, too.

Vel comes up beside me at Farah's gesture while Z continues laying down the ordnance. Explosions rock the palace steps as I fall back, supporting the man I love. Vel has his other side, and we keep moving until we're out of the carnage.

"All clear?" I ask, hunkering down.

"I believe so."

March comes to, then, and he's swinging until he realizes he's not in enemy hands. "Easy," I tell him. "The La'hengrin can take it from here. We fought hard enough."

It's funny that the enemy commander doesn't suspect what we're up to. As directed, the rest of my unit stays put, keeping up the pressure now that we're at the base of the steps. Loras shoots with single-minded ferocity, like it soothes his soul, every centurion he kills. But we don't push, even when he takes off the commander's head. The surviving centurions look almost ready to put down their weapons.

And then the signal comes.

The front doors explode outward. I stifle a smile. Sasha's dramatic as hell. He marches the Imperator out with the surviving members of his Special Forces unit. I'm so proud of them all. We stood knocking at the front while they crept in the back. They've all got their weapons trained on the supreme commander of Nicuan forces. Then, deliberately, Sasha forces the man down, and Loras executes him.

In the immediate vicinity, the fighting quiets; guns fall silent. As the Imperator's body tumbles sideways, Loras stands. He shouts, "Lay down your arms and nominate one of your people to handle peace talks on your behalf. There will be no negotiation, but I am willing to permit your immediate surrender and retreat. Who will speak for you?"

"I'm a legate," comes a familiar voice. Gaius. "I have the authority, as the governor is dead, the Imperator is dead, the primus is dead—"

Not surprising. We've been killing them for months.

With my helmet on—and from this distance—Gaius won't recognize Mishani. It's best that way, but I wish I could tell him, so he can move on. I hope he doesn't make the mistake of idealizing her, seeing her as a beautiful martyr who nobody else can ever equal. But maybe I'm overestimating her importance to him. I hope so.

Loras doesn't smile. "Yes, I'm aware."

"If you trust me, I will confer with the remaining nobles and send you a message with the particulars. Call a cease-fire, please."

"*Do* you trust him?" Farah asks.

Loras doesn't answer. He's thinking. Finally, he shouts, "You'll have your truce. But if you consider betrayal, remember Kayro. The bulk of my people are safe in the provinces, and we can survive an airstrike."

"You have broken the beast's back, sir. Give me two days to get an agreement ratified by the survivors, and we will leave at the first possible opportunity."

Loras glances at Farah, who nods, then he calls, "You have a deal. I will await your message. If it doesn't come in a timely fashion, I'll finish what I started today."

"Understood." Gaius turns and calls the few centurions

alive at the top of the steps back into the wreckage of the governor's palace.

Sasha destroyed a whole wall getting inside, and he looks exhausted as he leads Special Forces down toward us. March claps him on the shoulder, and says, "Good work, son," in a husky voice that reveals how worried he was. No matter Sasha's skill, he's still only sixteen. In March's head, he'll always be the little kid who clung and needed him.

Loras gets on the comm. "All units, stand down. Maintain position and set up perimeters wherever you are right now. We'll hold the city until we hear from the enemy." Then he outlines the unilateral victory . . . and I can hear the cheers even without technology; the streets ring with them. Then it quiets.

"They're still listening," Farah whispers. "Say something."

"Thank you for your patience, belief, and sacrifice. Without each one of you, this would have been impossible. Tonight, La'hengrin, we celebrate our freedom!"

CHAPTER 57

Today's the day.

The message comes down through channels, after what seems like an endless war. After the airstrike on Kayro, they know we're not screwing around. Loras *will* kill everyone in the cities if he has to. Wipe the slate clean. Obviously, some of us don't want to, but he's willing to make the hard choices.

And the nobles understand that.

So we play the vid, the terms for peace, over and over. Gaius looks sincere in the message. If it were anyone else who promised to lead this initiative, I might suspect a trap. But they're at the end of their ropes. Most just want to get out with their skins intact; La'heng isn't a vacation colony anymore. It's hell.

"What do you think?" Loras asks, once we've heard their offer.

Farah looks thoughtful. "We have to risk it."

That's all he needs to hear. He trusts her judgment implicitly.

"Publicize the meeting," he tells us. "I want big numbers. Witnesses. *No* chance for betrayal."

"You got it," I say.

Vel heads to the comm to get started on that. The others go to work on other aspects of ending the war. Ships must be made ready, but only enough to carry those who are withdrawing. Even if each noble had a private yacht, they're not leaving with them. The resistance starts working out a forfeit-and-seizure policy. Long into the night, I hear arguments about enforcement, and it's chaos all day long, with couriers running in and out, hammering out the official agreement that will go into effect. Meanwhile, there's a cease-fire, so everybody's tense, on edge, and hoping it holds.

Four days later, here we are.

Today, it ends. Gaius stands before the assembled nobles, looking older and harder than he did when I first met him. Loss has tempered him, made a man of him. If we hadn't been on opposite sides, we might've been friends. We can't be now, of course, because he thinks I'm dead.

There aren't many Nicuan left. Many died in the city bombings. Others tried to flee to their estates and were gunned down by LLA patrols. I wish I could say I felt heroic, but I'm just tired, now. Ready to move on.

A fragment of a quote nibbles at the edge of my mind. *The beacon fires burn and never go out,/ There is no end to war!* Sometimes, victory is bitter on the tongue like ashes and salt, the taste of tears after a fire. The dead know no defeat. Their ghosts linger in the twilight with accusing eyes, and you learn not to stare directly into the shadows.

He waits until the drone-cams hover in position, then says, "I am here to offer unqualified surrender to the people of La'heng. We request only sufficient time to make a permanent retreat and ships sufficient to contain the survivors. All accumulated material goods will be left behind to be redistributed by the La'heng Liberation Army in lieu of wages owed. All financial assets stored in planetary banking institutions will likewise be remaindered in restitution. It is insufficient for the harm we caused here. I only wish I had known the extent of the hardship sooner, or I certainly would have worked to end it."

Loras stands with him, listening to the recitation, then he inclines his head. "We find these terms acceptable. You have one week. Should any Nicuan personnel remain on world at the end of this cease-fire, they will be considered enemies of the people and executed on sight."

An aide brings agreements forward for e-signature, and they both initial, then shake hands. A cohort of centurions escorts Gaius away. He can't see me in the crowd, but I wonder what he'd think if he spotted Mishani. Soon, the soldiers contain the Imperial officials and commence the diaspora.

But the gathering doesn't go to waste.

Loras is a natural statesman, and he won't waste this crowd. He glances at Farah, who inclines her head. Even though I know what's coming, I can't repress my smile when he address the people. "I invite all of you to witness my union with the woman who has consented to make me the happiest man alive."

The crowd goes wild, and the drone-cams, permitted to bounce news for uplink with ONN for the first time in so many turns, record it all. They pan across the glad faces, cheering men and weeping women. In a few hours, the whole galaxy will know that La'heng is enslaved no longer.

A male I don't recognize steps forward as Loras takes Farah's hands on the steps, the ruined palace behind them. Above, the sky glows like a pearl, with smoke rising from the craters where the nobles used to live. It is a vista that simultaneously imbues hope and breaks your heart that progress came at such high cost. By the man's dark ceremonial robes, I take him to be a priest of native faith. La'hengrin was polytheistic before conquerors came and went, destroying more of their culture each time. It's good to see the doors opened to the old ways again.

Someone affixes a mic to his robe, and his voice booms out through speakers set up at the bottom of the steps. "We are here today because of love . . . and hope. In making this union, you promise to love one another today and forever.

"Loras and Farah, as the wheel turns, dark times may come. There will be strife and joy. I bid you, cleave to one another. Never put pride before devotion. Always believe the best of your beloved and remember that trust is the bedrock of any relationship. The house cannot stand without a strong foundation."

The crowd goes very quiet, and March slips his hand into

mine. He won't ever ask me to marry him, I know. I made it clear how I feel about such commitments. I'm like Kai in that regard; promises have no weight without the power of desire behind them. I'd rather have the passion than the pledge.

You sure? March asks silently. *Look how beautiful Farah looks.*

She's glowing, I agree. *But not because of the ceremony. Because she loves Loras so much.*

March nods. *He loves her, too. I can tell.*

The priest addresses the happy couple. "Are you ready to speak your vows?"

Farah and Loras nod in unison, then he speaks. "Farah, I take you as my wedded wife in the sight of all our people and beneath the sky blessed by the goddess. She hears my words, knows that I will love and keep you, forsaking all others, no matter what fortune holds. You are the brightest star in my soul's firmament and I will ever navigate by your light. I could ask nothing more than to stay by your side, so long as I draw breath. Will you have me as yours?"

"Yes," she says firmly.

She looks every inch the princess, and the people *adore* her. They lean in to catch her vows.

"Loras, you gave me strength when I thought all was lost. You led us all from darkness and into the light. When I would have faltered, you drew me on with gentle hands and caring words. You are the center of my heart, and I will always follow you. Will you have me as yours?"

"Yes," he answers.

The priest turns to an assistant, and he passes each of them a lit candle. In the soft wind, the flames flicker slightly, casting small shadows on the ground. This is a romantic, primitive tradition, but some part of me thrills to it. I know what's coming.

"These flames represent your love. You must nurture it and never let that brightness die. Its brightness rests forevermore in your hands." He steps forward with a bigger candle, this one with a dry wick. "Together, you must kindle a new flame to represent the journey you undertake together."

Smiling at one another as if they're the only ones present instead of surrounded by thousands, as if there isn't an enormous picture of them projected onto one of the buildings nearby, they lean in together and join the flames, lighting the bigger candle. The priest nods in approval and hands the candle to his aide, then murmurs, "Take care with it."

Then, louder, he intones, "Now you will feel no rain, for each of you will be shelter for the other. Now you will feel no cold, for each of you will be warmth for the other. Now there will be no loneliness, for each of you will be companion to the other. Now you are two persons, but there are three lives before you: His life, Her life, and Your life together. The goddess blesses your union, and to you, the people, I present your First Lord and Lady of La'heng, bound and blessed by their love and yours."

The cheers are deafening.

After the ceremony, Loras stops to give us the good news. "I've allotted you a ship from the vessels impounded from the Nicuan as reparations. I think you'll be pleased."

"Thanks," I tell him. "I'm looking forward to flying."

"It's the least I can do," he begins, but the press want a piece of the new leader of La'heng, and I watch him go, smiling.

CHAPTER 58

After victory comes pomp and circumstance. I doze through the speeches until I hear Sasha's name. While he receives his medal, I acknowledge how grown-up March's nephew has become. He looks so handsome in his dress uniform. The rest of his SpecForce unit is on point, fast to march, fast to salute. They do some tricks for the crowd, showing off their amazing cohesive ass-kicking expertise . . . and then, at long last, the ceremony ends. It's a *grand* finale.

People file out.

March and I lose the others in the crowd. I spot Tiana with a group of other survivors. She lifts a hand to me, and I salute her. Deven, too, lived through the epic Battle of Jineba, but he's full of sorrow without Darana; he lost so much. I saw his profile on the bounce, and it made me cry.

On the steps outside, I stand on tiptoe, looking for Sasha. Eventually I spot him. He stands with his unit. They're talking, clasping each other on the shoulder and promising to keep in touch. Though March and I are standing to the side, watching, I can guess what's being said. Now that it's finally over, they're going their separate ways.

Some of the squad will remain together. I hear that Loras is creating an elite police force to make sure all the foreigners depart in a timely fashion. SpecForce will be given first crack at that cush civilian posting. Some of these soldiers prefer to remain part of the first standing army that La'heng has mustered in over two hundred turns. It's a proud tradition commencing again.

Sasha, on the other hand, well, his future lies elsewhere. As if he senses my regard, he breaks away from the throng and comes toward us in long, graceful strides. He's taller than March by four centimeters now, and he might well keep growing. He's only sixteen, after all, but how many kids his age can say they've done what he has?

Amazing.

March shines with a pride that he doesn't bother to conceal. "The medal looks good on your uniform, kid."

"Yeah, well. I can't have you hogging them all, old man."

"Have you given any thought to where you want to go now?"

He's fully trained. And he's been using his powers professionally for the last two turns. I'd bet he can pass any certification test Psi Corp throws at him.

"I didn't want to tell you until I was sure I'd get in, but . . . they accepted me on New Terra. I'm going into an accelerated work-study program. In three turns, I'll be trained to help engineers stabilize dangerous tectonics on worlds that need a little tweaking before they're suitable for colonization."

By March's expression, he had no idea this was cooking. I glance between them, thinking the job sounds exciting as hell, probably dangerous, too, which might be why a frown's building between his dark brows. I lace my fingers through his, squeeze them. He growls silently in my head. *I get it, Jax.*

You have to respect his choices. If he was old enough to fight—

Remember, we weren't exactly in accord on that.

March. That's all it takes.

Fine.

"Do you still need Psi Corp certification?" he asks.

Sasha shakes his head. "The university has its own program to determine whether my TK's both strong enough and controlled enough to prove useful in a terraforming environment."

Holy shit. This kid will be *building worlds* in a few turns. After what he's achieved here, knowing that his future is going to be even more remarkable? Well, I think Svetlana March would be proud. And I don't think I hurt him any, wandering in and out of his life.

March proves why he's such a fragging amazing parent, all over again. "What do you need from me to make this happen?"

"Just some credits in an account and passage to New Terra. Edun and Suni helped me with some of the preliminary applications. It's looking good so far."

That was good of them. I hope we get a chance to say good-bye. They've become dear friends over the past few turns. Neither one is as hard as they pretend, and they're devoted in a way that warms the heart in times like these. They can't take the place of the ones I've lost, like Doc, Rose, and Evie; nor can they supplant the ones who went away to chase their own dreams, like Hit, Dina, and Argus. But they matter more to me than I would've expected, considering one is a politician and the other his pet spy. Not my usual sort at all.

For a moment, I remember the fallen. Rikir, with his quiet determination. Bannie, with her fierce pride. Xirol, with his ready smile. Nothing will bring them back, but we made it worth the sacrifice after all. I was so afraid we'd fail.

Sasha interrupts my thoughts with, "Don't tell me you're going to cry. I knew you'd miss me, but this seems like a little much."

I shake my head. "I'm just thinking how far we've come."

He puffs out a breath, his jade eyes sober. Sometimes, he's all mischievous youth, but he has a hidden core that reveals that he grew up the first time I let him blow up drones to save our lives. That was so long ago.

"Hard to believe," he murmurs.

"You all right with this?" I ask March.

He sighs, eyeing me, then he turns to Sasha. "Do you want us to take you—"

"*Seriously*, Dad? You think public transport is too much for me to manage? I might get hijacked on the way to New Terra?"

"You could take the ship right back," I mutter.

I've seen him in action, after all.

"That's exactly my point."

I touch March's arm. *I know it's hard for you to let go, but he needs to do this. He needs to prove to himself—and to you—that he can. It's time to let the baby bird spread his wings and fly away.*

He'd hit you for calling him a baby bird.

You think maybe that's why I didn't say it out loud? I grin.

"You have an account already," March says. "I'll transfer enough credits for your first turn of school. If you want extra stuff, you can work for it."

"Are you going to tell me the stupendously entertaining story about how you had to work as a merc on Nicuan to save up for your first ship? Because that's so edifying. I could listen to it a *thousand* more times."

I snicker.

March cuts me a look. "He gets that from you."

Since I'm as far from a mom as any woman could be—yet I might be the closest thing to it that Sasha will ever have—I don't deny it. I've lost my knee-jerk desire to deny all connection to this kid. He's not an anchor around my neck. Shit, he saved us more than once. I owe him. And I care about him. Not just because he's March's flesh and blood, either.

"And you think we're both adorable," Sasha says.

"Less so, every minute." March gets out his handheld, starts tapping away. "There. You have funds . . . and I booked you passage to New Terra, leaving first thing in the morning."

"Glad you didn't say tonight." Sasha glances back toward his unit.

"Why?" I ask innocently. "Are you planning to watch the fireworks with us?"

The kid aims a scornful look at me. "Sure. That's exactly what I had in mind. Wait, no. I'm gonna go drinking with the guys before I ship out."

I think that might draw a reprimand from March, but he only says, "Don't go too far from the spaceport."

"Don't worry, old man. There are tons of seedy bars where I can find trouble."

He baits March openly, cheerfully, and I can see what a fine thing that is.

"If you need us," I say, "here's the ship's comm code." Sasha offers me his handheld, and I key the numbers in.

March is looking forward to having our own ship; I can't wait to see grimspace again. It's part of me, just as much as the people I love. I can't change myself, and I don't even want to, anymore. I like the person I've become. No, I'm not perfect, but I do my best. That's all anybody could ask when the ride comes to an end.

Sasha checks to make sure I've saved the information, like I'm some relic who doesn't know anything about modern technology, then says, "Yeah, I figure you're dying to get out into the great beyond again."

The longing digs deeper, sharp as shards of broken glass. "You have *no* idea."

"Sasha! You coming? We're heading out, brother." For a La'hengrin male to term a human so, it's the highest compliment they can offer.

From the kid's expression, he knows. "On my way!" He adds to us, "You don't mind, do you?"

Even if we did, he'd still go, because it's time for him to find his own path. March, and sometimes I, have pointed him in the right direction. He's a strong kid with his head on right. He'll be fine.

But I wait for March's reply. It's simpler than I expected.

"Have fun. Love ya. And I'm gonna miss you. But you're gonna kick all kinds of ass on New Terra."

The kid flashes both fingers in a V for victory, then jogs over to join his buddies. These guys have been through hell together, and now it's time to cut loose before their final farewell. La'heng better hide its daughters tonight.

I lean my head against March's shoulder. "That was pretty hard, huh?"

He mutters a curse. "Hardest fragging thing I ever did, apart from leaving you."

I'm walking a thin line with this jibe, but I can't resist. I cant my head at him, eyes narrowed. "Which time?"

With a playful growl, he kisses me until the sky explodes.

CHAPTER 59

A free La'heng is a beautiful sight.

Fireworks arc up, and this time, the booms don't mean *take cover.* As I pull back from endless kisses, a glorious kaleidoscope of color unfurls like a fan. Red sparks to blue, then to melting gold, gilding the sky in La'heng's joy. Higher up, the departing Imperial ships show as streaks of light, growing ever dimmer until there are only stars to mar the dark tapestry of this fresh start for which we've fought so hard and sacrificed so much.

In awe, I admire the cheering crowds of La'hengrin embracing as Imperial troops withdraw from their homeworld. Not surprisingly, they want all aliens gone as soon as possible, even those who fought for their freedom. There will be no more overlords, no more *shinai*-bond. After so many turns, these people are free.

It's a magical night, leaving all of us buoyant. March stands on one side; Vel guards the other. Though they both stare up at the fireworks along with me, they're both on alert, just in case something goes wrong, in case my infamous Jax luck kicks in, and someone wants to rumble. But that's not going to happen. Not here. Not now. I feel utterly at peace, completely whole. Content. That's the word—not one I've invoked often before and certainly not in conjunction with myself, but Adele would be proud of what we've achieved here, and that's my measuring stick for all good deeds.

"I cannot believe it is over at last," Vel says softly.

His talons curl through my fingers and he gives a squeeze, a learned gesture, but one he knows I appreciate. March slides an arm around my shoulders, protecting me from the push of the crowd. I'm bound to both of them, but we've worked out the balance.

Zeeka bounces before us, indefatigable as ever. Though I feared combat would change his personality and darken his outlook, he's lost nothing. Instead, he's only gained a patina of experience that teaches him it's right to fight for those who need our aid. His mother, Dace, would be pleased with that lesson, I suspect. Maybe we'll have a chance to ask her. At this point, our destination's written in stardust—anywhere and everywhere, that's where you'll find us.

"Isn't it fantastic?" Zeeka asks.

I nod.

The celebration will go on for hours, but we can't stay for the finale, which comes at dawn. That's only for the native La'heng. And so it's time for us to tie up our loose ends and head toward the starport. As if privy to my thought, Loras and Farah fight past their admiring public to join us. Even now, I catch my breath at her beauty. She's the incarnation of joy, glowing with love for him. The First Lord and Lady of La'heng will serve their people well in the turns to come. For my friend, this ended well—in all ways. Together, they'll build a life and a tradition of independence.

"Jax . . . thank you for everything. I couldn't have done this without the three of you. And for what it's worth, I'm sorry to make you go. It's not that we are unappreciative," Loras explains. "But it's time for La'heng to stand alone. We cannot do that with foreign advisors whispering in our ears."

I shrug, smiling. "I've been grounded long enough. It's beyond time for me to get back out onto the star roads."

March nods. "With Sasha settled, I'm ready to ship out."

Farah bows to us formally. "Foreigners will not be welcome here for many turns. The council thinks it best for us to close our borders and make certain we're strong enough before we entertain diplomatic envoys."

Given their experience with outsiders, I don't blame them. This time, the Conglomerate will respect those wishes. Leviter and Tarn will see to it. I wonder where they'll go. With a past like Leviter's, though, it's best for him to run silent. So strange to think the people with whom I worked and struggled and schemed for so long—Loras, Farah, Leviter, and Tarn—I may never see again. We've come to our final parting of the ways.

A pang of melancholy pierces me. I ignore it and puff out a long breath, determined to be brave. So I smile for Loras and Farah. "Will you see us off?"

"That's the best part of the job," he cracks.

His consort raps him on the arm. "Loras!"

"Jax knows I'm kidding. If she hadn't brought her special brand of chaos to bear, none of this would've happened. I know that . . . and I'll never forget her."

The tears threaten, and I almost can't contain the burn this time. "Just . . . bounce me a message sometime. Maybe when you have your first kid . . . or shoot down your first ship for violating La'heng airspace."

Loras nods. "Either, or."

The crowd clears as I follow Loras. They esteem him so highly that they don't shove toward him. I'm sure he seems almost a god in their eyes; and I hope he doesn't grow to take such adulation for granted and abuse it down the turns, changing his wreath of laurel leaves for a tyrant's crown. But that's not my worry.

At long last, *I'm* free, too.

Grimspace's clarion call thrums in my veins. *Come home, Jax. Come home.*

Each footfall brings me closer to that ultimate goal, but I'm no longer thinking of how I might die. No, now I consider the ways in which I might live. It's a huge universe, and I intend to see *everything.*

To pass the throngs more easily, we fall into pairs with Loras and Farah forging ahead, March and Zeeka in the middle, and Vel beside me. *As it should be.* He seems happy tonight, though I'm not sure if it's the satisfaction of a long-held goal achieved or if he's looking forward to our future.

There's nothing to fear with Vel. There never has been, even when he was hunting me. He's the most honorable person I've ever known.

So I ask.

"Both," he replies.

I should've known. "Where do you want to go first?"

He lifts a shoulder in an easy half shrug. "Wherever you please."

I need to think about it, but there's time. Or maybe I don't. That's never been my strong suit, after all. Perhaps I'll just twirl a finger over a random star chart, and off we'll go. That sounds right, given my history. More often than not, nobody can predict what comes next in my story, not even me.

After ten minutes of walking, we reach the spaceport, already stuffed with other foreigners being politely escorted to their ships. In the flurry, I spot Tarn and Leviter standing together. They make a handsome couple, one distinguished with salt-and-pepper hair, the other a silver fox with a clever face. Their affection is obvious in their stance, the gentle tilt of their shoulders, and it lifts my heart to see them safe.

I weave through the crowd. "Thank you both for everything. If it was coincidence that found you here, then I suppose I ought to thank Mary for it instead."

Leviter smiles. "There is no such thing as coincidence, my dear Jax. Only immaculate planning."

They're not the sort of men you hug, so I content myself with a hearty handshake for each of them before I turn to Tarn. "I count us square now, you know. I've even forgiven you for trying to have me killed for doing my duty."

Tarn throws back his head and laughs. "You've always been adequate at putting yourself in harm's way, no special help needed on my end."

"Take care," I say. "Both of you."

Hurriedly, I rejoin the others before I can get even more emotional. Loras and Farah are waiting, hand in hand. They won't leave until we board the ship. It's a fine vessel with sufficient space for all of us. By some chance, we've ended up with two pilots and two navigators, which means we can travel twice as fast, twice as far. Serendipity, you might call that, or some master plan to which I'm not privy.

All I know is, I'll take it.

I've lost so many people along the way. This is where I draw the line and tell the universe: *You will take nothing more from me.*

"Mary bless and keep you," Loras says.

They don't believe in Mary on La'heng. It's a human story, but he speaks the words to honor and comfort me. Farah echoes them. There are no phrases sufficient for what I want to say or to encompass the way we were, so I keep silent. Anything else would be inadequate.

I lift a hand in farewell and turn to the others. "Are you ready?"

Zeeka nods. "Can I have the first jump?"

He's the bright light; I'm the old saw. Navigating isn't new to me, but it will thrill Z to have this moment. Even if he gets it wrong, well, it's not like we had anywhere to be, and he's been looking forward to this for such a long time. Over the turns, I've learned to share and to step back from the spotlight.

"Of course."

"I'll take us up," Vel offers, "so you can watch with March from the observation deck."

A glance at March tells me he's okay with that. He confirms, *I'd love to see the stars with you. We'll find a place to get those matching tatts along the way.* I couldn't have put it better myself. The four of us board the ship without looking back.

I stop Vel briefly with a hand on his arm. "Bounce a message as soon as you can and set up a rendezvous with Dina's crew."

"Understood, Sirantha."

"Great idea," March says. "Wonder what they've been up to."

"We'll find out soon enough."

Vel and Zeeka head for the cockpit then, and we turn toward the observation deck. *You're sure this is what you want?* I ask silently. *It won't be safe or settled. I'm never going to live in a house again. And I won't age like you do. It may be hard.*

March's warmth fills me with unshakable certainty. *You and me, until the day I die. Absolutely. I don't* care *if it's hard.*

Anything worth having is worth fighting for. I forget where I first heard that, but it's true. He's worth everything. His agreement echoes in my head.

After all this time, March knows what I want and what I can offer. He gets me down to my breath and bone; he will not try to change me. For him, I need not yield that which makes me Jax; I need not surrender the universe for March's sake. No, he will give it to me. He will *share* it with me.

I take his hand as the ship powers up, and La'heng recedes below us. At this point, I've gotten my name in enough record books . . . and I want something other than notoriety. Now, so far as the galaxy's concerned, I'm going quietly off the charts. After all, the adventure has only just begun.

The power swelled inside me, burning, hurting, but I let it center me. Pain means I'm still here, fighting. *I envisioned it swelling in my hand in a seething rush, gathering, gathering, and then I sent it out on my resolve like a dark and winged thing riding the magickal wind.*

From National Bestselling Author

ANN AGUIRRE

DEVIL'S PUNCH

A Corine Solomon Novel

As a handler, Corine Solomon can touch any object and learn its history. Her power is a gift, but one that's thrown her life off track. The magical inheritance she received from her mother is dangerously powerful, and Corine has managed to mark herself as a black witch by dealing with demons to solve her problems.

Back home, Corine is trying to rebuild her pawnshop and her life with her ex, Chance, despite the target on her back. But when the demons she provoked kidnap her best friend in retaliation, Corine puts everything on hold to rescue her. It's undoubtedly a trap, but Corine will do anything to save those she loves, even if it means sacrificing herself. . . .

penguin.com
facebook.com/ProjectParanormalBooks
annaguirre.com

M1079T0412